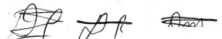

Shadowstorm

A Novel of the Shadow World

Dianne Sylvan

Part One
The River in Flood

Chapter One

SignetPulse News Update:

This week, another stunning development in the ongoing struggle between the Signets and the Order of the Morningstar's assassination squads: William and Virginia Larimer, Prime and Queen of the American Midwest territory, were killed on a crowded street in Denver in view of at least two dozen humans.

It is widely believed that the Morningstar soldiers are operating under a form of mind control that directs their attention solely to the mission objective; they are, according to rumor, under the ultimate control of a human calling himself the Prophet.

Another less shocking move came from the South as Prime David Solomon swept into the Midwest region with hundreds of Elite from all over the continent and subdued the riots in Denver before the week was out. Over the past two years Solomon has taken over all but one of the American territories; Olivia Daniels, the first female Prime in Signet history, shows no signs of relinquishing hers, and remains one of Solomon's staunchest allies.

Others in the Council are not convinced of the South's benevolent intentions. An unnamed source from one of the untouched Havens in South America reported, "We all know what's really going on—he will have the entire Western Hemisphere piece by piece before the decade's out. He has to be stopped."

SignetPulse was unable to reach Prime Solomon or his Queen for comment but will continue to investigate the situation in Austin and how its consequences will affect all of our honored Signets.

*****

Much like its children, darkness knew how to make an entrance.

Night walked in with a sweep of its long dusk-blue coat, parting the daylight with its commanding presence. The fire of sunset became pale and insubstantial before it and then withdrew altogether.

While in the city most people were just finishing up the day, out in the curvaceous landscape beyond Austin, the nerve center of the Shadow World was just waking up.

Unfortunately parts of that world had already been awake for quite a while.

The Prime of the Southern United States...and the West...and the Mideast...and the Midwest...woke from a fitful day's sleep an hour before the sun was well set, and after trying in vain to enjoy the quiet dark of the suite and the warmth of his Queen's presence draped halfway over him, he gave up and got out of bed.

A hush still held sway over the Haven while its leader pulled on clothes and paused to smile at the woman who still slept soundly, her wild red hair run mad all over the pillow, her expression surprisingly peaceful considering everything that stood against them now. Life wearing a Signet was never simple, never had been, but compared to now, just wearing a Signet seemed like an idyllic time long past.

Just shy of two years had passed since California had fallen. In that time, another seven Primes had been attacked, but at long last the Council had decided to act on his warnings and increase security, so only three of the seven went down. Many of the rest had barricaded themselves in their Havens, only emerging when absolutely necessary.

Since admitting he'd been right all along about the Order of the Morningstar's threat, the Council had been after him to return to the table. They cited tradition and history and how Signets must stick together, but he knew that was nonsense—they wanted to find a way to make him relinquish control of all the territories beyond his own, and without the ultimately empty ritual of parliamentary procedure they had no real way to pressure him. The Council had always prided itself on maintaining individual autonomy. In David Solomon that pride had backfired spectacularly. When their cajoling failed they turned to veiled threats.

He was quite happy to point out that if a group of "mere humans" had sent the all-powerful Council of Signets scurrying into its holes like little mice, the Council opposing David was as pointless as it was hilarious.

He left the suite and headed down the hall to his recently-redesigned office. Other Primes always looked at him patronizingly for his attachment to technology, and a great many didn't even have their Elite connected in any meaningful way, depending on handwritten reports.

Handwritten! They might as well carve everything into stone tablets.

It turned out that, thanks to that derided attachment to technology, running four territories wasn't that much harder than running one. The first thing he'd done was have three of his contractors start building sensors...lots of them. The West already had a network of his design, and within six months the other two territories were linked as well. All four now had the software patch that let the sensors detect humans whose speed and vital signs were similar to the Morningstar soldiers.

He hadn't had to use that, though, because there hadn't been a single attack in any of his territories since he'd taken over. Morningstar was active all over the world, not just taking out Primes but inciting violence among vampire syndicates. They were doing it covertly, but he was not fooled. They had apparently, however, adopted a wait-and-see attitude with him, possibly believing he would lose control as fear gripped the Shadow World and they could just sit back and watch him stumble without risking any of their own people. Clearly they had no idea who they were dealing with.

The door clicked open and the lights and equipment began to switch on as soon as he entered the room. David sat down at the long desk with its bank of six monitors in varying sizes; there was also a 52" screen on the far wall. It and four of the others were all touch-screen, and one ran the holographic generator he used to examine structural diagrams in 3D.

Miranda had taken to calling his office the Batcave, and wasn't terribly surprised when he started calling it that too.

The smallest screen, which gave him security readings for the Haven and Austin alone, was the only one that lit when he took his chair; a glowing box with the shape of a hand in the center waited to verify his identity.

He touched it, and after scanning his handprint the rest of the system began to load; he felt the beam of the scanner run from his head down to his feet, affirming fourteen additional measurements, vital signs, and energy signatures. If his handprint didn't match exactly his body in exactly this chair, the system would lock the user out. Miranda, of course, could access it too, and knew how to use most of the system.

He'd been amazed that so few of the warriors he'd taken in from the fallen territories had protested the change in leadership. Those who didn't want to stay were allowed to resign without any repercussions. David knew each territory had different needs that an outsider might not understand. Keeping Seconds and high-ranking lieutenants in charge and having them report straight to him, being sure to take their counsel as often as appropriate, kept the power structure in place. That way the things he did change—like installing the sensor networks and making sure everyone had the most advanced communication hardware and software—were easier for everyone to accept.

The summary reports for all four territories came up on a monitor, and just as he'd figured, situation normal all over. Things had been unsettlingly quiet for the last two months, not just here but all over the world.

Quick check of the sensor network, coms, other databases, phones: all systems nominal.

He sat back, tilting the chair and crossing his arms. The great stalemate...they had no way to destroy Morningstar, and Morningstar wasn't moving. He had his own house under control but in the global Shadow World Morningstar held all the cards.

At least, that's what he wanted them to think. The Circle had, here in these walls, a secret weapon.

David left the office and headed down another hallway in their wing; only one suite had a guard in front of it, and there he stopped, nodded in acknowledgment to the guard, and knocked softly on the door.

Before he went in he made sure to reach into the room with his senses and confirm that there was, in fact, only one person inside. He'd learned the awkward way that he had to double check.

4

As he'd expected, there were candles burning, and the room's inhabitant was awake, sitting up in bed with books and notebooks in a semicircle around him. Dark auburn hair, tucked behind two pointed ears, fell down all the way to the comforter.

He looked up at the door's opening, and smiled. David felt that smile all the way down to his toes.

"Good evening," Nico said. "Why am I not surprised to see you up so early?"

"Pot, kettle," David replied. He crossed the room and sat down on the bed, trying not to disturb the arrangement of research materials.

The book directly in front of Nico was ancient, its pages filled with strange symbols and, it turned out, at least four languages. Nico had a notebook in his lap and had half-covered a page with a mix of more symbols and modern English.

The task that they'd all expected to be quick and easy for the Elf had in reality taken months; to Nico's astonishment, the Elvish used in the Codex of Persephone was not his own, but a version at least as old as the earliest Elysian Greek. He had believed, as all the Elves he knew believed, that their language had remained mostly unchanged throughout history. This, though, wasn't just old, it was *weird*. It was as if Nico had grown up speaking modern French and then tried to read a book in 16th century Spanish. He was puzzling his way through it, but it was slow going.

David leaned over the pile of books and kissed his forehead; the Elf gave him an affectionate smile before returning to the matter at hand. "Our book is 60% sacred texts and rituals in Elysian Greek, 20% first-person history written by various members of the Order over the centuries, and 20% in Elvish…some of that I can read, but over 2/3 of that section is that odd second dialect…and now I think there may be a third in here too. I started a new section last night and it makes no sense whatsoever—it's written in Elvish characters, but it's gibberish. It's either encoded or it's useless."

David shook his head, frustrated. "I already ran CIA code-cracking software on that entire half of the book last year, and it didn't even recognize the dialectic differences, much less that there were *three* in there. Have you spoken to Kai?"

Nico sighed. "Not since he left for the harvest. I sent samples of the text with him. Hopefully he can find someone familiar with this dialect without calling attention to himself."

There it was again...the sadness. It had become a second skin to the Elf, dulling his luminous eyes, slowing down his movements. He had worn it since those first days of trying, trying anything, to reach his new Prime...but even then he had known the futility of that effort. They'd all been doing what they could to keep Nico going, but the more time passed, the more depressed he became. If Elves weren't so dependent on the natural world for spiritual sustenance—they needed it like air—Nico might have stopped leaving his room entirely and simply stayed in bed for weeks at a time.

The crux of the problem was the barrier between him and Deven: it allowed just enough energy through to keep them both alive, but made it impossible to share the way Pairs were supposed to. The imbalance wasn't catastrophic the way the Trinity's had been, but it was proving just as agonizing, with symptoms as physical as they were emotional. Nico was pale, drawn, eyes shadowed with dark circles; and while a lower body temperature was normal for vampires, he was constantly cold to the point of shivering. In addition to the chills he ached all over intermittently for no discernible reason. He was also constantly hungry...which presented another problem.

The first few days he'd been a vampire he had seemed to deal well enough with his new appetites. David remembered the irresistible dark creature he had become—how powerful he was, how beautiful. That, too, had drained away, leaving a wraith of an Elf who found blood revolting and could barely force himself to drink it until the hunger was too overwhelming to deny. The few times he'd tried to feed off a live human he had panic attacks, so he was subsisting on bagged blood...and that wasn't helping matters. He needed strength, and he sure as hell wasn't getting enough from his diet.

David had never heard of an anorexic vampire before, but then, he'd never heard of an Elven vampire either. It might be the inherent contradiction of nature between Elves and vampires—they had, after all, been created as polar opposites—but David suspected it was psychological, and if they could just set things right with Deven, Nico would work through it.

Once again, David felt a surge of anger...bordering on rage...at the elder Prime. If Deven wanted to hate himself and live in misery, fine—it was his MO, after all. As his lover David had tried for ten years to help him, and Jonathan had done the same for seven times that long, but neither had succeeded. Doing this to Nico was unforgivable. Nico had given up his entire life to save Deven's...and this was his reward, to barely live at all, chained to someone who hated him, and the world, but nothing so much as himself.

While the others had tried various ways to talk to or otherwise engage Deven, David had stayed away from him, which wasn't hard given he was rarely seen by anyone at all. David didn't trust himself not to throttle Deven or at least say things that would make the situation even worse. As it was, all he had to do was think about him and his teeth started to ache with the need to tear out a throat.

"Hold on there," Nico said quietly, looking at him with a slight smile. He lifted a shaky hand and laid it against David's face. "Don't do that to yourself."

"Sorry." David took the hand and kissed it, then rubbed it between his own, trying to warm the fingers. "It's just...you know how I feel about seeing you in pain."

The smile turned sweet. Nico kissed him lightly on the lips. "That's because you are wonderful, my lord."

"So are you."

Nudging the books out of the way, David shifted closer and drew the Elf into his arms, trying to give him as much warmth as he could. Nico burrowed close, and for a while neither spoke.

They had found a few things that helped the Elf cope, and physical affection was at the top of the list. He had Stella, of course, who spent at least two nights a week in his room. David spent as much time with him as he could spare, though unlike Stella he wasn't sleeping with him; and every few weeks, Kai visited from Avilon.

The Elven Weavers had banded together and generated enough power to send Kai to Earth, hoping that Nico would be able to send him back once he'd ascertained that his twin was safe. Seeing Kai had been so good for Nico that Miranda had convinced him to find a way for the Bard to come back, and Nico had gathered power from Stella, David, and Miranda to create something called a Gatestone that would open a portal directly to Avilon whenever Kai wanted one. Nico had been unconscious for five days after performing the spell.

David had thought a visit home might also do Nico a lot of good...until Kai had told Miranda privately that it would be impossible.

When they found out what Nico had done—turned into a vampire, something unheard of that went against everything Elves supposedly stood for—the Avilon ruling council declared him an abomination...and excommunicated him.

Nico didn't know yet. They had agreed not to mention it unless Nico brought up the idea of going home, but so far, he seemed to feel the same way the council did, and didn't want his old friends to see him as he was now.

"Maybe you should call him," David said into Nico's hair. "Your brother."

Nico chuckled. "You don't even like him."

"That's because he's an arrogant dick. But to be fair people have said that about me most of my life too."

"Well that isn't fair at all," Nico replied. "You're far less of a dick than Kai. And I wouldn't call either of you arrogant, just...extremely self-assured. You're a powerful being who knows he is and owns every inch of it, and Kai has been an object of fascination since birth."

"Fine, then, I'll take back arrogant. But dick still stands."

"No argument."

David went on, "The point is, no, I don't especially like your brother, but that's irrelevant. You need him, and he obviously adores you. Whatever it is that binds twins together is particularly strong with you two, and the minute he gets here you look and sound a thousand times better. That alone is worth a bit of dickishness."

Nico smiled up at him. "He'll be back in a few days—there are festivals and rituals practically every night during the harvest season. As the lead Bard he has to organize all of it." At David's dubious expression, he added, "In our tradition the most talented Bards are ranked on par with the high priesthood...and my brother is very, very talented."

"So I hear." There was another pause before David said, "I should leave you to your evening."

"You're looking at my evening. I don't have the energy to be up and around...and I haven't worked on this nearly enough. I could have been finished months ago if I weren't laying around feeling sorry for myself."

Irritated, David flicked the Elf's ear, eliciting a yelp and then a quiet laugh. "Don't start that. You're ill, Nico. You're doing the best you can—and it's not as if Morningstar has made a move lately."

"I just have so much trouble concentrating..." Even as he said the words Nico's voice became slightly slurred with sleepiness, and he became a greater weight against David's shoulder. Some nights were better than others, but often it seemed almost like the Elf had been drugged. Tonight, he all but crawled into David's lap, desperate for warmth and connection, and murmured, "Stay a little while...please."

"Of course I will. You rest. Let me move all of this off the bed."

He twisted so he could lay Nico down and then gathered up the books and set them on the bedside table where they usually were when not in use. David stretched out next to him, pulling him close again.

"I'm sorry," Nico murmured.

"You have nothing to be sorry for, *caraia.*"

Nico smiled, eyes closed. "Your accent is getting better."

"I'd be learning a lot faster if you didn't distract me."

"Distract you how?"

The Prime laughed quietly. "You should have warned me Elvish was so sexy."

"You have very interesting predilections, my Lord."

"Tell me about it."

David waited about twenty minutes after Nico had fallen asleep to gingerly untangle himself and leave the room. He told himself the delay was to make sure the Elf was all the way under, but he had learned the hard way not to deny having feelings for someone, and he had a lot...God, did he have a lot...for Nico.

He certainly hadn't owned up to it until Miranda had informed him quite bluntly that he wasn't fooling anyone, not even himself—but he admitted openly now that he was...what was the word the Queen had used? Twitterpated.

The realization had left him terrified, no longer knowing how to act around the Elf, or how to talk to Miranda about it. This kind of thing simply wasn't in his wheelhouse—he'd learned a lot from his Queen about the heart, but his own was still a willful little bastard who spoke one of the few languages he didn't. Miranda hadn't been upset about his flirtation with Olivia—but his feelings for the Elf were much, much worse than mere attraction. That was a whole different beast, and not one he'd anticipated they would have to deal with yet. Sex could be negotiated, could be fit into a structure of rules; love, however, was its own master, and the master of all it lay down with. He couldn't deny it, especially not to the strongest empath on the planet.

Miranda had been right when she'd predicted his relationship with Olivia would stay at an affectionate friendship level, with neither really inclined to push things. They had the kind of close friendship both Primes desperately needed, and talked on the phone at least twice a week. He had missed that kind of friendship so much since Faith had died...but he had also learned from his mistakes, and had laid his attraction to Olivia out on the table as frankly as he could, insisting on mutual honesty.

He only wished he could have done the same with Faith— pushed for open discussion, gotten things out, so that they could have dealt with them together and grown stronger as friends. It had worked with Olivia.

He'd asked Miranda if she thought the same would happen with Nico.

Miranda had snorted and gone back to her guitar.

Those first few weeks before Nico's strength had faded, David hadn't really been aware of any growing attachment to the Elf, so he'd missed the opportunity to act on it. Nico no longer had the energy for sex...but that was just fine with David. He didn't have to worry about things moving too quickly, and there was plenty of time for the Pair to figure out how they were going to deal with it.

Before he left, he added another log to the fire and another blanket to the bed, and kissed Nico on the forehead. A smile flickered on the Elf's lips, but he didn't stir. For a centuries-old being, he looked so young and vulnerable. David let his index finger follow the line of the tattoo on Nico's face, then moved away with a sigh.

Then he returned to his own suite, where Miranda was awake and dressed. He had to pause and watch her for a moment before she acknowledged he was there—over their brief span of years together he'd seen her covered in blood and sweat after a battle, flushed and trembling after five hours of intense lovemaking, fierce and mesmerizing on stage with her guitar...but one of his favorite Mirandas was this one, freshly showered and wearing one of his t-shirts, wet hair held back in a large pronged clip that looked like it was on the verge of running for the hills. Her face was caught in concentration as she stared down at her laptop, the light from the screen making her green eyes glow. She always bit her lip when she was reading. Everything from her expression to the curve of her back made his heart turn somersaults.

Next to her was the cat she had rescued two years ago, whom she was rubbing absently with her purple-polished toes. The grey tabby, no longer tiny and adorable but rather enormous and ill-tempered, ignored everyone but the Queen, though she acknowledged David on occasion if she was feeling magnanimous. They had a sort of détente in which he pretended not to notice when he woke up with a cat on his stomach, and the cat pretended not to know how she got there and walked off in a huff, digging her claws in when she jumped down for good measure.

David hadn't been thrilled when Miranda brought the cat home—even knowing how she had come to do so. The Queen hadn't been able to heal anyone again since; that power seemed to be partly asleep, much the way Nico was constantly partly asleep. Once David explained that he didn't really like cats, but if she really wanted the sorry little creature he'd learn to live with it as long as he didn't have to deal with the litter box, Miranda had let him name the cat as a peace offering.

She really should have known she'd regret it. She now had a cat named Jean Grey.

"You can't keep that shirt," he said with a grin as he closed the door behind him. "It's part of my fictional educational institutes collection."

Still looking at her screen, she smiled. "I know, I know." She glanced down at the shirt, which boasted the crest of Ravenclaw House, Hogwarts School of Witchcraft and Wizardry. "This one, the Jedi Academy, Starfleet Academy, Top Gun, Sunnydale High, Xavier's School for Gifted Youngsters...oh, and the University of Gallifrey, which doesn't exist."

"Well, none of them exist, that's the point."

"You know what I mean, you dork!"

He laughed, but his frustration from earlier crept into the sound. Miranda looked up, saw his face, and cringed sympathetically. "That bad?"

He sighed and dropped into his chair. "I don't know what else we can do."

"He's strong," she said. "He'll make it through this...something has to give, and I don't think it'll be him."

"I don't know where you get that much optimism." He sat forward and leaned elbows on knees, shaking his head. "I want to think things can get better, but...I know Deven. He doesn't get over things. He's his own archenemy...and you know what he's like in battle."

"Then we need to try something different," she said. "If there's any part of him that's still alive on the inside, there has to be a way to reach it. Now that it's been a few months since we tried, we might catch him off guard. Even if all we do is make a tiny crack, create a weak spot, maybe he'll do the rest."

"How do you suggest we do that?"

Miranda set aside her computer and pulled the cat onto her lap, who promptly rolled onto her back and stuck both back feet in the air, demanding belly scratches. "I don't know," she said. "We can start by figuring out what he's doing every night. I know he's going into town—Chris is driving him. She says he gets out at the same place every night, but knowing him he has her drop him off a long way from where he's actually going. We can track his com from that point."

"And then we follow him?"

"I will. Whatever he's out there doing I want to get an empathic read on it. That might tell us where to go next."

"You'll need to do it soon," he pointed out. "You'll be awfully busy after this week."

Miranda's second album had debuted at #1 on the charts and stayed there for weeks; her management had all but begged her to tour, so after a good deal of discussion she and David had decided she would go out for three weeks, playing in small intimate venues where security could be easily handled, with quick runs home every few days so they could rebalance their bond when necessary. The new jet was extremely fuel-efficient, so it wouldn't be as impractical as the idea had been last time around. She'd stop off in the Haven cities of each of their territories while she was out and make her presence known. David had done much the same earlier in the year, but this would be the first time she'd been to all four.

It was going to be arduous for them both, but Miranda was determined to do it for her fans, she said, the people who had given her such an amazing career. He had about a thousand misgivings, of course, but how could he argue with that kind of love?

Needless to say she would have guards. Lots of guards. Every sword he could spare. The whole thing would be tightly coordinated from start to finish.

Miranda grew silent, thoughtful, hands absently attending to the cat but her eyes on the fireplace, attention somewhere else. The last two years had been hard on her, though that deep inner well of strength she had found had yet to run dry, and despite the fact that her empathy should have made every moment torture, she seemed to be weathering the storm better than any of them.

A chill ran through her, and she came back to the room. "What are you working on tonight?"

"The new com system. I think it's ready to road-test; I'll just need volunteers."

Now she grinned—it was a rare enough expression these days that he felt warm from the inside out—and said, "Oh, sure— 'Who wants to be injected with a microchip like a pet poodle?' You'll have them lining up."

He grabbed the pillow they always threw at each other and mimed a toss, not wanting to risk the cat clawing Miranda's thighs in fright. "Just wait. The idea of not having to wear a wristband anymore will appeal to them."

She held up her own wrist. "I don't know...I'll kind of miss it. But you're right, it's time for an upgrade...plus there's something satisfying about using Morningstar's transmitter technology against them."

"How about you? You're home for the night, right?"

A nod. Jean Grey stood up in the Queen's lap, arched her back Halloween-cat-style, and hopped down onto the floor, taking a moment to weave around David's legs and leave hair all over his pants before heading off to cushier napping pastures. Miranda, meanwhile, stretched as well, hands clasped and arms above her head. As she lowered her arms the clip fell out of her hair.

"I need to work on the new arrangement for 'Last Words.'
Oh, and I have a sparring session with Avi."

"You've had a few with him now—what do you think?"

Miranda considered. "He's good. Very good. He's quiet,
but the others respect him implicitly. He's not the kind of leader
who barks and bitches; a few words and everyone falls in line. As a
teacher he's not quite as solid, because he doesn't really give
enough feedback for beginners, but I think if he's training more
advanced warriors he'll do fine."

"I'm glad to hear it. His technique is a thing of beauty. It's
enough like our style to fit in, but still his own. I heard such fantastic
things from the Mossad I had to at least give him a shot." David
toyed with his Signet and asked, "Do you get anything from him
empathically that we need to worry about?"

"He's got expert shielding. Apparently he's run into empaths
before; he's actually trained to block out all but the most superficial
sensory sweeps. But if you want my gut reaction...we need to keep
him."

"Second material?"

"Maybe."

It would be a tremendous relief to finally have a new
Second. David had his eye on a woman who had joined the Elite
only a couple of months before Avishai Shavit had shown up out of
nowhere a year and a half ago with an impeccable resume and
blown everyone in his training group out of the water. Extensive
background checks were performed on all incoming Elite, but Avi
received nothing but glowing praise from all of his references, most
of whom were high-profile and not given to exaggeration. Once
Avi and the other candidate had both proven themselves for a few
months on patrols and other routine duties, David had promoted
both to instructors—one of the best ways to know if someone was
equipped for leadership was to watch them try to teach.

If there was any hope of that, however, David needed to
spend more time with both candidates. He knew finding another
Faith was unlikely; she'd been a confidante as well as a right arm.
But he had to at least trust his Second's character as much as her
skill. He needed to get to know them better.

No time like the present. "I think I'll drop by Intermediate
Training and have a peek. I need to talk to him about heading up
your security detail on the tour anyway." He rose, bent to kiss the

Queen on the forehead and nose. She smiled and nipped his lower lip.

"You might want to change clothes," the Queen pointed out. "I don't think that outfit says 'scary-ass megavamp and the boss of you' so much as it says 'yes I can fix your printer.'"

David looked down at himself: barefoot, jeans, and a moderately ratty t-shirt emblazoned with 'If you're telekinetic and you know it, clap my hands.' "Point taken."

Just like the Elite, his work clothes were black from head to foot, including the coat that was finally seasonally appropriate. The main difference was style and quality; everything he wore was hand-tailored, and a lot of his wardrobe was custom made. Miranda had laughed about him having a closet full of bespoke blue jeans until she'd had a pair made for herself. He'd always been something of a clotheshorse, but he hadn't realized the full value of dressing the part until he got involved with the Signets.

The ritual of arming himself was so old and familiar he could do it in his sleep...and had, a couple of times, when an emergency hauled him out of bed.

He could feel the Queen's eyes on him, and turned to her with a smile. "Better?"

She gestured for him to come closer, and pulled his mouth down to hers. Kiss achieved, she reached up and ran her hands through his hair. "There. Scary and hot as hell." Then, as he turned to go, she slapped him on the ass. "Now, go get 'em, tiger!"

Luckily for his image, he managed to stop grinning by the time he reached the training center.

He tried everything.

Drinking was unreliable. The intake had to be constant, yet not enough to pass out; it required too much supervision to stay drunk particularly when one had an Irish constitution and a vampire's metabolism.

There were places in every city where their kind could get high and stay that way for as long as they wanted, provided they could afford it. What he was looking for cost nearly five thousand dollars a night...but what was money for? What purpose did keeping it serve? There was always more to be made when one was a murder pimp. He was already a billionaire; five grand in a night was pocket change.

Inquiries at the Black Door directed him to a place with no name, run by a woman who was called simply the Doctor.

Having known David Solomon for decades the first thing that came to mind when he heard her title was "Time Lord," but no matter—whatever she really was, the Doctor knew her patients' needs and tended to them diligently.

An unmarked door off a downtown alley led into an unadorned, dimly lit waiting area, where a bored vampire with tattoos all over her face signed patients in and alerted the Doctor to their presence. The Doctor, or one of the other trained staff, beckoned to whomever was next, leading him or her down a long hallway lined with curtained rooms—cubicles, more like, as they were about the size of a typical urban clinic exam room.

Passing each room, there was no telling what sort of sounds one would hear. There was a marker at the doorway with three designations—one for vacant, one for private, and one for "open to guests."

His kind of money earned a private room. Regardless, he was always stared at when he bypassed the waiting area; he kept his Signet hidden, but even here, addicts weren't a sophisticated or particularly hygienic lot. They were trying to escape reality, deny the physical world; there weren't just a whole lot of junkies wearing John Varvatos, and even fewer who walked like a Prime.

He took the same room every time, on the end at the left. It was mostly taken up by a hospital bed draped with disposable exam paper. There was a small fridge with various beverages to combat dry mouth or sobriety, a sink, and a low cabinet containing basic medical supplies, but other than that, the only other furnishings were an IV stand and volumetric pump.

The Doctor had a businesslike manner and wasn't much on conversation, which pleased him. She carefully pulled back the tape that kept the cannula in his arm from dislodging—he kept it concealed beneath his sleeve when he had to be back at the Haven. A human couldn't keep an IV in the same place for more than three days, but a vampire could go for up to two weeks before the body pushed it out.

She hung a bag of what was labeled saline, and was mostly saline, on the stand and entered a time and rate on the pump. The

Doctor and her associates—a network of chemists, dealers, and clinicians—ran a large and high-tech lab creating purified solutions specifically for the Shadow World, and they were very, very good at their craft. Within a few moments of her switching the pump on, he could feel a slow but steady drizzle of vampire-grade heroin snaking its way through his veins.

It was a delicious high, near-total oblivion. One bag would last nearly six hours.

For months, it worked perfectly. For most of the night, depending on how long it took to get through Austin traffic to and from the Haven, he could simply...stop. Occasionally he'd hand his credit card to the Doctor and stay all day too, but she warned him against doing that often; vampire systems acted the same way human systems did, gradually needing more and more of the drug. Her recommendation was to take a night off every week to ten days, let the needle wound close, and then start over.

He didn't listen. She didn't press the issue.

Everything was going fine until he woke up with a dick in his mouth.

Sometimes the first dose would wear off before the Doctor made it back to his room to check on his levels, and he'd come out of it for a few minutes, practically sobbing in pain until she brought more. It was a depressingly familiar situation; back in California he had been no stranger to opiates, and begging for a fix was not new.

Neither was this.

His first impulse was to ignore it and drift back off—he was just high enough yet to do that, and pretend he'd dreamed the whole thing. But the stink of sweat on an unwashed body and the raw feeling in the back of his throat that told him his guest had been at it for a while hit him all at once, and the high evaporated into something far less pleasant.

Rage.

The man molesting him swore up and down that the marker by the door said "open," and that the room was designated for E-21...or at least that was what the Doctor interpreted from his screaming, sobbing denials as he scrabbled on the floor in his own blood after Deven bit him and nearly severed his penis.

Deven ignored the screaming long enough to fetch a bottle of vodka and wash his mouth out. Then, he stood over the man, impassive, until footsteps ran down the hallway and the Doctor threw the curtain open.

She was a petite brown-skinned woman with a potent mind and an odd sort of compassion for her patients, even through her desire for profit. She knew that the only thing that would make a vampire lay in a clinic for twelve hours was intense and interminable suffering.

She did not, however, have compassion for people who broke the rules. There were two very large, very muscular vampires with her—security staff.

"Get him out of here," the Doctor snapped. The thugs seized the man from the ground and dragged him out of the room, leaving a long smear of blood behind.

She turned to Deven. "My sincerest apologies...I caught that scumbag humping one of my clients six months ago and put him on the blacklist, but we have a new girl up front and she must have missed him sneaking in. I'll comp you the night—can I set you up in another room for now?"

"No, thank you." He walked out without another word. He knew he wouldn't be back.

It was hardly the first time he'd experienced that kind of thing—he had, after all, spent half a century as an opium whore, offering whatever was asked for in return for drugs. It was just business—he wanted something, they wanted something, he didn't care all that much about what they wanted from him, so why not let them have it?

Even as a human, he had learned that the Inquisition might burn every faggot it could find, but when the clergy wasn't looking few guards would turn down a blowjob—a mouth was a mouth. No one in those cells died without having been raped or, at least, traded sex for food or protection and preferential treatment. Prison math: sucking one dick willingly instead of five forcibly.

Something about this was different. He stalked off down the street, angry—not even at being violated, but at having his one respite from reality ruined. He wouldn't be able to relax there now, thinking someone might ignore the door marker again and he'd wake up being gang-banged or worse. That, too, had happened before. Now he had to find something else, something else to make it all go away, before...

He paused, dizziness rocking him back and forth.

...before he started to feel. Before he felt the barrier he had
built with the steel of his will start to crack; before he could feel the
sadness and isolation he had inflicted upon the pure and beautiful
soul on the other side. He had to make it stop...or it would build,
and build, and destroy him again.

He returned to the Black Door and tried a few other drugs,
but none of them worked like heroin. He had to settle for another
clinic, this one less comfortable and its staff less professional; but its
rooms had doors that locked.

The drugs, at least, were grade-A quality, and as soon as he
was hooked back up, he shut his eyes and started to slide...

...until *he* ruined everything.

"Seventy years," came the voice, "And in all that time I never
realized what a fucking idiot you are."

Deven spun around, confused—but this wasn't reality, it was
dreamtime. He shouldn't be here—the drugs should have sent him
deeper into unconsciousness, past the reach of either memory or
dream. He didn't want either. He didn't want...

"Me," Jonathan said, crossing his arms and leaning against a
tree—a redwood. "You didn't want me."

Deven backed up, shaking his head, shutting his eyes
against that face, slamming his heart shut against that voice. "No.
Go away. If I can't see you in the real world I don't want you here."

"Are you sure you aren't just ashamed of your spectacular
lack of coping skills?"

He had expected, if he dreamed about Jonathan, it would be
full of longing, tears, and the comfort of the Consort's arms; instead,
he felt only anger. "*You left me,* you bastard. You *knew* you were
going to die and you left me alone—alone, in this world I wanted
more than anything to leave. Now I'm trapped here for God knows
how long—forced to fight, every waking moment, for sovereignty
over my own soul. How I cope is none of your goddamn business
anymore. You gave up all right to approve or disapprove."

"Hate me then, do you?"

"Yes!" Deven took another step back, both hands fisted at
his sides. "Yes, I hate you. I hate you for loving me. I hate you for
showing me I could be happy when you knew you were just going
to take it away!"

"No," Jonathan said reasonably, "you're the one who's
refusing happiness now. You could take that barrier down at any

moment, open yourself up to him—to all of them. You could have a whole host of Consorts, every last one loving you as much as I ever did, if not more. Listen to me, Dev..." He stepped away from the tree, coming closer—like all the ghosts of this plane, he didn't have feet, but glided, his form just translucent enough that the wisps of trees beyond showed through him. "I loved you with all my soul, but you could never give me all of yours—and that's how it was supposed to be. I wasn't your ending."

"You were to me!" He found himself batting at his eyes, and realized he was impatiently wiping back tears...of shame...of anger...and above all, of sorrow, that he had once been happy, once the most powerful of his kind, and now here he was, a drug addict and pathetic mess. "I don't want any of them. I just want you."

He was still, now, and felt the ground hit his knees; the scent of dust rose up though there was no dust here at all. He looked up through his blurred vision to the man towering over him.

"Well, you can't have me," Jonathan said gently. "I'm gone, my love. I'm gone. And you can hang on to that hate you have for yourself, for the world...but please...for me...don't punish the others for it. If you had any idea how much they love you...all of them..." Jonathan reached out and caught a tear, held it up, and as it fell, it brightened until it shone like a star. "I can't give you the love you deserve now...but I can take you somewhere you might start to find it. So what do you want?"

Down on his knees, shaking, arms wrapped around himself and fighting sobs, he whispered, "What do I want?" The question made no sense—what he wanted had never really mattered.

"Do you want to go on living like this, whoring yourself out for a fix and being degraded by lesser men...and you know that's what's coming, you've done all of this before...or do you want to take a chance that maybe...just maybe...there's something else out there worth living for?"

He lifted his head. It felt like his heart had been reamed out with a wire brush, leaving a great cavernous space in his chest that echoed even as the ragged edges of flesh fell down like leaves from the tree of his ribcage. "I can't let him in," Deven whispered. "I can't. It will kill me."

"I thought you wanted death."

He knelt in silence for a while longer before slowly straightening. He honestly couldn't tell what would be worse, waking up in the middle of being fucked by strangers or waking up knowing he was surrounded by people who loved and treasured him—because if they could see the reality, if they could see what he truly was, he would lose that love as violently as he had lost Jonathan.

"I wouldn't be so sure," Jonathan said, moving closer.

Now, they were within a couple of feet, and Deven found himself memorizing his Consort's face, the way he stood—yes, just so, unless he was on duty he tried to pretend he was shorter than he was. The scent of him—books, leather, whiskey, cigars...the faint strains of Amy Winehouse...It was all so much a part of the section of Deven's brain roped off and dedicated to Jonathan...how could he let anyone else have even an inch of that room?

Jonathan saw the vision Deven had created and smiled. "That's a very sweet way for you to hate me," he said. He reached down and touched Deven's face, and Dev had to drag up every ounce of strength not to try and crawl into his arms.

He couldn't look Jonathan in the eye right then, and fixed his gaze on the Consort's hand...his wedding ring. The real one had been badly damaged, unfixable without melting it down. It was locked in a trunk in his room back at the Haven with the few other items that had been salvaged from their home. As with the ring, so with Deven.

"I'm broken, Jonathan," he whispered. "I'm broken. Just pieces held together with spite, torn off one by one by the wind. Nothing can fix me—not Elven magic, not you...I can't help them. I'm not worth hanging on to."

"Like I said," Jonathan replied, the harsh words tempered with an all too familiar tenderness, "You're a fucking idiot."

Defeated, Deven bowed his head. "What do you want me to do?"

"Straighten out your coat a bit. Try to look presentable."

"Why?" Dev asked, but he let Jonathan move him around like a doll until the Consort was satisfied. When Jonathan found the IV port, he stared at it for a moment in silence.

"You had one of these when we met," he said softly. "You were hiding it from David."

"What are you doing? No, don't—"

Jonathan took hold of the cannula and with one quick movement pulled it out of the vein, causing Deven to gasp at the sharp pain. Black-shadowed blood fell in rivulets over his fingers, into the pale ground that looked like either snow or dust; either way, the blood shone out like it was on fire. Jonathan dropped the needle on the ground as well.

"I just want to go back to sleep," Deven said, bending to try and grab the discarded needle, but before he could reach it, it vanished. Deven whimpered, desperate—he had to leave here, now, so he could get a new one put in, or he was going to wake up sober and scream his life out.

But Jonathan was leading him somewhere, he realized, deeper into what turned out to be Muir Woods. There was a particular part of the forest path that wound through the Cathedral Grove, a stand of trees that stretched so high their tops were barely visible, especially at night. Inside the Cathedral even the human tourists fell silent; there was something there, even if they had no idea what to call it. He had known what it was...but he had lacked the language to name it. He had the words now but would not speak them aloud.

He followed Jonathan because he didn't know what else to do. There was no place to go, no drug that would end this...he understood that more and more with each step. To return to the Haven in this state was unthinkable.

The paths through Muir were man-made and smooth, as were the bridges that crossed back and forth over the stream that had been burbling its same song for at least a hundred years. He had seen that stream grow and shrink, overflow its banks and dry down to a near-trickle, but it, like the trees above, was always there.

They walked without speaking for a while until the path rounded a bend and he suddenly realized there was someone else there—a dark figure on the next bridge, leaning on the rail.

He started to ask Jonathan what was going on, but looked around to find the Consort was gone.

Gone again. Gone.

Wake up. Wake up now. Don't think about it...

"How old would you say this tree is?"

Deven frowned. It was a woman's voice, smooth and oddly familiar, and he moved a little closer, not sure what to make of the situation but sure he didn't like it.

Out of habit he reached down, but there was no hilt at his belt. He hadn't picked up a weapon in months. Still, edged metal and wood weren't the only deadly implements he had.

She looked over at him and smiled, and again he felt something familiar about her; the way she stood, perhaps, or the glint in her black eyes. She was wearing a long cloak of some sort that hid her clothing, but had a long tumble of hair the color of old wine. The ends of it faded into the darkness, as did her cloak.

Another spirit, then. Someone dead. That wasn't helpful; he had lived seven centuries. Nearly everyone he'd ever known was dead.

When he didn't answer, she said, "Eleven hundred fifty-three years old. It sprouted the year Paris was burnt by the Vikings. Imagine that."

Wary, he joined her at the rail, keeping several feet between them. "Who are you, and what are you doing in my mind?"

"It's a lot like you," she went on, ignoring the question. "Well, much older, but still—you were born in the year 1248—right around the moment the Aztec empire was established. You've outlived entire civilizations. That's amazing, when you think about it."

"I try not to," Deven said coldly. "Where did you get that year, anyway? Not even I know what year I was born."

"Or the exact date, I know. It must be infuriating trying to throw you a birthday party."

He just stared at her.

Again, a smile. "May 10," she said. "So you are, in fact, 766 years old—and a Taurus, which would not surprise anyone who knows you. If you don't mind my asking...how did you do it?"

"What? How did I live this long?"

"Yes."

He put both hands on the rail—they were paler than they should be, almost translucent, and shaky. He started to say something sarcastic, but the sight of his hands made him pause, and in total honesty, he said quietly, "I don't know."

There was something in her expression that made him feel afraid—small, ashamed. But it wasn't an accusation, or disgust, or anything like that. It seemed more of a mix of sadness, affection, and humor, covering an endless reservoir of what could only be love. He shrank away from affection...from any feeling that might make him feel warm again. "I can only imagine how painful it must have been," she said.

He rolled his eyes. "Everyone's life is painful. But for most people life is only temporary. There's an end in sight, so they can tolerate the wait."

"But you're a constant," she said quietly. "The world turns around you and, like these trees, you stand even if the forest burns down."

He nearly smiled. It hurt his face. "You make it sound so noble."

Who did she remind him of? As she smiled again, he got it—Miranda. No...Cora. No, it was definitely Miranda. He imagined her holding a guitar and the picture made sense. Something about her reminded him of the Queen.

Or perhaps it was the Signet that did that.

He caught sight of it as she turned toward him: a heavy chain, a faint glow...and red.

"Who are you?" he asked again, this time throwing authority into his voice. Very few people survived ignoring that tone.

Or they hadn't, back when...he shook his head, confused. Too many lifetimes in one mind. Too many decades crammed together, too many memories clamoring to be heard, and out of the chaos, nothing.

"It doesn't really matter, does it?" she asked. "I think a better question is, who are you?"

He groaned. "Oh my God, you're the fucking Caterpillar. I *knew* this was the drugs."

She laughed. It was a ringing sound, especially here in the silence of the wood. Yes, very like Miranda indeed, though physically they didn't really look much alike. Miranda had leaf-green eyes, and of course the curls. This woman's eyes were...

Black...

No delineation of pupil and iris, just endless black, and they had stars in them...stars that went on, and on, and if he looked at them the right way, they formed...

They formed a Web.

"It's You," he said softly.

This time, She didn't smile. "It is."

"What are you doing here, then? I thought you couldn't talk to us yet."

"In dreams," She replied, "and other altered states, the distance is shorter."

"Close enough to show me visions of my dead husband, but not close enough to actually lift a finger to help him survive." He tried to keep the anger out of his voice, but failed, and let each word be a dagger if it wanted.

None of them seemed to cut Her. She nodded, obviously having expected something of the sort. "I gave him knowledge. Perhaps if he had shared it, you could all have found a way to avert fate—or perhaps not. My children have free will. Jonathan made his own choices. There is only so much I can do without violating natural order."

"That's a pretty pathetic excuse."

An eyebrow lifted.

"If we're supposed to be Your little private army, and destroy the people who were strong enough to put You in the ground last time, You're going to have to do better than some vague theological platitudes about free will. We need *help,*" he said. "Real help. No more codes, no more dreams—a plan. Information. Firepower."

He was trying to provoke Her, of course, but instead She looked amused again. "We? I thought you didn't care anymore."

Deven shook his head and turned back to the rail. "I didn't. I don't."

"Or perhaps you understand, underneath all your attempts at self-destruction, that eventually you will come out of this and take your rightful place."

He had to hold himself upright with all his will; exhaustion and sorrow were never more than a step behind him, but the thought of living again...it was too much.

"No more," he muttered, bending until his head touched the rail. "Let me wake up. Wake me up."

"I'm trying to," he heard Her say gently.

He tried to ignore Her, and reach out to the forest as he'd done so many times, to wrap the feeling of trees and rocks and water around him; there was nothing else in this place that might offer comfort.

But the memory intruded of the last time he had been here, in the real world, and whom he had been here with. This place, too, his last sanctuary, was tainted by the life he didn't want.

"Here without the burden of all your cares, you are brighter than the sun."

It's not real. It's not real. None of this is real. Wake up...wake up.

"You're going to have to try harder, dear one. Or...stop fighting, and rest."

Get away from me.

The dreamtime was swimming and lurching all around him, conscious and unconscious fighting for control, and both fighting against the drugs that were keeping them asleep. *That's what I get for buying the good stuff.*

Suddenly he felt something take hold of the forest, grip it in iron hands, and say in a voice that shook the dreamtime, *"If you think I will allow you to throw away what I have given you, child, you are mistaken. If it's firepower you want—"*

The energy that thundered through him—conscious, unconscious, the whole of damned creation—was so intense that, had it touched a wire, it would have knocked out the power to the entire Southern United States. It was lightning in a very fragile bottle that should have shattered. His vision was thrown into the Sight so hard he couldn't breathe, just in time to see the wave of power flood the entire segment of the Web visible to his gift, strike the edges, and ripple back, over and over until it finally began to settle, leaving every strand glowing the color of moonlight on snow.

Deven sat bolt upright in the chair he'd passed out in at the clinic, that soundless thunder deafening inside his head. He was drenched in sweat and panting. Bewildered, he stared around the little room, momentarily clueless as to where he was or why.

His eyes fell on the IV pump by the chair. Drugs. Right. Except...

...why wasn't there a needle in his arm? The IV tube simply dangled off the pump, attached to nothing. But if he wasn't taking anything, why was he even here?

He pushed himself up and grabbed his coat off the hook on the door, and all but staggered out of the clinic—no one noticed. People stumbled out of the place all the time.

"Jesus," he muttered. The sound made his head start pounding fit to split.

There was a bus stop half a block up the street, and by a miracle he got there and fell onto the bench, teeth chattering with the sudden blast of cold. He forced his coat on and curled up in a ball.

Oh, I must look like a proper junkie now. Well done, Prime.

He snorted at the last word. He hadn't been Prime of anything in almost two years.

He sat up, still dizzy, and tried to ground, but the dizziness only grew worse, as did the headache and the shaking. He might have mistaken it for withdrawal, except for one last thing:

His hands started burning.

"No," he said, crossing his arms. "Not this. Not now. No."

There was a frightening amount of power moving around in him, and he had no idea where it was from—a check of the barrier he kept over the Signet bond showed nothing had changed. Whatever this was, it had hit him alone, and with every passing minute it grew worse, and worse...

History repeating. There was only one thing to do.

He forced himself to his feet, took a moment to figure out which street he was on, and Misted from the bus stop to Brackenridge Hospital.

Chapter Two

"Bring on the wonder, bring on the song
I've pushed you down deep in my soul for too long..."

     Miranda wanted nothing more than to wipe the last two years from the calendar...to expunge its memory, from the night after Jonathan and Deven's wedding to now.

     There was no joy in it anywhere; every single night had hurt. Even the triumphs—her music career was soaring, she had two new Grammys and a host of other awards—were tinged with grey from the shadows in her heart.

     Here in the Haven time stood still, or rather, life stood still—the months wore on, and they waited for something to change. They prepared themselves for the war they knew was upon them, but no shots were fired.

     She couldn't complain. She was holding herself together better than Nico and certainly better than Deven. But she was surrounded by people she loved who were suffering. No one, empath or not, could withstand that forever.

     The only people in the Circle who weren't in constant pain were Cora and Jacob, who had the luxury of being on a different continent. Cora had found someone to help train her gift, and Jacob had been conducting his own research into the Order of Elysium—research that had yielded several books of linguistics and history that Nico was now using in his translation efforts, but that was about it. The Order seemed to have gone underground. Whether that was due to the threat of Morningstar, or because they didn't want to help the Pairs whose number included the Prime who had slaughtered their High Priestess, Miranda couldn't say...but she knew there would be no help from them, at least not unless something significant changed.

Everyone just *hurt* so much. It wasn't killing her, or driving her mad; she wasn't losing her will to live the way Nico seemed to be. She was strong enough to carry it. But it was so hard to be in her home, to go through the motions of her life as if things were the same—as if one of her best friends wasn't dead and the other nothing more than a shattered shell of who he had once been; as if her world wasn't under the threat of genocidal war that could break out any second...

...as if she weren't a serial killer.

Even with all the connections and relationships she had gotten into, she was lonelier than she had ever been in her life.

There was, however, one bright spot.

Twenty-two months ago, Stella had woken the Pair up to inform them, voice quivering, that they had a houseguest. Prime and Queen had immediately headed for Nico's room ready to decapitate invaders but also mad with curiosity, and had not been disappointed.

Miranda remembered standing there, staring, trying to maintain her authoritative cool—she'd learned how to project an unflappable facade from David, but she'd probably never be as much of an expert at it as he was—in the face of the strangest, and most fascinating, creature she'd ever seen.

He looked like Nico, yet not at all. They had similar features but totally different coloring; their eyes were even two different shades of purple. Nico had said once that he was an average-looking Elf, and as exotic as they found him, they would be amazed if they ever met his brother. Miranda had always thought Nico's opinion of himself was lower than it ought to be, and now she was pretty sure she knew why. Anyone, no matter how accomplished or beautiful, would feel like a homely sparrow next to Kaimereth Eleanari.

And damned if Kai didn't know it.

He had turned toward the Pair from where he stood by the window, taken them in with a single disdainful glance, and said coldly, "So it was you who did this to my brother."

Things didn't improve much from there.

David, who was used to being deferred to by the most powerful beings on the planet, had immediately bristled, and his power-aura flared up like some kind of animal threat display. Miranda had stared at her Prime as if he'd lost his mind, unable to decide whether the Elf or David's reaction to the Elf was more incredible.

"We are Prime and Queen of this territory," David said icily. "Who the hell are you?"

Elf and vampire had stared daggers at each other until David said, steel reinforcing every word, "Answer my question."

And Kai *rolled his eyes.*

Only a pleading look from Nico kept David from wringing the Bard's neck. After that, the Pair stayed as far away from Kai as they could when he visited—he obviously wasn't a threat, and his presence was a healing balm for Nico's frayed heart, so there was no reason not to let him come and go.

Over the months, things between Kai and David calmed down a bit and they could be in the same room without a venomous glaring contest; it helped that Kai clearly doted on his brother, and was as gentle and loving with Nico as Nico was with everyone. David was rather adorably besotted with Nico, and being good to the Weaver endeared Kai to the Prime...a little.

"My lady?"

The voice startled her so badly her hand banged down on the piano keys. "Yes, Harlan?"

"Ready to go when you are."

Heart still pounding, she got up from the bench, grabbed her bag, and hit the door. "I'm on my way."

She'd been using the coms to track Deven's movements in the city for three days now, and while the first night he'd been to several locations in town, including the Black Door and two addresses that weren't labeled as businesses, the second two nights he'd taken the exact same route. Chris dropped him off in the same place as before, but he walked almost two miles farther, up near the interstate and not far from UT campus: the University Medical Center, Brackenridge Hospital.

He was there for a couple of hours each night and then went to a nearby park and stayed there for several more. She wasn't sure specifically what building or floor he'd gone to; she might have been able to get a reading that precise but it would have required logging in to David's office, and for the moment at least she just wanted an idea where to find him and if there was a pattern.

Harlan bowed and held open the car door, and within minutes they were on the highway.

She pulled up the tracking app on her phone; they were about ten minutes behind Chris. Good. She hadn't told Chris what they were doing—even the slightest blip in her usual behavior would tell Deven something was up. Even now, Miranda knew there was little that he missed.

Miranda had no idea what Deven might be doing at Brack. She could only guess he was after blood—he might be hitting their blood bank, or worse, feeding on patients. But why? He'd never had a problem hunting live humans, and he hated bagged blood. Had he developed his own impulse to kill, and taken it out on terminal patients? It seemed unlikely—Miranda had entertained the idea herself until David pointed out that disease made blood unpalatable.

The thought of killing made her stomach tighten. Even now, two weeks out from the New Moon, her body responded to the idea as if it were starving; luckily it wasn't the overwhelming need it would be that night, just a momentary pull.

She was getting used to it...which bothered her, but what choice did she have? David had been absolutely right that the guilt would drive her mad if she let it, so she had focused on what positives she could: she had chosen exclusively humans guilty of disgusting or horrific crimes that had gone unpunished. Her empathy allowed her to find them easily, and there were always more. It wasn't really the fact of killing a human that she found so terrible...

...it was how much she enjoyed it.

Most of the month she could be a regular vampire—well, as regular as a Queen could get. She could hold on to her semblance of humanity and keep her darkest impulses reined in. On the New Moon those impulses broke free, and she hunted the way vampires were meant to hunt...the way their bodies had been *designed* to hunt. The fear, the panic, the will to survive filling the blood with adrenaline and power...and that last second as a living, breathing person suddenly *stopped*...that final burst of life energy was an undeniable high.

"We're here, my Lady," Harlan said from the driver's seat.

Miranda sighed. "Thanks, Harlan. I'll call you when I'm ready to head home."

"As you will it."

She hopped out of the car and stared up at the hospital's main building, dread burning a hole in her belly. Hospitals were not good places for her. She knew her shields could withstand the onslaught, but took a moment to shore them up anyway, adding an extra layer of protection between herself and the pain and sadness that were sure to pummel her from all sides as soon as she walked in the sliding doors.

Now that she was within a square mile of Deven she could get a laser-precise reading from his com, and there he was, up on the fourth floor.

Hospital security didn't even blink as she walked past; she had long ago learned how to deflect human attention, which came in extra handy when wandering around a hospital in a long black coat with five weapons and a necklace that glowed, all the more so when one was a global celebrity. A number of reporters had asked her over the years if she found it difficult being recognized everywhere, but the truth was, she was very rarely seen even when she was in plain sight. It was a subtle part of her protections, a veil rather than a shield, her own personal Invisibility Cloak. She didn't disappear, but people's awareness would slide right off her. It wouldn't fool a strong psychic, but worked very well on the paparazzi.

The building was quiet. Visiting hours had been over for a while, and she was far enough from the ER that she couldn't sense much from it. Brack had one of the busiest emergency rooms in the state, as it was a trauma center and got all the violent crimes in the area. Thank God Deven hadn't gone in there.

She hit the button for 4 in the elevator, and when the doors opened, ducked sideways around a corner to get her bearings.

The light in hospitals was so garish and painful to vampire eyes. The faint flickering of fluorescent lights always gave them a headache, and between the uniformity of the hallways and the smells and the undercurrent of suffering that made her skin crawl, she wanted to run back the way she'd come right then and there.

When she read the sign, however, curiosity banished the urge.

The children's ward.

Miranda checked her phone again and followed the signal until she heard someone talking, and stepped back again, this time around a rolling metal rack stacked with folded blankets.

She peered around the edge and saw a nurse's station. A doctor in a white coat stood there, holding a tablet and indicating something on its screen as she spoke in a low voice.

Standing next to her, looking at the screen, was Deven.

Miranda's first reaction was surprise. It had been a while...three months?...since she'd personally laid eyes on him, and he looked very different from the Deven she had known. The black had long since grown out of his hair, and he'd cut it off so it was all his natural color, a fairly ordinary dark brown. Gone were the Goth trappings, and there wasn't a single piercing visible anywhere. In fact, he was...scruffy. Actually scruffy.

She couldn't help the thought: It was really hot.

He was wearing what she could only describe as normal-people clothes: a leather jacket over a grey Henley, jeans, boots. Miranda had learned how to spot expensive clothes on men thanks to her husband, and knew the jacket alone had probably set Deven back two grand, but it was still so...ordinary. His Signet was mostly hidden, though its chain poked out of his shirt collar.

The doctor finished showing him whatever it was, and smiled. Miranda mentally leaned her ears toward them.

"Thank you," the doctor said. "Is there anything else you need?"

His voice was weary, lifeless. "Just keep everyone out."

The doctor nodded and turned to have a word with the charge nurse; Deven walked away.

Miranda waited a moment before following.

He walked past several doors before finding the one he was looking for, and eased it open about an inch and looked in. The room was dark. He slipped inside.

There was no way she could see what he was doing without giving herself away. Frustrated, she waited where she was.

He came out a few minutes later and moved on to another room.

She followed carefully as he made a circuit around the ward; he didn't stop at every room, and some took longer than others. She had a suspicion as to what was going on, but she wanted to *see*.

Finally, he reached where he'd started and left the ward altogether. She had to leave more distance in the bright hallways, but with her phone it was easy enough to catch up again. She looked up at the sign here:

Neonatal Intensive Care Unit

Same drill. Deven moved from room to room, but this area didn't take as long; there were only about 20 beds that she could see.

As she walked, she bolstered her shields again: even after visiting hours, she could still feel the lingering presence of sadness and hope. She didn't get much of anything off the inhabitants of the alien-looking plastic beds. She wasn't sure how to describe it. She guessed most of them were significantly premature, but it wasn't that they weren't alive, it was that while pain was physical, suffering was an emotion that depended on context these babies didn't have yet. She couldn't decide if that was comforting or not.

Finally, she saw her chance: an open area with curtained bays instead of closed off rooms. The room was dimly lit from a bright lamp that was shining inside one of the bays. She moved into the one opposite, which fortunately held only an empty bed. From there she had a perfect view.

Deven drew aside the curtain of the bay closest to the window, revealing a clear plastic bed—incubator, if she recalled correctly—with a variety of tubes and wires connecting it to the bank of machines nearby. She could barely see inside, but then a tiny pink hand flailed up in the air.

Her heart was held in her throat by a tangled net of emotions. She held onto the curtain with one hand and just watched.

Deven slid his hands into the holes in the incubator's side and gingerly plucked some kind of tubing out of the way. He didn't seem stymied by the equipment the way Miranda would have been. Miranda shifted a little to the right to get a better look at the inside of the box.

It was, of course, a baby, wearing nothing but a diaper and a pink knit cap on her downy head. Miranda didn't know much about babies but this one had to be pretty new—she didn't have that fat rounded-off look babies got once they'd been eating for a while. This one wasn't eating anything, though. She had a tube down her throat.

That little hand caught one of Deven's fingers for a moment. Miranda glanced up at his face in time to see a soft smile.

It occurred to her to wonder if he'd ever wanted children of his own; she doubted it, given his monastic life, but she wasn't sure. It wasn't the sort of thing vampires usually talked about. David hardly ever mentioned his son, though she knew he had loved fatherhood.

Deven closed his eyes.

She knew what he was doing before she even felt the wave of energy rising up through him. She had seen this before, that night when he knelt on the street beside Kat's bleeding body. This time, though, the amount of power she sensed dwarfed that by a factor of ten at least—she had no idea how he could control that much power, but somehow he modulated it, feeding a little at a time into the tiny wrinkly creature in the bed.

Miranda had no idea what was wrong with the baby, or how he knew when she was better, but after a couple of minutes, he withdrew his hands and placed them on the lid of the incubator to steady himself, breathing hard. She had counted: he'd been to thirteen different patients tonight, and by now had to be on the verge of collapse. Where had all of this come from?

Taking a deep breath, he rubbed his hands together, flexing the fingers. While he did that the machines around the baby's bed began to beep faster or slower or whatever they had to do to indicate something was very, very different.

This time when he left the ward he headed for the elevators. Miranda stayed where she was for a good five minutes before doing the same; he would probably be on his way to the park now, and she had a good idea why—to rest, and possibly hunt.

She was thankful to get outside again in the free air; the more distance she could put between herself and the hospital, the better she'd feel. She started to call Harlan, but before she could dial, she heard,

"I suppose you think you're clever."

Miranda turned toward the voice. "How long did you know I was there?"

Deven, leaning against the outside wall of the hospital's front driveway, looked like absolute hell; wherever he was getting his power from, it was using him pretty hard. He looked a lot like Nico did these days. "The whole time."

She deliberately asked a stupid question just to see how he'd react. "How did you know?"

The exasperated look he gave her was, for a second, one hundred percent Deven. Rather than answer, he asked, "Why are you here?"

"I needed to know what you were doing. I thought you were off doing drugs, or killing people, not..."

She wasn't sure he was capable of genuine laughter anymore, but the noise he made was close. "You want to know why I of all people would do something as life-affirming as healing terminal babies."

"I am curious, yes."

"The drugs aren't working anymore," he said. "I tried everything...I only wanted a moment of peace. Death is denied me...I barely sleep...in the end only one thing makes it all go still."

She nodded slowly, wishing she could at least lay a hand on his arm, some gesture, anything, to let him know she understood. But even if he would allow it, to him it would be meaningless. "Healing," she concluded. "When you heal, you're at peace. I saw it that night with Kat."

He looked down at his hands. They were so pale, almost insubstantial, a ghost's hands. It was hard to imagine them wielding a sword, let alone belonging to the fiercest warrior vampire kind had ever seen. They shook the way hers had always shaken before she learned to master her gift.

"I can't stop...if I don't use it, it burns. It was like that sometimes when I was a child—mark myself a target for the Inquisition or end up screaming in pain. They sent me off to the monastery either to save or condemn me, I've never decided which. So you see," he said quietly, "It's the same as ever. I don't care about sick babies or ten-year-olds with tumors. It's purely selfish. I'm using them."

Miranda had to smile a little, because whatever private hell he was living in, she didn't believe for a second that he didn't care. She had seen his face when the baby grabbed his hand. "Somehow I don't think those kids' parents would care what your motivation was."

He pushed himself off the wall and started walking; she fell in step beside him. "Leave me alone," he said. The words were petulant but their tone was not—it was almost a plea. "Whatever it is you want from me, you won't get it."

"I just want to talk to you," she insisted.

He stopped, looked at her. "Why?"

"Because...you were there for me when David died. You kept me going. I want to be here for you. That's what friends do, and...I miss you. There's so much I..." After all those months, finally getting to talk to him even like this made her eyes ache with tears. "You were the one person I could tell anything—you never judged, never gave me anything but love. You don't know how hard it's been without you."

For a second, she thought she might have him, but his face hardened. "Talk to your Prime," he said, and started walking again.

"Won't you at least think of Nico?" she called after him. "He needs you even more than I do."

He didn't stop. She followed.

"Don't you care what you're doing to him?" she wanted to know. "If you could see him--"

"He doesn't need me," Deven snapped. "He's got the rest of you to keep him warm."

"But you're his Prime—"

"That's his problem, not mine."

"Do you really think this is what—"

He rounded on her, eyes gone pure silver with anger. "If you say a word about what Jonathan would have wanted I swear to God I'll break your neck."

She knew better than to continue the sentence. "Just let me help you," she said softly. "I know you're in pain—every single breath must hurt. I can't make it go away. I don't even know if I can make it any better. All I know is that you don't have to be alone."

Again, she saw it...the barest hint, just a glimpse...no matter how shattered he was, part of him still cared about her. She tried to reach out with her empathy, just to offer connection, but as soon as he sensed she was trying to touch him, the barriers slammed shut again, and that trace of softness became distant and cold.

"You can't save me," he said. "Stop wasting your time."

Then, he vanished.

Miranda's heart sank down to her feet. It wasn't so much that she'd expected him to exclaim "My God, you're right, let's hold hands and cry"—it was seeing what he had become, compared to the strong, imperious creature made of leather and snark she had met that night so long ago. She'd hated him back then, but his power and allure were undeniable. He'd swept in and rescued her in Rio Verde, fought at her side. She remembered sobbing her heart out in his arms when David was dead. Waking up in what should have been a cold, empty bed without David, to find another presence beside her, the scent of sandalwood she had grown to love…pressing into the warmth of a body there only to give her comfort, knowing she might be broken, maybe forever, but she wasn't alone. And though none of them had discussed it, she remembered the night David had made her Thirdborn, and how in her seeming delirium she had put her mouth to Deven's and felt a surprising welcome, perhaps desire but at the very least affection. And now…

All she could do was hope that what she'd told David was right: that if she had managed to put even the tiniest chink in his armor, it would start to crack.

It was such a faint and fading hope that she found her eyes filling, and after Harlan picked her up, she cried silently in the back seat the entire trip home, wishing for the kind of healing ability she didn't think existed…the kind that could work a miracle.

David followed the Queen's distress to the music room, where he found her sitting at her piano, arms up on the lid, head in her arms.

He laid a hand on her shoulder. "Beloved? What happened?"

Miranda looked up at him through her hair. Her eyes were red and swollen from a long cry, but dry, so it must have been on the drive home. "Babies," she said.

David blinked. "Babies happened?"

She nodded. "I followed Deven. We talked for a minute—I tried to get through to him, and for a second I thought maybe I had. I don't know. But…with everything he could be out there doing, every form of self-destruction at his fingertips, he's going to Brackenridge…and healing dying babies and children. He tried to play it off like he was just doing it to make himself feel better, but I could tell it was more than that."

David found his own heart aching, perhaps from relief, perhaps from...he had no idea. "That sounds like the Deven I knew," he said softly. "I saw him doing it once a long time ago, but I never let on. What...what do you think it means?"

"It means he's still in there," she answered. "It means we can't give up. Not yet."

"Then we won't give up," David replied. Just that tiny ray of hope was like a sweet summer sunset. "We'll find a way to reach him even if we have to start throwing sick babies at him."

Miranda giggled in spite of herself. "That's a horrible mental image. But it might be worth a shot."

He brushed the hair from her eyes, and wiped the tears from her face with the cuff of his shirt. She smiled up at him, taking his hand and holding it to the side of her face. "I thought you'd like to know," he said casually, "That Kai's back."

"Oh. Good."

He was trying not to put her on the spot, but also felt compelled to ask: "So, are you two..."

Miranda flushed, and then looked angry with herself for flushing. "No, it's not...it's not like that."

David raised an eyebrow.

"I mean it! I mean, of course he's disgustingly hot. But it's not anything. Or if it is it's not going anywhere."

He was laughing at her, and she punched his shoulder. "You do realize how ridiculous you sound to me of all people," he pointed out. "It's all right, beloved."

"No it's not!"

"Why not?" he asked. "I seem to recall someone telling me we have no control over our emotions, only our actions."

"I don't want to sleep with him, David—we're friends. Maybe like how you and Olivia are friends. But that's it. I don't want anyone besides you—ever."

"Oh?"

"I mean it."

"All right." He kissed her forehead, deciding not to press the issue, though he knew perfectly well there was at least one circumstance in which she would feel very differently. "Well, we made rules about extracurricular activities, and they apply to both of us. If you think it's going somewhere, we'll talk about it before it does, make sure everything's out in the open. You're every bit as entitled to lovers as I am—and you're also entitled to have none at all. I'm all right with either."

"But you don't like him," she reminded him.

He shrugged. "I don't have to. I know he wouldn't hurt you. And if he did I'd rip his lungs out. I'm sure he knows that too. Regardless, I'd recommend you start a conversation before things get awkward. You and I both know how unspoken feelings turn toxic."

"Yeah." She leaned on him for a minute, sighing. "Thank you for being... you."

He smiled and kissed her. "I wouldn't be me if you weren't you, so thank you too. Now, you go back to your song, and I'll see you later. I've got three Elite ready to try out the new coms. But try not to put so much pressure on yourself."

Miranda sat up straight again, pulling her hair back from her face with one hand. Her energy seemed a little lighter, even if her expression wasn't. "I love you," she said.

"And I, you, my Queen."

As he left the music room, he paused at the end of the hall, waiting; he wasn't about to leave her alone until he heard music. Just the piano was all right, but singing would be even better.

Finally:

"Sometimes, I think you want me to touch you
How can I, when you build the great wall around you..."

Relieved, David nodded to himself and headed for the workroom, where his three volunteers would be waiting and probably hoping fervently that their boss wasn't about to electrocute their heads.

About thirteen months ago, the Queen had been at her piano, finalizing the set list for a performance she was giving as a benefit for the Porphyria Foundation. It was the end of a blistering Texas summer, and the Haven air conditioning worked better if there was airflow, so she'd had her music room door open.

She'd felt someone watching her as she ran through one of her new songs.

"It's rude to stare," she said without looking over.

"My apologies."

"Aren't you supposed to be glued to your brother's side, pretending we don't exist?"

She was ready for the cold arrogance, the disdain, but instead, the reply held actual emotion: "He is asleep. I needed a moment to clear my mind from his suffering."

"So you thought you'd come and make me suffer."

A pause. Then: "You must understand...when he returned home to Avilon last time he was heartbroken. And now, I see the pain he is in, the unending grief—knowing he has been cast out by his own people, and denied by the one he loves yet again...is it truly surprising I would feel an aversion to this place and to those who, even for the most loving of reasons, brought him to such a pass?"

Miranda finally looked up at the Elf standing in the doorway, frowning. "Cast out?"

He was wearing dark purple, the exact color of his eyes, with a black cloak; his hair blended into the velvet so it looked like he was wearing a hood. He had the bearing of a king, and if Nico brought to mind a wild creature in the forest, Kai made her think of the trees themselves, regal, casting shadows over everything around them. She wondered if he was capable of slouching. "Yes. The ruling council of Avilon has decreed no vampire may set foot in our realm...not even one that is also Elven. He can never go home again."

"Oh my God." Nico already hated what he had become, and knowing his friends and family did too... "How could they do that? I thought he was loved by his people."

"He is. That love is the reason they make no objection to my coming here—not that they could stop me, now that I have the Gatestone. But it is an old, old fear that drives them. Vampires were instrumental in the near-extinction of our race. They were paid by the human authorities to hunt us down, and because we are apparently quite a delicacy, they murdered us by the hundreds. The human world itself terrifies my kind."

"Your kind, but not you."

Kai smiled. It was the first time she'd ever seen him smile; it made the distant, untouchable neutrality of his face seem almost human...and it made her heart skitter through her chest in a way she didn't like. "I fear very little."

"You're obviously not afraid of me," she observed. "A lot of people are."

Something she could only describe as a sparkle appeared in his eyes. "No, I am not. I confess I find you fascinating."

Miranda had to look away from his steady gaze, and to her horror she realized she was blushing. "Oh?"

"Well, you, and this...whatever this is."

She realized he was indicating the Bösendorfer. "Don't Bards play instruments where you come from?"

"I play six," he said. "Some are similar to those—" He gestured at her row of guitars. "But this enormous musical box is strange to me. Its sound drew me to you just now."

Miranda recognized the look on his face. It was, in fact, fascination, but with the piano, not her. *Thank God.* She'd seen musicians get that same keen-eyed interest over new instruments at music stores, and seeing it in Kai made her opinion of him shift a bit. Dick he might be, but he was a musician, and she couldn't resist sharing a little. "It's simpler than it looks," she said, standing up and lifting the piano's lid. "It's just hammered strings."

Kai gazed down into the piano's inner workings, eyes lighting up when she played a bit of the chorus of one of her songs. Then his eyes shifted to her hands, absorbing, analyzing, and cataloging everything about how the instrument was played. It reminded her very strongly of how David learned things in seconds that would take other people weeks.

She explained the pedals, and the black keys, and to her own surprise found herself scooting over. "Try it."

His eyebrows shot up. "You would let me touch her?"

Miranda shrugged, trying to downplay the impulsive suggestion. His wonder at it made her face heat up again. "Sure, for a minute."

He sat down. A familiar scent—trees and cookies, like Nico. She'd asked Nico once why he smelled like that, and he'd looked at her like she was crazy. Kai's presence, however, was massive and ostentatious, where Nico tried to make himself seem as ordinary as possible. The twins had apparently taken what made them different from the other Elves and gone in totally opposite directions with it. She could imagine how their people would adore them both even as they feared their potential darkness.

Kai's hands, which she could only describe as *elegant*, lightly pressed a few keys, the touch practically reverent. He looked up at the music stand and frowned at the pages she'd propped up there. "Your system of notation is very different from ours."

"How so?"

"Well, it is horizontal, for one thing." He stared at it for another moment, the analysis returning, then nodded once to himself...

...And started to play...

...Perfectly.

She knew she was gaping, but she couldn't help it; she'd never seen anything like it. She had to stop herself from applauding when he was finished.

"That was amazing," she said.

A fluid shrug. "The skill itself is only half of the work—the gift is the other. Only using the former is child's play."

"What kind of gift would a Bard have, if not playing like that?"

"Anyone willing to devote the time and work can play an instrument," he said. "I have been doing so for four hundred years, remember. What makes a Bard a Bard is the ability to influence emotion through music; to create a mood, or a vision, and thread it through the sound."

Again, she stared. "You're an empath."

He met her eyes and smiled. "And you are a Bard."

Since then, every few weeks when Kai visited, he found her in the music room while Nico was asleep, and they talked about their art. She introduced him to the idea of recording songs and played one of her albums to show him the difference between studio-produced and live. He brought her Elven sheet music, which was an art in itself—they illuminated their music, and the staffs were, as he'd said, vertical rather than horizontal. Elven musical vocabulary was full of plant metaphors—the words for different tempos were related to the speed at which a particular flower opened.

She found him oddly refreshing after dealing with so many vampires and their secret agendas. He had nothing to hide and wouldn't have bothered if he had. Unlike most people his self-confidence wasn't hiding insecurity. When he spoke of being talented, attractive, or popular, it was a simple statement of fact, as if it would never have occurred to the rest of the world not to admire him. Perhaps it was arrogance, but Miranda didn't think that really described it. Kai was just...Kai. He completely inhabited his own identity.

She also got to hear him sing. His voice nearly undid her. It wasn't just that it was beautiful; she'd heard plenty of lovely voices from talented singers. There was a quality there that was just not of this Earth—literally. The song was in Elvish, which might be part of it. Every time he heard Nico speak Elvish David had to take a cold shower.

After the song ended, Kai looked at her and frowned. "Are you all right?"

She stammered for a minute. "...amazing," she got out. "You should sing something in English next."

He smiled, and something in the expression said he found her sudden awkwardness endearing. "If you like."

"I've been meaning to ask you—how did you learn English so fast? Yours is way better than Nico's was when he first got here."

Kai blinked. "I took it from his head," he replied; to her mystified expression, he asked, "Do you not do that?"

"No, I think that's probably a twin thing, or maybe an Elf thing. Although...David and I do share a lot of our abilities now. But we've never tried doing it on purpose."

"Does he share your Bard's gift?"

"Empathy? A little. Just enough to hurt—but he keeps it blocked unless he needs it for something. Since it's fairly weak it's easier to control."

He looked thoughtful. "My gift has never hurt me," he said. "Perhaps because the darkness and tragedy inherent to your world does not exist in Avilon."

His tone surprised her. "And that's not a good thing?"

Kai absently ran his fingers over the piano's keys. "My kin would think me mad for saying so, but Nico and I have agreed that our lives there were good, and peaceful...but boring. There are only so many times one can play the same song. Our people cling to their peace so hard it has no space to grow, and so we stagnate. Long ago, we understood this, but after genocide and war we have willfully forgotten. Yet the truth of the universe remains: without darkness, light is meaningless."

"Maybe so," she replied, "But that darkness nearly destroyed me when I was still human. My gift ran wild and drove me mad, and I was already running out of time when...if David and I hadn't met, and he hadn't taught me to control it, I don't think I would have survived."

The Bard sighed, and said with mock irritation, "You must stop telling me things like that about your mate, or I will end up liking him in spite of myself."

She laughed. "Oh, I think you already do, you just don't want to admit it."

A conspiratorial grin. "Of course I do. How could I not at least acknowledge a man who so obviously adores, admires, and respects both you and my brother? He is wise enough to know how blessed he is to call you his Queen; that, at the very least, I can appreciate."

She knew, by how hot her face was, that she was blushing crimson, but thankfully he didn't comment on it. He did, however, kiss her hand when he left, and she stood there unable to move for a minute, her skin tingling where his lips had touched.

Oh, hell.

That was two weeks ago; after that, Kai had gone home for the Harvest. She spent the next two weeks in a knot over her sudden and unwelcome attraction to the Elf until David called her on it the night Kai returned. When the Prime left for work, she stayed on her piano bench with her thoughts, trying to make sense out of them before she had to deal with the Bard.

She had, without really saying so, come to the understanding that one day David would have a lover. Whether it was Deven, or someone else, she had long felt a sense of inevitability about it—it was common in Pairs, though the romanticized legends about the Signets made it seem that they were exclusive for all eternity. Very few remained completely monogamous, but historically it was the result of adultery, not a polyamorous arrangement of equals. Over time, starting after that night with Deven and developing further after David's crush on Olivia, Miranda had unconsciously come to accept the idea, but while that theoretically opened the door for her own pursuits, she hadn't thought for a second that any such pursuits would ever exist. David, it seemed, saw right through her, just as she'd seen through him.

Thank God he'd brought it up, though, because she would have had no idea what to say.

Hey baby, you know that Elf you think is a stuck-up bastard? Well, turns out, not so much. In fact I kind of want to...

No.

Okay, so, you know how you get the hots for basically anything that moves these days? I guess you're a bad influence, because...

No.

Hey, I was just thinking, you know what we've never done? Twins!

Oh lord.

She stuck her hands in her hair, trying not to pull it in aggravation. It was all so ridiculous. She had gone up against a dozen armed opponents at a time, recorded two platinum albums, learned how to operate not one but two psychic gifts, and overcome assault and murder—but give her a crush on a ridiculously attractive Elf, and she turned into a gibbering idiot. She'd been telling the truth when she told David she didn't intend to shag the Bard, but Elves were sexually permissive—to put it mildly—so who knew what Kai was thinking?

There was a soft knock at the door, and she swallowed hard. "Come in!"

She knew who it was, of course—there was no mistaking the moonlit presence of an Elf in the room.

She turned, about to try out the Elvish greeting he'd taught her...and froze.

"Are you okay?"

Her gift, it turned out, was not necessary at the moment. Kai's face was haunted, almost dazed with sadness; he sank down on the loveseat back against the wall, unspeaking.

She left the piano and sat down next to him, peering into his face with concern. "What happened...is it Nico?"

A vague nod.

"Tell me."

He took a deep breath, grounding himself. "It was bad tonight," he said softly. "The worst I have seen him. I could feel him losing heart...he fell into a shadow so deep I could barely sense his presence. Then he said..."

"He said he wants to die," Kai went on. "He has no more to give, and just wants rest. What am I to say to that?" He put his face in his hands for a moment before saying, "In all our years, I have never seen him like this. It was always my task to watch over him. Now all I can do is watch him die."

"He is not going to die," Miranda said firmly. "We'll do whatever we have to—even if we have to bind him to us. We'll find a way."

"Can you do that?" he asked, frowning. "Wouldn't that kill his Prime?"

"I don't mean separate them...I just wonder if there's a way to link someone else to Nico to give him energy, like a temporary one-way bond." It was one of the few ideas she'd had that didn't immediately sound ridiculous. Miranda nodded to herself. "I'll talk to Stella—she's better acquainted with that sort of magic and by now I bet she's strong enough. It might work."

"You can use me," Kai said, new determination in his voice. "We are already linked—widen that link and he can have all I can give him."

Miranda smiled. "It's really amazing how much you love your brother. I've never had a twin, but I had a sister, and...well, we definitely weren't like you two."

He looked a bit baffled. "How can you not be close? Blood binds to blood."

"Yeah, not so much here. Maybe things were different back before people were so spread out, and they had to stay closer to each other to survive and thrive—we prize our individuality to a fault. Most families are pretty disconnected."

"Your people are not," Kai pointed out. "There is a deep and still growing connection among all eight of you, binding you more and more tightly."

Miranda froze. "Eight? You can See eight?"

A blink. "Well, I do not have the level of Sight that Nico has, but empathically I can sense all eight of you, yes. Can you not?"

"No. I mean, I don't think so..." Miranda turned her attention inward, seeking out along her bond to David, and from there slowly around the Circle: Deven, Nico, Cora, Jacob, Olivia, and...

"There's someone there," she said softly. "I mean, the bond hasn't formed yet, but there's definitely a person in that spot. That's not how it was a year ago—it was a blank space then. He must be getting closer...I wonder if knowing that would make Olivia feel better or worse."

She shook herself out of it and gave him an encouraging smile. "We're going to save your brother. You have my word."

He took a deep breath and let it out slowly, then smiled back. "I believe you."

"Good. Let's think about something else for now, then."

She sat down on the piano bench, and a moment later he joined her, waiting expectantly for her to either play or talk about the song she wanted him to hear. She looked up at the sheet music. It was, all of a sudden, the last thing in the world she wanted to play.

"Is something wrong?" Kai asked, concerned. "You have a very odd look on your face."

"Well..." Time to be an adult, she supposed. She shifted on the bench to face him. "I have to ask you something. I know you guys are pretty forward when it comes to...interpersonal relationships."

"You mean sex."

"Yes. See? We're repressed, even when we're not. But the thing is, I'm even worse at it than most people. I don't know what to do when I'm attracted to someone. So I guess the best thing to do is just flat out—"

Kai sighed, and sounded somewhat weary as he asked, "Do you intend to take me to bed, Miranda?"

There she went again—her face became scalding hot. "Um...no. Not that I...in theory, I would, and could, but...no."

He nodded. "That's all I need to know."

"You're not going to try and change my mind?"

An eyebrow shot up. "Why would I do that? You said you're not interested. Perhaps one day you will be, perhaps not. If you do, you will say so. I am your friend regardless, as long as that is amenable to you."

She blinked for a second. "You know, you're not like any man I've ever met."

"That's because, thank the Goddess, I am not a man," he pointed out. "Now, the question I do have is this: We have in our friendship been affectionate with each other. That can change if it would make you more comfortable."

"No, no—I don't want anything to change, I just wanted to be honest."

"I appreciate that honesty. Shall we then return to our musical pursuits?"

"Wait, there's one more thing I want to know...how do *you* feel about this? What were you hoping for?"

"In our relationship?" He took a deep breath, which she could have interpreted a number of ways. "I find you deeply alluring, funny, kind...and of course beautiful in ways I had quite literally never seen. If you were ever to desire more than friendship I would be more than happy to oblige. Am I going to pine away for you, celibate and miserable? No. I am not a youngling given to fits of swooning. You need not worry, as I am sure you will, about hurting my feelings."

Miranda sat blinking at him again for a minute. "Okay."

When he saw her face, he started laughing—another thing she rarely saw. "You do realize you are not obligated to keep up with your husband, don't you? Unless of course you have a scoreboard over your bed, in which case I must know how many points an Elf is worth."

She slapped his arm. "Shut up!"

Another laugh. Then, something in his expression changed, sobered; he stared down at the piano keys, and after a moment he said quietly, "He really does love Nico, doesn't he."

Miranda nodded. "Yes. Very much. Your brother completely blindsided him. Even I didn't see it coming—I thought if anyone ever caught his heart it would be Deven again. I mean, of course he thought Nico was attractive, and they had a connection from the beginning. Nico needed to feel safe, and there's nobody better for the job. Then one day I finally realized it was way more than that. Despite appearances David doesn't open his heart to just anybody."

"He would have to be made of sterner stuff than stone to avoid it, surrounded by such remarkable creatures," Kai observed. "And clearly the feeling is mutual. Even with his sorrow and weakness, when Nico speaks of him, a light returns to his eyes I had feared would never spark again."

Miranda smiled. "That's pretty much what happened to me."

Their eyes met for a moment, and thank God, the awkwardness Miranda had been feeling was gone; they could get back to what they both needed, friendship, without her being in a twist every time their hands touched.

"Shall we, then?" Kai asked.

The Queen nodded. "We shall." She hiked her leg back over the bench to face the piano, and picked up the sheet music she'd had waiting there. "I wanted you to see this piece—it's a duet I did with another musician a while back, but we did some interesting things with the harmonies…"

Chapter Three

By the time dawn arrived, Nico had fought his way through five more pages of the Codex, and his head hurt so badly he wanted to scream.

He barely heard the knock, but what few people ever came to see him were always welcome, so it opened and closed without his having to look up from the book's swiftly-blurring pages.

There were the usual sounds of someone taking off a jacket. Nico looked up and offered a smile. "Back safely, I see."

Stella grinned. She tossed her hooded sweater on a chair then paused on the side of the bed to pull off her rather enormous black boots, revealing striped knee-high socks that matched her fingernails. Then she slid around behind him and rubbed his shoulders, eliciting a sigh. "Glad to be back, actually. I love my dad, but all the questions are getting old. When are you moving back to Austin? What about college? A job? A boyfriend?"

"Did you tell him you're sleeping with a vampire Elf who's been teaching you magic?"

A giggle. "Maybe I should—he'd probably stop asking then."

Nico closed his eyes. "Even though it isn't really true."

"It is true! We are, literally, sleeping together, and you *were* teaching me magic. You will again soon."

He tried to agree with her, but all he could get out was, "I hope so." Hoping to change the subject, he asked, "How is Lark?"

"She's doing great, actually. Foxglove promoted her to manager of the store, and she met a girl at the last Full Moon potluck—a geology teaching assistant at the university. Lark's even writing again. She says hi, by the way."

Nico smiled. He quite liked Lark, whom he had met several times on her visits to the Haven. The two young women had made a concerted effort to spend more time together, so Stella was often in the city for a few days at a time—a relief, he imagined, from playing nursemaid to a languishing Elf.

"Anything good tonight?" she asked, indicating the Codex with one foot.

"Actually, yes...I seem to have finally reached the part of the book that is relevant to our current situation. This, for example, is the beginning of the story of the original Circle. There appear to be three separate accounts, but I could only read one of them. That first coven was led by two of what we would call Thirdborn, though they weren't named as such. It's hard to say exactly what made them different besides being stronger—the text alludes to other qualities that set them apart, but it's not specific, at least not yet. They aren't named, but the author of the story, Galatea, was one of the Circle's Primes, and her Consort was named Cybele."

"Galatea...you mean they were both women?"

"They were."

"I'll be damned," Stella said, a smile in her voice. "So it's not as novel as we thought. You should tell..."

She trailed off, and he had to smile a little himself at that despite the ache it caused in his chest. "You can say his name, you know," Nico told her. "David does the same thing—like it's a secret invocation."

Stella laughed and kissed his ear. "It's more like Voldemort at this point."

"Who?"

"Never mind. Anything else interesting?"

"There's a ritual..." He held the Codex at an angle so she could see it and turned to a page covered in a complicated diagram of circles and spirals. Like everything in the Codex it had an Elvish feel to it, but was still distinctly its own creature. "When the entire Circle is complete, they can then dedicate a room—one in each Haven if they like—to communicating with Persephone. All eight together have to consecrate it, but after that any can use it alone or in groups. I just got to the instructions tonight, but I was too tired to continue."

"So as soon as we find Olivia's Consort, you guys can finally get the rest of the way across the bridge and find out what the hell Persephone wants from you."

"The ritual does something else, too. Apparently after it's performed, we'll be able to translate dialect number three. What we see here is *supposed* to look like nonsense. It's not encoded, it's bespelled. That's how the Order ensured that only the next Circle would be able to read their secrets. The book will only allow those who have stood in that dedicated room to know what it says."

"But they are assuming we can figure out dialect number two."

"So it would seem. And I will—it's just taking forever."

Nico leaned back against the Witch, giving up on the need to be vertical for a while. Her arms wound around him, along with her legs. He thought back to the night he'd first met her out walking the grounds of the Haven—she, like all of them, had changed so much in these months. The power in her had put down roots and was growing upward; she was still brightly colored and refreshingly young, but a certain sophistication had begun to creep into both her wardrobe and her demeanor—influenced, he suspected, by the Queen. As her power rapidly matured, so did Stella.

He shut his eyes against a sudden tide of sorrow. "I miss how things were at the beginning," he said softly. "When I still had the strength to teach you Weaving...when I could still Weave. I miss those first few weeks when you and I were all over each other. That time was so painful, in so many ways—I never thought I would look back on it fondly."

"Me too." Stella nuzzled his neck, breathing in slowly. "But it's okay, you know. Things will get better."

"They've only gotten worse so far." Nico laced his fingers with hers. "I don't know how much longer I can go on, *caraia*...the other night I actually began to wonder how much it would hurt to walk out into the sunlight...I made the mistake of telling Kai, and he nearly had a panic attack."

"Oh, sweetie..." Stella squeezed his hands. He tilted his head back and saw tears in her eyes. "You deserve so much better than all of this. I just want to kick little Voldemort in the junk sometimes."

Nico blinked—he had gained fluency in English rather quickly, but some of their idioms were far over his head. Still, her meaning was easy enough to deduce. He had to smile. "I appreciate the solidarity...but I don't think there's anything you could do to him worse than what he does to himself every waking minute."

There was another knock, and a second later a red head poked in the room. "Nico, are you up and decent?"

"I am, my Lady, come in."

Miranda and David both stood in the hallway. It was rare enough for both to come see him together that he was immediately put on guard, but he couldn't sense anything new had gone wrong with either of the Pair...not that his senses were good for much these days.

"We need to have a family meeting," the Queen said. She sat down in one of the armchairs, resplendent in what David called their "work clothes"—mostly black, made to look elegant and powerful but still able to fight. Nico could see the hilt of the Queen's sword, Shadowflame. It was odd...before coming here the idea of being around so much weaponry had made him deeply uneasy, but now, seeing either of them in their Signet regalia of leather and steel was comforting. His own life might be fading into utter uselessness, but there was someone in charge, someone taking care of things. He imagined that was why the vampires of the world were willing to put their faith in their leaders; when a Signet was in their corner, they were safe from all comers.

David remained on his feet for the moment but shot Nico a warm smile touched with a hint of promise that hatched a dozen or so butterflies in Nico's stomach. At least that much he could still achieve; he might fall asleep mid-kiss, but he did still feel that desire.

In truth, Nico had never wanted someone so much in his life, but for the first time in his life he was unable to do more than touch and flirt like a youngling. He had been relatively solitary in Avilon, but he'd always had lovers aplenty when he wished. It was nearly impossible to live celibate in Avilon except deliberately. Now, he was craving that sweat-bathed dissolution, that joining, a gasp in the darkness of a cool Autumn night...and his body had declared what Stella had dubbed a shag embargo. It would have been amusing if it had not been so face-clawingly frustrating.

Stella moved out from behind Nico and sat cross-legged on the bed beside him where she could see everyone. She and Miranda grinned at each other.

Kai arrived last, sweeping in with his usual grandeur. He greeted Stella with a smile and took the other chair near the fire. He'd warmed up to the Witch considerably over the months, in no small part because Stella's forthright, witty personality was so different from most Elven women. To most living in Avilon she would come off as brash, but to Kai she was adorable, and to Nico she was perfect.

The Queen turned the tiniest bit pink when the Bard smiled at her, but there was no real awkwardness in their demeanor upon greeting. Kai had related their conversation to Nico, and though Kai clearly thought the matter settled, Nico had to wonder how an empath of his caliber could be so blind to his own emotions. Everything the Bard had told the Queen was certainly true; it would never occur to Kai to be dishonest about that kind of thing. But Kai normally went through lovers like harp strings, and in the last year— by his own admission—that number had dwindled significantly. Kai said, and Nico knew he believed, that the change was due to splitting his time between Avilon and Austin…but did he truly believe that was *all?*

Nico looked over at David, who was watching the two with an unreadable expression. It was his Prime face—perfectly neutral so that no one around could tell what he was thinking or feeling. David had told Nico more than once that he was fine with the idea of Miranda having a lover…but that was when it was just an idea. Nico fervently hoped he *would* be fine with it, because if not, it was a distinct possibility that David would terminate any romantic intentions toward Nico and the Pair would go back to the theoretical simplicity of monogamy. For very selfish reasons, Nico prayed it wouldn't come to that. He had little enough to look forward to as it was.

"All right," Miranda said. "I have an idea, but I need to know if it's ludicrous, so I want to run it by the magic-workers of the household. My idea was that if we can find a way to connect you to one of us, Nico, we might be able to stabilize you—counteract some of the effects of all this. Up until now we've been looking at this like the only solution was to change the Signet bond, which we just don't have the power to do. In this case I'm not talking a Signet bond, just an energy lifeline."

"So it's come to this," Nico said, leaning back against the headboard and closing his eyes. "A year ago I was one of the most powerful Weavers among Elvenkind, and now I am an invalid who can't even manage my own energy."

"Do not be an ass," Kai said. "You need help and we want to help you. It is not a reflection on you, it is a reflection on that self-loathing little ingrate you have been saddled with."

Miranda's eyebrows shot up, and Nico saw David tense up in his peripheral vision—it would seem the Pair was not previously aware of how Kai felt about Deven. David was angry at the Prime, but would hardly talk about it, and had never been quite so blunt about his feelings.

Kai, of course, could always be counted upon.

The Bard noticed their discomfort and said firmly, "I make no apology. You all had the luxury of knowing him before, when he was redeemable—all I know of him is what you see here. I have no reason whatsoever to make excuses as the rest of you do. It is absolutely right for him to mourn the loss of his beloved, but it is not right to make Nico suffer for it. He does not care if he hurts my brother, and thus I care nothing for him."

Everyone was silent for a moment before David said quietly, "He's right."

The Queen gave her husband a look of astonishment— probably as much from the sentiment itself as hearing David agree with Kai.

"All I mean is," David amended, "We can't treat this problem as if Deven has anything to do with the solution."

Miranda said, softly, "I thought you said you weren't giving up on him."

Nico saw the pain in David's eyes. "It's not a matter of giving up. It's a matter of facing reality. Maybe there's hope for him and maybe there's not, but we have to move on and stop waiting. We could have done something months ago, but our fear of causing Deven more pain has caused Nico more pain—how is that better? It made absolutely no difference to Deven what we did. Nico, Stella—is Miranda's idea feasible?"

Witch and Weaver exchanged a look. "Sure," Stella said. "We've all been giving him energy when we could, just not in a steady dedicated stream. But it would have to be someone pretty damn powerful or they'd end up drained too, and we'd have two problems instead of one."

"I volunteer," Kai said immediately.

Nico smiled at his twin and said ruefully, "I'm afraid that wouldn't work, brother. We have a psychic connection, yes, but you've seen how much weaker it is when you're home. Unless you want to live here permanently, which I would not allow even if you claimed you did, you cannot provide the continuous support I would need."

"As much as I'd love to do it, I don't think I'm strong enough," Stella said. "I've gotten a lot more powerful this year but I'm still human—I think if we want the best outcome for an immortal we need an immortal."

Miranda nodded. She didn't seem surprised. "The advantage of using one of us is that you won't just be connected to one, but to the other indirectly. Believe me, we have all the energy you need."

"No doubt," Stella said. "Nico—do you think there'll be a problem since you're not the same sort of vampire?"

Nico thought about it a moment. "No. As long as it's a superficial link the difference won't matter—it's only when dealing with something as profound as a Signet bond that it becomes an issue."

"You're about to leave town," David said to the Queen. "We shouldn't wait three weeks—I guess that leaves me."

"It's logical," Stella told them. "You've already got an emotional connection; that can give us an advantage, like using a needle threader when you're sewing. And since Nico's not strong enough to actually do the work, and I'm the only person around with Weaving experience, that added link would be really helpful."

"You're sure you can do it?" Miranda asked. "It won't hurt you?"

"It shouldn't. It's pretty straightforward, magically speaking. It's not very risky for me, but it could be for you guys. A link like this always sets you up for nasty consequences if something goes wrong—look at what happened when you guys were a Trinity. This won't be anywhere near that deep or strong, but with the Circle connection and your Pair bond, there are a lot of unknowns. I doubt any of your people have done this before. We can't even be sure how much it will help."

Nico looked at David, who was looking back at him. "He's worth it," the Prime said, and then glanced at his Queen.

"I agree," she said with a smile.

"Are you sure?" Nico asked, lifting his eyes to the Prime. "You would be willing to link to me, possibly for a very long time, even without knowing what the side effects might be?"

Miranda rose from her chair and came over to the bed, sitting down beside him. "Nico," she said, reaching out to take his hand, "We love you. All of us. And we will fight to the bitter end to keep you with us and make you well. Don't forget that, okay?"

Nico started to nod and reply, but all that came out was a sob—the state of his life right now, the possibility that this really could help, knowing that they were all willing to do it for him...his damaged, worn-out heart couldn't take it. He wept.

Arms began to wind around him: First Stella's, then Miranda's, then David's, and Kai's.

Miranda rested her forehead against his and said to him gently, "You are loved, silly Elf. You're worth kingdoms to all of us."

Unbidden, the memory arose of Miranda's voice working its honeyed way through a haze of pain, giving him something beautiful to hold onto while Elven nature and vampire nature fought one another throughout his body. He could not doubt her words; he had felt their truth already.

"So when do we do it?" Kai asked.

Stella did math in her head, and replied, "Friday. It's the Full Moon. I know you won't be in town, Miranda, is that okay?"

"As long as you don't need me for the work itself, it'll be fine."

"All right then. Friday night, we'll meet in the ritual room. Be there or be square."

The others left for their own quarters, except for Stella. The Witch gathered up the Codex and its associated research paraphernalia and moved it off the bed; neither spoke until she'd shucked her clothes, put on the tank top and cartoon-cat-festooned pants that she kept in his room, and climbed into bed beside him.

She settled into his arms with a sigh that turned into a yawn. "Do you really think it's a good idea?" she asked. "You didn't say much about it, but you didn't contradict what I said, so..." The last word rose into a question.

Nico turned toward her, sliding one hand over her hip and up to her waist. He loved the landscape of her body—human curves rather than Elven angles. "I honestly don't know," he said. "I've done something similar back in Avilon, but those were Elves, not Thirdborn vampires. I don't know if any of the usual rules apply to the two of them. You've seen their part of the Web."

Stella nodded. "Scary as hell," she affirmed. "The strands keep getting darker and stronger...I don't even think they realize it's happening. My main worry is that connecting you to them might...do things to you."

He didn't have the energy to feign ignorance. "It might. And it might do things to David. Such a small amount of power shouldn't cause any measurable imbalance in the Pair, and I doubt any side effects will be truly dangerous in the short-term, but there could be long-term alterations in both of us, and even Miranda, if it goes on long enough."

"Plus there's the sex thing."

He raised an eyebrow. "I sincerely hope the link gives me the wherewithal."

She laughed. "That's not what I mean. Do you remember when we first hooked up, and every time, I'd walk around in a bliss bubble for days? That wasn't just the multiple orgasms—that Elf Tantra you do is pretty intense magic. That scar on my knee disappeared, remember?"

"Yes...I admit I don't really understand it. You're the first non-Elf I've been with; I didn't realize there would be such a difference."

"Exactly. Whenever you and David finally get down to it, if you're already linked, a bliss bubble might be the least of his worries."

"We'll just have to see," he murmured, wriggling as close to her as he could, hoping to steal some of her warmth. He was so tired of being cold...David had promised to bring him something called an electric blanket that apparently generated heat. Nico would prefer just to sleep with him—he was like a very, very attractive furnace—but he did his best not to demand too much of David's time, or anyone else's.

"I hope it works," Stella said softly, kissing his ear. "David's right—whether there's any hope for Deven or not, you need to move on. You need your life back."

Nico wanted to feel hopeful at the prospect. It would be good to feel something besides exhaustion and sadness, to work magic, to muster more than the most anemic affection for those he loved. The thought of feeling like himself again was too cruel a hope to accept, so for now, he closed his eyes and listened to Stella's breath even out, letting the sweet vanilla scent of her hair and the so very human sound of her heartbeat draw him along into another dreamless sleep.

"Sire? We've arrived at the Haven."

He started at the sound of her voice. He hadn't intended to fall asleep. "Thank you, Chris."

He was still trying to force his brain to wake up when Chris opened the door for him. He had to sit a moment, feet on the driveway but still sitting in the car, until the world stopped spinning; these long nights wandering from hospital to clinic to hospice all over town were taking their toll.

"Are you all right, Sire?"

"Fine," he muttered. "Just give me a minute."

She stepped back without comment. She'd been driving him for weeks, and working for Signets had gotten her used to odd requests from grumpy rich people. She was probably regretting that he'd picked her instead of the other secondary driver, even though he tipped in hundred dollar bills.

The Haven employed three drivers: Harlan, Chris, and a man whose name he could never remember. Harlan of course had a permanent assignment, so Deven was left to choose between Chris and the other one. Truth be told he didn't really care who was behind the wheel as long as they kept their mouth shut about what he was doing. He had picked Chris over the other driver for one reason: her Adam's apple.

Deviant solidarity, he thought irritably. The Haven was probably one of the most diverse workplaces in Texas, which wasn't really saying much, but it was one of the few Havens he knew of that had a Muslim doctor, a Jewish near-Second, at least two transgendered employees he knew of, and a dazzling variety of other religions, ethnicities, sexualities, and now even species living under its roof, all on the payroll of the most powerful bisexual on the planet. It was well known, at least in Austin, that David hired anyone who fit a position regardless of demographics, so minorities of all types flocked to him, which pleased him just fine. California had been similar, once.

Despite his mood, the thought of Avishai Shavit in charge of the Southern Elite almost made Deven smile.

David's suspicious eyes were on Carmine 2.3, a low-ranking warrior, as a spy—and quite rightly. She'd been in place since Lalita had been killed. But it had yet to occur to David that the Alpha might know Carmine was being watched. There was one Red Shadow operative in each Elite in most Signet territories; there had never been two at once. David kept track of most of them.

Bless his heart.

The main reason Deven had bothered keeping the Red Shadow running was that he felt an odd sense of obligation to his agents. He kept those on assignment in place, and as agents finished their work he put them on paid leave, the understanding being that they might be called back out again at any moment…though he hadn't taken on any new contracts in several months. He didn't know yet what he wanted to do with the Shadow, but he knew he couldn't leave his agents hanging mid-mission with no further contact or instruction.

He pushed himself up to his feet and grabbed the door for a second when the vertigo returned, but waved Chris away when she started toward him. She was used to his tendency to come home stoned or drunk out of his mind, and undoubtedly thought that's what this was.

Unfortunately it was nothing so enjoyable—it was burnout. Every night that he felt the power start to scorch his hands he had no choice but to use it…or, rather, let it use him. He had to scatter his visits around town so that nobody would notice a sudden rash of miraculous healings; he also held back as much as he could with each person, only taking care of the worst problems—he'd erase a child's leukemia but leave the side effects of chemotherapy alone, letting them resolve themselves.

If only he could use it up, and stay burnt out, but tomorrow night he'd wake up with just as much power as he'd had the night before, dragging him to the city, to sickbed after sickbed. There was no end to it. No relief.

Unless he were to try to balance it, and to do that...

He pushed the thought away and forced himself to walk. The hallways were a blur, but he knew the way so well he didn't need to think about it, and was back at his room and in the shower before he really had time to choose a destination.

It was a testament to how wasted he was that he didn't sense an intruder.

He walked out of the bathroom and froze.

The most logical question was irrelevant. He knew exactly who it was.

"You must be Kai," he said, walking past the Elf to fetch a shirt from the bureau. He felt dark eyes on him, narrowed, evaluating, and as he turned to face the Elf, those eyes didn't waver, but stayed fixed on him, still examining.

Deven pulled the shirt on and sank into a chair, grateful that the servant he'd been assigned had built a fire while he was gone. He had always been cold-natured, but now it was a constant.

He regarded his visitor without much enthusiasm either for or against his presence. "What do you want?"

The Elf sat down in the other chair without invitation, and they stared at each other in silence another moment before Kai said, in careful but clear English, "I thought it was time you and I met."

Deven raised an eyebrow. "You've been coming here for nearly two years and it just now occurred to you?"

"No." Kai rested his elbows on the chair's arms and interlaced his fingers. He was as coldly regal as any Prime, all the more impressive because of the insane length of his raven-black hair and the finely-woven clothes he wore, including a velvet cloak that should have looked ridiculous in this day and age but was the only thing that would look appropriate on such a creature.

"I decided from the very beginning to hate you," Kai went on, mincing no words, which Deven had to appreciate. "I love my brother very much and what you have done to him is unforgivable. Yet he and all the others have defended you to me time and again. And then, two nights ago, the Prime himself admitted that you might not be salvageable...and I could sense how much it cost him to say so. In spite of my best efforts I have come to value his wisdom, and for him to have held out hope for so long suggests there might be more to you than I believed."

"Well, trust your first instinct," Deven told him. "You were absolutely right."

Kai smiled slightly. "Perhaps I should have come months ago. I might have spoken more kindly of you all this while."

"Why? What evidence of my worth have you uncovered in five minutes?"

Still smiling, the Elf said, "I am an empath, my Lord. I uncovered what I needed within twenty seconds."

"Great," Deven muttered, looking over at the fire and avoiding that dark stare. "Now there's two of you running around."

"The Queen, too, is deeply grieved by your loss, but she has a much gentler heart than her mate's."

"If by gentler you mean deeper in denial of reality, I agree."

Another silence. Deven tried to think of a way to make the Elf leave, but he had a sense that nothing he could say would elicit much of a reaction. In fact, he had the distinct feeling his behavior was being tolerated by the Elf, as one might tolerate a child's.

Finally, Kai asked a surprising question: "Does this make you happy?"

"What?"

"The distorted vision of time and pain has made you believe you are worthless—if you can make everyone who loves you come to hate you, will you finally be satisfied?"

Deven had no answer for that.

Unfortunately that seemed to be all the answer Kai needed. "It will not work, you know. I cannot speak for the Pair, but I know my brother. His love is endless and eternally forgiving. It is his most remarkable and infuriating quality. You can torment him with this wall you have built, and drain him until he is nothing but skin and bone—as he is now—but you cannot shake his heart from yours."

"Then he's even more of a fool than I thought he was."

Kai didn't rise to the bait. Instead he rose physically, the movement graceful and silent except for the swish of whatever material his clothes were made from.

The Bard paused, eyes lighting on the fireplace mantel, where Ghostlight gathered dust in her sheath. "I am told you were a warrior once," he said.

"I was a lot of things once."

"A warrior, and a healer...a leader, friend, lover...one of the strongest of your kind...you must have saved so many lives back in those days. A pity." Kai looked down at him, and this time there was actually something kind in his eyes, as if he'd seen something in Deven in the last few minutes that Deven hadn't seen in 766 years. "Imagine what joy you might have found, and what miracles you could have worked in the world, had you not chosen to waste your time hating yourself."

Again, Deven had no idea how to respond. Kai merely nodded, bestowing another measured smile upon him, and left the room, closing the door behind him without the slightest noise.

Deven tried to focus on the fire and push the Elf's visit out of his mind, but to his horror, he felt his eyes starting to burn...not even because of Kai's words, but...

He looks so much like Nico.

Oh, Nico...oh, God...would you really forgive me? Even now? Why would you do that?

It would be so easy just to...

NO.

His knees nearly gave out twice between the chair and the bed, but he managed to get there, collapse onto the bed, and grope desperately in the bedside table for what he knew was there: a vial and a syringe.

That's right...disappear into a needle again. Show everyone how pathetic you are.

Except no one is listening anymore, are they. They're giving up on you. That's what you wanted, right?

He stared at the needle hovering over his arm for one minute, then two...and then a brief moment of sudden anger seized him, and with what little strength he had he threw it at the fireplace, followed by the bottle.

A faint pop, glass breaking.

And as much as he wanted to forget, to turn away from the memory, that tiny bit of affection in Kai's gaze took hands with the memory of Miranda's face outside the hospital, telling him she missed him...and before he could fall asleep, he had to roll over, away from a pillow damp with tears.

*****

Miranda and her entourage left Thursday night, and that Friday afternoon for the first time in a long time, David woke alone.

He lay listening to the eerie silence of the suite for a while, marveling at how different everything felt. There was something vital missing from the air, as if a light he hadn't known was lit had been abruptly switched off. It even felt colder, but that was mostly because she wasn't wrapped around him.

Miranda wasn't a noisy person, wasn't terribly messy...but she took up so much space here, and when she was gone, nothing felt right.

He knew if he dwelt on it that would only make the separation worse; if they were both in a good space they could stay apart a little longer. They were going to try and make her runs back home as infrequent as possible—laying here pining for her would not help matters at all.

Funny how once upon a time he'd been so used to solitude that having her in the Mistress Suite kept him awake—all her human noises, the scent of her reaching him at odd times. He'd shagged his way through a lot of redheads to avoid owning up to his feelings for her. As frustrating as those months had been, it was worth it in the long run. She had come to him when *she* was ready, and they had fit into each other's lives with a seamlessness that he wouldn't have believed possible.

She'd be in Dallas by now getting ready for the first show of her tour. A truck had carried her performance piano and other instruments, and she'd been driven, but after Dallas she'd take the jet over the larger distances to save time and fuel. Next was California. She was traveling clockwise around America, to all four of their territories and points between, and would end the tour with a show in Austin. There were a lot of places she wanted to stop and visit if she had time...including the bare, silent cliff where a year ago had stood a beautiful Mediterranean-inspired villa with a breathtaking view of the forest.

David had wanted to begin rebuilding the Haven right away, but Miranda had stopped him—how could he presume to know whether Deven would want the same design? He might, or he might want something totally different to keep from wandering around in the memories. It didn't seem right, she'd said, to build anything on that ground without its owner's permission.

Which meant it might never be built. But that might not be such a bad thing.

Again, as had happened a dozen times since Jonathan's death, David found himself praying, silently, to Whomever might be listening:

Bring Deven back to us. Back to Nico. Back to Miranda. Back to me.

Tell me the price and I'll pay it. Lay down your conditions and I'll fulfill them. Please.

Jonathan, if you're out there, thump him in the head for me. He might listen to you.

There was never an answer, but it still gave him small comfort to think the words—maybe that was why humans prayed even when their prayers met only the echoing silence of an indifferent universe.

Finally, before he could get even more mired in his own thoughts, David got out of bed. He had work to do before meeting the others at the ritual room, and since he wasn't sure how he'd be feeling after Stella was done doing whatever she planned to do, he wanted to check as many items off his endless to-do list as possible.

First a check on the new coms. He'd implanted four Elite with them, including Avi, who had agreed quite gamely to be part of the experiment. There should be reports from each; Avi was with Miranda, but it was a good opportunity to test the coms out in a closed sub-network that then connected back to the Haven.

He got dressed and headed for the office. Situation normal; no surprise there. All four Elite guinea pigs had dutifully dropped their reports on the server, answering the questions he'd sent with as much detail as possible.

No itching, swelling, or redness at injection site. Implant does not appear to have moved. Good. It looked like they couldn't feel the thing at all except from the outside, pushing on it with a finger. The transmitter was smaller than Miranda's pinkie nail, resembling a flat watch battery; they were injected under the skin just behind the ear. Each had to be individually calibrated, though, so it took a while to fully initialize them. The transmitters were tuned to a frequency only the individual could hear—the main purpose was to keep communication from being as obvious out in public. They could blend in completely by wearing a phone earpiece so it seemed they were just regular people talking to themselves as they walked around town armed and all in black, but in urgent situations they could simply speak aloud and be heard from afar. It was far less conspicuous than talking into a bracelet.

Better still, the Elite wearing the implant could give simple yes or no answers just by thinking them. The transmitter picked up low levels of psychic energy. If this system worked, he hoped one day to have the entire system use telepathy amplified and recorded by technology.

He wouldn't have thought it possible a few years ago. But once he'd figured out how to track spells and amulets like the ones Ovaska had used, he'd been able to create the sensor he'd used when they found the Codex; it was too complicated to be of much practical use until he'd done a lot more work on it, but it had occurred to him that they didn't need anything that complex for the coms, at least not right away. Ultimately, though, what had made it possible wasn't his geekery, it was magic.

Or, rather, it was Nico.

They'd been curled up in front of the fireplace one evening, just talking, and he'd mentioned the problems he was having. Nico had commented that it sounded a lot like the long-distance communication methods the Elves used. From there, they ended up with a drawing pad and David's tablet, sketching out the way the Weavers had set things up in Avilon, comparing it to the way David ran things here. The two were remarkably similar.

That was the night he had realized that Nico was not only beautiful and powerful—he was brilliant. David had always found genius incredibly attractive, whether intellectual or artistic. Watching Miranda play still had the power to melt his spine—so did watching her compose a song, frowning, the tip of her tongue sticking out the corner of her mouth...

Damn. He needed to think about something else before thinking turned into longing—longing would quickly turn into desperation and she'd be on her way back to Austin way too early. So: distraction.

Just in time, the phone rang.

He smiled as he picked it up. "Good timing."

Olivia's warm voice held its usual wry edge. "Poor baby," she said. "Twelve whole hours without Her Royal Hotness and you're climbing the walls. However will you last the week?"

"You can't see it, but I'm flipping you off right now."

A laugh. "So," she said, obviously feigning nonchalance, "Tonight you're getting your Elf hookup, right?"

"If all goes well, yes."

"And what's that going to lead to?"

"Well...hopefully it'll give him more energy, emotionally and physically, so he can at least have the strength to take better care of himself. I'm hoping that—"

"That's not what I mean, dumbass."

"Then what...oh." David chuckled. "You would want to know that, wouldn't you."

"Hey, it's just me and my battery operated boyfriend up here. Give me some fodder at least—the mental image of you and some pointy-eared sexy beast going at it would keep me buzzing for a while."

Now, he laughed outright. "You're incorrigible, woman."

"You're the one who passed out on my front porch and got me into this whole mess. It's all on you."

David leaned back in his desk chair, smiling. "True. I get such delight out of sucking innocent bystanding vampires into our collective madness."

"Not just vampires anymore. Witches, Elves...if I happen across a werewolf I'll send him along and you can have a complete set." He could hear her rustling papers around, meaning she too was at her desk. "So is there anyone you aren't planning to sleep with?"

He snorted. "I thought I'd stop once I got to Jacob."

"If you do manage to shag the Elf, that'll be three people in the building you've been involved with. Miranda has some catching up to do."

"Honestly, I don't really think her thing with Kai is going to get that far. I just can't see her going to bed with anyone, at least not yet. I worry about her getting hurt, but she's a grown woman who knows her own heart and mind."

"But you're sure she's okay with all of this?"

"I'm sure. We've talked about it at length. She comes first, obviously. And believe me, this isn't something I plan to make a habit of. I wasn't expecting this. I figured eventually we'd move in that sort of direction—but I thought that was decades in the future."

Too fast...everything these days was moving too fast, even though nothing was actually happening right at this moment. Why couldn't he and Miranda have had fifty or so years to rule in relative quiet before all of this?

"Well, just...be careful. All of you. And be careful tonight for different reasons. I know your Stella knows her stuff, but things could still go wrong. We're all rather attached to you, you know."

He smiled. "I know. It'll be okay, I promise. I'll talk to you tomorrow night, hopefully, or at least send a text."

"You'd better."

As soon as he hung up, David finished running through the various checks he did every night, returned his most urgent emails, and spent a moment reading through Jacob's report on the latest Council doings. There were no new deaths, thankfully, but several of the holdouts who had insisted Morningstar wasn't a real threat were quietly increasing security, hiring dozens more Elite and retreating to their Havens whenever possible. Morningstar might not have made a move lately, but they didn't need to right now—fear was doing their job for them, and soon they'd have the entire Council treed like a squirrel.

He wanted to take satisfaction from it, and he had for a while, but even divorced from the Council their fate was tied in with his. They represented the last bastion of traditional order in the Shadow World, and as antiquated as they were, their loss would usher in an era of civil war and worldwide violence until someone either took things in hand or their entire society was destroyed and there were no laws, nothing to stop vampire kind from killing en masse and quickly exposing their existence to the world.

It was not a comforting thought. Neither was the thought that the someone taking things in hand was probably going to be him.

He was, therefore, in a fairly dark mood when he arrived at the ritual room, where Stella, Nico, and Kai were already waiting for him. Stella had candles burning on the altar with a typical Wiccan array of tools and décor. They'd also piled a dozen or so cushions on the floor, and Nico was sitting cross-legged on one, looking tired and faintly sick. Kai was fussing over him as usual, and David caught himself having another moment of the tiniest bit of appreciation, if not affection, for the Bard. It was something of a relief, really—he and Kai might never really like each other, but they needed to be able to coexist, and if they could be friendly, so much the better, for Nico's sake and Miranda's.

Kai seemed to agree. He gave David a nod in greeting. Nico, on the other hand, smiled like the moon rising on a cloudless night, and all worries about the Council and vampire society vanished under that light.

Stella was in a more serious mood than usual. "Okay," she said, taking one last look at the altar to make sure nothing was missing. "If you guys will have a seat facing each other, we can get started."

Kai looked worried but determined, and squeezed Nico's shoulder lightly. "I'll be close by if you need me," he told his twin, and left the room, looking back at Nico one more time before closing the door.

David gave Nico what he hoped was a reassuring smile as Stella circumambulated the room, marking the boundary of a large circle with salt, water, and incense. Slowly David could feel something in the room changing; he didn't have the Sight the others did, but he could definitely sense the Witch at work. The room felt closed off, removed from the ordinary world.

Stella settled herself on another cushion so that the three of them were in a triangle. "Make sure there's one behind you," she told David. "Just in case this knocks you out and you fall over."

"Are you going to help, Nico?" David asked. He kept his voice low—the air in the room had taken on the feeling of a church, or a grove of ancient trees where no one would dare speak above a hushed, reverent tone.

The Weaver shook his head. "I am useless, I fear," he said. "I have not been able to Weave for a long time, and I lost my vision of the Web months ago. I get glimpses, and when Stella and I work together I can See more, but she needs her full attention on the task at hand."

David lowered his eyes, trying to stay grounded, but the matter-of-fact way Nico spoke of losing the gift that made him who he was, was heartbreaking. Sadness and anger both tried to claw their way up his chest, but he smoothed them over carefully before they could leak out.

"Tell me what you need me to do," he told Stella.

The Witch's eyes were closed, but she grinned. "Hold hands and shut up," she replied.

Prime and Weaver smiled at each other and laced their fingers together.

David wasn't the sort of person who was content to just sit still and let other people work—he felt like he ought to be doing something, especially since for a while it seemed like Stella was just meditating.

Then, she asked, "Nico...can I bring you in for a look? I have it narrowed down to two strands, but I could use a second opinion."

"Of course," Nico said, and closed his eyes. As if he sensed David's discomfort, he narrated what he was seeing. "There are two possible places in your Web where she can anchor the link between us. One is more powerful, but it runs deeper; the other is more superficial."

"Why not use the deeper one?" David asked.

The Elf smiled. "The deeper she reaches for the power, the more intimate the connection—we might get more than we bargained for, you especially. Connecting to that one will be less draining for you, as it's closer to the core of your being, but you run the risk of having me wrapped more tightly in you than you wanted."

"We're not talking Signet bond level, are we?"

"Oh, no," Stella said. "Even the deeper strand is way, way weaker than that. It won't come anywhere near your bond with Miranda, either in power or proximity. There are levels of connection a Signet bond reaches that go way beyond simple energy exchange. He might get echoes of it, but that's all. On the other hand if we use the superficial strand you won't be as solidly connected, but it will probably make you more tired than the other. It's like your bond with Miranda is your aorta, the inner strand is your femoral artery, and the other is whatever vein it is in your arm that they stick needles in."

"Femoral artery," David said firmly.

"Are you sure?" Nico asked. "We cannot predict the consequences."

"I'm sure—for one thing, if you're going to be yourself again you need strength, and some arm vein isn't going to do it. For another, I can't afford to walk around like I have an IV line in 24/7. I've dealt with chronic low-level weakness before; it's impossible to do my job if I'm draped over a fainting couch."

Stella chuckled, probably at the mental image. "All right," she said. "Let's do it. You can step back, Nico—if I need your eyes again I'll say so."

"Very well."

Nico squeezed David's hands. David wondered if the Elf was afraid; he wasn't showing it, but this had to be at least a little scary, the thought of being connected to a Thirdborn even on a mostly-superficial level. There could be just as many consequences for Nico as for him. At the very least he should be a little anxious.

Actually, he was; despite his calm exterior he was afraid that it wouldn't work, that he had gotten his hopes up for nothing yet again…or that David would hate being linked and want it severed…David could feel him resolutely staying grounded, but he was…

…wait…

"Did you feel that?" Nico asked quietly.

"Yes."

"Not quite there," Stella murmured. "The link is made but I'm holding it shut for a second while I make sure there aren't any weak spots. In a minute when I let it go you'll probably both get one hell of a head rush."

She was, it turned out, understating things a little. A moment later David felt like something was sucking his mind out of his head; the sensation was a little too familiar, a little too like dying, and he nearly panicked, the terror-laden noise of those memories thundering in his mind.

"It's all right," he heard the Elf say gently. "I'm not going to hurt you…just breathe…it'll stop in a…moment…" Suddenly Nico gasped.

David's eyes snapped open. "Are you okay?"

But Nico was smiling, and in a few seconds a tear fell from one of his closed eyes. "I can see it," he said. "The Web…I can see it. You've given me my Sight back."

David's heart leapt. He held onto Nico's hands tightly; he could sense the Elf doing what he couldn't for so long, looking over Stella's work with approval, then examining the link to see how deeply it—

Nico jerked his hands away from David, who was shocked at the abrupt change in Nico's face. It no longer showed joy or concentration.

Fear.

He was staring at David wide-eyed, breathing hard, and forcing himself not to shrink away.

"What's wrong?" David asked.

Stella looked worried, too, and put her hand on Nico's knee. "Sweetie, what is it? Is it not working?"

Nico visibly steeled himself to sit straight again, slowing his breathing inch by inch. "I'm fine," he said. It wasn't remotely believable. "Yes, it's working...I can feel things changing. In fact I...damn."

The Elf barely had the word out before he toppled over sideways. Luckily there was a cushion there too, and he didn't strike his head on the hard floor.

David looked at Stella. "What was that?"

She shrugged. "Not much telling. But it's as done as it can be. If it starts to cause pain, or you feel tired for more than a day or so, we'll have to undo it. For now you should probably stay together—physical contact can help seal this sort of thing, and at the very least he's going to sleep for a while. You should too."

Taking a deep breath, David nodded. "Thank you, Stella."

A smile. "You're always very welcome."

She got up and set to taking down the circle, returning the room to its ordinary atmosphere; meanwhile, David got up slowly, checking for dizziness before he bent to lift the Elf up off the floor.

"Once he wakes up send me a text just to check in," Stella told him.

David said he would, then carried Nico's far-too-light body out of the ritual room and back to the Elf's own bed.

It was several hours before Nico woke, and in that time David dozed off once or twice but started awake every time he heard a noise. He could feel things changing—something pulling at him almost delicately, working its way in to take root, then settling down and tapering off until he could barely feel it. It was a remarkably gentle kind of magic, even pleasant, and nothing like the immense drain when Miranda had bound them briefly to Deven. Stella had been right; this link was lighter, far less deep. Judging from the strength of the current he would have to be in physical contact with Nico to sense anything beyond what he could already read. That was good. David didn't want anything to compete with his bond to Miranda—he'd seen how impossible that kind of situation was.

He caught echoes of Nico's dreams, nothing specific but some watery images and emotions. He wasn't aware he'd drifted off again until he woke with a jolt and looked into Nico's wide, frightened eyes.

They stared at each other a minute. "All right," David said, "Tell me."

Nico sat up, then put a hand to his forehead in what looked like a vain attempt to stave off dizziness. He shut his eyes tightly for a few seconds and didn't look at David as he said, "When the connection opened up, I...saw things."

"What things?"

Nico met his eyes, took a breath, and said softly, "The New Moon."

David's heart tumbled down to the floor. He had hoped that, of all the things the Elf might learn about him in those brief moments, that that would not be one of them. It was one thing to know he'd done violent things in the past, but this was now...and was going to keep happening. "Oh."

Nico's hands held onto the comforter so hard they shook. "And the Queen, too. You're both..."

Now David sighed. "Just say it, Nico. Don't dance around it. I'm a murderer. Miranda is a murderer. That's just how it is. I had to accept what would come as the price of coming back from the dead as Thirdborn—it was the price of coming back to her, one we both willingly paid. That's why she and I didn't want to sire you through our blood—you would have been just like us."

Nico drew his knees up to his chin, looking utterly shell-shocked. "But...you enjoy it."

A flare of anger lit in David's heart—defensive, to be sure, but anger still. "Yes, I do," he snapped, sitting up. "It's what I was made for. What we were *all* made for. We live in denial of the fact that we were created to kill humans, to control their numbers. We failed at that mission, and they turned around and killed your people and ours, and Witches, and each other for centuries. And if the price of being able to stop Morningstar, or any other threat to our world, is that every month I have to drain some rapist until he shrivels like a prune, I will revel in it and walk away smiling."

He let the power in his aura flare as well, letting the Elf see just what he'd gotten into. "You knew what we were, what I am, when you came here."

He knew Nico could sense what he was doing; but the Elf was still staring at him, his fear turning gradually into sadness.

Nico nodded slowly. "Yes...I knew. I abandoned my own people and my life to help you, and even if I did regret it, there's no turning back."

Now, David lowered his eyes. "Fine," he said, defeated. "If you want I'll call Stella and she can undo—"

"No," Nico said vehemently, expression changing completely. "No, I don't want that." He turned toward David and lifted a hand to his face; the relief that Nico hadn't decided he was too monstrous to be touched was almost overwhelming.

They leaned forward until their foreheads touched. "I don't want that," Nico repeated. "I'm sorry. I knew there were things in your life I wouldn't want to see, but it was still a shock when it hit me. I can't say it doesn't hurt, but...I know you have no choice. At heart I know what kind of man you are, David."

"And what kind is that?"

Nico smiled. "The kind I love."

David stared at him, and the surprise on his face was apparently rather amusing to the Elf, who chuckled, kissed his nose, and stretched back out under the blankets. In the midst of trying to figure out what to say, David noticed Nico already looked better—his face was less drawn, and light had rekindled in his eyes. He was still moving slowly and still looked exhausted, but even a few hours had made a big difference.

Nico closed his eyes, still smiling, but now wryly. "David Solomon speechless," he said. "Surely a sign of impending doom for one and all." One eye opened partway. "Close your mouth and get in here. I'm freezing."

David nodded, still mute, and did as the Elf directed, sliding in next to him and drawing him close. His mind offered a comparison: Miranda preferred to be the little spoon, with her Prime against her back, both facing the same direction; Nico liked sleeping face to face. He thought back—no matter how they fell asleep he'd always woken to find Deven on the other side of the bed, connected only by a hand around David's throat or on his chest, anywhere he could feel a pulse.

It was the first time he'd really thought about the differences in an entire year of snuggling and kissing the Elf. Perhaps now that there was a real possibility they could give each other more, his thoughts were allowing themselves to wander...no, more like cartwheel...in that direction.

Not to mention it took his mind off Nico's words.

In most of his relationships David had been the one to say it first. Despite all of his emotional defenses, that had always come easily—by the time he made the declaration, it seemed like a foregone conclusion. It was logical to say it, because there was no doubt it was true, and it was important the other person know. Of *course* he loved Miranda. Of *course* he had loved Deven.

Did he love Nico?

Of *course* he did.

He had, in all reality, for a long time. Even in the first month of the Weaver's stay, David found he couldn't look at him without a sharp pain in his chest, breath catching, a visible shiver threatening to escape. As time wore on and Nico grew weaker, that pain softened into an ache that never left the Prime, letting him set aside that smoldering desire so he could be what Nico needed him to be until one day, he had hoped, things would get better for everyone.

But it had always been love. There was no doubt remaining.

By the time he reached that conclusion, of course, Nico was fast asleep.

That was all right. It could wait a little longer. For now, he followed his Elf's fine example and settled in to sleep.

Chapter Four

Here.

She took a step closer to the cliff, shifting left and right until she knew—she felt—she was in the exact right spot. The angle facing the trees was right, the elevation right.

Here was where she had been standing that night when the world went to hell.

The wind was hard and cold out here without a sprawling complex of buildings to break it. The land leading up to the cliff was scoured bare, piles of rubble like hulking monsters in the dark. If this had been a human home, there might still have been bone fragments in the dirt, but when vampires died, nothing was left but metal.

She thought of the shattered, bloodstained Signet David had held out to her that night, recovered from the tumble of concrete where one of the best friends she'd ever had was crushed, holding on to life just long enough to say goodbye.

Miranda didn't bother wiping her eyes. She'd known coming here would make her weep. She was, in fact, impressed with herself for holding it together as well as she was.

Everything about this place had been beautiful.

All of it was gone.

She looked out across the plain, picking out details: a boarded-over hole whose steps led down to the weapons vault door, and two more like it; one had held servers and other tech in a familiar system layout, and the other had been the odd variety of things you'd expect to find in a longtime couple's attic. Everything from all three vaults had survived, and it was all in storage at her Haven. David was keeping it all together in case...just in case.

Miranda carefully picked her way back toward the memorial, glancing over at Avi, who stood guard at the car. His presence was comforting; he was an imposing man, amazing in battle but with a gentle way about him she couldn't quite describe. He hadn't been here that night, but he understood he was standing at the edge of a graveyard, and maintained a respectful silence.

She wasn't sure who had built the memorial—probably the surviving staff or Elite who came back after the demolition crews to see the remains of their lives. Whoever they were, they had salvaged enough intact cinder blocks to build a semicircular windbreak, and inside that little enclosure were seven-day candles, crosses, cards leached colorless by rain, and other mementos of the people who had died here.

Among the tributes was a still-sealed bottle of Woodford Reserve. Miranda smiled, as well as at the small wood plaque carved with intricate Celtic knotwork—an offering for Deven, who she was almost, almost willing to concede had died here with his Consort. She still held on to that tiny scrap of hope, though it was shrinking more each night.

Her sigh was lost in the night air but the bricks caught her voice and held it well enough. "I didn't really know what to bring you," she said, sitting down cross-legged. "Everything I could think of just seemed so stupid. So I did what I do—I figured you'd like that best anyway."

Quietly, she began to sing.

She'd written the song just for this time, this place, this lost heart. As much as she hated songwriting she had to admit it was good; if she'd recorded it, she would have another hit on her hands.

She didn't need another hit. She needed to make an offering.

For just a moment the wind stilled and it seemed like the night was listening.

She hadn't intended it, but a capella with the chorus of crickets and the forest canopy beyond the cliff rustling in a sea of dark leaves, the song had an almost Elven feel to it, and on the last chorus she changed it up a bit to emphasize that. What had started as a fairly standard ballad now sounded haunting, hollow, and sorrowful, with the wind blowing through it. She tried to think of that emptiness as potential, not annihilation.

Kai would be proud.

As the song wound to its close—returning to the original theme in a kind of spiral, another Elven thing she'd learned—her voice faded out into the damp air.

"Sorry the candles are out," she said quietly. "I didn't bring a lighter. But…"

Curious, Miranda focused all her attention on one of the glass votives as if she were going to move it with her mind, but instead she concentrated on the wick drying out, heat gathering in its fibers and the wax around it, and—

It lit.

She got to her feet and stepped back, looking around in apprehension, but of course there was no one to see her except Avi, who had been resolutely not watching her in her private grief.

Her suspicion was confirmed, then—even with the Atlantic Ocean and a continent between them and Eastern Europe, their gifts were contagious. She had not yet heard Jacob, Cora, or Olivia mention picking up any of theirs, but if they were to try instead of waiting for it to happen, it might be a different story. They were all still a little spooked at the idea of their abilities merging. Miranda didn't blame them, but she'd had more time to get used to the idea.

Miranda absently dusted off her jeans and leaned down to unstick a leaf from the toe of her boot; as she started to straighten, though, something in her peripheral vision made her pause.

She held still and waited. There it was again: as its flame fought against the wind the candlelight had caught something metallic on the ground. The object was half-covered in dirt, but still flashed like a star, or a tear, against the earth.

Cautious, she reached over to brush the dirt away; it was probably just some kind of construction debris, but something about the way the light hit it made her close her fingers around the small object and pluck it from its resting place.

Her skin recognized it before her mind did, and her hand began to tremble as she took the hem of her shirt and cleaned off her prize. By the time she held it up to the light—unnecessary given her eyesight, but still, essential to verify to herself that she was looking at what she was looking at—the tremor had spread through her body, and she nearly sat back down in the dirt.

Silver, moonstone.

Nico's ring.

What was it doing here? If it had been in Deven's pocket that night it would have fallen out down below the cliff somewhere, and if it had been blown here all the way from their suite surely it would have sustained some kind of damage. The explosion had been intense enough to melt what metal it didn't pulverize. Aside from the dirt, the ring was flawless.

She turned it over and over in her palm, heart pounding even though she wasn't sure why. Yes, it was strange that it had survived, but it could be that Elven silver was stronger, or that there was some sort of protective enchantment on it.

Even thinking it, however, she knew better. Nothing in their lives happened by coincidence. In their world tattoos changed shape, ravens landed on the ground exactly when thought about, and Elves just happened to be holding magic communicator stones when the vampire on the other end made a call for help.

The moonstone rings were worn by the priesthood of Theia, the Elven goddess, signifying the bond between her and their souls. According to Nico the term "priest" could be applied to adepts of a number of different disciplines; he and Kai both were considered priests. As far as Miranda knew, the priesthood of Persephone had all been ecclesiastical in nature, but anyone who reached full initiation into the Order of Elysium received a labradorite ring a lot like this one.

Nico had given Deven his as a token of love and a promise to return...and Nico was no longer a priest of Theia, technically, as he was no longer a pure Elf and had been thrown out of his homeland. Was the ring useless now? Were they supposed to do anything besides look impressive? This one had opened the Codex of Persephone even though it was made for a different deity. What else could they do?

Miranda closed her hand around the ring and also closed her eyes, grounding herself firmly in the earth beneath her feet before reaching out with her senses and tentatively touching the ring. She no longer had the Sight, whatever David might believe, but she could still feel the tendrils of energy that connected things— changing their bond that night had changed her abilities as well, giving her senses a precision they'd never had before.

She felt the ring as a hum of energy in her hand, as if it weren't a solid object, but a vibration. David had told her during one of his enthusiastic verbal meanders about science that the whole universe was dancing every moment—at its most basic level all matter was in motion. Holding the ring, she could believe it.

"Why are you here?" she asked. "Are you magic too? I guess I should take you back to Nico."

She frowned. The stone was starting to feel warmer than it should. Each passing second it grew warmer and warmer, until it was genuinely hot. The energetic vibration she'd sensed became a real physical buzz that left her hand numb—and before she could really register what was happening, the ring grew so hot she cried out and dropped it.

"Jesus!" she gasped, clenching her hand against her chest. She heard footsteps rushing toward her; Avi had apparently decided to throw reverence to the wind and come to the aid of his Queen.

"My Lady, are you all right?"

She nodded, feeling dizzy, and looked down at her palm. An oval had been burned into her flesh, but it immediately began to heal, the searing pain fading until it was just sore, then itchy, then gone.

"That moonstone ring," she said, pointing. "Can you touch it—very carefully—and see if it's still hot?"

Avi was perplexed, but didn't argue. As he bent to retrieve the ring she wondered, briefly, if she could bear a Second who didn't argue with her when she did something dumb. Faith had been loyal to a fault, and had never disobeyed a direct order, but she had questioned her Pair regularly, just as they wanted her to. Signets who thought themselves infallible became complacent, and complacency had cost many of them their heads. Given the same rank, would Avi speak up when needed, or was he too obedient? Was she sensing a lack of willfulness where there was in fact just a quiet man who didn't feel the need to constantly hear his own voice?

He gingerly tapped at the ring with one fingertip, then touched it a second longer. "It is perfectly cool, my Lady," he said, picking it up. "Whatever possessed it is gone now..." He pondered the silver in his hand, frowning.

"Something on your mind, Lieutenant?" she asked.

Avi looked a little sheepish, but replied, "I believe you are mistaken about this stone. The Queen I served before had an extensive collection of jewels, and if I recall correctly, moonstones are white."

"Of course it's white—"

He held it up.

Miranda froze.

"No," she breathed. "That's not...how..."

Stupid question, really.

Sure enough, the ring Avi held out to her was no longer set with a moonstone, but with a labradorite.

There wasn't enough alcohol on the North American continent to satisfy a 766-year-old Irish vampire's drive for self-destruction, even if he could maintain the degree of falldown drunkenness he needed. Not only could he drink anyone in the bar under the table, he could drink them out the door, down the street, to another bar, and under one of *their* tables.

Still, Anodyne was as pleasant a place as any to waste a life; to run up a thousand-dollar tab each night, pretend not to notice when other patrons hit on him, and dodge the bartender's curiosity.

Since that night he'd met Kai everything had been wrong. After all those months working so hard to be too exhausted to dream, he'd begun having nightmares...nightmares of being trapped beneath a falling building, crushed under concrete debris, unable to reach help or find any comfort in his final moments...but those moments went on and on, an eternity under that wall, screaming into the pitch darkness long after the battery in his phone died and took the last light with it.

Then the dreams changed and he was digging—desperately trying to move the ruins, sure he had heard someone call him. He shifted mountains of rock every day until he uncovered the tomb...but it was too late, always too late. Sometimes Jonathan was down there, and sometimes Nico, sometimes even Miranda. She lay lifeless in the rubble, blood obscuring her beautiful face, sightless eyes fixed on the smoke-filled night sky. He pulled her out, holding her body close, weeping, thinking over and over, *I have to tell David...how am I going to tell David?*

Nico's fate was the same, but as soon as he was untangled from the wreckage Deven felt himself dying. He wanted to embrace it, to let go of this hateful life, but in the dreams he fought, fought for his Consort's life and his own.

He failed every time.

In another version of the dream, he found Nico alive, but when he tried to pull the Elf free, Nico pushed him away. "I don't want you," he said coldly. "I want him."

Deven turned in time to see David arrive and immediately dive in to free Nico without even looking at Deven. The Elf smiled at the Prime as if he were some kind of god come to earth, and they both ignored Deven entirely...he no longer existed in their world.

Worse yet, the dreams followed him throughout the night after he woke—he wandered around Austin like a sleepwalker, stopping here and there to heal humans, barely remembering having done it. He couldn't get rid of the power fast enough; all he could do was use as much as he could and then drink until the rest was dulled.

It wasn't hard to interpret all of the dreams. His psyche wasn't exactly a master of obscure symbolism. This pathetic creature he had become was trying to survive under the crippling weight of who he'd once been...who everyone wanted him to be again. Why couldn't they understand that, even if he were to lower the shield and let Nico in, even if he took up his sword and Signet again, it could never be the same? That life was over. It had died in the wreckage of his home, and now it died over and over again in his sleep.

"Another?" the bartender asked.

He lifted his head blearily and nodded.

She clunked two more ice cubes into his glass and then filled it nearly to the rim. "I know it's cliché and all," she said, "but you spend so much time here I have to wonder what your story is."

The alcohol had stopped burning a long time ago—in fact he barely felt its effects anymore, swallowed as they were by the other two bottles of whiskey he'd already downed tonight. "Do you know who I am?" he asked.

She shrugged. She was, he supposed, an attractive woman; tattooed and pierced, with load-bearing Germanic hips and hair dyed about eight colors, she was sort of a cross between Stella and Olivia, but more muscular than the former and more conventionally pretty than the latter. "A hot guy with a broken heart, who drinks his blood volume in really expensive liquor every night?

He lifted his eyes from his glass to her face. "Broken heart?"

"Happy people do not drink like that."

"You must not know a lot of Irishmen," he replied listlessly. "Birth? Drink. Wedding? Drink. Death? Drink. Tuesday? Drink."

She grinned. "So I can add 'Irish' to the list."

It occurred to him that she would have a lot more for her list if he actually looked like he had before. Right now he was ordinary, boring, blending in when he was used to standing out. "You should see me when my heart's not broken," he said. "I have a lot more piercings."

"So when you're feeling well-adjusted you put holes in your face."

He half-smiled. "I have to hurt myself somehow, don't I?"

She smiled back. "Do you do your own?"

Deven nodded, thinking of the wooden box back in his room, a box with a cracked corner—his piercing kit, one of a handful of things that had survived the bomb intact. His belongings were an odd assortment: the kit, Jonathan's copy of Les Mis, one of Jonathan's sweaters, a few other garments, and the sketchbook where Deven had been working out a new tattoo design. Everything in the piercing kit was cradled in foam, the box one he'd acquired in India that was as solid as a brick wall—more solid, it turned out.

The bartender had gone to fetch another patron a drink, but when she returned, she said, "Okay, let me just get this out of the way so I know where this is going—are you into women at all?"

He found he couldn't help a slight smile at that. His life had blown apart, he'd lost everything of who he was, except that...or, he was 95% sure of that. "No."

She nodded. "Okay, then, I won't waste time flirting."

"Flirt all you want," he replied. "I probably won't notice."

"Claudia," she said, extending her hand.

He took it. "Deven."

If she connected the name with an identity, she didn't say so; he appreciated that. "Nice to meet you, Deven," she said. "Thank you for all the awesome tips."

He shrugged. "What else is money for?"

"A philanthropist on top of that! Who'd have thought?"

Philanthropist. Hardly.

One of the first things he'd done once he'd come out of shock two years ago was to donate a million dollars to the Human Equality Coalition. He kept thinking about what he'd said to Jonathan about never doing anything to support the cause, and then about how that one night of marriage had made him happier than he'd been for most of his life. He'd gone from newlywed to widowed in 24 hours; he was in a perpetual fugue state and cared about nothing now, but that one thing haunted his thoughts until he picked up the phone and called his accountant. The money had come from the Pair's joint account rather than the Signet account or his private one where the Red Shadow's business flowed in and out; he had, therefore, made the donation in Jonathan's name. Then, at least one of his legion of demons was put to rest.

If only all the others could be pacified with money. He could have been a well-adjusted, happy man decades ago.

He snorted quietly, earning a look from Claudia.

"As much as we here at Anodyne value your patronage," she said wryly, "there must be a better way for you to deal with your baggage than what you're doing now."

"You think so? I haven't found one in 766 years."

That impressed her; now he was sure she knew who he was. This was a Signet bar, after all, meaning both the Pair and the Elite were its main source of income, so any astute bartender would learn all sorts of interesting things about the ruling class just by listening. To Claudia's credit, she didn't give any obvious sign, but he saw the ever so slight widening of her eyes, the quirk of one brow, the briefest pause in the midst of mixing a drink.

He sighed inwardly. He should have given her a fake name, should have kept his mouth shut, but he was too mentally wobbly from the alcohol to play things out logically.

"766," she said. "Really?"

He nodded...but...wait, where had he gotten that number? He didn't know what year he was born, or what day; he had it narrowed down to about a three-year range, but until the monastery he'd had no sense of what year it was. It wasn't important where he came from. He'd been born in early Summer, just after what modern Witches called the feast of Beltane. That was all he knew for sure. His mother had been in labor for almost two full days and he'd killed and resurrected her before he'd even cried; that had always added to the confusion. His people weren't stupid, but they were busy, and he and his birth were meaningless to everyone but his father.

"Why the tears, lad?"

"John and Finn were trying to hurt one of Báb's pups. I got in the way and they hit me. Then they laughed at me for crying."

"That's because your brothers are fools…there's no shame in having a heart. What about the pup, did…anything happen?"

He was an enormous man, at least to a scrawny child, with a beard as big as his laugh and callused hands that could bring untold comfort just by resting on one's head. He tolerated the other boys—they were needed to work the farm—but for some reason, the only one he really seemed to love was the runt of the litter who was useless for anything but the nightly Bible reading. And even with the backbreaking labor involved in keeping food on the table for seven people, he always had time to soothe hurt feelings, of which there tended to be many.

"I don't remember," Deven murmured, putting his head in his hands and leaning his elbows on the bar.

"Are you okay? What don't you remember?"

"His name," he said. "I don't remember his name. It's been too long and it hurt too much, and…the only person who loved me when I was human, dead and gone for seven centuries…no one even remembers he existed. There was no point to his life at all."

"You remember," Claudia said, reaching over to lay a hand on his arm. "Maybe not his name, but you remember. There's a point to every life—even if it was just that someone loved you."

It had been a very long time since he'd felt this kind of pain. He nodded vaguely, muttered a farewell of some sort, threw money on the bar, and stumbled out, fighting desperately not to fall down weeping.

"No, Da…nothing happened. I didn't touch the puppy."

"Good lad."

Then:

"We can't go on like this, Dónal…you heard what they were saying. The Church is sending people here to flush out heretics— one look at the boy and they'll know there's something wrong with him."

"There's nothing wrong with him except your bloodline, Elendala, and there's naught we can do about that. But you're

right; he's not safe here anymore. I'll send a message to my brother..."

Dónal. It was Dónal. Of course it was—where else would Deven have gotten his old surname? Relieved, Deven sagged back against the outside wall of the bar, ignoring the inquisitive looks of the bouncers. He was here enough that they knew to leave him alone.

Dónal...I remember you, Da. You lived. If that has any meaning at all...I remember you.

Something odd about the memory gave him pause, though. He could remember his mother's name, Sorcha...but the night he'd been eavesdropping on their conversation, his father had called her something else...something that was not Irish.

He'd had no context for it until now. Now he understood.

Elendala—it must be Elvish, her birth name. He knew nothing about her break with their people, but it seemed strange that her husband would still call her by that name when she had denied her entire heritage out of fear. It confirmed that he'd known who his wife really was, though, and that opened a whole new set of questions.

For the first time Deven realized he could find out more. Nico had said his grandmother still lived; he could meet her. She could tell him...

...what, exactly? What difference did it make what the story was? They were all dead, long gone, into dust and shadow, as he should have been.

Angry for no reason he could really define, he shoved himself off the wall and started walking toward the rendezvous point. He was done with Austin for one night.

He was a mile from Chris and the car when a wave of dizziness hit him, along with the assault of another long-forgotten memory—no, memories, twisted around each other, some he wasn't even sure were real. He put his hands on his temples, trying to force the images back into the dark, but they kept pushing back, and soon he had wandered into an alley and sunk down on the ground with his back against a wall.

"Hello, little one. It is lovely to meet you."

He stared up at the strange woman, heart pounding. She was so beautiful—her hair was dark brown like his own, but it shone and fell down to her knees. Her eyes were deep violet and full of moonlight.

"He has the gift, Elendala. You must let me take him. He would be safe among us."

"No...I told you before...my boy is human. He's cursed with your demon powers, but he's not one of you any more than I am. He can learn to block it out."

A sigh. "Daughter...your child is not human. You would condemn him to a life of fear and probably a horrific death at the hands of your Church...he could be at peace with us. He has enough of the blood that the Enclave would allow it. Please...do not damn your son to this world because you hate what you are."

"No. I'll not have him learning all your heathen ways and praying to your false gods. I'll not coddle his life in exchange for his soul. He'll go to the monastery and live away from normal people where it's safe."

There was a long pause before she replied quietly, with sadness and resignation: "You will teach him to hate himself as much as you do...and all so that he may burn at the stake, wasting a powerful gift and a kind heart. He is a beautiful child, Elen, worthy of your love and compassion...if you could see what I do...if only you would let yourself see."

"I think it's time you left..."

No...come back. Please take me with you. Don't leave me here...they're going to hurt me. Take me with you. I'm scared. Don't leave me here alone.

Don't leave me here alone...

"Shhh...it's okay, baby. It's just a dream. You're safe. I'm here with you...no one's going to hurt you as long as I'm beside you. Go back to sleep."

Don't...don't leave...

"Child."

It was a voice he knew, and didn't know. Deven lifted his head, but what he saw wasn't the alley—it was a forest...a redwood forest...and the night was soft, sweet, tranquil.

He felt a hand on his head—lighter than his father's, but with that same affection and reassurance.

"Why are you doing this to me?" he whispered.

"As with most of your suffering, you are doing it to yourself." Her voice was loving, gentle. "I can help you, child, but you must invite Me in."

He no longer had the strength to fight, nor the desire. He would have given anything in that moment for peace, even happiness; he was tired, so tired, of hurting, of wandering alone in the dark.

"Please make it stop. Just let me have one night where nothing hurts...please."

A kiss on his forehead, and he looked up into those endless eyes. There was nothing but peace there, peace and love resting quietly in the arms of the darkness between stars.

He waited for Her to deny him, or at least demand something in return, but She didn't. Instead, She sat down next to him on the ground, the shadows of Her garments flowing out all around them like mist crawling through a valley, and put Her arm around him, drawing his head to Her shoulder.

It occurred to him that in the real world he was sitting in a grimy alley—was She there too? Or was he now leaning sideways looking like a drunk?

It didn't matter. None of it mattered. He had asked for a reprieve, and in a moment, it began: those shadows lapped at his feet, then began to rise, their tide whispering in a million voices. It almost tickled, but was so soothing...he closed his eyes.

She was rocking him back and forth, and singing very softly. He recognized the song...had his grandmother sung it to him? Had his mother, in a weak moment when no one would overhear? He had forgotten it, until now, but the words were clear, as clear as the knowledge that they, too, were not in a human tongue.

"*Eth Luna amasti embra es argena estelli,*
Eth es aurum Sola amasti adoro es azur,
Eth Prinaver amastes amoriel es nuve vertis ista di,
O mes cari, ile amast amori, ili'thur."

Hours later, he woke on his side in the back seat of the Escalade, a very concerned Chris in the driver's seat speeding through the streets of Austin.

"Where are we?" he asked groggily, sitting up.

"Oh, thank God, my Lord...are you all right? I couldn't wake you."

"Wake me? Was I asleep?"

"I have no idea—I got a signal from your com for an urgent pickup, but when I found you, you were unconscious."

"No, that's...that's not right. I was at a bar in the District."

"You were four miles from the District, my Lord. I assumed you blacked out from too much alcohol, but then I couldn't rouse you...Mo is standing by at the Hausmann to check you over."

"I'm fine," he muttered, but even he couldn't muster the energy to make a forceful denial; he wasn't fine, and he knew he wasn't.

"All right," he finally said. "The Hausmann...okay."

Chris seemed even more alarmed that he wasn't arguing with her, and a look of determination set on her face as she hit the accelerator.

Deven lay back against the seat and closed his eyes, losing awareness of the world for a while longer, wisps of melody and a dark, sweet voice lifted in song that wrapped around his mind like ebony wings, feathery and protective. Sometimes the words were in one language, sometimes another, but they were always full of love and comfort, and he held onto them even after he let go of wakefulness.

"*As the Moon embraces the silver stars,*
As the golden Sun adores the color blue,
As the Spring loves the new grass and the rain,
That is how much, my darling, I love you."

Chapter Five

By now, the Haven guards were used to their employer striding purposefully down the corridors in moods ranging from preoccupied to homicidal; in recent months they had no doubt grown accustomed to their resident ghost's comings and goings as well. Still, the guards were somewhat alarmed at the sight of their Prime carrying that ghost in from the cold, rainy night.

Mo and Chris both had called, one from the Hausmann and one from the road, to alert him to what had passed in the city; the urgent pickup call had sent up an alert on David's phone, so he was already waiting for further information from Chris.

"Sire...Prime Deven is...hurt...I think. I don't know what happened—he's been in and out for an hour. I'm on my way to Mo now."

And not long after, Mo: *"Sire, you need not be alarmed—he is in rough shape, but not in any danger. I have fluids running through him now; he was severely dehydrated."*

Dehydrated. Not the same as starving, an important difference for creatures on a liquid diet. Dehydration in vampires wasn't usually caused by a lack of blood, or insufficient water intake, but by something actively leaching water from the body. For it to be severe it had to have been happening for a while. Unfortunately David knew exactly what it was.

Vein running, they'd called it in the 40s. The equipment was more advanced now but the principle was the same—hold the vein open to allow for a near-constant stream of drugs. It hit harder than a normal injection, straight for the brain. Deven's poison of choice, heroin, was especially known for its dehydrating effect on their kind. David was well aware that before they had met Deven had been in the habit of spending days high, only coming out when he had to pay for more...whether that was with money or his body, whichever would get him another hit faster.

There was no reason Dev would be whoring himself now. He was a billionaire, after all, and could afford all the drugs he wanted with barely a blip in his credit line. But the mere thought made David's stomach clench with impotent anger. No lowlife drug dealer should dare lay a hand on something as exalted as a Prime...even a fallen one.

Exalted. As David brushed past the door guards at the suite and deposited Deven on the bed, the word was bitter in his mind. Deven was a mess: he was pitifully thin, and worse yet he was *dirty*; he looked like he'd been rolling around in an alley. The Deven he knew would never have left the house in anything but the finest hand-tailored clothing from studded collar to steel-toed boots. He would be armed to the teeth and look like a creature who could cast a room into terrified silence just by walking in the door...not like this. Aside from the grime his clothes could have come from any average man.

Horrifying.

Without actively making the decision, David picked Deven up again and this time bore him to the bathroom, where he ran hot water in the tub while gingerly picking the clothes from the elder Prime's thin frame.

He tried to be clinical about it and not notice everything that had changed since the last time he'd seen this much of Deven's bare skin. Strange how once he had known every centimeter, every line of ink, but in the intervening years he'd added several images— David hadn't even seen most of them that night five years ago, as they'd been in too much of a hurry to linger. Most of Deven's tattoos grew out of the stained-glass-patterned sleeves of saint and sinner; their edges twisted into Celtic knotwork, and hidden among the lines were symbolic animals, like the white stag that had been the emblem of Deven's clan. Dev designed them all himself—just as he did the carvings and ornaments on his weapons. It would surprise most people to know he was such a talented artist.

Deven didn't stir when David lowered him into the water. He just slept, as he had slept the whole way back from Austin. That was fine; David didn't especially want him to wake up until he was clean and safe in his own bed. David worked quickly but carefully, scrubbing the smears of mud away.

Another time in another place it would have been unbearably arousing, but all David felt in that moment was a choking vine of sorrow growing up through his chest.

It had come to this. The powerful, beautiful creature he had loved so dearly had become this empty shell he barely recognized.

A memory intruded, one he wasn't expecting...kneeling beside another tub just like this one, with Faith next to him, silently washing the filth of rape and murder from Miranda's skin. He had been focused on her hair; it became the symbol of what he was trying desperately to save. He hadn't even known her last name, but the pain at seeing what had been done to her—not just by those humans, but by months of encroaching insanity and despair—had clawed at him, as it did now. Thinking of her like that, blood on her thighs and vitreous humor under her fingernails, her hair matted and her face gaunt...he nearly dropped the washcloth and dug out his phone to call her, but she would be onstage right now, just about to finish her show.

She's safe. She's healthy and strong and she'll be home soon.

But the juxtaposition of that night with now had done its damage, and he found he could barely breathe.

Too much grief. Too much. He held onto the side of the tub with both hands and leaned his forehead against the cool porcelain, trying to ground.

He heard movement behind him, but immediately knew who it was, and a moment later felt a hand on his head.

He looked up into Nico's eyes. "I can't," he said, voice strange and hollow in the humid little room. He wasn't even sure what it was he couldn't do.

Nico didn't need to know. He nodded, knelt, and slid his arms around the Prime. "You're not alone," he said softly. "I will help you."

David hadn't considered that Nico would be able to give him energy along their link; he'd just assumed that it would flow one way, since the Elf was the one who needed the help. But Nico sent a wordless pulse of strength and love along the thread, and David took it gratefully. Within minutes he felt like himself again, able to master the assault of emotions.

Nico found another washcloth, and together they finished cleaning Deven up. David dug around in the bathroom drawer until he found a razor, and Nico moved Deven's head around like a doll's so that David could—almost gleefully—get rid of that godawful scruff. Dev could be mad about it if he wanted, though chances were he wouldn't care either way. David knew he hadn't grown it deliberately; he'd simply not bothered to shave.

Finally, they got the elder vampire washed and dried and dressed and in bed. David watched the Elf surreptitiously off and on, seeing the sadness, but also the love in Nico's hands, caring for his Prime as if he were a holy relic. A tiny glimpse of how things should be...except that Deven should be awake, smiling that little half-smile that meant he was a combination of amused and contented at being fussed over.

It shouldn't be like this for any of them.

Neither spoke as they left the suite and walked around the corner and down the hall to Nico's rooms. David was thankful for the silence. He had no idea what to call what was happening in his heart, but he was pretty sure speaking was a bad idea right now.

Nico closed the door behind them and sighed. When David looked at him, the Elf's eyes were bright. "That's the first time I've touched him in months," Nico said.

The servants had been in and gotten the fire going, as well as turning down the bed and straightening up—Nico was generally fastidious, but his pastimes involved large stacks of books and papers that seemed to breed in his room. The Elf was uneasy about having people wait on him; it wasn't that such a thing was unknown among his people, but that he himself had never been taken care of, Weavers not being the rock stars that, say, Bards were.

Nico had given up protesting after Esther commanded him to stand back and let them do their jobs. Not even powerful sorcerers from idyllic forest worlds argued with Esther.

David shook his head slightly. His mind was trying to latch onto anything to think about but what it needed to think about. He wanted to ponder refinements to the camera system, or sensor performance fluctuations in Dallas, or even trying to figure out what the hell the writers of Doctor Who were smoking, but it was all denial.

He felt Nico's eyes.

"I wish you could have known him like I did," David said quietly. "Back before everything got so complicated. I'd never seen anything like him before: this intense and commanding warrior who had never been bested, with a presence that swallowed up an entire room when he wanted it to...or disappeared without disturbing the air...I learned so much those first few years about how being powerful really worked—how much of it was glamour, attitude. And even with all the nightmares and shadows and history, he burned like the sun to me. And now..."

Nico heard the catch in his voice and came to him, resting his hands on David's shoulders. "It's not too late."

"Maybe not. But no matter what...he deserves better than this. So do you. And there's nothing I can do to save him. It's my job to protect my kind, Nico, and my life's work to be a force that stands between those I care for and the violence inherent to our existence. I've failed miserably."

"Nonsense," Nico replied. He took gentle hold of David's coat and slid it off, draping it over the chair where it usually ended up. Next he reached down and unbuckled The Oncoming Storm, placing her reverently on the bookshelf nearby. "Not even the Thirdborn are strong enough to force someone to want to live."

The Prime sighed and let Nico steer him over to the other fireplace chair, where the Elf dropped gracefully to his knees to start the laborious task of unlacing David's boots. First came the buckles and straps that wrapped around, and then his nimble fingers began to unweave the laces themselves.

"I wish I could hate him," David went on, unable to enjoy watching Nico work as he usually did. Elves—or at least this one—devoted themselves fully to whatever they were doing, and gave that depth of love and attention to everything they touched. It was, David supposed, inspiring, but most of the time he just found it incredibly hot. "I tried. And I've been angry...but after tonight I don't think I can even manage that. God, I wish I could."

Nico looked up at him with a sad smile. "A futile endeavor," he said. "Believe me, my Lord, you might as well save your energy. I have learned in all this that a heart can only truly be broken from inside. If he can still break your heart, he still dwells within you, and there is no cure for that particular affliction—at least, none you can accomplish by force of will. Sometimes time and distance are enough, but if it wasn't for you last time when he had cast you aside and treated you so cruelly, it certainly won't be enough now."

David put his head in his hands, feeling a thousand times his age just then. "I don't know how to do this. How to feel this much and still function. I'm not as strong as Miranda—I never have been."

"Be grateful for that," Nico told him. "Think of the fire that strength was forged in."

"I suppose you're right." David lifted his eyes to the Elf's, and their gazes held for a silent moment; David laid one hand against Nico's face and Nico leaned into the touch with a smile. Nico covered the hand with his own, and turned David's palm to place a kiss over his lifeline.

Then he seemed to make some sort of decision, and with a nod, rose from the floor. He smiled. "Come to bed, my Lord."

"It's early yet," David pointed out. "I'm not really tired, either, and I should—"

"David," Nico said firmly, a surprising glint of mirth and mischief in his moonlit eyes, "Come to bed."

The Prime blinked. He mentally sputtered for a moment. His eyes fell on the Elf's outstretched hand. Such a simple gesture...he'd been imagining this moment for months, but...

He took a deep breath and reached out, folding his fingers around Nico's. "As you will it," the Prime said softly, and rose.

Miranda was sitting behind her piano finishing her encore when she realized she never wanted to tour again.

She had no idea how normal human musicians survived months and months on the road. Granted, they didn't have a mystical bond slowly starting to itch and ache in the back of their minds, but the stress of being away from home and performing night after night...even without an empathic gift it had to be exhausting.

Her friend Jane Cassidy, with whom she'd recorded a wildly successful duet not long after her first album, claimed she loved touring. The travel itself was boring and repetitive and she never got to see as much of a city as she wanted, but the high of performance, the love of the audience, was Jane's favorite drug, the love of her life as she called it. Jane sold out large venues all over the world; Miranda had stuck with small spaces where she could manage the crowd without draining herself. Smaller venues better suited her far more intimate style—Jane was a rocker chick, all spiky hair and electric guitar.

Big crowds made Miranda nervous. The last time she'd done a really large concert, a charity event for the relief effort after a hurricane decimated the Gulf Coast, she'd nearly had a panic attack out on stage—every noise was a gunshot, every face an assassin. She still remembered the bullet hitting her chest, remembered having to fall. That night at the Austin Live Music Festival had nearly ended her career...which was what Hart had wanted. She was glad that she'd won that round before she finished the battle with her sword; he'd never have the satisfaction of seeing whatever finally did drive her offstage.

Her security team, with Avi in the lead, surrounded her and escorted her from the theater as soon as the encore was done. She wasn't doing much publicity this time around, aside from a few radio and print interviews and a few meet-and-greets with contest winners. After three hours of singing she wanted nothing more than a hot shower, warm blood, and a decent night's sleep.

The first two she could get. The third, not so much. It was really amazing how difficult she found falling asleep without David next to her and without the familiar sounds and smells of her home all around. His presence anchored her, helped her relax—there was nothing to fear if they were together.

That night came another complication, though not an unexpected one.

Once upon a time not very long ago, David had had sex with someone else, and Miranda had been forced to experience it vicariously, overcome with a combination of betrayal, rage, and arousal she hoped to God she'd never feel again. Knowing what was happening, and knowing what was about to be destroyed, she had been through one of the worst nights of her life, third on the list after the attack that had brought her to the Haven and far, far worse, feeling David die.

How could five years have changed everything so drastically? She was, by any standard, still very young for a vampire and even more so for a Queen. Only a few women had taken the Signet under the age of 100. But that night, only three months after their wedding, she had been sure it was over—even if there was no way she could physically leave him, neither could she forgive him.

Funny.

She was, luckily, settled into her hotel room for the night, replacing a string on her guitar that had broken in the middle of the show and forced her to finish on her backup instrument, when she felt it start, and instead of sinking onto the bed in mute horror, she couldn't help but smile.

This time what she felt was *relief*. Relief that her Prime could be happy for a few hours and that Nico might be able to shed some of the burden of his broken heart, even if just temporarily.

Of course, the relief very quickly turned into something else— and this time, she was able to feel what he was feeling without her vision clouded by anger. She wondered, if she bent her mind closer to his across the miles, would it—

...long-fingered hands, nails scratching lightly along skin pale in the candlelight...kisses at once unhurried and intense, one article of clothing falling away at a time, everything so slow and euphoric...a soft chuckle at his impatience...waiting for this for so long...I love...need...want...NOW...

Miranda gasped and "jumped" back, the rush of feelings—and the feeling of phantom teeth sinking into her thigh—a little more than she'd bargained for. Her whole body was buzzing from the inside, like a gradual electrocution.

A wave of need and appreciation hit her. She managed to strip herself down to the t-shirt she'd had on after the show, and tumbled onto the bed. Experimentally, she mentally nudged herself farther away, and the sensations toned down, but didn't stop. Still, if she had that much control without even working at it, that was a good sign that she could learn how to regulate the energy and even channel it into something useful like sparring or performing.

Not this time, though. This first time she'd just have to let it happen, and try to observe as impartially as possible so she could learn more about how the links among them worked together. She and David were bound to each other, David to Nico, Nico to Deven...and that was ignoring any emotional ties. Deven had mentioned hearing Jacob and Cora in bed together once. There was too much to learn, and so few opportunities to really study how they fit together.

"That's my story and I'm sticking to it," she murmured.

This was going to go on for a while—she knew her husband, and that same drive for excellence he applied to his technical wizardry applied to amorous pursuits. He'd had 350 years to practice, after all. She remembered how Nico had tasted the night they'd turned him, and how she'd wanted to shove David onto the bed and tear into him...and now they were together, and when she imagined it...or better yet imagined she was there too...

Miranda groaned. It was going to be a long night and her hands were already tired from three hours onstage.

If only she'd had the foresight to bring Mr. Shaky.

Once again, Deven dreamed.

At first he was wandering alone in the dark like always, but somewhere just past the reach of his vision he could sense something...something warm, something safe.

He struggled toward it, realizing he was soaked to the skin like he'd done a swan dive into a lake, so cold his teeth chattered audibly in the silent darkness that gradually took the shape of a forest.

It was a familiar one, but this was not Muir. These were shorter trees, broader, massive old oaks that were both younger and more stately, in their way, than the redwoods. A forest like this one had housed the Cloister where Eladra had brought him to heal and learn...God, was that where he was going?

Dread fell into his stomach, but he couldn't stop moving. If he did he would surely freeze. Freezing wouldn't kill a vampire but would put him in a sort of stasis, and if he didn't manage to lose consciousness before his body became paralyzed, he would be trapped, immobile, until something brought him out of it. Freezing was one of those unspoken horrors among their kind he pretended not to be terrified of. He had to keep walking, on and on in the dark and alone, until the blurry not-quite-a-thing in the distance took the shape of a building.

Light flickered warm and golden in the windows. Carved stone walls, a fountain somewhere within, a sense of solace held safely in the arms of the forest...it wasn't the Cloister he knew, or the one he had destroyed, but it was very much like them. It seemed to be empty except for one entrance whose door stood open, beckoning him into the dry comfort under its roof.

As dreams were wont to do, as soon as he stepped up to the threshold the scene changed—inside, the building was in fact a bedroom at the Austin Haven, one he recognized by the number of potted plants and books covering every flat surface. The air was verdant and held a touch of the greenwood, the faintest wisp of incense, the smell of vanillin from the books and...

...sweat...

He moved into the room cautiously, heart beginning to pound. Like most Haven bedrooms this one was dominated by a large bed hung with light-blocking curtains; on one end of the room was a fireplace with seating, and the doors to closet, bath, and hallway stood shut tight on the other three walls.

The dreamtime wavered, shimmering like heat from the pavement, and though physically he didn't move, the shifting in and out of phase with the room made him dizzy. He groped sideways for something to steady himself, and found the back of a chair.

He realized, then, that this wasn't a dream—or at least not fully. The forest outside had been imaginary, but this room was real, and what was happening in it was happening now in the waking world.

Astral projection. Body in one place, mind in another.

Fantastic.

He started at the sound of a quiet chuckle at the other end of the room.

The voice was soft but clear, and its familiarity made his chest hurt like he'd been staked. "Where did you learn how to *do* that?"

The second held a smile in its lilting accent. "Kai may be the popular one, but I've hardly been celibate these centuries."

Pulse clanging so loudly he was sure they would hear it, Deven moved closer, until he was beside the foot of the bed, holding on to the post to keep from drowning.

Oh God.

He saw exactly what he expected to see, and yet, it was still a shock. He'd seen David naked a thousand times, of course, and was intimately familiar with every inch, but he'd barely ever even seen past the Elf's forearms. It turned out that the tattoo on Nico's face didn't stop at his cheekbone; it took up again over his clavicle and wound over and around his shoulder, down to his wrist, and then started again at his hip. The tangled sheets obscured a few spots, but it was clear the scrolling vinework went all the way down to his ankle; there were lines of flowing Elvish script twined around the vines, and there was a quiet power to the ink that meant it must have been done ritualistically.

He kept staring at it, mesmerized, unwilling to let himself think about what was going on here until he had no choice. David closed a hand around Nico's chin and drew him in for a kiss, the Elf groaning softly into his mouth and digging his fingers into the Prime's shoulder where there were already mostly-healed half moons in blood.

They were both bloody—not messily so, but with obvious bite marks and fingernail scratches all over that were moments away from disappearing. Sharing blood, drawing pain…they hadn't just fucked, then, they had *devoured* each other. David was a cruelly accomplished lover; he knew how to draw out every second of pleasure until it was almost unbearable…until his partner was begging, every moan a plea for more and more. He was the one man Deven had actually *craved* in his entire long life, and that constant need had been as terrifying as it was exhilarating.

Standing more firmly in the room Deven could feel it; the air was humming both with sexual energy and the lazy satisfaction of two people who'd been holding back from each other for far too long. There was so much love and pleasure permeating every inch of the room it was almost impossible to breathe—even though he wasn't really there.

"Already?" Nico said with a smile as David edged down and left kisses along his throat. "You have a remarkably short refractory period, my Lord."

Deven almost smiled through the snarl of emotions he was feeling. Truer words had never been spoken.

David lifted his head and looked down into Nico's face. The Elf's adoring gaze traveled from David's practically glowing blue eyes down to his lips, then back up again. Something passed between them that was almost too subtle to feel, but Deven recognized it—a link. They'd been magically bonded at some point. When? Who had done it? Why?

Why. As if he really needed to ask. Everything happening now, from the thinness of Nico's face to the link that was currently feeding the Elf enough power to live as more than a wraith, was Deven's fault, born of the suffering he'd been only too glad to force on everyone around him.

Kai's words came back: *"If you can make everyone who loves you come to hate you, will you finally be satisfied?"*

"I only have you like this for a little while," David said, nuzzling Nico's ear and then nipping the point, eliciting a hitched breath. "We'll figure out how to negotiate everything once Miranda comes home, but I want to enjoy these few days as much as fate will allow."

"As do I."

"Glad you agree." David curved one foot around Nico's calf, one hand around his arm, and pulled him closer, kissing him hard and deep—a tremor ran through Nico, and he gripped David's biceps with surprising strength. There was a brief, and only partly serious, struggle for control, Nico switching their positions with lightning quickness and pinning David's wrists above his head, then the Prime doing the same to him, both growling faintly.

Deven had to cling to the bedpost even harder. It was unbearable to watch—so incredibly beautiful, and so agonizing, seeing two people he had cast aside in so many ways find in each other what he had been unable to give either.

Again, David held the Elf beneath him, this time saying in a harsh whisper, "Whatever happens tomorrow…right now, right here…you're *mine*."

"Yes," Nico murmured. "Yours. You have this night made me your own, by blood and flesh alike…" He locked eyes with David and all but hissed, "Now it's my turn."

The emotion that surged through the room—through Deven—as they tore into each other was too much…too much for his weakened and already shaken heart to bear. Panicking, Deven shoved himself backwards, out of the room, out of the dream, and a moment later gasped himself awake and sat bolt upright in bed.

He was shaking, and couldn't catch his breath, disoriented— the last time he'd been thrown back into his body so forcefully was when Miranda had created the Trinity and dragged him back from death. The feeling was too similar, the shock of what he'd witnessed overwhelming the logic that he had nothing to be upset about, and he curled up in a ball, trying desperately to get warm.

He should be glad. They could have each other and stop trying to get through to him. They could give up, and live their lives while he faded into the shadows beneath the trees where he belonged, his sustained heartbeat enough to keep Nico alive. That was all they needed. They didn't actually need him. Nobody did. Not now. Maybe not ever. All he had to do was stay alive, forever, giving

Nico the only thing he could even if it meant being chained to the world for centuries, decade after decade rolling out endlessly...

Freezing. He was freezing. The room wasn't cold, but ice was forming in his veins. He could give in to it, it would be so easy...

Then something...it was difficult to know what to call it...his soul, perhaps, or at least the tiny wasted part of him that was still longing so deeply to feel again, stumbled out of hiding, its sorrow combined with a thousand other kinds of despair and grief, and it felt like his entire being became one concentrated plea, whispered harshly into the still air and screamed into the void:

"Help me...please...help me."

He had made that same entreaty a hundred times over the centuries until finally he had accepted that there would be no answer. Either there was no one to reply, or Whoever was there had dismissed Deven as Deven had dismissed those he had once claimed to love. He knew the words would fall flat on the deaf ears of the universe. It was folly to try, foolish to grasp at those last frayed threads of faith that had clung to his heart even after all else had fallen away. Chained to a table at the mercy of a Dominican, or feeling the knife-blades of grief when the words *Call Ended* flashed on his phone and his world shattered...he had been begging for mercy for hundreds of years and received no reply.

From what seemed like a thousand miles away, he heard wings.

He didn't look up—he was too afraid to find out he was imagining it. He kept his head bowed, breath coming shallowly, as something heavy and warm was drawn over him, rustling, tickling the skin where it touched.

Feathers.

He must still be dreaming. She couldn't show up in the real world like this, only in the dreamtime. The power to intervene directly in their lives was still denied Her. She had to act here, or through someone.

He was grateful to be asleep, though. The real world was so empty and cold. Here he could dream up love from the past, or a Goddess to hold him, or a moment of peace in ten lifetimes of loss.

But when he lifted his head, he gasped; there were no wings around him, no waterfall of blood red hair...the eyes that met his were not star-flecked black, but dark violet, filled with their own quiet power.

Deven pulled back, feeling suddenly exposed, flushing and grabbing at the comforter even though he was clothed. "Kai."

The Bard, who was dressed in the sort of lounging robe one might wear while surrounded by adoring Elven lads and/or lasses, merely held his gaze a moment, unspeaking. What was it about him that was so goddamned unnerving?

Finally Kai said, "I was passing by. You cried out—it sounded as though you were in agony. I felt compelled to come to your aid."

"I'm fine," Deven replied automatically...but he wasn't fine, and he and the Elf both knew it. His voice shook, as did the rest of him...why was he still so cold? The fire was still dancing, and with the endless rain of an early Fall—for Texas anyway—the central heat was set pretty high.

Kai picked up the thought easily, which was even more unsettling than his being here at all—Deven's shields were seven centuries old and well nigh impenetrable, but to an empath as powerful as Kai apparently was, they seemed transparent. "What you are feeling is not external," he said. "You have driven all the love from your life, or tried to—without it nothing can be warm."

Deven tried to roll his eyes, but a headache slammed right between them and wrapped itself around his skull, squeezing hard. He put his head in his hands. If this were his old life, he would have been able to turn to the other side of the bed and give Jonathan a look of entreaty...the blonde would touch a hand to Deven's forehead, and in seconds the bond between them would banish the pain.

That was all gone now. Gone.

He tried to dredge up the strength to tell the Elf to leave. He didn't want those dark eyes stripping away all his defenses. Kai looked too much like Nico and felt too much like David, and both of them were together now, touching, kissing, lost in each other while Deven wasted precious months he could have been in that bed...he could be there now...no...never. That part of him was dead, and lucky to be dead.

He tried to speak again, to order Kai out of the room, but what came out of his mouth was completely unexpected.

"It hurts," he whispered. "Help me."

He didn't know Kai at all, but he had a feeling that the expression on the Bard's face wasn't one often seen. Kai drew a surprised breath, the cultivated stillness of his countenance softening into genuine emotion. If it had been pity, Deven would have shrunk back from it; but it wasn't pity, it was the same compassion Miranda had offered outside the hospital that he had thrown back in her face. An empath's love. All she had wanted was to love him. So many people wanted to love him. Why? *Why?*

Again, Kai read the thought without effort, and again a surprise: for just a moment his eyes grew bright, and he closed them and took a deep breath.

"Why?" Kai asked quietly. "How can you ask such a thing? Do you think we are all too stupid to know better? Do you value our love so little that you think it born of delusion?"

"You don't know me," Deven said. "You don't know what I've done to everyone...I break things. I break people. I don't deserve your love. I don't understand why none of you can see that."

"Then you are the delusional one," Kai replied. "I am an empath, like your Queen. It is what makes me a Bard, the ability to affect emotion through sound, but I can also read people on sight as I did you. Your Queen is one of the most powerful empaths I have ever met, and I outmatch her only due to age and experience. Both of us can see to the truth of someone's heart in seconds. We know who is evil, who is kind, whose soul is black and whose is gold. Miranda loves you more than you can conceive of—she, who would know immediately if you were worthless or irredeemable. What do you say to that? Is she a fool?"

Deven had no answer for him, so he went on. "Your fear has turned to poison in your veins, and now it has become hate, toxic and slowly killing what cannot die...but what you will not see, we all see. I see."

His mind was swimming in circles, caught in the quiet storm in the Bard's eyes. "What...what do you see?"

A touch of amusement and sadness both together in Kai's voice: "I see that for all your faults, in spite of whatever crimes you have—or believe you have—committed, no matter what you do or how hard you push everyone away, the fact remains, and is obvious to anyone willing to truly see you: You are beautiful, my Lord, in every way possible, and we would all move heaven and earth to make you see it too."

Damn it...damn him... Deven couldn't stop the first hot tear from falling, or the second, and though he tried to turn away in shame at being so weak and broken, a hand took gentle hold of his face and held him still.

Kai leaned forward to rest his forehead against Deven's, and that familiar scent that David claimed was "trees and cookies" but was really just "Elf" seemed to ease something in Deven's chest, letting him exhale. He could feel the Bard's energy moving over him, lightly, like the barest lover's caress; it had the same "flavor" as Miranda's, but was infinitely deeper and wiser, and Deven realized he had completely misjudged the Elf, as he suspected most people did. There was a well of love in Kai that perhaps only his twin and Miranda knew existed.

"I am sorry," Kai said softly. "I am sorry you hurt...I am sorry you have lost so much...sorry that I thought so unkindly of you all this time when I might have been able to help you. And I am sorry that you make it all so much harder on yourself than it needs to be."

"How can you help?" Deven could scarcely speak above a whisper, but the quiet and intimacy of the moment demanded an equally intimate tone.

"At this moment? I can stay with you and help you rest. You need not worry any farther than that. Just let me do what I can for you."

Deven closed his eyes tightly. He didn't know what to do or what to say. But though he might be temporarily paralyzed, Kai was not; he slid his arms around Deven and eased him back into the pillows, settling in close and drawing the comforter up over them both. He didn't make any sort of move beyond that, but coaxed Deven's head to his shoulder, and lay back with him, silent again for a long while.

Deven felt all the remaining tension flood out of his body, and for the first time in months he was completely relaxed, finally touching something of the peace he'd craved. Without really meaning to he burrowed into the Bard's neck, wanting to be as close to that peace as possible, and heard a quiet chuckle followed a moment later by a half-whispered voice twining itself around the lyrical Elven language, a melody Deven knew so well it felt like Kai had drawn it out of Deven's own soul.

"As the Moon embraces the silver stars,
As the golden Sun adores the color blue..."

It should have been astonishing, Deven supposed, that Kai would just happen to choose that song at that moment; but Deven was simply too weary for surprise, and accepted it as he accepted the fact that it wasn't just a lullaby, it was magic. The old words took on new meaning now that they were clothed in such compassion. That power asked nothing of him; it only wanted to touch him and gently wash some of the pain away.

He let it. He could not do otherwise. And true to the Bard's word, Deven felt sleep rising up over his mind and body as slowly and gently as a summer sunset. Deven closed his eyes, smiling with relief.

He felt one long-fingered, strong hand glide over his face. The fingers were callused from untold years of playing musical instruments. The Bard's lips, however, were like silk—he kissed Deven softly on the mouth, again demanding nothing, only giving.

Then Kai whispered against Deven's lips, "Sleep," and that was the last thing Deven knew for quite a while.

Chapter Six

From the very first night Miranda had been told she was in a mansion surrounded by vampires, she had come to expect surprises, usually unpleasant ones, around every corner.

Two nights before she was due back in Austin, just after arriving in New York, she got a surprise that knocked her for a bit of a loop...and for the life of her she couldn't decide if it was a good one or a bad one. In the end she supposed it must be a little of both.

She was to spend two nights at Prime Olivia's Haven. The first was a night off for her and her Elite; she could get a little rest and recharge for one last show away from Texas, and have a chance to spend some time with Olivia, whom she had always wanted to know better. Even if David hadn't been so attached to the dreadlocked Prime, Olivia had been the one to bring him home to his Queen, and that alone made her a worthy friend. And as with everyone in the Circle, Miranda felt drawn to Olivia both empathically and on a deeper, more instinctive level she imagined only the elder children of Persephone would understand.

Still, as much as she wanted to visit Olivia, Miranda's nerves were damn near shot. She'd managed to go the entire three weeks of her tour without running home to Austin, a minor miracle for any Pair. A big part of the reason was that David's end of the bond was currently very well grounded in a certain lovely pointy-eared boy. The Prime had, in fact, been in bed with said boy for nearly 72 hours without leaving the bedroom except to deal with the most strictly necessary Signet business.

Miranda was still surprised at herself. She didn't feel resentful of his time with Nico, though she very well might once she got home and actually saw them interact now that they were lovers. She was prepared for jealousy or whatever might come up, but at the moment she knew this thing they had was new and burning bright, and it wasn't as if the Elf was taking attention away from her. They were getting the first intense few days out of the way while she was out of the house...and even with the allure of endless Elven shaggery, she could sense David was starting to lose it as well—an edge had crept into his voice, and she could feel his energy reaching across the miles, trying to touch hers with increasing need. She might have called a halt to things but there were only two nights left, and she really wanted to prove—to herself? To the world? She wasn't sure—she could survive on her own, mystical bond or no.

Curled up in the back seat of the car, Miranda felt a chill. She *had* survived without him, once. It had been hell.

That wasn't what she wanted. She just valued her independence too highly...and what she'd seen of most other Queens had made her doubly determined. She was no doting housewife, no trophy.

David had given her the over-the-phone equivalent of an "are you mental" look when she confessed that.

"I don't think anyone on the planet would mistake you for a typical Queen," he said. "Why would you?"

She didn't have an answer at the time, though she had something of one now. With everything in flux—her identity, her marriage, the Shadow World itself—she needed to be sure of certain things about herself. In a way this tour had been one of them. She needed to be Miranda Grey, multiplatinum musician, as much as she needed to be Miranda Grey-Solomon, Thirdborn vampire and Queen of the Southern United States.

"Are you feeling well, my Lady?"

Miranda looked over at the other end of the seat. "Yes, Avi...I think so. How far out are we?"

He checked his phone. "About twenty-five minutes with the traffic."

"Good...I could do with a night off. I'm sure you could too."

"Only if you are comfortable in the hands of the Northeastern Elite," he replied. "If for any reason you prefer me to stay on duty I shall gladly do so."

She chuckled. "Do you ever relax, Avi? Do you have hobbies, sport, anything like that?"

He gave her a rare smile. "I paint."

Her eyebrows shot up. "Really? I would not have pegged you as an artist."

"Few would. That, I think, was why I was drawn to it. That, and my wife encouraged me."

"You're married?" she asked, genuinely shocked. "You don't have any dependents or next of kin listed in your file."

"No, I do not. It was a long time ago."

She realized what he meant, and chagrined, said, "God, I'm sorry. I had no right to ask such personal questions."

Another smile, this one thinner but no less sincere. He really was quite handsome when he wasn't so Very Serious Indeed. "As I said, it was long ago. I devoted myself to the Signet shortly thereafter in order to channel my emotions over the loss."

"And you were Israel's Second until he was assassinated." At his nod, she said casually, "Have you thought about taking on that kind of responsibility again?"

Now, his eyebrow lifted, but if he got her meaning, he didn't say so. "I believe it would depend entirely on who I was fighting for, my Lady. I have in my life given my loyalty to four people, and each time it was unbreakable. Such a commitment is a grave thing."

"Israel, Israel's Queen, your wife, and…who was the fourth?"

She couldn't help but ask, even though it was a highly inappropriate question. He was such a cipher, and she couldn't resist poking at someone that shielded, even if he weren't in the running for Second. This trip had given her ample reason to recommend him for the job, but not only was she an empath, she was Queen; if she wanted this man to work for her that closely she could leave no stone unturned.

He started to answer—and she knew he would dissemble, which was fine, but she wanted to hear his choice of words—but the intercom buzzed, and the driver announced that they were at their destination.

As the car rolled to a stop, Avi nodded to her and got out, coming around to open her door. Miranda unfolded herself from the increasingly uncomfortable seat and looked around with interest.

It was her second trip to New York, but the first hadn't exactly been a vacation. She and David had slipped into the city and made a beeline for Hart. Not a lot of sightseeing involved in decapitation, though the view through Hart's window with his blood spattered over the glass was rather morbidly beautiful in the torchlight.

Olivia's Haven wasn't even in the same part of town. One of her first acts as Prime had been to relocate her forces and have the old Haven demolished. She refused to live in the same building where Hart had abused and tortured so many women. The only way she could have made it clearer that she was in control would have been to piss on Hart's remains. Miranda would happily have joined her.

Olivia, though, was all class; she'd reached out to Hart's many enemies and dedicated her rule to restoring the New York Shadow District, which had been driven into the ground by Hart's illicit trades in drugs, slaves, and weapons. Olivia had swept the District clean in a few months of bloodshed and fire, and not only sealed her reputation as an ally of her people, but shown the world that the Signet's will was still absolute and a woman's fist could be made of iron the same as a man's.

David had said that Olivia's ascent to the Haven reminded him of Deven's, back in the 40s; Dev, too, had had something to prove to the Shadow World, and had done so without hesitation or remorse. Olivia however seemed a lot more...well, sane.

Miranda stood as tall as she could as she walked down the aisle flanked by the Northeastern Elite that led from the street up to the Haven's front doors. Olivia had chosen a modern yet classic building, reflecting the progress among vampire kind that had led to her rule, and she already employed twice as many swords as Hart ever had, in a diverse assortment to rival Austin's.

She noted how Avi checked out the entire scene before falling into step just behind her. The rest of her personal guard surrounded her, and thankfully between them and the Northeastern Elite she was mostly invisible outside the fence that surrounded the Haven; Miranda was so beyond done with reporters she had come dangerously close to snarling at the paparazzi hanging out at the airport. Showing her teeth in public was no way to end a successful tour.

Up at the top of the steps Prime Olivia Daniels waited for her, smiling; she was as impressive as ever, her olive skin nearly glowing with vitality and her tattoos practically alive as they twisted and climbed all over her body. She was armed, but for a diplomatic meeting rather than battle—enough weapons to mean business but not so many as to indicate she anticipated a threat. The Signet that had once hung from Hart's throat—after a good deal of cleaning and polishing—now hung from hers, its sapphire shining in the street lights. She was, quite honestly, the sexiest woman Miranda had ever met.

Miranda stopped at the foot of the steps and bowed. "Queen Olivia Daniels of the Northeastern United States," she said clearly, letting her voice fill the courtyard, "I bring you greetings and goodwill from the Haven of the South."

Olivia bowed in return. "Your goodwill is returned with gratitude, and my own offered," she replied. "I bid you welcome to the Haven of the Northeast. I hope that your stay…will…"

Miranda frowned. Olivia trailed off, her formal greeting sputtering to silence on her lips as she went suddenly pale. Her wide eyes went even wider, and she took an involuntary step back.

Miranda's hand went to Shadowflame's hilt and she flipped the leather strap, drawing the blade as she spun toward whatever had spooked the Prime. She heard dozens of Elite around her doing the same, but no one charged—one look at Olivia told her why.

The Prime had one hand on her sword, the other over her mouth, and Miranda's eyes fell on the one thing she had not expected to see tonight:

Olivia's Signet…

…flashing.

Miranda turned again, following Olivia's thunderstruck gaze, but she knew what she would see, intuition hitting her like a punch in the gut a second before her gaze fell on her would-be Second, Avishai Shavit, who was staring at Olivia with astonishment, awe, and fear…but above all, with *recognition*.

David lowered the phone slowly, and he knew by the concern on Nico's face that his own expression must be hilarious.

"Are you all right?" the Elf asked, sitting up. "Is it Miranda? Is she hurt?"

He shook his head, still numb, but dropped the phone on the chair and put both hands on the chair's back. "She's fine, just..."

"Come here," Nico told him. When he didn't respond, the Elf said firmly, "Now."

The command broke through David's paralysis. He rejoined Nico in the bed, letting himself be tucked in and drawn close. Nico was silent for a moment—an impatient moment—before he couldn't help it anymore: "What the hell is going on? I did not think you capable of shock."

Finally David found his voice. "Miranda's fine...but something happened, and..."

Nico caught his gaze and held it. "And?"

David had no idea whether to laugh or cry, feel satisfied or disappointed or simply freaked out—but there was really only one thing to say, regardless. "The Circle is complete."

"Well," Jacob said, amused, *"I guess we won't have to hold a ball after all."*

"How are you, Liv?" David asked. "What can we do for you?"

Olivia's image over the holographic com line was actually clearer than digital video would have been, so he could see the play of emotion over her face—still in shock, obviously, and while a part of her was turning cartwheels of joy, another part was terrified.

"What am I supposed to do now?" she asked a little more softly than usual. *"Do I go jump in bed with him? Do we date? We don't know anything about each other, but we're supposed to be soul mates. How does it work?"*

Jacob took the lead on this one, as he was the only person on the conference call to have had a traditional thunderbolt Pairing. *"Cora and I had a lot of baggage going in—she didn't want a man within twenty feet of her, and I didn't want her to ever, ever think of me the way she thought of Hart. We had to go very slowly—very. That was fine with me. Aside from respecting boundaries, the best thing to do is talk. We started getting together in the library, or out by the horses—an hour here, an hour there. We told each other our stories, and from there moved closer into hopes and fears. It was very organic—I suspect that's how it works for Signet Pairs. God guides us together and then nudges us toward the right way to court one another."*

"May I ask a question, Prime Janousek?"

The holographic Jacob turned toward the three-dimensional Nico, who was sitting in on the conference call as a representative of the West.

"The Signets and vampires themselves were created by Persephone," the Elf pointed out. "What do you expect to happen once the Oracle is awakened and we can speak to Her? Do you imagine She is a demon, a trick? I ask only out of curiosity, not to put you on the defensive. How do you two feel about all of this?"

Jacob was silent for a moment. David knew that Cora, while not present in the call, was physically present with her Prime, and he sensed that they had discussed this very thing more than once. David was madly curious about the answer as well but he hadn't wanted to force the issue.

"I honestly do not know just yet," Jacob finally replied. *"Much will depend on how this Persephone presents herself to us. David has said she has no intention of demanding our obedience, or for us to abandon our beliefs to worship her, and that does help ease my fears. But I think I will have to speak to her, to hear what she truly wants from all of us, before I can decide if taking up her mantle is something our creed will let us do. Cora agrees, though she is perhaps a bit more enthusiastic about a potential meeting since she's had dreams of the Raven Mother before."*

"The Raven Mother," Nico murmured. "I like that. In our tongue She would be called the Kaiathea Mari."

A quiet chuckle, and Jacob said, *"Cora would like you to know she thinks that's beautiful."*

Nico smiled. He and Cora had never physically met, but he was already obviously quite fond of her.

"Has anyone told Deven about what's happened?" Jacob asked. *"I know he has ears everywhere, but I doubt he's paying much attention to them."*

"I'll go by his room and let him know," David said with a sigh. "If by some chance I can get him talking, Liv, he might have some insight—he and Jonathan had the at-first-sight sort of bonding too. In the meantime we'll spread the word around what's left of the Council; Tanaka will probably want to make a state visit if you're up for it."

"I think I might need a little time," Olivia replied.

"Don't worry just yet—just like with the first Magnificent Bastard Parade there's usually a waiting period of a month or two depending on the circumstances. Nobody will even bring it up until you publicly give the okay."

"Good...this is all just...God, I don't know. I was going along, running everything the way I wanted it—what if this guy wants to take over? What if he's some kind of sexist dick who thinks women should be making sandwiches and giving head 24/7?"

David heard Jacob cover a laugh.

"That's not how it works," David reassured her. "You're not just Paired with some random person. You're already a partnership; you just have to find it together. Contrary to myth it's not always instantaneous. Even if you fall in love that second you still have to work out who sleeps on what side of the bed and who wins the thermostat argument."

Aside from trying to make Olivia feel less trapped by the whole situation, there wasn't much any of them could say; she and Avi would have to find their own way, and they couldn't do that if they didn't talk to each other. David all but ordered Liv off the phone at that point: "Stop stalling, grab a bottle of Scotch and go talk about something—favorite movies, battle tactics, whatever." Something Miranda had mentioned popped into his mind, and he added, "Apparently he paints—that's a pretty significant commonality. Show him your gallery."

"He does?" Olivia perked up a tiny bit. *"Does he have any tattoos?"*

David laughed. "That's for you to find out, my Lady."

Then it was just David, Jacob, and Nico on the call, and Jacob said, *"This is going to be interesting. I've never really been privy to the inner workings of a new Pair aside from Cora and I, and our circumstances were drastically different."*

"Same here. I'm the only Prime alive who knew his Queen before she was a vampire. Well, unless you count Nico, of course."

The Elf offered a tired smile. He was still easily worn out, and the last few days hadn't exactly been an orgy of naps. David saw the faint edge of a bite mark just inside Nico's collar, and was suddenly hot all over, barely able to concentrate on the conversation.

"...getting in?"

Luckily he'd long ago learned to multitask. "Miranda? She's in the air right now, and will be here around 3am. Now that we have the airstrip it'll be ten minutes, not an hour, between plane and Haven."

There was a grin in Jacob's voice. *"I imagine you're counting the minutes."*

"Damn right I am. The seconds, in fact. This whole thing was a worthy experiment but I hope to God she never wants to do it again."

"Once everyone's situated, we need to talk about everyone gathering together for this summoning ritual from the Codex."

"I'm working out the specifics on when it must be performed," Nico told them. "If I'm interpreting the text correctly it requires a Solstice, most likely the Winter when the night is at its longest. That gives us a few months to prepare, and for me to make absolutely sure the translation is accurate."

"Let's hope it is—I don't fancy being turned into a frog or anything."

Jacob's words were light but David knew there was genuine trepidation beneath them. This whole Goddess business was worrisome for the Eastern European Pair, and even though Persephone had told David quite clearly that none of them were required to bow to Her, only to work for Her to destroy Morningstar, he couldn't really blame Jacob for having reservations.

After a few more items of business, mostly concerning what Jacob had heard this week about the Council, they ended the call, leaving David and Nico alone in the Bat Cave.

The Prime went about the usual routine of shutting down the conference system and locking down everything else for the night. He felt Nico's eyes on him.

"You're staring again," David said mildly without looking over.

"It is downright wicked to have hands like yours," Nico pointed out. "Watching you work is maddening—I love how clever and capable your hands are, but I cannot help wishing they were on me instead of on the keyboard."

"Give me a few more minutes and they can be."

Nico gave an exaggerated sigh of frustration. "You are so difficult sometimes."

David laughed. "I am, aren't I? I don't know why people keep falling in love with me."

"I suspect it involves that thing you do with your tongue."

The Prime watched the computers go into standby mode, the entire system still running but locked, and he sat back and held still while the scanners verified it was in fact he who had ordered the status change. The primary security screen's icon went from red to green, flashing "IDENTITY CONFIRMED: PRIME DAVID L. SOLOMON. STANDBY MODE ACTIVATED."

Nico was grinning. At David's inquisitive eyebrow, the Elf said, "A few months ago Stella was introducing me to television, and there was a film on about humans traveling in outer space—just now you reminded me of the captain of their ship."

"God, tell me you mean Picard and not Kirk."

A blink. "I don't know what that means."

"Never mind. I'll take it as a compliment regardless." He rose from the chair and extended a hand to help the Elf out of his own; Nico took the opportunity to take firm hold of David's shoulders and kiss him breathless. David slid his arms around Nico's waist and pulled him even closer, luxuriating in the taste of his mouth, the scent of his hair.

Faintly dizzy, David said, "Damn...I need to go by and tell Deven about Avi—why don't you meet me in your suite...unless you want to come with me."

"No, I don't," Nico replied quietly. "You go ahead...I'll be waiting for you."

Outside the office, they parted ways for a while—Deven's room was in one direction, toward the Signet suite, and Nico's was in the other direction.

Halfway down the hall, he had to stop walking and grab the nearest chair as Nico sent a slow, feathery caress along the link between them, and the whispered command, "Hurry."

That boy is going to be the death of me...but as deaths go it wouldn't be the worst I've had.

Taking a deep breath, David did as he had been told, and hurried.

Or at least he tried to.

For the first time in a long time, Deven felt...okay.

It was such a pathetic word for such an immense relief, but he wouldn't claim to be happy, or healing, or anything so ambitious.

He didn't think any of those things were possible for him anymore. But okay, he could manage, as long as he had help.

Nico and David had been so immersed in each other that the former barely noticed his brother was at the Haven; Kai wasn't offended, as he was grateful to see his twin so happy after all these months of tormented sorrow. As Kai said, he didn't come here for himself, but for Nico; and if Nico was getting better, that was what mattered. Plus, it left Kai free to devote himself to his new project: Deven.

Kai slept beside him nearly every day, letting Deven fight his way out of nightmares to find a strong shoulder ready for his tremors; he sang the Prime to sleep most mornings, going through the long, long repertoire of songs he'd gathered in his centuries as a Bard. Kai mostly kept to old folk songs from the era Deven had been born, seeing that the first lullaby he'd tried had resonated so deeply.

Mostly, Deven slept, but now he truly *slept*, rather than tossing and turning fitfully until he had to turn to drugs to silence the monsters under his bed. He felt like he was sleeping off years of insomnia bracketed with terrible nightmares. His dreams now were watercolored, blurry, and soft; they were woven from the darkness of rest and renewal, like the time before birth.

Between sleeps, he talked. Kai didn't pressure him to—in fact the Elf never asked for anything, but let him decide what to reveal— but he listened, without judgment or shock, only with acceptance. Sometimes he asked questions, wanted to hear more about something, laughed at the surprising number of funny stories Deven had forgotten until now, but mostly he just listened, giving no sign of boredom or impatience. As far as it seemed from outside he found every word out of Deven's mouth utterly fascinating.

Whether that was part of Bardic training or was actually true, Deven didn't ask. It was just such a relief to be heard...and to be unafraid to speak.

He found himself remembering things, both good and harrowing, that had slipped from his memory centuries ago. He remembered moments of his childhood; he remembered moments with his father, and his grandmother; his brash, cruel older brothers; the long and lonely journey to the monastery. He remembered even worse things his uncle had done in his quest to beat the queer out of him, for there was no hatred so easily turned on another as that already pointed at oneself.

He remembered being hauled from bed in the middle of the night, naked, his young lover dragged away after only a few days of awkward touching and a single hurried blow job in his chamber. He never saw that boy again, and never expected to see anything. The soldiers had dragged him to the House of God, as the Inquisition's headquarters was called, and sins he had thought were secret—his healing a friend's broken ankle, the way his eyes turned colors—were thrown in his face along with his perversions. That lover had been beaten until he gave up every secret passed to him over the pillows in the damp Irish night.

He wept into Kai's shoulder for that boy whose name he didn't even remember, but also for the boy he himself had been once, back when he'd sat at his father's knee reading the Psalms to the family, Dónal's big hand on his head, rumbling deep voice reciting passages with him. They were a well-regarded family because of the size of their farm and because his mother was a midwife...had they come for her, too, eventually?

Then there was Lesela, who begged her daughter to let the Elves take her son...he would be safe among them, and his mixed blood would eventually be forgotten, but here...here, he would be murdered.

At that point, Kai spoke. "Lesela?"

Deven looked up at him, surprised at the surprise. "Yes."

"Lesela is your grandmother."

"Yes. Why?"

Kai chuckled. "I know her. She is a powerful, and formidable, woman. A healer, as are you, as well as a prophet...and my brother would no doubt turn scarlet if I told you this, but, he and she were lovers once, a long time ago."

Deven frowned. "My Consort slept with my grandmother. Just when I though this whole thing couldn't get any more ridiculous."

Kai sobered, however, and said, "I should have noticed the resemblance right away—you have her pale eyes and that stubborn chin. She would, I am sure, be pleased to meet you someday."

"I don't know...I..."

Kai heard the fear, and kissed it away, touching his lips lightly to Deven's closed eyes, then his lips, then his forehead. "You need not fear, I'lyren. She would not come unless you asked. But if you are ever ready, you should do so. I think after the family you were stuck with all those years ago you should get to have one that knows and accepts you."

"Accepts me? The way they accept your brother?"

The Bard nodded thoughtfully. "Lesela is not like the others. She has never once been afraid of either of us, and she sought Nico out herself wanting to learn more about what makes us different. Apparently he chose a pretty direct way to show her."

"Do you know what happened to my parents?"

"No. But I imagine Lesela does—I can ask her when I am home next."

"No, that's…I don't think I really want to know, I just…I've been thinking so much about my father lately, but I barely knew my mother. She was always afraid of me, but looking back I think she was afraid of everything. She lived in fear that the Church would come for her, even though she didn't manifest any arcane abilities."

"Yet she sent you off to live with that Church?"

"She thought that locked away in a monastery I would be hidden, protected. Being in a constant state of prayer might balance out my demon blood and save me from perdition. In her way I think she was honestly trying to help—I wanted to be a priest, but a position like that would have been too public. She knew I could spend my life with God, and with books, and maybe be happy. She didn't know my uncle, didn't know what she was sending me into. She and everyone in the village…they weren't bad people. Their world was small and they had a lot of fear dogging their steps, even without Elven blood. Human lives are so easily destroyed."

Kai took gentle hold of one of Dev's hands and began rubbing it; the vampire carried a lot of tension in his hands, and massaging them was one of the most soothing things the Bard could do for him. Nico had done the same, once, after an intense healing session had left Deven emotionally wrung out and shaking…Deven remembered how later he'd thought about it over and over, something very different from comfort in those thoughts.

Kai once again intuited what was on his mind, and said, eyes on Deven's palm, "You know, even if he and the Prime are spending most of their time together, if you were to ask to see Nico, he would be at your door in moments."

"I know." Deven sighed, shut his eyes, and for the first time, said hesitantly, "Maybe…maybe someday. I just…not yet."

A nod. Kai didn't push. He continued his work, eventually switching hands, and again that feeling of well-being settled in Deven's mind. Outside this room everything was still broken, still wrong; but for a while every day he could lay it down and feel safe with his...counselor? Healer?

"How about 'friend,'" Kai suggested.

He was getting used to the Elf overhearing his thoughts—in fact if he'd wanted to he could easily have stopped it, but he found it strangely reassuring...less lonely.

Their eyes met. After a moment Deven gave him a tentative smile. "All right," he said softly. "Friend."

But there was something he needed to know before he could completely accept that word. He hated to bring it up, to potentially destroy whatever this was, but... "Kai, are you...I mean, do you..."

He deliberately trailed off, hoping Kai would hear the rest of that sentence too so he wouldn't have to say it aloud.

Kai frowned slightly. His expression darkened, and though it wasn't anger, it made Deven's heart skip with anxiety. *Have I ruined this too?*

"You think that I am only helping you because I want you as a lover? That I would take advantage of your pain in such a despicable way? And even worse, that I would bed down with my brother's soul mate when he cannot even come near you? That is what you think of me? What is *wrong* with you people?"

The expression made sense suddenly—it was hurt. "No, no," Deven said, mentally kicking himself for not being clear about his meaning. "Of course not. I just...I know that your people are all bisexual to one degree or another, and you're very...affectionate. I don't mind—I like it a lot actually—but Elven culture is very different when it comes to this sort of thing."

He still felt like he was making a total mess of the explanation, but Kai nodded slowly. Some of the hurt faded from his eyes, though they were still stricken.

"I'm sorry, Kai. I didn't mean to..." This time, Deven simply didn't know what to say, and averted his eyes, trying not to lose what little composure he had regained. Still, he heard the pleading in his own voice, hating the sound even as he said, "Don't be angry. It's just...I've only known you a few days, but you've been...amazing. I don't want to fuck this up like I do everything else. Don't...don't leave. I..."

Kai let out a breath and nodded again. His empathy was clearly able to find the meaning behind the words even if Deven couldn't express himself like an adult anymore.

The Bard placed a hand around the back of Deven's head and drew him close again, his presence wrapping around the vampire like the wings Deven had imagined that night he'd first woken with Kai beside him. Kai might worship Theia, but Someone else seemed to have borrowed him for a while.

"It is well, *i'lyren*. Do not be afraid. I think I understand."

Relieved, Deven closed his eyes, breathing hard from the near-panic that had gripped him for a moment. He thought back to what Kai had said, and told him softly, "I never meant to hurt Nico. I still don't. Tell me you believe that."

A sigh. "I believe you. I would not be here if I truly thought you had intended any of this. You have been bleeding for most of your life, and losing your Consort was one wound more than you could bear. I understand that. And I understand your fear."

If Deven had been upright he might have sunk into a chair with relief, but instead he just buried his face as deeply into Kai's neck as he could. Gradually he felt the Bard relax, returning to the level of comfort they'd been enjoying with each other.

"You are a treasure," Kai said, his voice vibrating against Dev's temple. "And, just to alleviate your fears, no—I am not looking for another lover, and my history is made up of, let's estimate, 80% women. I have lived too long to stick to the same thing forever, of course, but for the most part it is females with whom I walk into the woods."

"Good...I mean, that we have incompatible preferences. I have this tendency to do stupid things that hurt people if I'm left alone with a mutual attraction."

He'd told Kai about his history with David, and with Miranda—clearly the Elf was smitten with the Queen, and when Kai said she had confessed to similar feelings, Deven was surprised. He had always been taken aback with Miranda's acceptance of her Prime's voracious heart, but hearing she was even remotely entertaining the idea of a full-on polyamorous arrangement of four, even just as a dalliance, Deven had been genuinely shocked.

She must have been so confused by all of this...God, no wonder she said she needed someone to talk to...I should have...what am I

*thinking? I'm the last person she should look to for relationship
advice. Look what I've done to everyone I've touched.*

Kai raised an eyebrow, not liking the direction Deven's mood
was headed. "I find it interesting," he said, "that you place the
blame for all of these events on yourself, when there was always at
least one other person who participated. Why is it more your fault
than theirs? The Prime is an adult. So is my brother. So was your
Consort. We all make our own decisions, my Lord. You give
yourself too much credit—unless I am gravely misinformed, you are
not a god, nor have you ever forced anyone to lay mouth or hand
upon you."

Before Deven could frame a reply, a knock at the suite door
nearly sent him flying out of the bed. He turned over to face the
room's entrance, about to ask who on earth would come to see him,
but the door was already opening.

"I know you don't want visitors," came a familiar voice, "but I
thought you should at least know...that..."

David stared at them for an uncomfortably long moment.
Deven realized with a lurch that this must look like exactly what he
and Kai had just established it certainly wasn't.

Sure enough, when David finally spoke again, it was in that
deadly quiet voice that Deven recognized all too well from a
thousand nights that had ended in beheadings.

"What...the hell...is going on here?"

Kai's temper flared. "It is none of your affair what is going on
here, and if you are not going to give Deven the respect of waiting
to enter until invited, there is certainly no reason for him to explain
himself to you."

David's eyes grew cold, their irises starting to pale, and his hand
moved to the hilt of the Oncoming Storm.

Deven winced as Kai made a disdainful sound. The Elf was
brave, and could be a match for David in the energy department,
but no one, not even a cocky Bard, should ever, ever attempt to
stand up to the Prime of the South once his hand was on that hilt.

"Go ahead," Kai told David. "Attack me. See what your Queen
and your lover have to say about that."

The silver edge in David's eyes spread deeper, and their
perimeter began to darken to black.

"Wait just a goddamned minute," Deven snapped, sitting up.
"Both of you need to calm the hell down. Kai—you are powerful

and treated like a demigod in Avilon, but I will remind you whose house you are in. Whatever you think of him the Signet should command your respect if nothing else. And David, there is nothing going on here but talking—we're friends, that's all." At David's dubious eyebrow, Deven said, "I give you my word."

David looked a little shocked that Deven, who had barely lifted his gaze from the ground in months, had at least for the moment become something of himself again. He didn't back down, but he did take his hand off the sword, and after a moment his eyes started to fade back into blue.

Kai's aura also pulled back into itself—God, they were like a couple of bulls butting heads over a cow.

Deven took a deep breath. "All right. What do you want?"

David continued to stare daggers at the Elf for another second before answering. "I came to tell you that Olivia has found her Consort."

Now, it was Deven's turn for shock. "Where? Who?"

"Miranda's tour stopped in New York last night—the man we were hoping would eventually become Second was her head of security, and the moment he and Olivia saw each other, her Signet lit up like a marquee. Miranda says they have absolutely no idea what to do with each other, and are just sort of sitting and staring—I told her that's the first stage and she should let them be."

"Wait...Second?" Surely he didn't mean...

"Yes, Israel's former right hand, the one the Mossad recommended. Avishai Shavit."

Deven stared at him, mouth dropping open, the sheer ludicrous enormity of the news causing something in his brain to flatline for a moment. *"What?"*

The Prime sighed. "I don't know much about him, on a personal level, so I have no idea whether to be glad for Olivia or worried. Obviously the Signet wants the former, but...you mentioned once you'd heard of Shavit. Do you know anything about him that we don't?"

Deven couldn't help it—he laughed. Again, David looked astonished, and glanced at Kai, then back, tacitly acknowledging the change in the fallen Prime just in the last few days.

"Yes," Deven said, shaking his head wryly. "Yes, you could say I do."

Chapter Seven

She took the stairs down two at a time and hit the ground running, handing off her guitar to Harlan—he and the other guards would make sure her things got where they belonged, but she couldn't stand another minute anywhere but in her Haven, or rather, with her Prime.

He'd said he was going to meet her at the airstrip, but she didn't give him a chance; it was only a ten minute walk, or a five minute run, from there to home. They'd had the strip built last year to bypass questions about weapons from TSA. It had saved hours from every trip they'd made, and if she'd really tried she could have Misted from there, but she still hated Misting unless it was necessary and after hours stuck on that plane she wanted nothing more than to run, hair flying, boots thudding quietly on the ground.

As she came around the corner to the Haven's front entrance she saw the doors open, saw a dark figure emerge no doubt intent on going west along the same path she'd just run east, and before he could even reach the steps, Miranda had flung herself into him, only centuries of practice and immortal strength keeping the embrace from becoming a tackle.

He laughed, and his arms wrapped around her and held tight as he spun her around, absorbing the impact. His heart was pounding with hers, and she pressed into him as hard as she could. By the time her feet hit the stones again his mouth had already claimed hers.

In that kiss she felt the slowly-encroaching misery of the last three weeks, a pain he'd been fighting off less and less successfully the last few days…and, with a long exhalation, she felt that pain ease as the energy between them balanced itself, restoring their precious equilibrium and setting everything right with the world again.

Miranda kissed him harder, pushing three weeks' worth of pent-up desire and vicarious pleasure back at him so he'd see just what she'd been dealing with. He'd had the novelty and wonder, not just of new love, but of learning how to be with an entirely new race, so his level of sexual frustration was a tiny, rather smug thing compared to the howling demon horde that had taken possession of her hips.

"I must beg your forgiveness, my Queen," he murmured, kissing down the side of her neck. "Allowing you to sleep in a solitary bed day after day is torture of the cruelest kind."

"I accept your contrition…but penance must be paid."

"Name your terms, my Lady. I am your humble servant."

"Damn right you are." She grabbed him by the arm and hauled him into the house, ignoring the grins they got from the door guards.

She didn't remember the trek from the front door to their suite being so goddamned long before.

By some miracle, her luggage had reached the suite first—the Haven staff was arcanely efficient. That was good; it meant no interruptions. She had no place to be until after sunset, giving her the entire day to repeatedly accept her husband's penance.

He was disinclined, or perhaps too wise, to argue, and instead of telling her how much he missed her, he picked her up and set about stripping off her clothes between the door and the bed. Once there she took hold of his belt and hauled him down with her, trying not to claw off his shirt—it was one of his favorites and she'd already left nail holes in much of his collection.

She had intended to just let the fever she'd been battling rise up and engulf them both, and to spend hours biting and screaming, and frightening the servants, but she found that, when she finally had his body against hers again, blue eyes locked on her green, that driving need had become something different, and she slowed down, putting both hands on his face and locking gazes for a moment.

"Welcome home, Miranda," he said softly.

Suddenly she couldn't speak—there was too much tumult in her heart, emotion after emotion trying to take over. It all became a single ache, one she couldn't articulate even if she'd wanted to. She nodded silently, blinking back tears.

He smiled and kissed her again, this time taking her cue and slowing down, removing what was left of her clothing little by little and nipping lightly at the newly exposed skin. She snaked her arms up to do the same to him.

Curious, she ran her senses over him to see if his attention was at all divided, but whatever extracurricular activities he'd been occupied with these weeks, there was only one lover on his mind right now, only one heart whose happiness he would break the world to ensure. Sighing, she lay back and closed her eyes, hands drifting—one up around the headboard, the other around his neck as he devoted himself to re-learning her skin with his mouth.

At the center of a world spinning off balance into war and destruction, with sadness and fear waiting to attack at every crossroads, there was one thing, the stillpoint of darkness and light, that mattered above all else. Two red stones glowed in the candlelit room, two pairs of black eyes for just a moment filled with stars, two heartbeats fell into a single rhythm.

All of Morningstar could have poured into the room and lit the bed on fire—she could have destroyed them all with a glance. There was no force evil enough to overcome the simple truth that together they were unstoppable...now, and always.

"How do I look?"

Stella grinned. "Kind of weird, but also kind of hot."

Nico looked down at himself, biting his lip. "Are you sure this is necessary? I feel like a clown."

She giggled and came up behind him, sliding her arms around his waist. "Honey, if you go to Miranda's concert in Elf robes you're going to stand out way more than in pants. Don't worry—I think Kai's dressing in human drag too. I have no idea what he's going to do with all that hair, though."

Nico toyed with his sleeves nervously. He had only been out in the city a handful of times, back at the beginning when David had been trying to teach him to hunt. The Shadow District had been too much for him—all that darkness and hunger, and he so vulnerable—and large groups of humans had terrified him.

Tonight, though, he was feeling a lot better, and it would be a pretty simple outing; they only had to walk about a block to the theater's rear entrance, and they'd be up in a special seating area apart from the crowd. He'd be surrounded by Kai, Stella, and David, and if anything could get past all three of them, he was doomed anyway. He had to start somewhere.

Kai appeared in the doorway. He was splendid as always, in his usual dark colors chosen specifically to set off his eyes. He'd pulled his hair back and braided it in the Elven fashion—younger Elves loved doing their hair up in complicated configurations, but after about 200 most opted for the simplicity of unbound hair, or a couple of braids on each side to keep it out of the face for important work. Kai often kept his back when he was practicing or teaching, so it wasn't entirely strange to see, although the way he'd doubled its length on itself to make it appear shorter was odd.

"Very nice," Stella told the Bard. "You don't exactly look human but I think you'll both pass."

Stella for her part was rather amazing to behold. She'd reverted to her pigtails and striped arm warmers, big platform boots, and a ruffled skirt with what looked like polka dots but were in fact skulls. Nico was amazed at the sight of her with eyeliner and black lipstick, tiny sparkling gems dotting her temples. It looked like several different fashion styles had mated hastily in a closet and fallen out covered in glitter.

Nico absolutely loved it.

Kai gave the Witch a once-over and shook his head. "You would scandalize our entire population," he said. "Excellent work."

"You seem excited," Nico observed of his twin.

"I am. I've been wanting to see Miranda work her gift on a crowd—I want to see how it compares to the way I use mine. She mentioned so casually that she'd influenced audiences in the thousands. That kind of power...I cannot wait to see it."

"That and you get to stare down at her cleavage all evening," Stella pointed out dryly.

Kai laughed. "You said it, Mistress Witch, I did not."

A moment later, there was a knock, and the Prime stepped into the room. He, too, looked beautiful, but there was nothing terribly novel about that. He would set hearts and loins on fire whether in a formal suit or one of his comical shirts about television. This time, he was in a slightly dressier version of his work clothes, including the coat, and smiled as he looked the three of them over.

"Not bad at all," he said. "Stella, you might be the cutest thing I've ever seen."

The Witch blushed furiously but said, "If I can't be smoking hot like some people, I'll take cute."

David gave her a lifted eyebrow and, "You are perfectly beautiful, but the word doesn't seem quite fitting for an outfit like that."

She looked at herself and shrugged. "Point taken. One of these days I'll show up in an evening gown and none of you will know what to do."

"I will," Nico told her.

She blushed again.

David moved over to Nico and drew him close for a moment, sighing contentedly at the scent of the Elf's skin. It was the first day they'd spent apart in a week, and while Nico certainly didn't begrudge the Pair their reunion, it had been a lonely day. He'd get used to it; one way or another he would be able to continue seeing David, and whatever arrangement the Queen approved would be good enough given that the alternative, not ever tasting that mouth again, was unthinkable.

"Chris is out front with the Escalade," David said, reluctantly releasing Nico and stepping back. "Miranda's gone ahead in the limo so she can do her sound check and so forth. We should get going too."

Kai asked, "Has anyone thought to invite Deven?"

David shot him an unreadable look. "What, you didn't?"

Nico took a deep breath. David had told him that Kai and Deven had struck up some kind of relationship—not a romantic or sexual one, the Prime had been very clear on that—but something more akin to a counselor and client. Nico hadn't had time to ask Kai for details, but despite the stab of jealousy that was inevitable upon finding out his Prime had taken up with his brother even just as friends, Nico knew that if Kai had decided to help, that meant the Bard had decided Deven was not beyond hope, and not only could be healed, but should be. That was such a radical departure from how Kai had felt about Deven only days ago that Nico was dying of curiosity to find out more, but it would have to wait, perhaps until they got home tonight and things quieted down.

Kai's attitude toward David had also changed pretty significantly; instead of a sarcastic retort, the Bard said only, "I did not think it was my place."

And even more surprisingly, David replied, "Perhaps I should have. I assumed I knew what the answer would be—do you think I'm wrong?"

Kai shook his head. "I think he might have appreciated the invitation, but I do not think he would have accepted it. Not yet."

The Prime nodded, then made a sweeping gesture toward the door. "Shall we, then?"

Nico, a bit dazed watching his brother and lover suddenly getting along, turned to Stella. She chuckled at the look on his face and kissed his cheek as they left the suite.

"One big happy family," she whispered.

He held back a snort, took her hand, and followed the others to the car.

Every time she played in Austin Miranda found herself thinking back. From the night she had been attacked leaving that dive downtown, to her performance at the Austin Live Music Festival that culminated in a gunshot, to the night Marja Ovaska had first attacked her disguised as a reporter, her beloved city had taken and given in equal measure.

Here she was again, on a stage she'd walked out onto a dozen times—the Paramount, a cozy venue on South Congress with a mere 320 seats, an historic theater that had hosted vaudeville, movie premieres, and all sorts of performances. She'd had two fundraisers for the Porphyria Foundation there. Stepping into the dressing rooms felt like coming home.

It was a fitting end to the tour—after playing in venues scattered around the country, most with at least three times the capacity, and spending most of a month feeling utterly disconnected from her own life, she was back at the Paramount, with her family in attendance, and the moment she slung her guitar around her shoulder she couldn't stop grinning.

She could feel David close by, up in the box with the others; and she could feel them too, Nico's verdant energy growing stronger at last, Kai's attention riveted to her presence on the stage, Stella and her starlit magic so reassuring despite her youth.

And now, if she were to reach beyond them into the Circle, she would find all eight places filled.

She still didn't know how to feel about that. It was amazing, on one hand; on the other, it felt...portentous. Her precognitive sense had kicked into overdrive the minute Olivia's Signet began to flash, and since that moment she'd had a low level of anxiety that at first she couldn't explain.

She had figured it out on the trip home. With the Circle completed, their respite was over. They needed to prepare, to be ready for Morningstar's next move—one that would surely come soon. However he and Olivia worked out their newfound Pairhood, Avi joining them was a stone dropped into the relatively calm pool of life at the Haven—dreadful as much of the last year had been, at least it was a known quantity. Soon they'd have to do the summoning ritual Nico had found, and enter into Persephone's service as a group. What then?

She was getting ahead of herself, of course. It could wait at least until tomorrow. Right now she had work to do.

It was easy to hold the audience in the palm of her empathy. They were already happy to be there; she just wanted them to have a phenomenal time, a night to remember. All she had to do was wrap her attention around the room as a whole, take gentle hold of the positive emotions, and breathe into them as if blowing up a balloon. Amazing that once something like this had drained her for days, and that her gift had nearly killed her. That Miranda seemed so far away now, like a character in a book she had left on a shelf so long the pages were yellowed.

She was Queen now. Powerful, skilled both on stage and in battle. She was one of the strongest of her kind. And her family was as well—each had her own gifts, something to contribute. They were all the stuff of legends...some more than others, now that there were Elves in the mix. Witches, warriors, strategists, geniuses: her Circle, and its allies, stood strong. New connections were blossoming everywhere, and there were even signs of hope for Deven. Once they were united, how could they help but win the war?

Miranda had to smile at herself. The audience affected her as much as she did it, when she allowed it. Tonight, that's what she wanted more than anything. Joy, triumph. Certainty. Right now it was hers to grasp.

The crowd's roaring farewell rang in her ears as she walked off stage, and again as she returned for her encore. She returned to her piano for the last two songs, giving them two of her favorite covers: "Bloodletting" by Concrete Blonde and Sarah McLachlan's "Possession."

"The night is my companion
And solitude my guide
Would I spend forever here
And not be satisfied..."

By the time she got back to her dressing room, she was so high off the audience's radiant energy that when someone knocked on the door it didn't occur to her to wonder who it was—that's why she had bodyguards, after all, to make sure only approved individuals got within twenty feet of her.

"Come in!"

The mirrors were all covered, as per protocol, but she sat before them anyway intending to pull her hair back and take off her stage clothes, put on something more sane, and then wash the makeup off her face and neck.

She looked up, and smiled. "Detective Maguire! This is a surprise."

The minute she saw his face, and his expression truly registered, her euphoria burst like a soap bubble in a cactus garden.

Maguire was not a man who smiled easily, which was a shame, since Stella had inherited his bright grin and lively eyes. Investigating murders took its toll on even the most upbeat person. Just now, though, he looked genuinely upset, as well as a little embarrassed, and she had no idea how to interpret it.

"What's going on?" she asked. "Did something happen?"

Maguire cleared his throat and started to speak, but another man stepped up in front of him and flashed a badge. "I'm Detective Myers with the Austin Police Department. Ma'am, I'm going to need you to come with us."

She frowned and looked at Maguire. "Explain."

Her tone was not one to ignore, and to give them credit, they heeded it. "We need to take you in for questioning," Maguire said. "Technically I'm not the lead here—conflict of interest and all."

"What interest? What's going on?"

Detective Myers shot Maguire a venomous look, then asked, "Mrs. Solomon, where were you on the night of April 24 of this year?"

"I have no idea," she replied truthfully. "I'd have to look at my calendar—may I?"

At Myers's nod, she pulled out her phone and brought up April. Not much had gone on; she'd had a charity performance in Houston on the 16th, but that was about it. The 24th...

Her heart froze in her chest. Whether it was precog or plain old fear, she went cold, and she knew she had paled. She carefully stowed her phone back in her coat.

The 24th had been a New Moon.

"I was at home," she replied steadily. "About 50 people saw me."

"Were you home all night?"

She sighed. "No, I don't think so. I think I came into town that night."

"What brought you to town?"

"A Cadillac." Realizing now wasn't the time for a joke, she added, "I don't remember...you might have to ask my husband. He never forgets anything."

"So you're saying you don't have an alibi."

She met Maguire's eyes, even though he hadn't spoken and was trying to avoid looking at her. "An alibi for what?"

She heard the metallic click-and-snap and saw a flash of steel—but it wasn't a sword being drawn from its sheath.

It was handcuffs.

"Miranda Solomon, you are under arrest for the murder of Annalise Vitera. You have the right to remain silent—"

"I waive that right," she snarled as he approached her with the cuffs. "Lay a hand on me and you'll regret it."

"Miranda—" Maguire gave her a look of entreaty. It occurred to her that if she really were a murder suspect, his relationship with her people would throw his whole career into jeopardy.

She could end this with one swipe of a blade, but that would end her life as a musician irrevocably; besides, she wanted to know what was going on, and how the APD had come to believe she had killed someone.

Especially since she absolutely had.

Shadowflame was still in her sheath among Miranda's things, so the detective didn't see the sword and demand it be handed over. She did however have two knives and a small stake for close-up combat, and removed them from her coat and handed them to Maguire without explanation.

"I'll go without a fight," she said firmly. "But you're not cuffing me."

A surprising number of uniformed officers were waiting outside the dressing room. They formed a tight circle around her and escorted her from the building, through the gathered post-show crowd of fans. She heard cameras snapping and questions firing at her rapidly from reporters.

She could imagine the headlines now: *Miranda Grey Arrested for Murder.*

Better still she could imagine the follow-up: *Miranda Grey's Husband Goes Completely Batshit and Kills Entire Police Department.*

The police shepherded her into a waiting patrol car—its lights were flashing and everything—and shut the door, letting her look out at her fans who milled around in confusion, some angry and some clearly worried at the sight of their idol being snatched up and driven away, and with her the happiness she'd worked to give them...and herself.

Chapter Eight

Maguire took custody of her once they arrived at the station so that Myers could do something paperwork-related; he and several of the officers led her toward a doorway where she could hear a lot of crowd noise—Holding. They were going to put her in a cell.

"Is this really necessary?" she asked.

Again that pained look. "It's just for half an hour or so—none of the interview rooms are open right now, and we have to wait for your lawyer to get here since you asked for one."

"And David," she noted.

Maguire swallowed. "Yeah. Hopefully he'll understand I'm just doing my job and not have me strangled and tossed in a shallow grave."

She leaned a little closer as the right hand guard moved forward to run his badge over the scanner and open the door to Holding. "What the hell is going on, Detective? Why do you guys think I killed someone? I know you—you're a good cop and an honest man. You must have compelling evidence to do this."

Maguire looked at her. "I'm afraid we do."

The heavy metal door slid out of the way, and the Detective and the other cops led her in, down a long hall with cells on either side.

For the first few steps there was a good deal of hooting and yelling, some whistling, various appreciative epithets for her various body parts. The emotions of several dozen men and a couple of women, most who had committed various sorts of crime and many of those violent, shoved up against her mind, and she nearly stumbled.

Anger seized her—an anger born as much from alienation as anything else. She didn't belong here among these mortals. They looked at her and saw a weak little woman in a black coat. She could feel it...that oily black energy that tried to glom onto her like tar. These were the people who fell at her feet dead every month. Some of them would recognize her as a celebrity, but she was still an object to them, a pair of killer breasts and thighs wrapped snugly in vinyl. She'd been treated that way once...the misogyny inherent to human society was a part of her own, yes, but at least among her own people she was something more than a collection of parts. The Shadow World *knew her*. Even Hart in all his insanity had known not to underestimate her.

Miranda felt her teeth press into her lip. She allowed just the barest edge of her true identity to seep out from behind her shields, touching each human she passed. One by one they fell silent and shrank from the bars. They wouldn't know why, they would not even be able to articulate it, but they would spend days jumping at noises after dark and feeling watched. The weaker among them would have dreams about black wings and dark water.

She smiled thinly and, just for fun, met one of their gazes and held it so long the man started sweating. When she looked away she could hear him panting and falling back onto the bench in his cell. She wondered what color her eyes were right then.

Maguire steered her into an empty cell and moved back so the bars could shut. The lock engaged, and Maguire gave her a parting look of mixed emotions—if he'd seen the evidence, whatever it was, had it changed how he felt about her? Or did he maintain her innocence no matter what?

She'd find out soon enough, she supposed. For now all she could do was sit and wait for the cavalry to arrive.

"Miss Maguire, if you'll all come with me," the uniformed woman said, holding the stage door open. "I've been instructed to escort you back to the car."

"But what happened?" Stella asked. "I heard the police took Miranda away—why would they do that?"

"I honestly don't know, ma'am. I just have my orders."

Stella gave Nico a helpless look. "I don't know what's going on."

"Then we should do as the Pair have requested, and return home," Nico told her, squeezing her hand. "I am sure an explanation is forthcoming."

Kai, who emerged last from the venue, was smiling wryly as he said, "Besides, do you honestly think human authority could bring the two of them to harm? Inconvenience, perhaps. Consternation, undoubtedly. But genuine harm—I should like to see them try."

Stella couldn't help but think about Deven, wherever he was right now, and remember seeing him unconscious after his Consort was crushed by a building. That explosion had killed dozens of people and destroyed lives…it had led to Nico, one of the most powerful beings she'd ever met, suicidally depressed while Deven took massive doses of heroin in a desperate attempt not to feel.

Humans had done that.

A chill of foreboding ran through her. She didn't have precog like Miranda did, but she wished she could knock on some wood.

Downtown Austin was practically boiling over with people that night. Nico's hand in hers tightened every few minutes as he fought down panic over the crowds and the noise. It had been the chaos as much as the darkness that had freaked him out so badly back when David had tried to get him to hunt; this was one of only three times she could think of that he'd been in town since. They should have had the Pair and their bodyguards with them—they were all supposed to depart at the same time, and both vehicles had been parked together. Miranda would have had no trouble parting the sea of humans without even saying a word. Anyone who got too close to Nico would get the patented David Solomon Death Glare. And Stella would feel infinitely safer—funny, that she would worry way less in the care of vampire warriors than her own species.

The woman who'd taken charge of them had a backup guard, so at least they weren't totally on their own. After a few minutes they finally broke through the crowd and angled off toward 11th. She remembered they'd parked there not far from the fortress-like Travis County Courthouse. Ironic considering where Miranda was now.

"Are we going all the way to the garage?" she asked their guard. "Usually Chris comes and meets us."

"He is," the guard replied absently. "Just up the block here."

Stella stopped walking so abruptly that Nico ran into her back, but luckily Kai's arm shot out and caught his brother, steadying them both.

The guard gave her a look of impatience with a touch of condescension. "What's the problem?"

Stella looked her over head to foot—no anomalies, but... "You're a lieutenant," she said warily. "A lieutenant on public guard duty...which means you should know Chris is a woman. So either you're a jerk playing pronoun roulette, or you're an impostor. Which is it?"

The woman rolled her eyes and reached up to her ear. "Now," she said.

Stella heard several tiny somethings whistling through the air, and felt one impact with the side of her neck. She slapped it like a mosquito, and her hand came away with a small wooden dart with a needle. The wood had been marked with symbols only a few millimeters tall, and even from her hand the dart smelled like...

"Magic," she said hoarsely as the world began to swim around her. "Run—call—"

She heard the others sinking to the ground, but stayed on her feet desperately, dragging words out of her body as fast as she could and speaking into her com: "Star-One, Star-Two, this is Stella Maguire—we've been attacked, I think it's Morningstar, we've been drugged and..."

She caught movement on a sort of time delay—she felt the fist hit her face before she saw it.

After that, darkness.

Miranda Grey had a reputation, in the media, for being rather weird. Most of it was blamed on her "illness" and the rest usually chalked up to the strangeness of celebrities.

Her husband, on the other hand, was hardly ever seen, and a wide variety of rumors circulated about why—the most popular was that he was the leader of a drug cartel, or possibly the Mafia, and stayed out of the public eye to avoid being targeted by rivals. That one had always given Miranda the giggles: *Watch out for that ex-British ice cream addicted nerd Mafia. He made a fortune on the black market in World of Warcraft and will leave your avatar to swim with the fishes.*

Overall they were considered an odd couple. Any married people who wore matching necklaces had to be a little bit batty. But for the most part David was an enigma wrapped in a mystery wrapped in a black leather coat...which made his arrival at the police station that much more hilarious, in her mind.

She sat in the cell with her eyes closed, listening to the natural ebb and flow of noise outside Holding, and when she sensed that glowering storm cloud of energy approaching, she smiled.

Apparently he'd decided to hell with anonymity. He walked into the station with four guards, not even attempting to look human or blend in. Much of the conversation in the foyer went silent, so it was even easier to hear his low, dangerous voice directed at the front desk clerk:

"Take. Me. To. My. Wife."

"Sir, if you'll—"

"*Now.*"

"...yes sir. Just, um...Johnson, would you lead Mr....um...to Interview 3? I'll page Maguire and Myers."

Someone, Johnson apparently, coughed and said, "I'm afraid you'll need to leave your...escort? Outside, sir."

"Fine."

She knew that he'd have gestured at the guards to take up position on either side of the interrogation room door, and no doubt their obedience would make the whole situation that much stranger to the humans.

A moment later a harried-looking Detective Myers appeared and unlocked the cell.

Wordlessly, Miranda rose and walked past him, following the call of her Prime's anger to room 3, giving a nod to the guards as she did.

It was a relief to notice that the room didn't have the two-way mirror one often saw on TV. It was just as bleak, though, with that industrial green paint that seemed to coat the walls of every government building in Austin, one ancient office table, four chairs...and a laptop.

David stood when he saw her. "Are you all right?"

She smiled. It wasn't something she'd admit often, but she loved it when he was angry. That killing light in his eyes was better than porn. "Yeah, I'm fine. Confused, pissed off, and I smell like a urinal, but fine."

Maguire and Myers came into the room and closed the door; all four sat down, but Maguire said, "We should wait for the lawyer."

"She'll be here in 20 minutes," David told them coldly. "But don't worry—I have a law degree. Get on with it."

Maguire shot him a look of surprise. "You do?"

He shrugged. "I got bored in the 90s."

Miranda had actually forgotten about that—he had six or seven degrees, though just the one doctorate from MIT. That was the important one, in his mind. In fact the motto inscribed on his version of the Signet Seal was *Mens et Manus*, the same as the school's.

"All right," Myers said. He slid the laptop over and clicked a few things. "This will take a minute to load."

She held back a giggle as David glanced at the logo on the laptop and made a faint, probably involuntary derisive sound.

Miranda knew she shouldn't find this whole thing hysterically funny, but she did—a defense mechanism, she supposed. Like her mother had been wont to say, it was either laugh or never stop crying.

It was just so surreal...she'd been *arrested*. Like a human. For murder. There were paparazzi waiting for her outside the police station, probably already branding her the next crack-addled falling star. They wouldn't know why she was here yet, and speculation would probably turn first to drugs or a disgruntled ex-employee.

Maguire was fiddling with the recording device, which looked pretty ancient. She knew that APD had some sophisticated tech at its disposal for forensics, but they had to cut corners somewhere.

He got it working, however, and said, "Please state your name for the record."

"Miranda Grey-Solomon."

He went through a quick list of mundane questions: birthdate, birthplace, a few basic facts. Then, he produced a photograph and slid it over to her. "Do you recognize this woman?"

She looked down at the picture—a laughing, bright-eyed Hispanic woman in a UT shirt. "No."

"You might recognize her better here."

The second picture was dramatically different. It was clearly the same woman, but she was emaciated and had huge dark circles under her dull eyes. She was pretty clearly strung out on something.

"I'm sorry, I don't know her."

Maguire nodded. "How about here?"

The third picture made her stomach twist on itself with dread. In this one the woman was dead, lying on top of a body bag, filthy. She had clearly been dead for a while, though Miranda didn't know enough about decomposition to say how long.

What made her insides lurch, however, was the pair of neat puncture wounds in her throat.

"Annalise Vitera, aged 34, found in a dumpster behind a Korean restaurant downtown. Cause of death was exsanguination, most likely through those two punctures you see in the picture."

"How exactly is that possible?" she asked. "There's no blood on the body."

"We were hoping you could tell us," Myers said. He turned the laptop around to face her.

Miranda stared at the screen, schooling her expression to a careful neutral, but behind the mask she was shaking. A grainy video, apparently shot from a security camera, showed a woman in black with curly red hair leading the woman from the pictures into the alley, then pinning her against a wall and very obviously biting her throat. About three minutes later the woman slumped down to the ground.

The camera wasn't stationary, however—it switched to a different angle after a minute, then to another, then two others before returning to the original frame...and by then both redhead and dead woman had vanished.

"You think that's me, in the video," she said. "Because there aren't any other redheads around?"

"Watch it again," Myers said. "Pay special attention to the 2:52 mark."

This time, he put that section of the recording in slow motion. Miranda watched, holding her breath, as the killer in the video turned her face toward the camera for just a second—long enough, though, to capture the image in several frames of the recording. It still wasn't 100% clear, but it would be hard to argue with anyone who said it was Miranda...especially since when she looked toward the camera, something red could be seen glowing at her neck.

Shit. Shit shit shit.

David spoke up suddenly, and as often happened, he startled both detectives; he'd been playing invisible, basically, so they wouldn't pay any attention to him. "What led you to this woman's body, exactly? Was she reported missing?"

"No," Maguire said. "We received this video anonymously several days ago."

"If this is all you have, Detective, you're wasting our time," David told them.

"As it happens, we were able to get a saliva sample from the wound." Myers placed a piece of paper in front of her. "This is a court order for your DNA sample."

She looked at David, close to panicking, but he gave an almost imperceptible nod; he knew way more about the strange quirks of vampire anatomy, and he thought she should go along with it. Fine.

"All right," she said. "Whatever it takes for you to figure out this is ridiculous—I mean, what's my motive? I don't have any connection with this woman. Do you really think I'm walking around the city killing random people by biting them?"

"As a matter of fact I do," Myers said. "Let's add it up: you can't produce a solid alibi for the time of death. You're famous for people thinking you're a vampire, and that disease you supposedly have is known to affect people's mental state. Fame does things to people—everyone knows you have some strange habits. It's not that hard to imagine you might read all these stories about yourself, go over the edge due to your condition, and start believing it's all true."

She couldn't help it. She laughed.

Both detectives looked at her with alarm. She fell silent immediately; so, laughing at a murder accusation wasn't a good thing. Good to know.

Maguire wouldn't meet her eyes. She made sure to address Myers—the fewer lies Maguire got caught up in the better. "I'm sorry, I just...you are honestly telling me that I think I'm a vampire, and I'm going around sucking people to death. Do you hear yourselves?"

"We have you on video, Mrs. Solomon. We're currently combing it, the alley, and Ms. Vitera's body for any and all trace evidence, and if we get so much as a speck of DNA that looks like yours, you're done."

There was a knock, and one of the deputies poked her head in to let them know their lawyer, Grace, was there.

"All right," Grace said, striding into the room, the force of her presence silencing the detectives. "This interview is over—I spoke with Judge Markdale on the way over here and bail's been set. If you brought your checkbook, Mr. Solomon, we can get you out of here."

He took out his phone. "Give me the amount and a routing number and it's done."

Miranda barely paid attention to the conversation. She was staring at the pictures, and at the frozen image of herself on screen. She kept trying to think back to that night and remember this woman...why had she picked her? She'd never chosen anyone who qualified as any sort of decent human being; this one had to have been carrying some kind of deep, dark sins.

But she couldn't remember. In fact when she thought back, it was hard to distinguish any of the people she'd killed from each other. There were a few so reprehensible they stood out, but she should remember all of them, shouldn't she? Was she really that far gone—had excusing their deaths become the same as dismissing their lives?

If she was going to be brought down by one of the criminals she'd taken off the streets, she wanted to know who it was. She wanted to remember how it had felt, what she'd known that made it okay to sacrifice this specific human to her own bloodlust.

The thought that she could do this, kill without caring, just drop a body in the trash and not even remember why...it made her feel sick.

You don't have a choice. You pick the worst you can. Most other vampires wouldn't even bother.

Just keep telling yourself that, Miranda.

She was so caught up in her own mind that she followed David mutely out of one of the side doors—Maguire had led them there, taking pity on her public image, for which she reminded herself to thank him. Did he really think she was a killer? What if he told Stella?

"Miranda."

She shook her head and ignored him for a minute, head swimming. What were they going to do? If she wasn't acquitted her career was over. It might be over anyway—or it might get a boost thanks to all the publicity, if it turned out they couldn't prove it. And what about—

"Queen, *ground.*"

Her attention snapped back to the present moment, and within three breaths she had regained her mental footing. She'd tipped

143

.

dangerously off her axis just then; that scared her more than almost anything.

She looked up at David, who was calm as always—and none of the signs of actual distress were in his eyes.

He pulled her close and squeezed her around the middle. "Don't worry," he said. "I already have an idea. Three ideas, actually. Well, two ideas and a long shot. But at least two solid ideas."

"This is so unreal," she said. She waited until the limo door had shut and they were in a soundproof space to say anything else. "I thought I was being careful. But the truth is I wasn't—I was being arrogant. I honestly didn't think anyone would miss the people I killed. I don't even remember this woman. What if she wasn't as bad as I thought?"

"Has your empathy ever been wrong?"

"No. But I might have misinterpreted it. Or maybe...I don't know. I just don't know what to do with being arrested for a murder I actually committed but don't remember, for reasons the cops think they know that are almost right. It's crazy."

David looked preoccupied—and worried. He hadn't been concerned with the murder charge, but something was wrong now. "What's up?" she asked. "You have Serious Prime Face on."

"I don't know," he said vaguely. "Something doesn't feel right. I mean besides all of this." He looked at her, and the heightened tension in his eyes made her feel tense too. "Are you getting anything? Precog, empathy, anything that feels wrong?"

Miranda had doubled her shields the second she reached the police station, and after that her emotions and ungrounded state had gotten in the way of her usual external feelers. She started to reach out—

"...Two...Stella Maguire...Miranda, can you hear me?"

Heart thudding to a halt, she hit her com. "Stella, it's me! What's going on?"

"I don't know where I am," she replied, her voice hoarse and weak. She also sounded like she was trying not to fall into hysterics. "On the street...I can't see the signs."

David already had his phone out. "11th...what the hell are you doing there? Chris was supposed to meet you a block from the venue."

"...someone pretending to be Elite...led us away...she attacked us. I just came to a minute ago...I feel like I'm dying, Miranda. Please...please help us."

"Us? Nico and Kai are with you, right? Is anyone else?"

David vanished. Miranda was glad—he was practically a virtuoso at Misting. She signaled to Harlan, but he was already turning the car around; David had automatically sent the coordinates from his phone before leaving the car.

"Kai's here...he's hurt, too, but mostly just dazed...Miranda..."

Oh God. Don't say it. Don't say it.

Now her precog was firing on all cylinders, just in time to be good for absolutely nothing.

"I don't know why, but...they took him. Nico's gone."

Chapter Nine

The Elf's room was utterly silent except for the shallow, uneven breathing of its occupant. A half-dozen Elite had swept into the room, deposited the Bard on his bed, and swept back out to render their other houseguest unto Mo at the infirmary.

When he was sure they were finally gone, Deven moved back around the corner he'd been hiding behind and made his way to the bed to see what was going on. He hadn't been able to get much out of the Elite except this was almost certainly a Morningstar attack and that Nico had been taken captive while Kai, David, and Stella were out for the count.

He sat down on the edge of the bed and gingerly checked Kai's neck for wounds. It would take a keen eye to find the single tiny puncture mark, and it did; so they'd been darted with something. The Prime, too, had been brought down, as had Stella, and therein lay a mystery: Stella had been darted but was coming out of it. David hadn't even been there for the attack but had passed out the second he came out of Mist on the scene.

Nico himself was the obvious answer. When he was hit, anyone with an active energetic connection to him had gone down too, and would be drained very quickly if more harm befell the Weaver. Stella loved Nico, and was his friend, but they weren't twins, and they didn't have an energetic lifeline between them. She'd been the one to link him to David, and that might have been enough to pull her in temporarily.

146

Deven had barely felt anything other than a growing sense of unease until he heard the call for an Alpha-Five go out over the network. In another time he might have been impressed with himself; the barrier he had created against Nico had been even stronger than he'd intended. No wonder Nico had been in such sorry shape all year. If the block was so powerful his own Prime hadn't felt him attacked...Deven hadn't meant for it to be that strong. God, how was Nico even *sane*?

"Are you happy now?"

He'd been so focused on his thoughts that the voice startled him. He looked up at the Queen, who sagged against the side of the doorframe, her face pale but her eyes full of anger.

"I mean this is what you wanted, right?" she demanded. "What you've been hoping for?"

"I don't understand," he said faintly, standing up to face her.

"They're probably going to kill him. He's one of the Circle, so all they have to do is take him out and we're done for. He was the weakest link, after all. Not a warrior, only barely able to do magic anymore, a pacifist...and undefended."

He stared at her, feeling a sick tremor spread from his skin inward toward his heart. "You think I want him to die?" he asked softly.

"Don't you?" She pushed herself off the frame. "If he dies you get to die, but you don't have to outright kill yourself, so you don't get the blame."

He tried to come up with something to say, but the combined shock of her anger and her statement shattered any resolve he might have had. He just shook his head.

She wasn't done.

"You made him suffer for two years—and the rest of us suffered too. You couldn't cope so you got to spend months high out of your mind while people who loved you dealt with the fallout. We tried to be there for you. And now this—tell me something, Deven. Would this have happened if you'd been with us, with Nico, like you were supposed to be?"

They both knew the answer to that, but he had to make some sort of confession, even if it meant nothing to her anymore. "No."

"I'm the only hope he has now. David can't rescue him. Stella can probably help but she can't fight her way through Morningstar. And I have *no idea what to do.*"

He could see how terrified she was, how lost—it was far worse than taking the brunt of her anger. In that minute the futility of his behavior hit home even harder than before; what was point of any of it? What had he proven? All this time, he could have had as much warmth and love as anyone could ever need.

He could have had Nico. And now...

"What do you want me to do?", he asked.

Miranda either didn't hear the genuine entreaty in his tone, or didn't care anymore. She took a step back and shook her head.

"I want you to go to hell," she said, and walked away.

When the drug finally loosened its grip enough that he could fight his way awake, and he could at last open his eyes, Nico immediately wished he were still unconscious.

He didn't have words for most of what he was looking at. The only term he could think of for the kind of room he was in was *clinical*; it bore some resemblance to the infirmary at the Haven. He was in its center, on his back, but had enough freedom of movement to look from side to side.

Freedom of...

That was when he realized he was tied down. He pulled upward against the restraints on his wrists—surely even a vampire at half strength could undo most human engineering—but he was held down tightly at wrist, ankle, and neck...by steel.

He didn't remember anything after feeling the affects of the dart crawl through him. It could only have been Morningstar's doing...but what about Stella and Kai? Were they here too? Had they been killed? The idea made him nauseated.

"Good evening, pretty one," came a voice. "It's nice to have you with us."

He jerked his head upward to look, but couldn't. Obligingly, the speaker moved around to the side until he was in Nico's line of sight.

It was a human...probably. Male, relatively young, at least on first glance. Looking more closely Nico could see his skin was a strange, sick greyish tone, and was wrinkled...no, not wrinkled. Cracked. Long seams ran up his bare forearms and over his face, following the contours of the bones, the skin so thin and dry it was splitting bloodlessly from what was either old age or magic.

He couldn't be that old. That meant something very powerful was keeping that body together...or something very powerful was attempting to rip it apart.

"Who are you?" Nico asked, keeping his voice calm. "What did you do with my companions?"

"Oh, Good, you do speak English," the man said, nodding with approval. "This would have been so much more difficult if you didn't. As to your friends...I assume they're back at the Nightwalkers' home. Putting them out was really just for convenience; you were the only one I needed."

"And why do you need me?"

"My associates and I have questions which you are uniquely qualified to answer."

Nico's blood went cold. He knew what that meant. He'd heard David tell enemy captives *I have questions for you* and it always ended in screaming. "I won't tell you anything," he said in what he hoped was a brave-sounding tone.

"Oh, I don't expect you to—not with your voice. But perhaps introductions are in order—I know you're called Nico, and that you used to be an Elf. We certainly were surprised to find out you all still existed! You were supposed to have been wiped out centuries ago."

The man was cheerful, friendly. It was a contrast both to his somewhat ghoulish appearance and the way he was looking at Nico, slowly from head to foot and back again, evaluating something, coldly, calculating. It was a look Nico might have called lustful, but there was nothing sensual in it—*covetous* was a better word.

"Here among my people I'm known as the Prophet," he said. "And you see...I need to know more about you, Nico. There's no data on your people anywhere anymore. I know what I can expect from a human, and I have no use for vampires, but Elves...you might be the answer I need."

"I don't understand," Nico said. "What could you possibly need from me?"

"As I said...data. Obviously you're of no use to me in and of yourself—you're a halfbreed, the worst of both worlds. But there aren't just a whole lot of real Elves running around, and before I go trying to find one, I need to know if I'm wasting my time. You might be an abomination to your own people, but there is something you have that makes you unique, and ideally suited to my...explorations, let's call them."

"What do I have?"

The Prophet made a gesture, and two other humans appeared. They began bustling around, opening drawers and tearing open packages. Nico could just barely see what they were doing, but one was filling a row of at least a dozen syringes from at least that many vials. The other produced an ordinary pair of scissors, and, with a nod from the Prophet, began cutting through Nico's shirt.

"You can't possibly be comfortable in that costume," the Prophet said reasonably. "As to what it is you have that I need...why, you have vampiric healing ability. It gives me free rein to learn what I need to without fear of killing you, at least, at the outset."

"Why not just kill me?" Nico demanded. "Kill one of us and we're beaten, remember? Your whole war would be over with in minutes."

The Prophet made a dismissive noise. "There are ways the survivors could still be a threat. In the time before, there were only four of them left when we were defeated. It's just a matter of what they're willing to sacrifice. But you..." He helped the other human peel back Nico's shirt, cutting through the sleeves entirely to take it off in pieces before moving on to the rest of his clothes. The air in the room was freezing, and Nico's heart was pounding in his throat. "I'll need what I learn from you regardless. Your sacrifice will help the righteous once again take control of the Earth. We were so very, very long asleep."

Nico tried to make sense of that, but the only thing he knew was fear—mad instinctive terror was crawling all over him, the ancestral memory of all his people who had been dragged away by Inquisitors and chained to a table to scream their lives out. He thought of Deven, who had been a hundred times stronger than Nico, suffering the same fate until he was thrown into a dungeon to rot from the inside out. Now here Nico was...he was going to die just as his people had, alone and afraid—

No.

I will not give them the satisfaction. If they want to kill me, so be it. But I will not make it easy for them.

As one of the humans moved closer, a scalpel in his hand which he touched lightly to Nico's chest, wrath surged through the Elf, and he shoved outward with his power.

Both of the assistant humans flew backwards; one hit the wall, the other managed to steady himself on a cabinet.

The Prophet chuckled.

It was a nasty, reptilian sound.

He stood at the head of the table and leaned down so his face was two inches from Nico's. The closeness made the Elf's skin crawl, as did the dry cold feeling of the Prophet's hand sliding down Nico's arm...but not nearly as much as the near-sexual satisfaction in the Prophet's voice.

"Good boy," he said. "Now...do it again."

Miranda wanted nothing more than to turn around the minute she walked out of Kai's room and go back—she'd never seen the look on Deven's face before, and it made everything inside her hurt. But if she was going to help Nico she had to hurry before—

Her heart sank as she heard the faint slip-and-rattle of the outside shutters closing down. It was nearly 6am.

There was nothing she could do to help him until sunset; the only person she could even send out to the scene was Stella, but Stella was still unconscious.

Exhaustion nearly knocked Miranda over. The show at the Paramount, the arrest, now this...even a Queen's energy tapped out after so many blows.

She returned to the Signet Suite, defeated, praying to anyone who might listen that Nico would be okay until they could find him...she dreaded the thought of what they might do to him in twelve hours.

David lay on the bed where the Elite had left him, on his back, hands on his stomach. He looked awful. Not just-returned-from-the-dead awful, maybe, but still ashen white with dark circles around his eyes.

She managed to peel off her clothes and force herself into the shower so she could rinse off the stink of the jail; then she fell onto the bed and dragged herself up next to him, taking his hand and wrapping a leg around both of his.

Before she could drop off she grabbed her phone and told it to wake her in five hours.

`   She must have hit the wrong number, though, because just as her eyes fell shut, the alarm went off, blitzkreiging her awake. She groped for the phone to see what had gone wrong and nearly sobbed. The alarm was right. Five hours had passed.

She checked over David quickly: still out, but he did look better in some indefinable way. Maybe the effect would prove to be temporary and both he and Kai would wake up. She could use all the help she could get.

Miranda pulled on clothes and all but sprinted to the Batcave.

David had programmed her into the system for just such an occasion—well, maybe not the occasion of him being under a coma spell, but incapacitation of any kind.

The room lit up as she entered, and she sat down and put her palm on the security screen; it took a minute for the network to scan and recognize her with all its various metrics, but chirped and beeped to life obligingly as soon as it was sure she was who her handprint claimed she was.

She had no idea what a lot of the system did, much less how to work it, but luckily it was programmed to respond to her voice.

"Give me sensor grid data for…12:42 am."

The city of Austin appeared in front of her. She touched the screen to zoom it, and dragged the image around until she identified the street corner where the attack had taken place. 12:42 was when Stella's distress call had come through.

"Scan back twenty minutes and replay at 1 ½ speed."

She watched, biting her lip. There they were: five dots moving in a cluster along the street. One human, one vampire, one classified as "other" since David hadn't felt the need to program in "Elf" just yet, and two…well, they read as vampires, but their vitals were off. That should have sent up a flag.

A moment later the group stopped. The human's heart rate soared; then one by one she, vampire, and Elf all disappeared. So did the two "guards."

An alert flashed on the screen: COM MALFUNCTION STAR-ONE.

Sure enough, at the same time some distance away, the light that represented the Prime went out, while hers stayed lit.

Mere minutes later Stella and Kai reappeared, as did David. 12:42.

Stella's first call hadn't failed—whatever was on those darts had blocked it.

Years ago David had reprogrammed the network to recognize magic, but he couldn't plan for everything. If there was one way to fool the sensors there must be more. Morningstar had found a way, and used it to snatch Nico. There was no trail—she had the system look for any signals that appeared out of nowhere somewhere else, but nothing came up. Wherever he was, he was still blocked; Signets were pretty obvious on the grid.

How had David caught Ovaska? He'd explained it, but it was hard to visualize, since she hadn't been there—she'd been bleeding in a cell at the time. It was something to do with pressure and temperature...he was looking for something that *wasn't* there instead of what was.

Trouble was she had no idea how to do that, or what to look for. That was way past her programming pay grade—he'd written search algorithms on the fly in order to track them down. She was hardly an idiot, but she didn't have an armload of degrees and take things apart for fun. She was not in her wheelhouse.

God, if only they'd all been in one group like they were supposed to be! Even without Deven there, Morningstar wouldn't have dared try to take Nico if he had the Prime and Queen of the South with him. They would have...

Understanding dawned. She put her head in her hands.

"We received this video anonymously several days ago."

"You bastards," she muttered. "You absolute bastards."

It had all been a diversion. The murder charge...Morningstar had gotten their hands on that video somehow and sent it in knowing exactly when she would be arrested. They must have someone working in the Department who could get the evidence into Maguire and Myers' hands at the right moment—and at a moment when everyone in Austin knew exactly where to find her. And knowing she and David and their personal guards were all occupied, that left them free to lure the others away and kidnap their intended target, Nico.

But what did they want him for? If all they wanted to do was kill a Signet they could have done that right at the scene. Nico wasn't recovered enough yet to do any serious magic, and he had no other defense against trained killers. It would have been easy. But no, they took him, and went to a lot of trouble to do it. Why?

Information, perhaps. Directions to the Haven, secrets of the inner workings of the Shadow World...which they could have gotten more easily by capturing an Elite. No, logic and her instincts told her they wanted him for something very specific, something they could only get from him.

Whatever it was it couldn't be good. Whatever it was...it was unlikely they planned to let him walk away.

Stella might know some kind of location spell like all the Witches on TV. If nothing else she might be able to identify the magic used and that could lead them to occult shops, well-known practitioners, something...anything.

First she had to wake up, though. Miranda had no idea when that would be or what condition Stella would be in.

She kept playing the footage, changing the target statistics over and over to find something that would point her in the right direction.

Miranda closed her eyes. "Hey...Persephone?...You probably noticed a rather large pile of shit has just hit the fan, and...Nico's Your child too...maybe the one who needs Your love the most. He gave up everything he knew to be part of this fight. Just...I don't need a miracle, although I wouldn't kick one in the head...just...please help. Help me find him. Maybe You can act through somebody, send me news, or...I don't know. But please."

She didn't feel like anyone was listening. But a minute later there was a knock at the Batcave door, and a pale, clammy-looking Stella poked her head in.

"Mo told me not to leave," she panted. "But I'm okay. Really. I don't feel any magic on me and my energy's coming back. I can help."

Miranda sat back and pulled her feet up into the chair. Stella came into the office and leaned on the desk; she was, in fact, looking better by the minute, although the worry on her face made her look ten years older. "How?"

"I don't think I can do a straight-up location spell for this—I probably have the juice, but there are whole parts of town I don't know, and with something this emotional I'd have trouble focusing. But you know what can focus like a motherfucker? *That.*"

Stella was pointing at the monitor. "Nico helped David redesign part of the grid here in town as a prototype for the other territories. He was telling me about it a while back—they used Elven magical architecture as inspiration. That means if I can see what the computer sees, I might be able to follow the patterns since they're modeled after magic I already work with—Weaving."

"I have no idea what most of that meant, but I get the gist. How do we go about it?"

"Not a clue." Stella put her hands in her disheveled hair. "I was hoping you'd be able to come up with the next step."

Miranda's heart sank, or rather, plummeted. "I don't know enough about networks, vampire or Elven, to even venture a guess. We need—"

"You need me," came a tired voice from the doorway.

She nearly threw herself across the room and tackled her Prime, who looked way worse than Stella and sounded half dead...but he was *awake*.

"How did you come out of it?" Stella asked. "You guys were both way under."

"I don't know for sure," David replied, carefully moving from door to desk and taking the chair Miranda happily vacated for him. "It felt like being trapped in a locked room knowing there were monsters all around that I couldn't see—I kept trying to open the door and couldn't, until out of nowhere it fell open and something shoved me through."

"Star-Two, this is Elite-44...um...you asked to be notified when the Prime woke. He seems to have vanished."

"Yes, thank you, Elite-44," Miranda said wryly. "You can stand down."

David was switching the system over to his profile without even looking at the monitors. "I'm pretty sure I know what you need, Stella—it'll take a minute."

Miranda moved around behind the chair and threaded her fingers through her Prime's hair, sending energy into him to help him recover. He took a deep breath and bowed his head a moment while the network beeped and blinked to itself.

"I'm glad you're here," she told him softly. "And glad you're okay."

He looked up at her. "I think 'okay' is pushing it," he replied. "I don't know what they're doing to him, but thank God I can't feel it...or I can't over the worry." He kissed her hand, and asked hesitantly, "What about Deven?"

She held his eyes a moment and then shook her head. "He may come around. But I said some pretty ugly things...and it might have worked. I just hope I have a chance to apologize." Miranda looked over at Stella, something horrible occurring to her. "I hate to say this out loud, but if Nico doesn't make it, what will happen to David?"

The Witch frowned. "Nothing. I mean, it'll probably hurt like hell, and it might take you out of commission for a while, but it won't kill you. The link is deep but it's not a soul bond like you guys have."

"He's not going to die," David said firmly in that tone that the heavens themselves would roll over to obey. "I won't allow it." A faint smile crossed his face. "Even if I can't pick up a damn sword." He gestured for Stella to come closer. "All right...tell me how your spell usually works."

"Sort of like you see on TV. I get a map and focus on it. Some spells use the blood of the lost person, or of a relative, and the blood draws a path to the destination. Others actually burn the paper. I don't really want to get blood or fire anywhere near all of this."

"I should say not. It took me months to build it and a flat out ridiculous amount of money."

"The third option is light, either from a candle or a bulb—I think given everybody on the grid is represented by a dot of light that would be our best bet. I just need a way to interface with it."

David clicked something and one of the monitors flashed from the screen full of code it had held to a palm print scanner like the one they used to log on. "Touch recognition," he said. "Put your hand there and I'll have the system scan you. After that it will allow you programming access. I hope that's enough."

Stella stepped forward and did as he'd said, and with another click, he set the system loose on the Witch's identifying details. While it ran David leaned his head into Miranda's hands again, looking sick and exhausted.

She didn't say anything. They both just waited. Miranda's heart was racing—this had to work. It had to. The computer wasn't any different from a map or a candle; it was a tool, just one with more modern technology. It would work.

A cheerful beep, and the system indicated a new profile had been set up for Stella.

"Okay," David said. "It's all yours."

Stella swallowed hard but kept her hand on the screen. She closed her eyes, grounding, and Miranda felt her pulling power up from wherever Witches got it. Stella started murmuring something that sounded like Latin, but it obviously didn't need to be heard, as to Miranda's ears it was unintelligible. But the Queen felt Stella's energy reaching toward the computer, seeking a point of contact.

For a long minute Miranda held her breath, sure nothing was happening. But then she saw something move in her peripheral vision, and looked over; the image of the sensor grid was moving, spinning out and then in, as if trying to reorient itself—or as if Stella was reorienting herself.

Miranda glanced at the Witch. Sweat had broken out on Stella's forehead, and she was biting her lip, but the grid continued to move, zooming in closer and closer on Austin, passing by street after street.

The image moved away from downtown, headed north, past the old airport and over to Lamar Boulevard, deeper into an older and more run-down part of the city. There were a lot of government buildings there, including the sprawling Department of Public Safety complex, and a bit farther than that, a number of half-empty or abandoned strip malls and office buildings whose inhabitants hadn't weathered the last recession.

Stella homed in on a single building. The grid fixed on what, based on the name, was once an Indian grocery store.

"There," Stella said weakly. "That's it. It's underground...the whole building is shielded really strongly, but I could feel...God, Miranda...they're hurting him. I don't know what they're doing but they're hurting him."

Miranda memorized the address. "On my way," she said. "David?"

The Prime shook his head. "You're going to have to do it," he said. "It took all the energy I had just to walk here. I'd be a liability."

"All right—stay on the grid, back me up. Stella—stay here, but sit down and try to rest. I might need both of you." She squeezed David's shoulder, kissed his forehead. "I'll bring him home," she said. She looked from him to Stella. "I promise."

Then she hit the door at a run, calling Harlan and summoning all available Elite to the coordinates. She didn't want to hit the building with all her resources—if they were underground they probably had surveillance, and a herd of vampires converging on the spot would definitely tip them off. But if she was going in alone, she'd want them available.

She texted the coordinates to Harlan before she was even in the car, and he floored it the second the door shut.

"Hang on, Nico," she murmured. "I'm coming."

"You really are a fascinating creature...I apologize for the discomfort, but it was important you were awake for our work. I need to know how much pain you creatures can feel, and how much you can tolerate. Also, sorry for the gag—the noise was distracting my associates here. Let's move on, shall we? Dr. Porter, let's go ahead and pump the blood back in so I can have a look at the circulatory system. I'll need a Y-incision..."

Even through a barrier strong enough to almost totally block a Signet bond, he could feel shades of what was happening. He could feel pain, almost enough to make his knees weak, and once in a while he heard the faint, distant echo of a scream.

Deven sat with his elbows on knees, face in his hands, wanting to scream himself but paralyzed with too many emotions at once.

The sounds in his head. The familiarity of that pain even centuries away. The look of disgust in Miranda's eyes. All the nightmares of the last year and a half, digging through rubble, searching in vain for what he had lost or worse, finding it bleeding out in his arms.

"It's time."

He lifted his head. "Kai...you're awake."

The Bard didn't acknowledge his words, but held onto the doorframe much as Miranda had, only so much paler, so weary. Deven had seen less worn-looking corpses, particularly given how Kai's black hair emphasized his pallor. But his violet eyes were alight as he said, "It's time to make a choice, my Lord."

He didn't have to ask what Kai meant. Live or die? Warrior or coward? Prime or dust?

Kai held his eyes. When he spoke again, it was softly, shakily. "Save my brother," he said. "Please."

Then, he left.

Deven wanted to hide. To wait until it was over, then embrace whatever fate awaited him. Whatever rescue mission the Pair had planned, they might be too late. He could just wait, and see.

He turned his gaze to the mantel, fixed his eyes upon Ghostlight.

It's time to make a choice.

Accept the worst of yourself or reclaim the best.

Fear or love? Which is it?

Which would it always, always be?

Slowly, Deven stood, not looking away from the mantel for fear he'd lose what nerve he had. He took a deep breath and walked over to the fireplace.

The sword was exactly where he'd left her, only still clean because the servants gave her a quick dusting when they came through. Memories of all the heads he'd severed with her, the battles…taking down nearly a dozen Morningstar in Sacramento, fighting alongside Miranda and David in the barn…he'd carried dozens of blades over the centuries but none had ever been such a part of him. She'd been the sword he put David down with the first moment they'd met; she'd been the model on which he'd based the designs for The Oncoming Storm and Shadowflame. The world might fall apart but there was one thing on which he could completely rely.

The sight of his own hand shaking as he extended it toward the mantel brought a flash of anger to his heart. *This is what we are, now? A hundred fights and thousands of enemies left in their own blood, and now this? They've taken one Consort from you. They took your home. Will you let them have your soul?*

Practically snarling, he steeled himself and reached out again. No tremor this time. Better.

His fingers closed around Ghostlight's hilt.

Chapter Ten

There was no light, no warmth, no solace—after the first four hours, it wasn't even pain, because that word had lost all meaning. Everything lost all meaning.

"It's said that Rene Descartes used to vivisect dogs in a public display to show that their shrieks weren't real pain, but a mere reflex, response to stimuli. Documented evidence of this is slight, of course, but it is a strong indicator of attitudes of the time. I wouldn't go that far, myself—this is the modern world, and we know anything with a nervous system can feel pain."

The voice droned on and on, destroying any hope of silence—it was its own form of water torture, a constant flow of words.

Different parts of his body went in and out of focus as the endless hours crawled by. The itchy trickle of blood on the side of his head when they took a scalpel and sliced off his ear—only to reattach it, letting the healing process do its work as they did with every incision, every broken bone. The dull crunch of those bones...one rib, then another, cracked and removed, then put back in.

And through it all, the Prophet never seemed to stop talking. His diatribe was at turns pedagogical and disgustingly intimate—he would lean close and describe in loving detail what they were doing, what would happen next, how it would probably feel. He would praise Nico's pain tolerance one minute and then call him a halfbreed demon the next.

His strangely hot hands would lie on an unbloodied patch of skin and knead the muscle, or caress the skin, murmuring appreciation.

Then one of the "doctors" would send an electric shock through Nico's body, and Nico would lash out with magic, throwing them to the ground with a feline hiss while the Prophet laughed quietly in the corner.

That wasn't the worst part. The worst part was the feeling of human hands inside his body, digging around, touching where no hand should ever touch. They discussed his body as if he were a particularly interesting insect pinned to a board. One made notes while the other cut, or scalded, or carefully peeled back patches of skin. Pain, he had felt before, the night he was turned. He didn't understand this kind of humiliation. Over and over he asked himself, *Why?* Even though there was no why, even though the pretense of scientific inquiry eventually gave way to flat out sadism, it simply wasn't in his nature to comprehend causing pain just to cause pain.

At least, it shouldn't be.

At some point he heard the Prophet say, "...yes, it's in the way—go ahead and cut it, and get the bone saw ready...what is it, Barnes? ...Fine. I shall return in a moment."

He heard the "doctors" muttering to each other, then felt the cold shadow of one fall on his face. The human reached down and took hold of the Elf's hair, and with rough sawing motions, chopped it off. The comparatively mild but sudden pain of the human pulling on it sent Nico's senses into sharp focus.

That was it.

He had been abandoned by everything he'd ever believed in. All this time he had fought against the darkness, running from it in fear.

In the end, it was all he had left.

He was weakened from repeated mutilation and healing, mutilation and healing...but there were resources he could call upon that even these filthy humans and their knives and saws couldn't touch. The image of the men scrabbling on the ground in their own blood, begging for their lives...he drank it in greedily, letting the satisfaction add fuel to the fire.

Then he reached to the closest source of power he could access, and *pulled*.

"All right," one doctor said to the other. "While we're waiting let's get some more samples. Get the opaque vials for the blood, and I'll—"

He never finished the sentence.

Nico's vision went red.

The power he had drawn streamed into him, healing his wounds and filling every last cell with renewed strength. He didn't care where it had come from or who it might be draining. That was irrelevant. Only one thing mattered now.

Blood.

The restraints snapped as if made of paper. Nico hauled himself up, and by the time the humans realized he was free, one of them had already flown across the room and into the wall so hard there was the sound of snapping vertebrae. The man did not get up.

The other was staring with huge, petrified eyes, backing toward the door.

"Y-you can't," the man stammered. He was groping for the door handle. "He said Elves don't hurt people—"

"Didn't you hear?" Nico snarled, his teeth digging into his bottom lip hard enough to bleed, holding out a hand and closing it into a fist, crushing the doctor's larynx. "I'm not an Elf anymore."

The other man was still alive, just paralyzed. Nico stood over him for a long moment, impassive, watching him struggle to get away without using his legs, pathetic. It was like looking at an insect pinned to a board.

Slowly, he reached down and took hold of the man's shirt collar, lifting him up off the floor.

The doctor tried striking out with his hands, but Nico held him farther away, letting him flail uselessly in the air.

Nico looked around the room. There were lines of containers full of his bodily fluids on the counter, his blood all over the floor drying in some places and still fresh in others. He saw a shred of his own skin on the floor. The second doctor's corpse was in a crumpled heap against the door. There was, he noticed, one thing conspicuously absent.

"What happened to your Prophet?" Nico asked, tilting his head to one side and holding the man's gaze. "He doesn't seem to be returning to save you, does he. It's almost as if he knew this would happen."

"His...will...be done," the human choked out.

"Not this time, mortal. This time it's my will."

He tried to say more, but Nico held a finger to his lips. The finger only just had a nail growing back.

The man managed to get one more half-syllable out before Nico's teeth ripped open his throat.

His blood was full of violence, hatred. He was a man who had killed before, just like this, slowly carving apart his victim. When offered the chance to do so to someone who wouldn't die from it— at least not immediately—he'd been ecstatic. His blood, hot and coppery, was bitter, but it filled Nico's veins with an almost explosive charge, and when he dropped the body on the floor, the doctor's face was contorted with fear.

It felt good. No, not just good: *Righteous.* Nico smiled.

Something—perhaps one of the men hitting an alarm—had summoned more guards, and he could hear the clamor of booted feet down the hall. The familiar pace and footfall of the Prophet, however, was not among them.

Yes, the bastard had known this would happen. Perhaps he had even planned on it. He might still be observing, collecting data on his prize. Clapping his hands like a delighted child over the deaths of his minions.

Calmly, Nico gathered both the ruins of his own clothes and what articles he could salvage from the men that weren't completely blood-soaked, and dressed, listening to the guards' approach.

His eyes fell on a glass jar that held an amulet with a green stone. He didn't remember them taking his Signet off, but it must have happened early, as it wasn't bloody.

He turned away from it, toward the door, which was hit hard with something and shuddered on its hinges.

No reason to stymie their efforts, he supposed, and pushed the corpse away from the door with his foot. He stepped back, leaning against the operating table with crossed arms, and waited.

The door slammed open and five, ten guards swarmed in, with more in the hallway. They had crossbows, for the most part—not the most graceful thing in close quarters but effective enough.

Whatever they'd been expecting, this obviously was not it; they were all staring, a few sweating. Perhaps they were soldiers, brainwashed to do the Prophet's bidding even if it meant murder, but most of them were young and clearly not accustomed to bloodshed.

They would get used to it. He was coming around pretty quickly himself.

Teeth, magic, or both? Tricky.

"Fire!" one of the soldiers bellowed.

Half a dozen clicks and whistles, and wooden bolts sailed at him.

Nico stood up and held up a hand.

Every one of the bolts burst into flame.

A second later, so did their associated weapons...and then the men themselves.

The screams were deafening. The remainder of the men bottlenecked the door trying to fight their way back into the hallway before the smoke—or worse, their prey—could reach them. They were trying to regroup outside.

Nico looked up at the ceiling. There were sprinkler heads there—he'd been staring at them for hours. He snapped the heads off of several with his mind, and water poured down on the burning men, putting them out, though the stench of burning flesh and clothing still hung in the air.

They'd burned him, too. If he were human, and had survived, he would have burn marks over most of his body from their experiments.

He stepped over the dead and out into the hallway.

There were men on either side, all aiming at him, many looking scared out of their wits.

Poor, stupid children. There were so many ways they could die. It was so difficult to pick just one.

He stood there, drawing in more of that delicious rage as if it were food, and he starving. The power he was still pulling into himself had the touch of kindness, of love; he ignored it, twisted it on itself. Such things were meaningless in this world. He had tried to love, and been spurned. He had tried to heal, and been excommunicated. And he had tried to belong...to find beauty in this place, in the stink and decay of humanity. And for *what?*

Very slowly and deliberately, he lifted a hand to each side, palm out toward the humans...and with a single hard jerk, tore the hearts from all of their chests, leaving nothing but empty shells clad in military gear, innocent lives taken over by evil and now spent, in pools of blood, at his feet.

*****

"Okay, talk me in."

"Around the west side of the building there's a security panel. Head there."

Miranda slipped through the shadows surrounding the building; there were no cars parked in front of it, no lights on, nothing to suggest people had been near it in a long time. Weeds had grown up around the foundation and through cracks in the sidewalk.

She stayed low, reaching back to gesture silently at the Elite who were back a safe distance and out of sight. *Stay.*

"Do you have the entrance code?" she asked quietly.

"Hold on," David said. He still sounded worn, but he was in his element. *"I'm decrypting their system now."*

"How good is it?"

"Not terribly. They're either incredibly stupid and don't think anyone would look here, or they have much better security inside. My money's on the latter."

"Seconded."

She hopped over the stair rail that surrounded the west side of the building, dropping down to the concrete and landing right in front of the panel. It was awfully unsophisticated-looking. "A Staedtler T-950? What is this, 1986?" She paused, blinked. "God, how do I even know that?"

"For better or worse," came the wry answer over her comm. *"Code: 666539."*

"666, like Satan?"

"I don't know. But it does spell 'monkey.'"

"I'm just going to assume that was the previous owner's idea." Miranda hit the code carefully, nodding in satisfaction when she heard the lock chunk open and the light went green. "I'm going in—"

Suddenly she heard a gasp, and a groan of pain, followed by a disturbingly loud thump. "David? You okay?"

There were several noises like someone fumbling with a phone, and to her surprise Stella said breathlessly, *"He passed out, Miranda—he sounded like someone stabbed him, and then just toppled over. He's breathing okay but he looks like he's having a nightmare. Something's really wrong."*

She could feel the pull of the bond, drawing energy from her to compensate for what must be a significant drain on him. She fought against a wave of dizziness, but once it passed there was no sense of emergency, just urgency. "Call Mo," she said. "I've got to go in—I can't wait or they're going to know I'm here. I'll check back once I'm out."

She didn't wait for a reply, but grabbed the push bar on the door and edged it open.

At first there was nothing to see but a staircase that went down into the darkness without a single light fixture. It was the only way forward, and she didn't like it—too much possibility of being boxed in. "Elite team 1," she said, "converge on my location and defend the door and stairwell behind me. Maintain distance until called. I don't want to spook them."

"As you will it, my Lady. Team 1 on the move."

She slipped inside and let the door close behind her; the lock clanked shut, so loud in the metal-walled room it nearly made her jump.

Advantage of being a vampire: her feet were soundless on the stairs. She stayed against the wall, hand on Shadowflame's hilt, not wanting to draw in such close quarters unless she had to—hand to hand would work just fine in here.

She really should have expected booby traps.

She'd barely placed her toe on the second fight of steps when it disappeared out from under her. Two treads folded back, leaving a huge gap, and at the bottom of it, God only knew. Miranda tried to jerk her foot back, but she'd lost her balance, and the dumbfounded surprise of being caught by such low-tech Indiana Jones bullshit cost her her hold on the rail. She braced herself for whatever was down there, praying it wasn't giant wooden stakes waiting to pierce her entire body and leave her hanging, blood draining down their shafts to the floor—

Her whole body jerked upward as a hand closed around her wrist and lifted her up out of the hole.

Her feet found the next step, and she stared up at her rescuer.

Their eyes met, but neither spoke; there would be time for surprise later. Deven moved past her and jumped, landing gracefully at the bottom of the stairs and turning back to her with a nod.

She followed, trying not to stare—she'd hoped her harsh words would jolt something loose in his brain, but she hadn't been entirely ready to see him look like himself again; he hadn't reclaimed his Goth wardrobe so quickly, of course, or stopped mid-crisis to dye his hair, but he was wearing the black-ops clothes his agents wore, and was armed to the teeth, though most people would see one sword and perhaps a knife. She could count probably about half his complement of weapons. The sight of Ghostlight nearly brought her to tears of relief.

She dragged her focus back to the matter at hand.

There was another security panel waiting at the interior door. This one looked way more modern...and with David passed out, she had no idea how to—

Deven took her arm and pulled her away, then spun and kicked the panel hard. Sparks flew, and it fell off the wall. Beyond the door, alarms started blaring all over the place.

Well that was one way to go about it.

So much for stealth.

A cadre of humans met them in the hallway. Miranda seized the closest man, who had a crossbow, and turned him, hitting the trigger and firing the bolt into another soldier.

Nearby, she heard the most wonderful sound possible: Ghostlight, drawn.

After two years without picking up a sword she kind of expected Deven to be rusty, but seven centuries way more than balanced such a brief span, and he didn't miss a step. As another group of men surrounded them, they fell into the fight together, just like that night in Rio Verde; she hadn't wanted to admit it but fighting with both him and David had been so enjoyable it was practically a turn-on.

It wasn't that hard to disarm the archers; their weapons were impractical in this much space, and their bulk got in the way. The soldiers were skilled both with weapons and without, and a few were very good; but Queen and Prime pushed them back, and back, into a junction of two hallways where there was more space, and once she had Shadowflame in her hand, the humans were done for.

It had been a while since she'd been in an actual fight, too. She wasn't a centuries-old assassin; still, she felt herself slipping into that trance space again, and her energy and Deven's connected with an ease that still surprised her. Without even speaking they were able to team up, the way she and David did—one of the men, a burly guy easily 6'8", apparently had it in his head to pummel them into submission with only his fists, and in response, Dev grabbed Miranda's arm and swung her around, giving her momentum and leverage to wrap her ankles around the man's neck and slam him to the floor. She hit the ground in time to see Ghostlight run through the human's throat.

They were down to three opponents when she noticed the smoke. It rolled into the hallway from another corridor, and with it came a totally different alarm and flashing lights up near the ceiling.

She put down two more humans roughly within seconds of Deven breaking the last one's neck, and they halted at the same time. With a shared glance, they took off toward the smoke.

The screaming started when they were halfway down the hall— very clearly human screaming. She could hear water pouring down like Niagara Falls, and orders being barked, but the sounds made no more sense the closer she got. The building itself was not on fire, and the smoke had stopped billowing but still filled the air with a choking haze.

Miranda stopped, coughing. What the hell was that smell? It was acrid and disturbingly familiar, and she had a flash of a 4th of July barbecue—

Burning flesh. It was burning flesh.

She gestured for Deven to go on, and was only a step behind, trying to clear her watering eyes. What was going on here? Some kind of accident? How close had it been to wherever they were keeping Nico?

As they rounded the corner, she found out, and skidded to a halt, unable to process what she was looking at.

She looked over at Deven. He was staring and had gone pale, eyes losing most of their color.

There were black-clad bodies everywhere in groups of four and five, their weapons scattered on the floor. Some of them were charred, some drenched in blood, all of them dead. She saw strange lumps of oozing, bloody meat...no, organs. Hearts. Something had ripped their hearts out.

"Oh, Jesus," she heard Deven say softly, the first words he'd uttered to her tonight. He was so openly astonished that she could actually hear his accent.

A figure emerged from a side room. It was not human. In fact, *inhuman* was the only word she could come up with for the way it moved, with a sinister stalking grace, one hand curving around the edge of the door, blood staining the fingers as if they'd been dipped in it.

Her mind flat-out refused to recognize him at first. She couldn't reconcile the gentle creature she knew with this...

"Nico," she said softly, "What did they do to you?"

He didn't acknowledge the name, or seem to recognize her, but he looked at her, replying only with an animal hiss.

Her heart went cold in her chest.

His eyes were black.

Deven's reaction was even more frightening; he stumbled back a step, groping for something to hold onto, and she grabbed his shoulder...just in time to see his eyes go black as well.

He blinked, and they had already returned to normal, though they were anguished as he returned his attention to Nico, taking a careful step forward.

"Nico," he said, "Do you know who we are?"

No answer.

Deven tried hesitantly, "Do you know who *you* are?"

After a moment came an answer, a harsh whisper with none of the lilt and moonlight she knew. "Yes...I believe I do."

"His hair," she said.

It had been shorn off, probably by a knife, almost at the scalp. She looked closer: everywhere his skin was exposed, there were scars, most already healed to an angry pink that she watched begin to fade. Some of them looked like burns, some like almost surgical cuts, perfectly straight. Some looked like the skin had been ripped.

David's unconsciousness suddenly made sense. If Nico had been torn apart as it looked like he had, the only way to heal all at once like this would be to flood his body with an enormous amount of power. Nico was hooked up directly to that power from two directions, and though he couldn't pull much from Deven, he could take whatever he wanted from David. If it kept up she'd start feeling the drain in less than an hour, and be unconscious shortly thereafter.

Deven took in the scene in an instant and said, "Telekinesis...pyrokinesis...what else?"

"Obviously not empathy," she replied.

Nico made a sound that might have been a quiet laugh if it hadn't been so cold and empty. "Oh yes," he said. "I felt it, all of it...terror, pain...their lives ending...I made sure they knew what it felt like even as they burned. Every second, every wound...their final minutes made up of nothing but agony and fear. They deserved it."

Miranda swallowed. She didn't know what to do. They had all killed, at one time or another, and some regretted it forever...but this was Nico. He couldn't even feed on a live human without getting sick because the darkness scared him so badly. To have gone from there to here in a day...how were they supposed to pull him back?

"Come home with us," she said. "We'll take care of you. Whatever they did, we can help."

"Can you?" Nico gave her a look that was full of rage, hate. It wasn't at her, exactly, more...at everything. "How exactly can you help me?" His gaze sharpened on Deven, and that time, the loathing was very, very focused. "Neuter me with your pathetic moping? Make me hate myself as much as you do?"

"We'll think of something," she said.

"You cannot help me," he snapped. "There is nothing left to help."

Deven caught her eye, and she got a very strong sense of *Keep his attention.*

"I know you don't mean that," Miranda told the Elf. "You're in pain, and you've been through...I can't even imagine. But you know we care about you. We just want you to come home, and be safe."

Another short laugh. It was a terrible sound, and she realized why: his voice was hoarse, like it had been dragged over broken glass. How long must he have been screaming that it still hadn't healed?

"Safe? There is no safe, not in this world. I threw away safety, threw away everything, and now look at me." Something shook in Nico's eyes—something she might be able to take hold of, if she was careful. He lifted both hands so she could see the blood that had dried on both of them. "Doing it with my mind wasn't good enough," he said, almost in a non sequitur. "I wanted to feel their ribs break in my hands. But they kept falling with their eyes open, *staring* at me...the only way to fix it was to burn them. Have you

170

ever crushed a human heart with your bare hands? They make more noise than you would think."

"Nico..." She took another step forward and held out a hand. "It's going to be okay. It's terrible—I won't pretend it isn't. Just...take my hand. You can come home and rest, and we'll figure all of this out tomorrow."

Anger flashed in his eyes, and she braced herself, but before he or Miranda knew what had happened, he drew a ragged breath and fell to the ground.

She ran to his side, kneeling. There was a dart sticking out of his throat. It wasn't another one of the little Morningstar specials; it was a more traditional looking syringe dart, about four inches long.

The Queen looked up at Deven. "Did you—"

"Tranquilizer," he said, looking as shaken as she felt. "Enough to put down an elephant. It'll only last ninety minutes. We need to get him out of here before more of them come."

"I don't think they will," she said, looking around. "I get the feeling like the humans left here were meant as cannon fodder while the others vanished. Hopefully we can get more information...later." She was about to call the Elite team in, but something occurred to her: "How did you get here so quickly?"

"I Misted. Chris had the coordinates."

She'd forgotten most Signets had way more Misting range than she did. David could reach the city from the Haven when he had to, though it took a lot out of him.

She didn't say any of the hundred things she wanted to; she didn't want to scare Deven off again. "Elite teams 1 and 2, commence building entry—I want this entire place swept for evidence and then the interior torched. Harlan, I need you here immediately."

Miranda barely heard the chorus of affirmatives; she was too busy trying to assess Nico's injuries, and fighting back both sickness and sobs as she did. "I don't understand why they did this," she said, tears in her voice that she'd kept at bay talking to her people. "Was it just for fun?"

Deven knelt next to her. She felt him raising healing energy— not along the bond, but via his gift—and pouring it gently into the Elf. The rest of the scars began to disappear rapidly. "I don't know," he said. "Look at his ear—they cut it off and reattached it. Most of this looks surgical."

His hand hovered just over Nico's face for a moment, so close to touching him, but he withdrew, clenching his lowered hand into a fist.

Miranda let out a breath and forced herself not to remark on it. "They went to a lot of trouble for this. It just doesn't make sense."

Near-silent footsteps heralded the arrival of the Elite teams, who all drew up short when they arrived at the scene. The carnage took them all aback, as did both the sight of Nico in such horrible shape and Deven armed.

Miranda rose. "27, 44—get him to the car. The rest of you know what sort of thing the Prime will want to see."

Because they worked for whom they worked for, all the Elite had evidence bags and a few other tools of that sort. Part of their training included learning the numbering system David used for specimens that would go to Hunter Development or to him. She'd thought it was silly when he first instituted the protocol, but it didn't take long to see she was wrong.

She stood back as the two warriors she'd indicated gingerly lifted Nico up off the floor and carried him out of the building. She and Deven both followed, neither speaking.

Harlan was waiting in the parking lot. They had to do a bit of maneuvering to get Nico into the car, as he was taller than the seat was long. They ended up with the Elf's head in Deven's lap and his feet in Miranda's, more or less.

She could see a tumult of emotion moving through Deven's eyes, but again, she held her tongue. It would be too easy to say the wrong thing and make him shrink back into his self-imposed exile. Best just to let him brood until he made a move.

"Miranda."

A knot in her chest untied itself. "David—are you okay?"

"No. Tell me."

"I don't even know how," she said. "He's alive, but...it's bad. I can't even—"

Suddenly Nico's entire body twitched, and his eyes flew open, black as hell. He tried to push himself up and at Miranda, teeth already extended, a combination of anger and mindless panic on his face. She threw herself back against the door, crying out, as he fought to get away from them like a cornered wild animal.

Deven's hands closed around Nico's throat and hauled him back. He twisted so that he had a knee on Nico's chest, pinning him solidly to the seat while he produced another tranquilizer dart and jammed it hard into Nico's neck.

The Elf struggled for a few more seconds, and then his muscles went slack.

She and Deven were left staring at each other and panting.

Miranda swallowed hard and said softly into her wrist, "Yeah...it's bad."

By the time they had Nico somewhere secure, which turned out to be the reinforced interrogation room they'd built after the explosion during the Council summit, he'd needed another two darts to stay unconscious, and each time fought like a rabid dragon to get free of them.

The room had a window for observation, though it would just look like a wall on the inside. The thought of making him sleep on the floor didn't sit well with anyone, so the Elite brought in a cot to deposit him on before making as quick a retreat as possible. The Elite were shaken by the situation too; Nico was unfailingly kind to everyone from servant to Signet, and while few really knew him, nearly everyone liked him.

David, who was leaning against Miranda while he regained his strength, watched Kai with unaccustomed sympathy. The Bard stood at the window with his hand against the glass, his eyes shining and periodically brimming with tears he didn't shed. He looked very young, watching his twin, and said only, "I knew they were doing this. I didn't feel it, exactly, but...I knew."

Miranda reached over and squeezed his shoulder but he didn't seem to notice. They were all a little numb by now.

David stared at Nico for a long time, his heart utterly lost at sea. All he could think was *I'm sorry...I'm sorry. I'm sorry.* The words were beyond inadequate. Nico, the most loving person he'd ever met, so past broken there might not be any repairing him...those elegant hands David had felt on his skin, now dyed red...that soft mouth whose kisses he'd fallen into so many times, bloody like the rest of him, some kind of indefinable innocence destroyed. In his sleep Nico couldn't lay still, and clawed at the blanket draped over him.

The link Stella had created between them still existed, and it wasn't blocked, but David had pushed himself back from it once he came to. He could feel Nico's mind affecting his; every few minutes something would twinge in David's head and he would crave blood so fiercely his canines extended partway, out of his control.

The rage was the hardest part to deal with. It was almost primitive, far too strong for David to wall up like he usually did with such emotions. David knew, watching him, that he wasn't dreaming of his own torture. He was dreaming of killing.

Stella was with them too, but she had turned away from the window and was crying quietly in the corner.

"Sire," came a voice. David looked over at the Elite standing a few meters away.

David lifted his chin inquisitively.

"We found this in the building and thought you would want it brought to you right away." She held up a 12-ounce jar...containing a Signet.

"Give it to Prime Deven," he said.

The Elite offered her cargo with reverence, bowing as she did. Deven stared at it for a moment before taking it. He unscrewed the lid, lifted the Signet out, and handed back the jar.

She bowed again and disappeared.

Deven held the Signet up where it caught the light...the stone was dark. That wasn't unusual, really, as when not around its rightful bearer's neck a Signet usually went dormant, but seeing it like that, almost the perfect symbol of the despair he knew they were all feeling, was insult to injury.

Bowing his head for a moment, Deven stowed the Signet in his pocket. David's gaze followed his hand and ended on Ghostlight, at her place on the Prime's hip as if she'd never been removed. Should that feel good, or not? David had no idea. He knew one night didn't automatically make Deven himself again, but it was a dizzying amount of progress. Somehow Miranda and Kai had gotten to him when it mattered most.

That had to mean Nico could come back. He could entertain no other possibility.

He hadn't thought they could all hurt any more than they did already.

Finally, Deven said, "All right...I'm going in there. He's going to wake up in a few minutes. I want to see if I can get a better read on his condition."

"Are you sure?" Miranda asked. "You're the one he was angriest at. It might be too soon."

Deven looked doubtful, and David said, "I'll go. I wasn't there tonight, and the last time he saw me was under positive conditions at the show. If he tries to attack I'll Mist out."

"Are you sure you're up for it? You still look awfully peaked." Miranda looked even more doubtful than Deven.

"I am. It's fine." He pulled away from her, squeezing her hand before he completely broke contact, and made his way around the side of the cell to its entrance. He put his hand on the scanner to unlock it.

The air inside the room stank of dried blood and scorched meat. They'd need to arrange a shower for Nico, and soon; the quicker they got that crusted gore off his body the easier it would be to remind him who he actually was.

Inspired, David called for water and soap. It appeared outside the door in minutes.

He carried both over and sat down on the second, empty cot. David knew the others were watching, but he couldn't think about that—he had to think of what Nico needed right now.

The water was blessedly warm, just the right temperature to scrub blood from skin without leaving it raw. He lifted one of Nico's hands and began to wash it, at the same time cataloging everything he saw.

Morningstar had, at the very least, broken all his fingers, pulled out his fingernails, and let them grow back. Measuring growth rates, perhaps? Comparing the speed of repair for the bones versus the nails? He kept his touch as light as he could, trying to get as much done as he could before Nico woke. Most of the scars were completely gone by the time he had the skin clean, but he had time to note their locations and likely sources.

How many times will I have to do this for people I love?

One hand, mostly clean; he switched to the other. On that hand a line from the bottom of the index finger made David think they had simply cut off Nico's thumb and then let it grow back onto the hand. That's what they'd done with his ear, and thank God they'd let it reattach; Nico wasn't vain, but Elven ears were such a fundamental part of their appearance that losing one might prove more than Nico could bear. All that was left of the wound was a

175

ridge of skin that might remain, or not; sometimes scar tissue acted oddly in their bodies if the wound was kept open for a long time.

Both hands clean. He moved up to Nico's neck, and his face, washing and rinsing off the remains of over two dozen men.

The intercom buzzed. *"David,"* Miranda said, *"Kai brought some of his clothes—something simple that won't be a big tragedy if he ruins it. It's got to be more comfortable for him than that mess."*

"Agreed." He waited until the door beeped, and rose quickly to retrieve the armload of fabric Kai had left for him.

He continued to work, continued his inventory. Some of the things they'd done made no sense on the surface unless one knew about forensic pathology…there were only a few uses for an incision like the one on…

David put his head in his hands. He understood.

"What is it, baby?"

He looked up at the window, even though he couldn't see anything in it. "These lines," he said. "They're not random, and not just for pain. They're very precise and follow a standard method."

"Method of what?" Miranda asked.

"Autopsy," David answered. The word seemed to weigh him down. "On the whole, I…I think they vivisected him."

He heart Stella retching.

David went back to his work, very lightly pressing on different areas of Nico's body to see if things were still where they went, and to his disgust…they weren't.

"Did the Elite destroy all the samples?"

"Yes," Miranda said. *"Why?"*

"I'm pretty sure the humans removed one of his kidneys. It would have been a fascinating thing to study if they could preserve it—ours are much larger than a human's, and more complex. Losing one won't kill him but it'll make him…permanently delicate."

He peeled off the foul remains of the clothes Nico had found at his escape, and checked for signs of sexual assault. There were indications that the humans had done…things…but he couldn't be sure if they were of a sexual nature or just exploratory. The abrasions and raw flesh could have come from either, though generally speaking rape required heightened emotion, particularly rage, and the rest of their work was purely clinical, suggesting detachment. Either way it was a violation…all of this was.

Nico's chest bore telltale marks besides just the y-incision. He could feel, when he pressed on the bone, that his sternum had been cracked, allowing them access to his chest cavity.

They'd cut him open, chained to a table, without anesthesia, and put their hands into him, reaching in to play around with whatever interesting toys they found inside.

Rage, again. This time David knew it was his own.

He had to fight it down. If it touched Nico, it might wake him, and he needed more time to finish his work. David grounded himself firmly, taking his emotions in hand and shoving them hard behind a shield.

Kai had brought one of the long tunic/loose pants combinations they favored while relaxing; light, with ease of movement, they were equally perfect for a midnight tryst or a week of convalescence. David was quite intimately familiar with how the sides tied up, and left them fairly loose, not wanting Nico to wake up feeling strangled.

David took a moment to wash the blood from Nico's sad mess of hair; they'd have to get in here and cut it when it was safe to have scissors around him. It wasn't ugly on him; quite the opposite, in fact. But it needed evening out, preferably by professional hands. By the time it was all shaped into something normal-looking it would be perhaps two inches long. David imagined that they had cut it off both for convenience and so they could shave it and access the Elf's skull, but it didn't look like they'd gotten any farther than the first step.

Work done, David took a pretty significant risk and leaned over to kiss Nico on the lips. "Rest, my lost one," he whispered to the Elf, touching his face very lightly. "You're home now, and we're here for you. Rest and come back to us."

Then he rose, tucking the blanket around Nico's inert form, and left the cell, dimming the lights and locking the door securely behind him.

Part Two
The Wind-Swept Cliff

Chapter Eleven

SINGER MIRANDA GREY SUSPECT IN AUSTIN HOMICIDE
GREY'S ATTY: ALLEGATIONS ARE "LUDICROUS"
GRAND JURY HEARING SET FOR NOVEMBER 14
FANS: WE'RE STICKING BY MIRANDA GREY
GREY'S HUSBAND TO REPORTERS OUTSIDE COURTROOM:
    "STEP BACK OR EAT YOUR OWN PANCREAS"

David had to admit the last one was fantastic.

The casual, noisy ebb and flow of humanity in the coffee house was a bit distracting, but it was also far more comforting than being home these days. He'd claimed he wanted to do this in a location completely unconnected to anyone in Miranda's life, on a disposable computer that could not be linked to the Haven, which was why he'd chosen Houndstooth; and while that was true it was also true that he just needed to get out of the house before he lost his damn mind.

"Mouse, are you online?"

A pause, then a voice in his ear: *"Yes my Lord. Already in the building, waiting for instructions."*

"Good lad. All right—remember the number one rule of industrial espionage?"

"Look like you belong there, walk like you own the place, and no one will blink."

"First you'll come to the fingerprint scanner that lets you into the secure elevator. Right thumb."

"Yes sir."

Mouse had been working for Hunter Development for a few years, and he had that awkward-teenager vibe that covered up his brilliance; he was a programmer, not a forensic scientist, but what David needed here was someone smart who could follow orders but think on the fly. Mouse was highly plausible as an employee at IntelliGenetic Labs. David had reviewed the files of every employee to build a profile for what he needed, and Mouse was almost a perfect match.

Getting into APD itself, or their forensic lab, was a bad idea, though it would be child's play. There were few enough employees that anyone he sent in might stick out. IGL had a staff of nearly 500 and ran 24/7, serving half the state of Texas. It was better to go to the source in this anyway.

"Sixth floor," Mouse said. "Lab 42 is to the right. Heading that way."

"You'll see a security panel in front of that door that requires another print and retinal scan. Don't hesitate."

David pulled up the next set of data, Mouse's retinal information, and slotted it into the gap he'd created in IGL's records. By the time Mouse reached the scanner, the system thought he'd been working there for 24 months.

"I'm in."

He watched the little dot that represented Mouse on the grid move through the building, approaching their target: Sample Prep and Extractions.

"Ready?"

"Yes sir."

"Okay, we're looking for ATX-APD-MIR-GRE-4095437262-187. The APD samples should all be in the fridges to your left, far end of the room, adjacent to the sink."

He waited, glancing at the internal photographs he had of the room. Mouse, clad in a white lab coat with the IGL logo embroidered over the breast pocket and a badge identifying him as Dr. Nick Tesla, would have to locate a single set of samples among thousands. Even a contract lab like IGL had a backlog of weeks, if not months, for the police. The technology had advanced to the point that a test could come back in 90 minutes, but it could still be months before prosecutors and defense attorneys had their data.

"Found it," Mouse murmured. "Removing now."

"Double check the Chain of Custody form and make sure you've signed it before you swap it for the original. Make sure every vial is positioned exactly as its partner."

"What about the cassette? It has custody seals."

"The kit you have should have dummy custody seals as well. Replace their cassette with yours and seal it the same way. Don't try to open the cassette."

"Gotcha."

It was the nature of their lives that David had vastly over prepared for every emergency he could think of, but it turned out it wasn't necessary; even the techs bustling around the labs, ducking into Sample Prep and out again, paid absolutely no attention to Mouse. Why should they? He'd passed external and internal security at six checkpoints, had a badge that unlocked the doors, and obviously knew what he was doing. There was not one case on record of DNA evidence being tampered with at the laboratory level in Texas. Most criminals didn't have the resources, let alone the brains.

"Replacing the case."

The case in question, a flat rectangular box containing vials of DNA separated from APD's blood sample as well as vials that had already been extracted and prepared for analysis, also had a vial that had been inserted into a plastic carrier cassette that could be plugged into an autosampler—a closed system free of contamination. That would be the first thing they ran; if they got a hit on that, there would of course be additional tests run to verify it. Nobody wanted to put someone in prison based on a single test.

Mouse reported in frequently as he finished his errand and pushed the case back into its neatly labeled slot in the fridge; he placed the original vials in an empty case from a stack nearby, and slid both the vials and the paperwork into it. He couldn't exactly shove the bottles in his pocket and walk off; there were cameras on all the labs, though where he was standing would give a limited view. Much less suspicious for him to take the case out of the lab like he did so every day, put it in a transport cooler, and walk out of the building without missing a step.

"Good work," David said. "I'm keeping an eye on the security system for a while, but so far you haven't so much as raised an eyebrow. You know where to go now."

"On my way, Sire."

Now that Mouse was clear of the building, David pulled up the IGL database and summoned the records for the sample they'd replaced. The police had an extensive list of tests ordered, including phenotyping that was so detailed it could provide hair and eye color of a subject. He accessed the preliminary markers and switched each one for the quantities in their replacement sample, as analyzed by Dr. Novotny's team. From here, IGL could run whatever test they liked.

He made sure to follow the data flow both in and out of the system just in case those few markers had been sent anywhere else, but they weren't considered admissible in court or even definitive, just enough to track the samples as they moved through the lab.

The chair across from him slid out, and Mouse dropped into it. He'd ditched his coat and was now in a nondescript hoodie and jeans.

"Twenty-seven minutes from door to door," David said. "Nice."

Mouse grinned and slid his badge across the table. "Dr. Tesla signing off."

"Well done, Mouse. I'm glad Novotny suggested you—you are kind of a ninja, especially for a human."

Mouse held out a shopping bag from Whole Foods; inside would be ice cream, Stella's favorite pesto and bread, a case full of vampire blood, some of the chocolate fudge that Miranda had vapors over...and even a package of candied ginger, which had been Nico's favorite...before. Mouse had also included a smaller bag containing the gloves he'd worn in the lab so they could be destroyed.

"So you said what they had was going to degrade," Mouse said, bringing him back to the room. "Degrade how?"

Glancing around to make sure no one was looking—of course not, everyone else was either waiting in line for a drink or staring into their phones or both—David opened the case and removed a single vial. Protocol was to keep the samples out of bright light, at temperatures less than 6 degrees Celsius.

"There's a reason you can't DNA test a vampire," he said quietly, opening the vial and turning it over. Mouse started, jerking his hands back from the spill, but what came out of the vial was thick and gloppy, and as a single drop hit the table and the overhead lights hit it, the blood began to essentially burn, though with only a tiny bit of smoke. It was ash in seconds. "As soon as it leaves the body the proteins begin to clump up. By the time they got to the PCR it was probably already badly coagulated. They'd get the prelim markers and that's it. It would never make it to the final analysis. The effect you just saw was caused by light. Ultraviolet is the worst, but any light of sufficient brightness causes rapid degradation. Novotny has had a lot of luck prepping the samples in a dark room, but there's no reason a normal lab would even try that."

"I'm guessing what we put in there was human, then."

"It was indeed. I ran facial recognition software on as many humans in Austin as I could find, then expanded the search to adjoining states. I looked for someone with the same general appearance as Miranda, then got hold of her DNA."

"You're going to frame somebody?"

"In theory, perhaps, but in reality this particular redhead was in Oregon at the time of the murder, and there are documents and witnesses of her entire trip. She works for a very prestigious law firm. APD will have the DNA of a woman who looks like Miranda but couldn't possibly be the killer, and they'll have DNA from the body that matches neither woman. Not to mention Miranda will have an alibi by then—she said she didn't remember the night of the murder, but her credit card records will remind her where she was, which was nowhere near that alley. The case will run round in circles and go cold."

Mouse was just staring at him. "Remind me never to try and screw you over. You screw back really really hard."

"That could be the title of my autobiography."

Mouse shook his head, impressed. "Well, scary as the whole thing is, I'm glad I could help. It was actually kind of fun."

David smiled and turned the laptop screen toward him. "There you have it: first payment of nine thousand, with one per month until you die, waiting in this account. You've got the card for it already."

The boy nodded. "Nine thousand—so the IRS won't flag it?"

"They won't anyway. But better anal than annoyed. If you need an advance on it at any time just call the number in your packet."

Mouse's face got a distant kind of happy expression, and David asked, "Planning to retire from Hunter?"

"Nah...not yet. I love my job. It's just... One of the first assignments they gave me was to run my own family tree to show how good I was at hacking records and analyzing data. I found my grandma. I didn't even know she existed. We met, and we've been spending time. She's in a shitty nursing home, or she will be for another week."

David smiled. "Well done, Mouse. Well done indeed. Now get out of here."

"Yes Sire. Again, thank you. I'm really glad I could help."

"You're welcome."

He watched the lanky young genius weave his way out of the coffee shop. Miranda would be happy to know that something good had come out of all this.

Speaking of which...he checked his inbox and found the video Miranda had just made for her fan site. Just like when she'd been shot, she wanted to reach out to her fans, both to thank them for their support and to encourage them not to harass the police. She was worried that Maguire in particular might be a target—not that they'd do anything violent, necessarily, but the poor detective's life was already hard enough without his car being egged or worse.

The camera system had improved by leaps and bounds. He'd refined the video to where once it was recording, it was almost crystal clear, albeit with periodic glitches and a slight graininess with too much zoom. It was certainly good enough for a home movie of the Queen at her piano, talking into her laptop and then playing an exclusive song for her fans.

He switched the audio output to his com, where only he could hear it, and hit play.

"Hi guys," Miranda said, looking up into the lens. She looked tired, and vulnerable...perfect. *"I know you've been hearing a lot of crazy stuff about me lately..."*

He adjusted the picture and ran a few filters over it to clear it up a bit and adjust the color.

She took a deep breath, steeling herself for the implicit lie. *"I can't say much about the case, but I want to make one request: please let the police do their jobs. I've dealt with APD a lot over the years, and the detectives involved are good men who want justice. There are always false leads and exonerated suspects. I'm confident I'll end up being one of those. Anyway, I love you guys and I'm so grateful for every one of you.   If we got through my being shot together, we can get through this too."*

Miranda offered the camera a smile, then reached up and tilted it down from her face to the piano. *"Since we're here, I thought you might like to meet my piano—if you've seen me onstage you've seen her twin, but this is my great love, the Empress. She was originally part of an inheritance of my husband's, but over time, she became mine. And just for you, here's a little bit of music."*
David grinned. Fans who watched this would be overjoyed.

He played the whole thing through another couple of times, tweaking settings here and there, before converting it to the format needed on the website and uploading it. Then, he reached into his coat and took out a USB drive.

It took a few minutes to completely wipe the laptop—it would have been easier to destroy it in some decisively violent manner, but he really hated to waste a perfectly good computer. That meant a bit more effort to make sure there were no fragments of data left anywhere, no strings of characters, nothing but a blank slate without so much as an operating system. The version of OSX he used was not exactly the bog standard model; he had it reinstall the original operating system, putting it in a state of cheerful readiness for whoever owned it next. It had, in fact, another owner lined up; Stella's friend Lark was in desperate need of a new machine.

He had no real reason to linger and every reason to head home. Miranda was okay for now—she'd finished recording the video about half an hour ago, and would probably stay in her music room with her audience of one Elf and one Witch. The Queen was trying, subtly, to keep both Kai and Stella occupied so they couldn't fret over what was really going on. David doubted it was working, but the two seemed pleased to be included regardless.

David reached up and tapped the implant behind his ear. "Harlan, I'm ready."

"Yes, Sire. ETA five minutes."

He was pretty sure Deven was watching over Nico tonight. They'd been taking shifts. After three days in the interrogation room Nico had made his demands known: He would refrain from hurting or killing anyone, and submit to monitoring, if they let him return to his rooms. If not, he would Mist out of the room now that he was strong enough to do so and the next they would hear of him would be a trail of bodies left across Austin.

They'd all braced themselves for whatever escape plan he'd concocted, but once he was back in his suite, he ignored them all completely. Mostly he just sat staring into the fireplace, seething. He hadn't made a move to injure any of the guards, or to circumvent the two cameras David had halfheartedly placed in his room; he didn't do much of anything.

The one thing they had in their favor was that as long as David and Deven were both holding back power from him, the Weaving he could do was limited; the thought of Elven magic of his caliber turned on the Haven was the stuff of nightmares.

Every night someone would go in to see if he needed anything, and try to engage him in conversation, just to make contact. He rarely acknowledged they were there unless he wanted something, and there wasn't much he wanted. A cloud of dark emotion churned around him every moment he was awake; when he slept, dreams took control and almost every morning he ended up screaming himself awake.

It couldn't go on like this, but no one seemed to know what to do. They had to tread carefully.

David had seen people he loved tormented in just about every imaginable way, but he'd never seen anyone react quite like this. Nico wasn't just letting himself indulge in the violent side of their kind, he was *reveling* in it. He'd left the gentle healer he'd been strapped to that table to bleed out, and all that was left was everything he'd denied about himself, all the parts of becoming a vampire he'd feared and hated.

They'd been dealing with Deven's breakdown for two years, but that one was, in a way, simpler: Deven had always been depressive and self-loathing, so his behavior was, while extreme, nothing new. Nico had done a 180 like nothing David had ever seen.

Harlan was waiting at the curb when David emerged from the coffee shop in a blast of espresso-heavy air conditioning. David sighed heavily once the Escalade was in motion and shut his eyes for a moment.

"Everything all right, Sire?" Harlan asked. "Or at least no worse than earlier?"

He had to smile at that. "Better, actually. I'll know in a few days if tonight's work was successful, but I have every reason to believe it will be."

"That's good to hear, Sire."

David did a network check on his phone: all systems nominal. "You don't happen to know any psychiatrists, do you?"

"Not personally, Sire, but surely you can find one—I assume you're thinking of someone who specializes in PTSD."

Frowning, David said, "You know, I was joking, but that's not a bad idea. I know there are a few vampire psych doctors here in town, and there are probably a lot more out there. It's a surprisingly lucrative field."

"I would imagine," Harlan said wryly. "We can't all be as well-adjusted as you."

David laughed. "True. Maybe I'll put feelers out. Even if I can just talk to someone about how to approach this, get some ideas, that would be helpful. We didn't do terribly well on our own with Deven."

"I think we're all treading in unknown waters here, Sire. We need all hands on deck."

"Aye, matey," he replied, half-yawning. He pulled over the bag Mouse had given him and dug out the swiftly-melting pint of Chocolate Therapy. In the absence of an ashtray the Escalade had a push-button compartment for phones and whatnot; this one contained, among other things, a stack of plastic spoons. "If you'll pardon me, Harlan, we're twenty minutes out from the Haven and that's just enough time for me to eat my feelings."

"Of course, Sire. Cheers."

It had been a long, long time since Miranda had last walked into the study to find Deven drinking. It was comforting, in a way, to finally do it again.

The Prime was curled up in the chair with his head against the armrest, a bottle of Scotch on the table...and an empty glass.

"You're not drinking?" she asked, kind of alarmed.

Deven glanced at the bottle. "Oh...I forgot it was there."

She had no idea how to react to that. The best course of action seemed to be fetching herself a drink and sitting down. She tried to look him over without being obvious.

Casual dress: jeans, t-shirt. He looked way more put-together than the night she'd followed him to the hospital. Clean-shaven, for one thing, and to her relief, he'd re-dyed his hair. It was just black, lacking the streaks or tips in red or blue or violet he'd always favored, but it was something. She wouldn't feel like he was really himself until she saw eyeliner.

Something random occurred to her. "Avi works for you," she said. "He's one of your agents."

"Well, he was."

"David said you had a spy in our Elite, but he said it was a woman."

He gave the tiniest flicker of a smile. "I had two spies in your Elite. David was supposed to make her."

She had to laugh. "You boys are ridiculous, you know that. Have you talked to Avi since New York?"

"Not directly. I sent him a message telling him not to worry about being killed as a deserter—Signets trump pretty much everything. I said we'd be in touch to discuss the end of his contract. It may seem unbelievable, but he didn't actually know who I am—I've been careful not to be seen since I've been here. He knows I'm familiar with the Signets—familiar enough to know their inner workings so I could assign him this detail. That's all."

"He's going to have kittens when he figures it out."

"An entire litter, yes. The second the Circle is together and he sees me it'll all be out in the open."

"Why not tell him now?"

Now she could definitely see the smile. "Mostly for the fun of seeing his face."

Miranda popped the top on her Coke and poured it over ice, adding two rather chubby fingers of rum. She didn't want to get drunk, exactly; she just wanted to turn down the dial on her anxiety for a while.

Finally she forced herself to ask: "How is he tonight?"

Deven closed his eyes. "The same. Not interested in talking, not interested in anything. I know he's thinking about something— maybe a plan, maybe just making sense of it all. I can feel his mind whirling underneath all the anger. There's nothing to orient him, no compass points. He may still be in there, or he may be dead and this is all that's left. I just don't know."

She knew she shouldn't say it. She'd been trying not to bring it up. But she had to. "Maybe if you lowered the barrier—"

"I can't."

"Of course you can!" Exasperated, she sat forward, holding her glass in both hands. "There's no reason to keep it up anymore—imagine if all that love were to reach him."

"Exactly," Deven said sharply. "Imagine it. Imagine I take the wall down, and he's hit with the full weight of power that's built up behind it. I don't have the strength to moderate a flow of that size—it'd be like hitting him with the entire ocean. It would kill him, or at least drive him even more insane."

Miranda stared at him as it started making sense. He hadn't kept refusing to lower the wall because of his own fear, at least not entirely—but because of fear for Nico, fear that the force of everything he'd held back from his Consort would dash Nico to pieces on the rocks.

An oddness again: Knowing that made her feel a little better. Deven wasn't being quite as obstinate as he seemed.

"I concur," came a tired voice, and Kai poked his head into the study. "I have looked as closely at the situation as I can without myself being a vampire, and I believe Deven is right. Without someone to help dampen the flow of energy, it would burn them both out in seconds. It would take a sorcerer of great skill to do so—at least Nico's level or better if we could find it. I do not even know anyone in Avilon who..." Kai trailed off, narrowing his eyes. "Excuse me." and he vanished.

"Do you think he's thinking of calling another Elf?" she asked.

Deven shrugged. "He's been a little scattered the last few days. It's hard to get him to complete a sentence."

She nodded. Seeing what this was doing to Kai was one of the hardest parts of an entire truckload of hard parts. Kai, Stella, the Pair, and Deven couldn't all have been more different, but they were united by their love for Nico. They'd all grown a lot closer in the last week as everyone tried to cope with yet another change in their reality. Nobody was dealing all that well, though she had caught Kai and David actually having an amiable conversation, and something in her chest had unclenched a little.

Surprising her, Deven asked, "You're not actually worried about this murder nonsense, are you?"

"I don't know. I know that in the long run it's meaningless. I could break out of any jail they tried to put me in. Texas is a death penalty state, but fat lot of good lethal injection's going to do them. Convicted or acquitted, I'm still Queen. But am I still Miranda Grey to my fans? That I don't know. I don't want to hurt them. The best thing would be if David's plan goes off without a hitch and the whole thing just goes away. It's not like Morningstar was invested in getting me put away—they wanted to split us up into smaller groups so they could kidnap Nico. He was what they wanted, not me. I just wish I knew why."

"Well, what's unique about him?" Deven prompted.

"He started out an Elf, not a human."

"And what were they interested in when they had him?"

"His body, mostly. Nico mentioned something in one of David's visits about how they really didn't want him at all—they just wanted to cut him open and play with his insides knowing he wouldn't die from it. David surmised that they want to do something to a full Elf, but didn't know enough about Elven anatomy for what they're planning. There aren't exactly a herd of Elves running around, so if they get hold of one, they have to be careful with her. But now they know a lot about how to hurt one without killing her."

"Comforting."

"Plus it still leaves the central question unanswered," Miranda pointed out.

"And unanswered it'll remain until we know more about this Prophet and what he wants. Jacob pointed out a while back that aside from killing vampires, nothing they're doing fits with the usual behavior of religious zealots; they're not turning their swords on entire Shadow Districts, but on very specific targets, the Signets. They don't want to exterminate us, not yet—first they want to destabilize our power so the entire system collapses, possibly to cause anarchy and widespread violence to make themselves feel righteous in killing us off wholesale."

"But that answer is incomplete," Miranda noted. "I don't know why, but it just is."

"I know. But I have nothing."

"We need to double the guard on Kai," she muttered. "He shouldn't leave the Haven again."

"Agreed."

They drank in silence—or at least she drank—for a while. A dozen questions fought for the first chair in her mind. There was so much she needed to tell him, months of sorrows and now all of this, but she was terrified to ask too much, to expect anything. She was so afraid to drive him away again—this time he might never come back. If she was careful he might be her friend again someday.

"I'm sorry," he said softly.

Startled, she looked at him. "For what?"

He looked down at his empty glass, whose ice cubes were slowly turning into a tiny lake. "I can't...I can't make up for everything. I can't fix who I am. But you deserved better—a better friend. Someone to talk to, about...everything. I could have been there for you. But I wasn't. I couldn't see past my own brokenness. And I'm sorry."

She smiled through a knot in her throat. "I forgive you."

He nodded. There was just the slightest shine to his eyes, but he wouldn't look at her. "I don't know how to help...but if you ask for something, I'll try to give it to you."

Miranda took a deep breath. "You know, there's only one thing, really, that I wish...right now, I mean...I think we could both use...shit, never mind."

But Deven had already intuited her meaning from the word salad, and with something oh so close to a chuckle, moved over, making enough room for her in the chair.

Miranda didn't give him a chance to change his mind. She moved over to the chair, drawing her legs in and snuggling up next to him while he draped the throw blanket around them both. She leaned her head on his shoulder, but rather than being content just to lean, Deven turned toward her—the chair was enormous, after all—and wound his legs around hers, drawing her head against his chest, his hand curving around the back of her head, the other around her hip.

One of his feet drew up along her calf, and she felt a shiver—there was just something so intimate about a gesture like that, but it felt right. Her reply was to slide her hand up around his waist, very carefully finding the hem of his shirt and letting just her fingertips touch the skin beneath.

"What are we going to do?" she asked in a whisper.

"I don't know."

She closed her eyes and listened to his heartbeat. "I missed you so much."

"And I you, though I wouldn't have admitted it. So often I wished for just this...just knowing someone cared who wouldn't judge me or cast me aside. Even as I railed against all of you for refusing to give up on me, I was desperately grateful that no one did."

She lifted her head so she could look down into his face. "Look, I know everything's not just magically fixed, and that's okay—let's just not lose this again. It's too important."

He smiled gently. "I agree."

"Good. You don't have to be the same you as before—even if that's possible. And whatever you you're going to be, it takes as long as it takes. I won't try to push you back to who you were, or anywhere—just don't shut me out again. Deal?"

The smile broadened ever so slightly. "Deal."

Miranda grinned and kissed him lightly, intending just to seal the deal, but...

Between one breath and the next, without a single thought, she had clamped her mouth on his. He made a faint noise of surprise, but didn't push her away—in fact, he kissed her back, and pulled her even harder against him, the hand on her hip sliding around to the small of her back.

She knew she should stop, knew it would be a very very bad idea to dig her nails into his neck—

"Whoa!" Deven jerked his lips from hers as if she'd electrocuted him. They were both breathing hard. "Jesus, woman, what *is* it about you?"

"Sorry," she managed. "The last few days have been awful, I guess we're confused about what we want—"

He snorted. "I know perfectly well what I want, Miranda." As an illustration, he took hold of her hips and rocked them forward. When she realized what he meant she felt herself turning scarlet. "What I want to know is *why.*"

In spite of her embarrassment, she grinned. "Oh, you mean cleavage like mine isn't enough to make a 700 year old gay man want a piece of this?"

They stared at each other a second, then both started laughing.

"Were I to shag a woman, I'd be more than happy for it to be you. I'm just a little leery for a number of reasons I'm sure you can understand."

"You think David would react badly?"

Deven rolled his eyes. "I think he'd ask to be included. But aren't you at all concerned why this keeps happening?"

"Not really. But then, you're a boy, I'm a heterosexual girl, you're unspeakably hot, my best friend, and good God, have you ever seen you fight? If that's not foreplay I don't know what is."

Her not being troubled was apparently troubling. "So you're saying you want to go for it right here, right now."

She sobered, sighing. "It's not that, sweetie, it's...you think I should take it more seriously, but I think you're taking it too seriously. So unusual for you, I know. Like David told me, we've all got odd energetic links galore because of the Circle—most of them are wobbly because we don't know what they're for. Not to mention you're in a rough state and have all that power moving around with nowhere to go, and I'm antsy as hell what with the murder charge and all. If you don't want me to kiss you again, that's totally fine. I don't want to make you even more uncomfortable than you are just by waking up. But really, don't catastrophize one of the few things that isn't a catastrophe. We make out, we don't make out, the world doesn't end either way."

After a moment of watching her, he commented, "You really have changed in the last two years."

"My priorities might have shifted a little, yeah."

"You're even entertaining the idea of an affair with Kai. I would never have expected that, even with David carrying on with Nico."

Miranda shrugged and settled back against his shoulder, carefully not touching anywhere that might be considered inappropriate. "I don't know," she said, and it was the first time she'd ever managed to get the foundation of her thoughts out loud. "I like the flirty stuff, but more than that...I don't think so, to be honest. I care about him a lot. But I look at David and Nico, the way they were before things went to hell, and they made sense to me. Not once did I ever question the way David felt—I kind of liked watching them get closer. I don't know what the difference is. When I think about actually sleeping with him, it doesn't feel *wrong*, but just doesn't feel right either."

"It's a bit of a leap, from flirting to shagging," Deven replied. "You've got a complicated history in that department."

"Maybe that's it. Maybe I'm just tired of everything being so goddamned complicated."

They were quiet for a minute before Deven asked, almost sounding afraid to hear the answer, "How does it feel when you think about sleeping with me?"

Miranda thought about it for a moment, toying with the button at his collar. "I think it sounds amazing," she confessed. "But I'd also be terrified."

"Terrified?"

"I'd be your first woman," she pointed out. "And more than likely your only one. That's a big deal."

"On the other hand I'd have nothing to compare it to," he reminded her. "I don't know if you've figured this out about men, but for the most part, if we get to stick our dicks in something that doesn't bite them off, we're happy."

It was Miranda's turn to snort. She burrowed closer, pulling the blanket up over her shoulders. "I only hope I could live up to such high standards."

They were both sleepy—it was hard to keep up enough energy these days for all the night-to-night issues of Signet life plus the added layers of drama.

"Oh, don't worry," he murmured, eyes already closed. "As beautifully as we nap together I'm sure we'll be magnificent lovers someday. Today, more napping."

Miranda couldn't stop smiling—not even as she fell asleep. *I have you back...you're here with me...please don't go away again...I need you and you need me and it's just so, so good to be here.*

A light, gentle voice touched the back of her mind. *I'm not going anywhere...now rest, my Queen, just rest.*

Chapter Twelve

"All right, now that we have him open, I'd like tissue samples of all the organs."

"...fascinating, the size difference in some of these. Sir, would it be all right if we kept an entire kidney? Even a human can live with just one."

"I don't see why not."

Gloved fingers closing around something inside his body cavity, the cold steel of a clamp and then—

Nico flailed his way out of sleep, just barely keeping hold on the screams that had built throughout the dream—he turned on his side, curling up, biting down on his forearm to silence cries he knew would summon the guards outside his room.

How he wanted to strike out at the source of those voices...but he already had. With a single exception, they were dead, by his hand, the violence of their ending as much a part of his nightmares as what they had done to him. Tearing a dozen humans apart and reveling in their fear was not the behavior of an Elf...it wasn't even the behavior of most vampires.

And one day...one day he'd do the same to the Prophet. He didn't have any way of hunting the human down, but he knew it had to be part of Persephone's plan, and as soon as they found him...Nico's few satisfying dreams were of standing over the Prophet in his final moments, hoping that, while his own belief in an afterlife was dwindling as quickly as his belief in the inherent goodness of Deity, for this human, at least this once, there was a Hell.

He clung to the rage and hatred as hard as he could because he knew they were all that was left. If he stood still, if he let his anger lose momentum, his armor would slide off, and the whole world would see...he would see...that there was nothing left beneath. The Prophet, whether as part of some greater design or just for pleasure, had brutalized the Weaver to death. What remained was made up of teeth and blood.

He remembered his words to the humans. *I am not an Elf anymore.*

The thought sent a hollow, desolate sob through his body. He pulled the pillow down over his head, hands fisting in the softness that was more comfort than he deserved, and lay shaking for a while until he could breathe again.

He had a sudden mental image of himself: a trembling, pathetic mess, craven and weak.

The anger flared again. He shoved the pillow and blankets aside and forced himself out of bed, numb hands seeking the nearest clothes. He had to get out of here. His insides felt like they were crusted with sand—he needed blood.

Two birds, one stone, as they said. Drawing power up around himself, reaching through space, he easily combined the magic he'd used to build portals from Earth to Avilon and the birthright of the Signets: Misting.

In a matter of breaths, he was in the city.

The others thought they had him contained; as long as they gave him relative freedom in the Haven he wouldn't wreak havoc on the mortals of Austin. But all he had promised was not to go on a killing spree. And what good was that promise anyway? They lived by stealing the life from other creatures, and since when was there honor among thieves?

Downtown Austin rose up all around him, but he had to ignore the towering buildings or panic would set in. He could feel them closing in if he stood still too long. He had spent his entire life among tall trees and the gentle rhythm of the seasons in a dream of peace; this place was built on violence and fear. Its inhabitants were frightened little children clinging to the surface of a planet that spun too fast for their lives to matter.

Nico moved out of the traffic path so he could evaluate the humans around him. It was a typical street corner, busy even this late, more so tonight because of the line of storms that had come through early in the evening. There was another on the way; the humans were therefore in a hurry to finish their business and get home.

He knew there were several hunting styles among vampires. Most of the truly powerful went for the quick and efficient hit; they sought out a clean, strong specimen and isolated them, afterward making sure the human's memory of the event was blurry or blank. David had said once that he'd often had sex with his prey to infuse the blood with pleasure and strength, but there were thorny issues of consent surrounding such a habit; Nico knew he'd had very firm rules about not influencing their minds until afterward, but the truth was, if the human was made to forget, any conceit a vampire made to the free will of his food was purely to make himself feel like more than a monster. There were plenty of vampires who would take what they wanted and leave whatever trauma they caused without a second thought.

In a way, the vampires the Signets looked down on—those who killed when they didn't have to—were more honest. They didn't have pretensions of civility. The Signets liked to think they were above those who indulged in their animal instincts, as if putting dinner in a wine glass somehow made it other than the lifeblood of a human being.

A young woman jogging across the street caught his eye. He focused his senses on her, and could almost hear her heartbeat—strong, steady, filling her blood with oxygen. She was healthy and bright-eyed. Perfect.

Nico tapped on her mind and pulled at her consciousness, causing her to veer from her original trajectory and turn right at the light, heading right toward him. He moved back into the alley; it wasn't one of those creepy dark areas, but was still empty, as humans from the surrounding restaurants used it to dump their garbage in a large metal bin. The amount of refuse these creatures produced was remarkable.

The girl came around the corner and skidded to a stop. She yanked the earbuds from her ears; he could hear the faint strains of some kind of dance music.

"What the hell," she said, blinking. "What am I doing here? I wasn't coming this way."

Nico didn't bother answering. He seized her by the shoulders and shoved her against the wall, clamping one hand over her mouth, his teeth already extended. She struggled hard—very strong indeed—but pointlessly, as he had her pinned to the bricks. Her entire body went rigid when he bit her, and her scream was muffled under his palm.

David had tried to teach him to hunt back when he had first come to the Haven, but Nico had been too weak and too cowardly to take his lessons to heart. He remembered that there was a definite signal to stop: as soon as the human and the vampire's heartbeats came into synch, it was time to let go, or within seconds there would be no return.

He'd managed not to kill anyone in the last few days since he'd been sneaking out to hunt. It wasn't so much that he cared, but that he didn't want to be as foolish as Miranda and get caught. She and David had no choice but to kill every month, but while David seemed able to handle it pretty easily, Miranda could not; that guilt she harbored had made her sloppy.

Tonight, as the girl's struggles became more and more feeble, images of that night in the Prophet's lair kept intruding, a frame at a time, flashes of his own struggles against the restraints, and then of the "doctor" begging for his life. He didn't remember a point of no return that night—there was no return from any of it.

No return. No way back, not for him, not for this poor child— so young, so unaware of what was waiting in every shadow of the city where she felt safe enough to run, alone, her fragile human body in jeopardy every second she was alive.

Her blood tasted like youth and a rainy night, like coffee. He was inclined to let her walk away...until he took a breath and caught a faint scent under her shampoo and sweat, something...clinical...plastic, chemicals, sanitizing products...

He couldn't stop the surge of explosive rage that took him. She probably worked at a hospital, or was a student, but all he could see was that ceiling, the sprinkler head he'd stared at for hours, the smell...metallic instruments clicking together...

Suddenly something took hold of his arm and hauled her off the girl, throwing him hard into the wall face-first. Nico managed to turn his head in time not to break anything, but the impact was enough to drop him to the ground, hands scrabbling against the bricks.

He snarled, his anger turning from the girl to his assailant, and lifted his head, taking in boots, long leather coat, sword, glowing emerald...pale lavender eyes that almost glowed themselves in the darkness.

"That's enough," Deven snapped. "Kill if you want, but keep your teeth off the innocent. There are lowlifes aplenty to satisfy your appetite if you aren't too lazy to look."

"I do not take orders from you," Nico ground out, poison in every syllable. He started to get back to his feet.

A boot came down solidly on his neck.

"Yes. You. *Do.*"

Deven held him down for just a beat, then moved back to let Nico struggle to his feet. "If you choose to act like an animal you will be put on a leash like one." Power mantled around the Prime like black wings—he could almost hear them rustling, almost see their edges in the flash of headlights driving by. Nico remembered the Queen doing the same thing, months ago when the newly-vampire Elf had attacked Stella. It was a dominance display, pure and simple, but there was a reason the Signets ruled the Shadow World...it worked.

Nico's resolve crumbled before the roiling cloud of darkness facing him. He might have tried to fight it—he was much stronger now than he had been that night with Miranda—but there was an added complication...he wasn't just confronting a Prime...but *his* Prime. Deven was the one who had built the barrier between them, and that meant he had power over it; if he wanted Nico to cower before him, Nico would. He couldn't stop himself.

He locked eyes with Deven for a long, wordless moment before slowly returning to his knees. The imperious, cold glare remained on him until he lowered his eyes first.

"Stay," Deven ordered. Nico listened, unmoving, as the Prime moved to the girl's side and he took quick inventory of her condition; Nico felt energy flowing into the human, healing the ragged tears in her throat and restoring her strength enough that she would easily survive the blood loss—Nico sensed he hadn't signed the girl's death warrant but it had been close. Deven murmured to her, telling her to return home and eat, and to call in sick for work.

Deven took a step back. Nico heard the girl's shoes on the gritty concrete as she straightened. "Damn," she muttered. "I don't feel so good. Sorry...didn't mean to run into you."

"No problem, my dear," the Prime told her. "You look like you might be coming down with something. You should take a cab home."

"Yeah...I'm probably coming down with something. I think I'll just take a cab home. Excuse me."

Footsteps retreating.

Footsteps approaching. "What the hell are you doing?"

Nico looked up. "This is what we do," he answered venomously. "It's why we exist, isn't it? To control their population?"

"How many have you killed since that night?" Deven demanded. "I know you've been slipping out of your room—" At Nico's expression Deven made a dismissive noise. "Please, Nico, remember who you're talking to. So are there bodies all over the city to be dealt with?"

A note of sullenness entered his voice. "No. I've let them all live. I didn't want to deal with the inconvenience."

He wasn't sure Deven believed him at first, but the Prime merely said, "Get up."

Nico obeyed.

A hint of emotion made its way through Deven's impassive exterior. "Don't let them do this to you," he said quietly.

"What?"

"What those bastards did to you was monstrous," Deven replied. "Don't let it make you a monster. Don't give them the satisfaction of letting your suffering become your identity. If you want vengeance you have to seek it as yourself or it's meaningless."

Nico made a derisive noise and started to walk away; Deven easily kept pace with him. "You do not get to lecture me on coping with pain, *ghost*," Nico said icily.

"It's only advice, Nico. And you *should* hear it from me—no one knows better how *not* to heal from trauma. You've seen me do everything wrong from the night we met."

"And somehow out of nowhere you're all better."

"No. Not even remotely. Right now the nightmares are staying in my sleep, but I'm not fool enough to think that will last. I don't think I'll ever be all better. But I can be better than I was. I think that's all any of us can do, most of the time."

Nico rounded on him. "So here we are, then. You spend all this time ignoring me, making me weak and sick and near suicidal, but now, because you paid attention to me for one night, you have the right to counsel me? You may have the authority to command me not to kill, but you have forfeited all right to the state of my heart. Too little, too late, my Lord." He infused the last word with all the spite he could.

To his surprise, Deven nodded. "Fair enough."

Nico started to walk away again, but Deven's voice called him back: "Do you hate me?"

He looked back over his shoulder. "Yes."

He had hoped the word would sting, but it was no less than Deven expected, apparently; he just nodded again. "I understand."

But Nico couldn't help it: he laughed.

One eyebrow shot up. "Why is that funny?"

Nico walked back to him, letting his far greater height give him some semblance of power in the situation if nothing else. "Because I'm lying. I *want* to hate you. I want to so badly. I want to dedicate myself to making you as miserable as you've made me. Everything would be so much easier if I could hate you…but I can't. I don't. And that makes me want to hate you even more. So no matter what situation we're in, you still have the ability to hurt me."

The anger he'd been wearing as a shield was swiftly unraveling into a tangled snare of despair as he went on, "Do you remember the night we walked in the woods, and you said that you feared your God would cast you into hell over whom you loved? Well, congratulations: that's what you have done to me. Your sad little broken heart possessed mine and dragged me down with you. And now here we are, both of us broken, a mockery of a Signet bond tethering us to each other until one of us summons the courage to end it. Well done, my Lord. Well done."

He saw that Deven was about to reply but didn't give him a chance. Nico shook his head in disgust, reached across the distance to the Haven, and Misted away before the Prime could say a word.

Stella was nervous as she slid into the booth opposite her dad, but she tried to be casual, not act as if he was trying to get the needle for one of her best friends and that there was no internal drama dragging the last shreds of hope out of everyone at the Haven.

"Hi Dad," she said.

He looked so relieved. "I wasn't sure you'd come," he said.

She didn't say that she didn't have much else to do these days. She had run from the Haven with both Miranda's understanding and Miranda's credit card, and the Pair had set her up at a ridiculously nice hotel for however long she needed a hiding place. They understood that she needed to be...away for a while, until she could get her head around what had happened to Nico and what was happening with Miranda. Guards followed her everywhere, but they were good at their jobs; if she hadn't been told they were out there she would never have noticed.

"I was worried about you," the Witch admitted. "You look kind of beat. And look, you haven't even touched your eggs."

"I ordered for you," he said sheepishly. "The Kerbey scramble with French toast, right?"

"Yeah." She grinned, leaned over, and kissed his ruddy forehead. "Thanks Dad."

They nursed their coffee for a moment; it made a good distraction with the pouring and spooning of sweeteners and whiteners.

The waitress arrived in record time with Stella's food. Once she had departed, Stella said, "I know you can't give me many details, so I'm not asking for any, but: how's the case going? I mean is it long hours, lots of pavement-pounding, or are you in a holding pattern waiting for lab results?"

Maguire considered for a minute between bites of his Denver omelet, while Stella loaded her French toast with an obscene amount of syrup. "Okay, this is off the record, because I shouldn't be telling anyone before they formally announce it...but..."
Stella held her breath.

"We're going to have to drop all charges against Miranda Grey. The DNA wasn't a match. It wasn't even close to a match. They fast-tracked it through the lab because it's such a high profile case. It led us on a wild goose chase, and the analysts finally deemed it useless."

"Did they double check?"

"And triple. They used up the entire sample running different tests, and not one iota of data supports Miranda Grey as the killer."

"Well thank God."

"Just for my own peace of mind, have they...has anything been said?"

"About you? APD? Not really. I promise, Dad, Miranda and David both know you guys are just doing your jobs. Their main area of concern is where that video came from that just happened to fall in your lap. They have some enemies that would be positively gleeful to see Miranda go down."

"Stella..."

She looked up from her fork, where she was swirling a piece of toast in the syrup-and-melted-butter puddle. "What's wrong, Dad?"

"I don't want to make things weird with all of you."

"Daddy, I don't think it can get any weirder."

"The evidence clears Miranda of this murder. But I was looking into the missing persons stats for the last year, and...there's a pattern. Two people go missing every month at the same time. Some are found dead in dumpsters or other out of the way places; some never resurface. The common thread is that they're all violent offenders or have hurt lots of people in other ways. Some get a cursory investigation, but none of them receive a lot of police attention."

"They're evil," Stella mused.

"You could say that. It's not drug users, or even average dealers. It's dealers selling to kids, dealers trading sex for product from kids. Rapists, child pornographers. The guy in charge of that big dog-fighting ring on the East Side last Spring was found half eaten by coyotes on the edge of town. Whoever's killing them knows exactly what they're looking for."

"So Austin has a vigilante?"

Maguire took a deep breath. "A vigilante who drains every drop of their blood. Every month there are two, found in separate locations. And it happens every month around the New Moon."

Stella felt the bottom drop out of her lungs. "Wow, that's...you think it's vampires?" she asked softly.

"We find puncture marks, but we already tried comparing them to Miranda's dental impressions; they never seem to line up right. The holes are almost always closed, leaving just bites like a great big mosquito. As they heal—even postmortem—they pull farther apart as the skin tightens. I asked the medical examiner's office if there's a way to calculate the distance based on the rate of decomp, but there are too many variables."

Stella knew where he was going, and as much as she dreaded what he'd say, she asked, "Do you think Miranda's the killer?"

"To be honest, Stell…I know it's probably going to get me killed if I speak up, but I think it's both of them. I don't know why they do it when they never did before, but they're out there killing evildoers every month, and leaving almost no trace."

"But isn't that good? I mean hypothetically…you get criminals off the streets that the system has let walk."

"But we have that system for a reason, Stella. And I know Signet authority is absolute, but I was under the impression that meant over vampires, not us. I know in my gut that somehow David Solomon tampered with the DNA, but our lab has airtight security and I can't prove it. But if he did it once he can do it a dozen times, so trying to prosecute either of them is pointless. There's really nothing I can do but step back and let it happen—even if every cop bone in my body knows it's wrong."

She swallowed her now-tasteless toast. "If you keep digging you can always find evidence—that's what you used to tell me."

"Well, that's before I had a beer with the things that go bump in the night. Myers's career and life are on the line here too. If we keep tilting at Miranda Grey and coming up empty it's going to ruin both of us. Once the charges are officially dropped I'm going to gather up everything on all of these cases and hand it over to Solomon, along with the original video of the murder. It's a huge breach of procedure and all the rules, but staying alive is more important to me these days—and keeping you safe."

"Dad, Miranda adores you," she insisted. "And David may be…scary…but he's fair. Neither of them is going to hold you responsible for anything APD does."

"They're not even my big worry. They have powerful friends, and powerful enemies who aren't as kind to humans. The fact is we don't know where that video came from. Someone did it to manipulate the police into investigating what they wanted us to. I'm not going to be somebody's dancing monkey just to give them a shot at the Signets."

Stella tried not to let her relief be too obvious, but she wanted to hug him until he squeaked—she was so, so grateful he was doing the smart thing, even if it wasn't the Law Enforcement Right Thing. APD was out of its depth here, and he knew it, and if he pushed too hard he could get good men killed in the pointless pursuit of David and Miranda Solomon.

As she made her way back to the hotel, though, a box of leftover French toast in her hand to warm up for breakfast, she wondered how to ask Miranda if any of it was true...and deep down, Stella knew it was. She wanted to know more—why they were doing this, what they gained from it. It probably had something to do with the Thirdborn thing, but why? What had they received in return for such a sentence? Or did the ancient instincts of the Thirdborn just need to kill? Was it food, or fun?

She couldn't think of Miranda murdering anyone. She just couldn't. David, she certainly could, probably because he was so much older and, as she'd told her father, scary. Miranda could certainly be fierce and dangerous, but she was still much closer to human. David liked Stella, but there were moments Stella looked at the Prime and knew without a doubt that the man in front of her was not human...not even a vampire the way the others were. The full extent of that had yet to claw its way out of its chrysalis, just as with Miranda...so what was it waiting for? And God, what on Earth could be waiting in there? It was all well and good to say they were an older form of vampire, made by the hand of the Goddess Herself, but...did any of them have a clue what that really meant?

And if Nico never recovered from all of this, could they ever find out? That summoning spell he'd half-translated made one thing clear: all eight members of the Circle had to be there, along with one additional participant to actually do the spell. Stella had assumed, perhaps naively, that the reason she kept escaping death was that Persephone wanted her to be that participant, to help open the gate between Her and Her wayward children. If Stella was chosen for that, Seph would do everything She could even from the other side of reality to make sure Stella lived to see that night.

Everything depended on that ritual. Naturally Persephone would want Her priestess protected.

Some Witches might have felt important, knowing that.

Stella was scared shitless.

And now, with Nico "gone," she had no one to talk to about it.

She'd missed those nights, back before Jonathan died and Nico had come to Earth, when she and Miranda had eaten ice cream and just laughed about the kind of nonsense young women laughed about. A few hours here and there of avoiding reality could be really therapeutic.

Come to think of it...when had that stopped? Right around that time...around the time things got busy, yes, but also when it became clear that David and Miranda were going to be the lynchpin around which the Circle spun...could that have been when Miranda started killing humans? It would explain why almost all of Stella's overtures were gently but firmly brushed off. Miranda knew Stella had the Sight, and who knew what Stella might pick up from a casual touch or an unguarded moment? Miranda had been trying to shield her from the truth, which was as touching as it was infuriating.

"You should be indoors by now," came a voice that nearly sent her out of her skin. "Storm's coming."

Stella spun around, hoping her guards were fast enough to— "Christ, Deven, don't *do* that!"

The Prime smiled slightly. "My apologies. I forget sometimes that your hearing isn't as good as ours."

Stella snorted. "I've seen you do the same thing to David. It's not vampires, it's just you."

The smile broadened a hair. He bowed slightly. "May I walk you back to the hotel?"

"Um...sure."

This was a weird one. She'd been in Deven's mind, was more familiar with what made him tick than a lot of people, but she couldn't think of a time they'd been alone together. In fact she wasn't sure she'd ever stood this close to him; walking beside her, he was a good inch shorter, and she wasn't even wearing platforms.

His reasoning for joining her became clear momentarily. "Is there something you want to ask me, Stella?"

She let out a breath. "I get it. Okay. But that means you already know the question."

"And if you're asking me instead of Miranda, that means you already know the answer."

Damn logic. "I guess I do."

"It's unfortunate that your father had to get mixed up in all this—there was no way it was going to end in a triumphant conviction and justice for all. Between David's IQ and their net worth, there was no way Miranda was ever going to jail—now or in the future."

"That's what my dad said."

"You don't seem terribly upset finding out your idol is a killer."

"My idol is a vampire," she pointed out. "Finding out she *wasn't* a killer was a shock. Most of my ideas about vampires came from TV, but I know you don't get as powerful as you guys are on the bunny diet." She looked around at the slowly-quieting city, the thinning crowds. "I feel bad for her, really. I know she's not the killing kind—in defense of what she loves, sure, but just for food...I can't imagine how hard that is, even if they find nothing but bad guys."

"She's dreadful at it," Deven affirmed Stella's earlier thoughts bluntly with a nod. "That's why she got caught in the first place— guilt makes people stupid. In this day and age, and given her husband has the entire United States wired up with sensors, it's foolish to think there's a corner anywhere without cameras on it. Very few can get a good picture of us, but all it takes is one at a lucky angle. David knows that. She's got to accept that dark deeds have to be done in the dark."

"Speaking of which..." She trailed off, but again, she didn't have to ask.

He shook his head, eyes on the ground. "He nearly killed a human tonight—she was lucky I stopped him when I did or she might not have made it. I don't think he really planned to...I could feel something...something set him off." A moment later he lifted his gaze back to her. "I don't suppose you have any ideas how I could reach him? You know him better than anyone else here."

"I did. But I don't think I knew anything different from what you know—he's—he was—endlessly kind, compassionate. Brilliant, really funny in a dry sort of way. He's always been a little sad, for obvious reasons, but underneath that was this kind of quiet, unquenchable hope that I think came from his spiritual life. Once he became a vampire he lost that—or, he ran from it, because he didn't believe Theia would want him anymore, and had no way to know if Persephone would take him in."

Deven had stopped walking, and she looked back to see a stricken expression on his face. "After he spent all that time trying to heal me from exactly that kind of pain...he drowned in it himself...and I had no idea."

She shrugged. "I don't know if that can help you now. But what will help is—"

"Taking down the barrier, I know. But unless you have a way to dampen the power that will flood him when I take it down, I have no way to do it without killing him. He could probably do it himself, but I'm guessing the likelihood of that is somewhere in the 'fuck off' area."

Stella shook her head, frustrated. "I wish I knew what to tell you. My magical career up to meeting you people was mostly tarot readings, money spells, and one really ill-advised love spell for a friend that luckily ended up getting her a dog instead of a dude."

"Lower maintenance," he remarked. "More comfortable to share a bed with. But men have their positives, too."

"Like reaching things on high shelves?" she asked, deadpan.

He grinned and inclined his head to the right. "We're here."

She grinned back. "Thanks for the company."

"Be safe."

He faded from sight, leaving her smiling at nothing in front of a ritzy hotel. Stella glanced over and noticed one of the hotel staff—a bellhop, maybe? Did people still use that word?—giving her an odd look. She cleared her throat, squared off her shoulders, and strode up the sidewalk to the grand double doors, trying not to look like a goat hopping up to a banquet and chewing on the tablecloth. Like Miranda had said, the secret was to walk like you need fear no evil because you were the biggest, baddest motherfucker in the Valley of the Shadow, even if you were, like Deven, a slight 5'7" eternal teenager or, like David, wearing a Donkey Kong t-shirt under your trench coat.

Miranda had said it hadn't come naturally to her. Stella wasn't totally sure she believed that—the Queen seemed like she'd been born with a Signet around her neck. But there was definitely something to the theory, and Stella imagined she could pull authority and power up around her like it was a black leather coat, sweeping in past the doormen with a smile and nod of acknowledgment, headed for the elevator like she already owned the place.

Are you out there? Can you hear me?

David didn't really remember his mother. He had fairly clear recollections of his father, mostly surrounding the forge and the sound of a hammer striking metal, but he also remembered his father drawing out plans for machine parts he was making for...a windmill, perhaps? Or something like that? It was something the town council had hired him to build. David's mother, however, had died when he was ten, expelling a stillborn child conceived far too late in life for her safety.

Still, that night as he lay on his side on the couch ignoring his inbox, he found himself wondering about her, trying to remember what she'd looked like. He'd been born essentially a carbon copy of his father, so she might have looked like anything, though most of the villagers were painfully drab and ordinary in appearance. She was probably a brunette, with brown eyes or hazel, skin milky pale from the lack of sunlight in their bleak region of England—but she might have been unusually tall. His father had been several inches shorter than David, as were all the men of their line. David wasn't exactly a giant but for the time, he was considered one.

He closed his eyes and tried to call up her image. The shape of a woman, round-hipped and strong-backed, began to form, standing on the far end of the wooden bridge that led into town over the burbling creek where everyone got their water. She was dressed like most of the women in town, in plain-colored and unadorned but beautifully woven and sewn clothing, her hair tucked up under a bonnet.

In his mind, she noticed someone was approaching, and turned toward him—and as she did, her clothing began to morph, turning black, its hem dropping down to the ground and losing its edges so it seemed to blur into the mist that began to rise around her. Hair as red as old wine cascaded down over her shoulders and nearly to her waist, scandalously unbound.

The bridge, the village, the creek all disappeared. They were standing in a forest, the sky above filled with stars. The Haven, too, faded from sight, the light of the fireplace concentrating into the jewel at her throat.

Silver-black, luminous eyes met his.

The reaction was as immediate as it was instinctive: he crossed the space formerly occupied by the bridge and knelt before Her.

Her hand touched his head, and a wash of power like nothing he knew in the real world spilled down over him. Everything that had been tense and afraid in the last week felt soothed, as if there was no such thing as fear in this place.

This place...

"No," She said with an affectionate smile. "You are not dead. Rise, child."

"Then how am I here?" he asked. "Is this a dream?"

"It is, and is not. There are avenues of consciousness down which I can walk even now, to drop into the dreams of the others, but you are the only one who can come here."

"Why me?"

She tilted her head to the side.

He had to smile at that, both because it was a dumb question and because her expression was such a Miranda thing to do. "Well, okay. But still. Why show up at this particular moment?"

"You have been calling Me."

"I have? Oh...I have, haven't I." He hadn't even realized that was what he was doing, but he'd been silently conversing with Her for months, embarrassingly the same way people often did with God, basically either complaining or bargaining. "Sorry."

"It is I who am sorry, My son. I want nothing more than to give you the help you need—the help you deserve after all you and your family have endured. Even were I close enough to speak to all of you face to face at will, there are limits to My intervention in the world of form. We are all subject to natural law except in rare cases. My power must come through one of you to affect reality."

"Like Drawing Down the Moon," he mused.

"Just so. I find it easy to work through young Stella as she has training in her Craft."

"So what kind of Craft are we going to need to help Nico?"

Sadness entered Her dark eyes, and She looked up at the night sky. He wondered what She was seeing—clearly something more than stars, or perhaps stars were wonder enough. "That is why I am here now. You already know: only one thing can help Nico."

"Breaking the barrier."

"Yes. Right now his mind and heart are dangerously imbalanced—until now he was able to maintain balance because of the strength of his heart, but no longer."

"He needs to be hit with that much love to balance out the hate?"

"Not hate. The opposite of hate is indifference, not love. Love informs the entire universe—its opposite is nonexistence. Love and hate are remarkably similar in that regard, but only one endures beyond death, and only one heals. Nico does not need a sorcerer; he needs a healer."

"But Deven said he can't lower the barrier without killing Nico. It's too much power."

"Deven is afraid."

"You mean he's wrong?"

"Far more often than he would care to admit."

"How am I supposed to convince him of that? I can't force him to take it down."

"Force is not necessary. There are much gentler, and more effective, methods of persuasion. You and your beloved have everything you need—yourselves. It is by your hands that Deven can lay down his fear."

"And what about Nico, in that case? The power wouldn't overwhelm him?"

"Are you certain that would be a bad thing?"

"It wouldn't kill him?"

"He is far stronger than even you know. Regardless... blackening eyes are not your only new ability, child. Channeling and controlling power of that magnitude is part of what you were made for."

"It is? Why?"

David thought he saw a slight smile. "That will have to wait."

"And where exactly do we learn to do that?"

"One of you already knows."

He raised an eyebrow. "Miranda. She learned Weaving before Jonathan died—but she claims she forgot how. She's wrong, too?"

Now She was definitely smiling. "Far more often than she would care to admit."

Slowly, he nodded. "I think I understand."

"Good. You are about to wake up—I would hate for our meeting to end without you learning what you needed to."

"I have about a thousand questions for You," he said. He could feel the vision, or whatever it was, beginning to dissolve, its edges unraveling like fabric. He held onto it as long as he could. "I don't even know where to—"

She smiled again, reached out, and touched his face. He fell silent; in fact, the urge to kneel again was difficult to resist...almost as difficult as the urge to throw himself into Her arms...but he sensed doing that, while probably as comforting as he hoped, would do far more to him than he was ready to deal with right now.

"Every time you come to Me, you will be further changed," She told him quietly. "You have always been a warrior—you are becoming My warrior, and that is an even greater burden than the one you bear around your neck. But I chose you for a reason. There are no four creatures in the World of Shadow more worthy or better suited to My lineage. Fear not, my son...by the time you need it, you will have full knowledge, and full power."

He nodded. "As You will it...wait, *four?* What do you mean four?"

Too late.

David jolted awake to see worried green eyes peering down at him.

"I said, it's after four," Miranda said, stepping back out of flailing range. "It's been a long night—you should come to bed."

He was breathing hard, momentarily confused. Where—the Suite, the couch. He'd fallen asleep. The sound of wind in trees was fading from his mind...but what he'd learned was not.

"Are you okay?" the Queen asked, sitting down next to him and taking his hands, drawing him upright. "You look like you've seen a ghost."

"Not exactly, but..." He met her eyes, a spark of hope kindling in his chest. He squeezed her hands, leaned forward and kissed her firmly; she was giving him a dubious look as he leaned back, like she wasn't entirely sure about his sanity.

"It's okay, beloved," he said. "I think I have an idea."

Chapter Thirteen

For a couple of days Miranda walked around fairly sure her husband had lost his mind.

Soon enough, however, she began to realize he might have stumbled on their only viable option at this point.

At first she'd flat-out refused to try the magic again. The first time she'd used it had been awful...but it had worked. She'd blundered through it, but she'd been able to un-bind the Pair and bind Deven to her and David. Compared to the magnitude of reworking Signet bonds, the idea of breaking through a barrier wasn't nearly as intimidating.

She didn't even have to bring it down all the way—just push it open wide enough that its own energy would break it like a dam. After that it was a matter of standing between Prime and Consort and helping dampen the wave to keep it from killing either of them. With her on one side of it and David on the other, their strength combined with whatever Weaving knowledge she could recall could do it. She knew, in her bones, that they could.

Honestly it was less the idea and more the execution that left her speechless.

Still, at this point it was just an idea. They didn't have a whole lot of time to waste before Nico did something disastrous and unrecoverable, but she couldn't just jump into it without at least *trying* to remember what she'd learned in her dreams two years ago.

She could hammer at the barrier with sheer force of will and probably knock it over, assuming she could get in past Deven's shields...but she didn't want to traumatize either of the Pair any further. She had to believe that magic as ancient as the Signets would find its way to balance once that initial surge had passed. Everyone just had to survive that long.

Miranda leaned her head on her piano and shut her eyes, groping after the vision. How had she found it before? She remembered little of how she'd done it; that night had been so catastrophic it was hard to hold onto any part of it willingly.

Nothing came to mind. She might as well have been trying to remember someone else's life.

On the other hand...she did remember another time that the Web had shown up in her mind. She'd been high as a kite, thanks to Deven's Better Living Through Illegal Pharmaceuticals program, but it was still before the explosion. The night of the wedding had been a good one...she'd felt happy enough to burst for her friends. She remembered the club, and its noise and teeming crowds; she remembered being surprised, and yet not really, when Deven kissed her, giving her the E-21 he had on his tongue. She wondered now...had that been an excuse? She was pretty sure the list of women he'd made out with was list-able on one hand.

Don't get distracted. Keep going. What happened then?

The drug had kicked in quickly, and she'd seen it...the curtain of reality parting, as Deven had said, letting her see behind it.

There it was. The memory glimmered in her mind's eye: thousands of threads of light, informing everything around her, herself included. She had been terrified at first, but he'd reassured her: *Find out what it wants.* It had just wanted to dance with her.

And if it could dance, could she play it?

Miranda didn't move her head, but reached down and lifted the lid off the keyboard, fingers finding their places out of years of practice. She knew the chords didn't really matter: it was the motion, the undulation of matter and space making love to itself. That's all any of it was, really. The universe in love.

She kept her eyes closed and started playing, improvising a slow and rolling melody. She held the image of the Web in her mind, not trying to do anything with it, just letting it be there; even though it was just a memory, before long, it started to move.

She didn't dare touch it. Not yet. And just playing wasn't going to be enough. But for now it was enough to watch from a place beyond fear. Before she could become too drained, she wound the music down, giving herself time to withdraw. It had been little more than a meditation but she had to be careful.

When she opened her eyes, she finally sensed she wasn't alone. She turned her head to see Stella standing in the doorway, eyes huge.

"What the hell were you just doing?" the Witch asked.

Miranda considered the piano in front of her. "I don't really know," she answered. "Just experimenting with something. What did it look like?"

Stella hovered in the doorway and said, "It looked like Weaving."

"It did? Good."

The Queen had to take a moment to ground, hands on the piano lid. She made herself breathe in fours: four counts in, hold for four, four counts exhale, hold for four.

She was tempted to ask Stella for help—Stella had been learning Weaving arts, after all—but she wasn't quite ready for the Witch to know what she and David were up to. Right now she wanted to get used to the magic on her own terms.

Finally she looked over at Stella and said, "You're back."

"Yeah...I didn't check out of the hotel, I just wanted to see how things felt here. I knew if anything had changed you'd call, but...this place feels like home now. It's hard to stay away. Funny, really."

"Not that funny." Miranda smiled, thinking back. "There was a time I was still human and fell in love with this place. This life gets in your blood somehow."

Stella half-smiled. Her demeanor was unusually serious—given the situation Miranda couldn't blame her for losing some of her sparkle. "Was it the place, or the owner?"

The Queen chuckled. "Both. I think even at the very beginning, when I was a screwed-up shell of a person scared of everything and without hope, I knew this—he—was where I belonged."

Nodding, Stella said a little too casually, "I bet you never thought you'd end up killing people."

At first, Miranda didn't get it, and jumped to the wrong conclusion: "The Blackthorn were killing all over the city, and they did kill me. I didn't think twice about defending what was mine."

Stella's eyebrow lifted. "But before that...the night you came here, you killed humans."

Miranda had been through enough since that night, and had learned enough, that talking about it wasn't as hard as it had been. "I don't know if I'd classify them as human. Or maybe human but not people. Either way...I regretted it for a while, the fact of ending lives. I don't anymore."

"Because of people like Annalise Vitera?"

The Queen froze. Suddenly Stella's behavior and tone made perfect, terrible sense. She'd been to visit her father, Miranda knew, and between whatever the Detective had said and what the Witch's intuition must be telling her...

Miranda sat back, crossing her arms. She cared too much for Stella to keep bullshitting her; and there was no way to sugarcoat it, either. "You know that when David returned from the dead there was a price. In order to serve Persephone he had to become something new. To regain our bond I had to make that same choice. Once in the month, on the dark of the Moon, we have to kill. It wasn't something we knew specifically going in, but it was clear there would be consequences. There's only so much power a vampire can attain without the power of death."

Stella didn't react quite the way a normal human would have. She looked down at the floor for a minute and then nodded. "You don't seem too upset about it."

"I hate it, Stella. I love what I am, and who I am. But I hate what I have to do. Please, please remember something: Every single one of our kind *wants* to kill. Every cell in my body fights with my will, every time I hunt, not to drink until there's nothing left. We're born starving. A lot of us are still good people in spite of it, but the facts are the facts. We were built as predators...hell, we're practically the ultimate predator. Not only are we bloodthirsty and fast and strong, we can pass among our prey unnoticed for years."

"So you enjoy it?"

"Yes." Miranda said bluntly, but added, "Not for the reason you might think. David and I use our empathy to find the evil ones so that we can live with ourselves and to make something at least marginally good out of a tough situation. But I'll tell you the truth...it's a *relief* to stop fighting for a night. It's like handing over this huge burden—putting it in Persephone's hands once a month.

Is it okay? Not even remotely. For a long time I haven't even been able to admit there was anything satisfying about it. But there is. In a twisted sort of way it's like She's given us a reward."

Strange. Up until this very moment she hadn't been able to articulate any of that. Was it telling Stella that made it easier, or was it what she'd just been doing with the Web? Those endless strands of light were the truth of the universe. Maybe touching that truth made all truth easier to speak.

"I suppose the question is whether *you* can live with it," Miranda told her. "You don't have to. You can go back to the hotel and then leave town—we can take care of it for you. You can even take your father if he'll go."

Stella smiled sadly. "No, I can't. I'm bound up in this too, remember? There's work for me to do. Knowing that you have no choice doesn't exactly make it better, but it does make it easier. Look what I'd be giving up if I walked away—you're my friend. And if we ever get Nico back...I want to be there for that. And I want to help you burn Morningstar to the ground if I can." She shrugged. "Just don't ask me to kill anyone."

"I would never do that."

"I know. That's a big reason I'm staying. I just had to hear the truth from you—I had to know you'd tell me the truth."

Miranda regarded her quietly for a while before saying, "Your father knows I'm guilty, doesn't he—he just knows he can't win."

"Yeah." Stella leaned against the doorframe; normally she would have come in and flopped into one of the music room chairs, but her emotional aura was more troubled than she was letting on in her words, and Miranda didn't comment on it. She'd need time to process it even if she thought she already had. Some people never could deal with the reality of what Miranda was...like Kat.

Miranda looked down and pretended to fiddle with the piano lid to hide the way her eyes started burning. She tried not to think about Kat, had stopped having her watched once it was clear the human was not a target of any kind. She had to let her friend go, had to let everything in her life that was human go, eventually.

Even if Stella was genuinely okay with what Miranda did, their friendship had an expiration date, and the longer Stella was involved with the Shadow World the sooner that date could come. Detective Maguire probably understood that and wanted to warn his daughter away in whatever way he could.

And worse yet…Miranda's always-helpful precog gift was buzzing in the back of her mind, telling her that soon Stella's loyalty would be tested by more than dead drug dealers and rapists…that along with the storms outside something was building in this house.

"What did David do, exactly, to fix the case?" Stella asked. "I mean I assume it was him, since Dad said the DNA wasn't a match and that seems like David's area."

Miranda finally summoned a smile. "I can't tell you that."

"You think I'd blab to my dad?"

"I would, if I were you. But what I meant was I don't really know how to explain it to you. I could just say the samples were switched, but that doesn't cover it. Ask David—he might tell you. Or he might just fire off a bunch of science-y technobabble."

Stella actually grinned at that. "Yeah I guess he would. And he'd think he was explaining it perfectly."

"Then he'd look at you like you were an idiot when you told him he was babbling, yes. It's one of his more infuriating qualities."

"Can I ask you something about you guys—all of you, I mean? Are there a lot of vampire computer geniuses?"

Miranda slid off the bench and picked up her coat, slinging it over her shoulders as she left the music room. Stella fell into step beside her without hesitation.

"No," Miranda began, heading toward the study where the ice cream stash lived. "Vampires are actually kind of hostile toward progress. You should have seen when all the Signets were here for the Council Summit—a bunch of sexist, racist, privileged assholes, with a few glowing exceptions. Jacob and Deven have always been David's allies, so he shared his tech with them, and also with a few others, like Prime Tanaka of Japan. The rest are basically old men sitting on the front porch waving rifles, yelling 'you danged kids get off my lawn!'"

Stella laughed, starting to lose some of her seriousness, which was Miranda's goal. For now, the less Stella thought about the fact that she was surrounded by killers, the better. "Best mental image ever."

"Then there was Prime Hart—that's the jackass Olivia replaced. I almost wish you could have met him so you could know the worst of what's possible for vampires of our caliber."

"I think I'll pass on getting to know the worst. He's the one that kept Cora as a slave, right?"

"Her and dozens of others over the years. Imagine how many amazing women and how much potential he killed with his tiny little dick and his massive ego."

"How do you know he had a tiny dick?"

"Well, for a long time I had no proof. I just figured a guy with masculinity issues like that, terrified of gays and women, had to have been compensating for something. But Cora confirmed it— blushed so hard I thought her face might explode, but she did, once she had something to compare it to. And Deven said something about the way he walked it was almost 100% sure he had, as Dev put it, a 'third pinkie.'"

Stella was laughing hard enough to lose her breath now, and Miranda understood why when the Witch said, "So...since David's openly bi and doesn't give a shit what anyone says about his masculinity...can I assume..."

Miranda grinned wickedly, holding open the study door. "You may," she replied. "And the boys have been vague about it, but if he's to be believed, Deven has nothing to be ashamed of either."

"I didn't need to know that!" Stella giggled. "How can I look at either of them in the face if I'm thinking about how they walk compared to the size of their...artillery?"

"You know what they say," Miranda replied. "It's not the size of the army, it's the fury of its onslaught. Hart let other people do his fighting for him. Both of my boys can take down a dozen Elite in five minutes. That's some fury."

They were both giggling madly as Miranda shut the door behind them.

MIRANDA GREY CLEARED OF SUSPICION IN AUSTIN MURDER

All charges against singer Miranda Grey have been dropped, representatives of Austin Police Department reported on Friday. Forensic DNA testing determined Grey could not have been the attacker in the murder of Austin resident Annalise Vitera.

Following the announcement, the reclusive singer released a statement to the media, saying, "I would like to thank the Detectives involved in this case for their professionalism and commitment to the truth. They are a credit to the Department and I wish them good luck in finding the killer and bringing him or her to justice. I hope we can all put this behind us and get back to work."

There was yet another line of severe thunderstorms charging over the Hill Country that night, but for the moment, there was a lull—a tense, almost creepy silence beneath a flat black sky. A tropical storm in the Pacific had strewn bands of storms across the Southwest and the rain would keep coming for another night or two.

The gardens around the Haven were saturated with days of rainfall, and anywhere one stepped off the path threatened to turn into a morass of mud, but Deven had no interest in wandering in the woods; he had been sitting on a bench for over an hour, knees pulled up, first reading the news report on his phone and then just staring at one of the night-blooming gardens where a few stalwart flowers had thus far resisted drowning.

It was as he'd told Stella several nights ago: the police had no hope whatsoever of standing up to the combined forces of wealth, privilege, and genius. It had been a kindness on David's part to put an end to the situation as quickly as he had—he could have let things drag out, wasting taxpayer money and time until he could make a far more dramatic gesture once the case went to court. Of course, that would require them to figure out how the hell to even try a case against someone who couldn't go outside during daylight. At least now, as Miranda said, they could all get back to their lives.

Whatever that meant.

The police had wasted little time: Stella had seen her father Wednesday night, and Friday afternoon APD officially dropped the charges. Miranda's statement had come just before sunset and was already all over the news.

He shifted uncomfortably on the bench. His skin felt like it was on too tight—he'd been trying to ignore the healing energy again. He didn't want to go into town tonight. He just wanted peace and quiet. He'd already spent most of Wednesday—before he confronted Nico about his feeding habits in such spectacularly unsuccessful fashion—slipping from clinic to clinic and looking for humans he could heal without causing a stir. He'd been to the Heart Hospital this week, and to a private children's cancer hospital, but then shifted his attention to the poorer sections of town where the ailments weren't as dire but their consequences could be. If the sole breadwinner of a household was too ill to work, the children couldn't eat. Older kids would end up whoring or selling drugs, or both. Having done both himself at a similar age Deven couldn't help but Mist past security and take care of the problem.

He smiled at himself sadly. Sentimental fool.

Jonathan would have been pleased. He had always thought Deven should use his power the way he was using it now; not on such a scale, and not at the risk of pain, but just as a way to do something good both for himself and other people. It might help him learn not to hate the gift. Vampires couldn't benefit from healing talent to the extent that humans could; it was a waste, the Consort said, to hold it back from those who needed it.

"You don't understand—it's not a gift, Jonathan. It's what got me tortured, imprisoned, cast out. You don't know what any of that feels like."

"It was seven centuries ago, Dev. Don't you think it's time you made use of what God gave you?"

"God doesn't give. He doesn't heal. God only kills. We were all made in His image, remember?"

He couldn't recall the reply. It was an argument they'd had a number of times before Jonathan had finally dropped it. Now, if he'd had a chance, Deven would have apologized to him...for that, for everything, a thousand times.

What he'd told Nico was true. More nights than not he still woke up screaming, and no wardrobe change or arsenal would take away the horror of feeling Jonathan trapped under the Haven, under the wreckage of their life together, crushed by it, only the light of a cell phone for comfort in those last moments. He dreamed of falling asleep in Jonathan's endlessly safe embrace and woke clawing in the dark trying to save him...or Nico...or Miranda...just like in the nightmares, not one of them had come away from loving Deven unscathed.

He wished desperately that he hadn't burned the last of his heroin. If he wanted more he'd have to go into Austin, and if he did that he'd just end up at the hospital again.

The thought of drugs, however, gave him an idea that might provide something of a distraction: Needles. He'd begun to miss the spike through his tongue lately, the familiar tap-tap of the metal against the back of his teeth. While he was at it he could put a ring back through one eyebrow, perhaps two.

He took a deep breath, let it go slowly, and got to his feet, thankful to have something to focus on. He couldn't let emotion creep back up over him and drag him into the black water of despair like before. He owed it to the others to keep it together, or at least together enough to function.

He only made it a few steps before he felt something very strange in the air.

It felt like lightning building in the sky, but the clouds overhead weren't to that point yet—centuries of reading the weather had taught him that they had another forty-five minutes before the storm arrived in earnest, and about thirty before cloud-to-ground lightning became a real threat. But there was electricity in the air...he felt the hair on the back of his neck standing up, and turned in a circle, one hand on Ghostlight's hilt while he tried to pinpoint the source.

There...

A few yards away, something weird was happening to a patch of the darkness. It became almost watery, shimmering, an incongruously perfect oval forming and blocking out the view behind it.

Deven's heartbeat stepped up. He had seen this before that terrible morning on the roof in Austin when Nico had teleported himself from the Haven covered in blood. Nico used the same power to augment his Misting ability, but when he did it there was no disturbance in the air like this, which meant it could only be—

He smiled and waited. It was about time. Perhaps—

A tiny shaft of light pierced the center of the portal, widening, becoming blinding. There was a blast of warmth, the scent of trees and wind...

...Deven stared.

The figure that emerged from the portal was tall, proud, dressed in long robes. Distinctly pointed ears poked up through waist-length dark hair. With the light silhouetting the Elf it could easily have been Kai.

There was just one problem.

The light faded, and he realized three things: One, the Elf's hair was not black, but a shining dark brown; two, where Deven was expecting deep violet eyes, these were paler, almost lavender; and three...this was a woman.

She was beautiful, but in a different way than the twins; her beauty was ethereal, every inch the creature from a distant world, spun delicately out of sunlight and stars. There was no shadow behind her eyes as they had. Even in the first few seconds it was obvious she was a very different sort of Elf.

She stared at him. He stared at her.

When she spoke it was in Elvish, and while her face had an indefinable familiarity, her voice was so familiar he couldn't breathe. There was a gentle sadness in her words. "You look so like your mother."

It took him a moment to find his voice. "You."

She bowed, just as both Nico and Kai always did. "Leselena Ithidaria," she said. "Do you know who I am?"

"I do."

She took a step closer, lifting a hand, but he moved back away from her reflexively.

"Long have I wished to see you again," she told him. "To ask your forgiveness. If I had known you lived—"

"It doesn't matter," he cut her off. "Why are you here now? Did Kai send you to help Nico?"

Her expression took on a level of urgency that immediately worried him. "What has happened to Nico? And where is Kai? I had assumed he would be meeting me at the portal."

"He's not here," Deven replied. "He went back to Avilon, I assume to find you, a week ago."

She paled a shade. "No...he never returned to Avilon. The Speaking Stone called to me, brought me a message from him days ago saying he needed my help, but he did not mention coming home to fetch me. When I heard nothing further I began to worry."

"But...then...where is he?"

Lesela shook her head. "I do not know."

They stared at each other again, realization and horror both dawning, and he held her eyes as he lifted his wrist and said, "Star-One."

Chapter Fourteen

An important part of staying in the Shadow World ruling class was making a sufficiently intimidating first impression. David Solomon was a master of the art...most of the time.

It just so happened that at the moment Deven opened the office door, David was leaning back in his chair, staring up at the ceiling, arms crossed over a Keep Austin Weird shirt he'd stolen from Miranda, reading glasses propped up on his head while he juggled a handful of miniature Nutter Butters with his mind.

Periodically he'd open his mouth and let one of the cookies fall in, while another floated out of the package and took its place overhead.

Thanks to centuries of practice he didn't drop them all when the door opened—instead they froze in midair as he sat up and started to say something about how it was considered polite to knock.

Deven stepped into the office, beckoning to someone behind him, and said wryly, "Allow me to introduce David Solomon, Prime of the Southern United States, Thirdborn child of Persephone...and his snacks."

David frowned, returned the remaining cookies to the package, and said, "Fine control is the same with telekinesis as swordplay—it takes constant practice. But you said you needed to tell me something -"

The sentence died on his lips as the figure behind Deven entered the room.

David's first thought was that she looked just like her grandson.

Deven hadn't mentioned a newcomer—he'd told David to stay where he was, that there was a problem he'd rather talk about in person. But how many Elves could there be who'd show up on his doorstep?

The resemblance really was uncanny. She had the same proud bearing, a spine that seemed made of steel; her eyes were that same pale lavender, and they had the same natural hair color, though Deven had gone back to black a few days ago. Seeing her, everything about Deven's appearance and demeanor made perfect sense—all he lacked were the ears.

"Leselena Ithidaria, Prophet and Healer of Avilon," Deven said. Lesela bowed.

David rose and echoed her motion. "Welcome to the Haven of the South," he said in Elvish, surprising her. "May I assume you're here to help us with our Nicolanai situation?"

She looked over at Deven. "I do not know much about the situation...but there is another that may be more urgent."

He lifted his chin inquisitively, but it was Deven who answered. "Kai is missing, David. He sent a message to Lesela a week ago that he needed her to come, but he never reached home."

"He went missing *a week ago?*" David all but exclaimed in astonishment. "And you're just now doing anything about it?"

Lesela's ears turned pink, and her expression guilty. "There was nothing I could do to come faster. Nico's power casts all other Weavers into the shade; it takes six of them days to build a portal he could create himself in hours. I tried using the Speaking Stone to contact either twin."

"Nico has the Speaking Stone," Deven said quietly. "God knows where it is now."

"Please," Lesela said. "Tell me what is going on with Nico. The things I have imagined must be far worse."

"I doubt that," David replied. "Why don't we escort Lesela to a guest suite and talk there."

"Where's Miranda?" Deven asked. "We need her here too."

"In town. She and her management held a press conference after the official exoneration announcement. She should be back in an hour, maybe two."

He led them out of the office and down the hall, grinning slightly at the way the guards stared at their newest arrival. They'd gotten used to Nico, especially once he was a vampire; Kai was stared at with equal fascination, but he'd been coming and going for months and had mostly been accepted as part of the family. But here was another Elf, this one female and an example of what they "normally" looked like, gliding down the hallway in a floor-length robe looking, David was sure they noticed, an awful lot like the Prime of the West.

He saw immediately that Deven kept his distance from Lesela. She darted a few curious looks at Deven—David could tell she had a hundred questions—but he determinedly avoided eye contact. His coldness clearly saddened Lesela but it was doubtful she'd expected tearful hugs and family bonding. Nico had said that she felt incredible guilt for leaving Deven in the human world when the Elves withdrew to their sanctuaries, but that once the Veil was sealed the governing body of Avilon had forbidden anyone return to Earth.

David had laughed at that—mostly out of pride—because Nico had not hesitated one second in punching a hole in the Veil when he learned he was needed. The Enclave had been furious when he returned. Nico hadn't given much of a damn about that either. David wondered if his rebellious spirit had inspired Lesela to step between worlds when the rest of her people wouldn't dare.

"You said the other Weavers sent you here," David said, turning to her. "Does that mean your travel was approved by the Enclave?"

Lesela sighed. "They were only too happy to excommunicate Nico, despite his power and renown, but were determined to keep Kai in the fold. It was only when he threatened to leave Avilon forever that they stopped haranguing him for visiting here. Finding out he was in trouble…they were not happy about my coming, thinking this world would swallow me as it has the twins, but if they wanted him back, what choice did they have?"

"Not to speak ill of your people, Lesela, but I think if I ever meet your Enclave I may kick them all in the Elf-business."

She blinked at the terminology, but the meaning was clear enough. "I would happily stand back and watch," she said in a low voice touched with surprising anger. "They are hidebound and afraid, and it has made them small in mind and heart. I understand that fear—many have scars, visible or not, from what the humans did to them. But we have remained too long in our idyll, and our people have stagnated. The humans did not end our race but our own stubbornness might."

"Well why would you want to come back?" Deven asked bitterly. "It's not as if you left behind anything that mattered."

Lesela closed her eyes for a second. "I did not know you were still alive. You must understand—"

"No, I mustn't," Deven cut her off. "I told you, it's not important. What is important is finding Kai and figuring out how to help Nico. The sooner we do that the sooner you can go back."

Wisely, she dropped the matter. David considered asking more pointed questions to force a conversation, but now didn't seem the time—Deven was right, for now. They needed to focus on the twins.

They reached the suite David had picked out; Lesela hadn't brought much in the way of luggage, and set her single bag on the bed before coming to sit with them in front of the fireplace.

It didn't take long to catch her up on what had happened. As Deven described what they had seen when they rescued Nico from the Morningstar lab, Lesela's face paled, and her hand rose up to her mouth in mute horror. Finally, she put her head in her hands.

"I want to see him," she said softly. "Can I see him?"

Deven spoke up, this time far more gently; perhaps seeing how upset she was made him more kindly disposed. "I don't think that's a good idea," he said. "He might hurt you, Lesela."

David agreed. "He's not himself. You wouldn't recognize him now."

"Then what shall we do?" she asked.

David looked over at Deven, then back to her. "We have to take down the barrier between the two of them, and hope that rebalancing their bond will bring him back. As long as they're so imbalanced there's no way for him to return to himself."

Lesela turned her gaze on Deven, and it became piercing; David had seen that expression before. She was seeing, or Seeing, more than just the physical. "I am a Healer, not a Weaver," she said. "I can see how badly mangled their connection is, but I am unsure how to fix it. I will help you in any way I can, any way you ask, but this is not my craft."

"Kai seemed to think you could do it," Deven told her, voice cooling off again.

She shrugged. "I cannot say what he intended—he might have wanted me to persuade the other Weavers to help, or he might have had a plan. I am powerful, as a Healer, but as you know, our power is of the body, not the mind. I can serve as a source of energy, of course, and I have a Healer's vision of the Web, which is strong but not as profound as a Weaver's."

"So you're as much use in this as a human." Deven stood up, agitated. "Maybe Kai was just desperate for any idea at all and you were the best he could come up with."

"Deven," David said tiredly, "I understand that you're angry at Lesela, and I don't blame you, but you're being a little bitchier than we really need right now."

"Perhaps it would help you to know—"

"You're right," Deven interrupted Lesela as if he hadn't heard her speak. "I need to take a walk and clear my head. I'll be back in a minute."

He was gone before David could say anything, but he wouldn't have disagreed anyway.

Left with the Elf, David said, "You do understand why he's angry."

"Of course," she said. "I hate what I did. His mother forbade me to take him when he was little, and I should have anyway. She could not have stopped me. I never should have let her send him to those people, that place. When I learned the Enclave intended to seal the Veil I went back to her and begged to know his whereabouts, but by then the Inquisition had already stolen him away and we assumed he was dead."

"He did die," David told her. "It was only by the intervention of the Order of Elysium that he woke again. If you had any idea what he went through in that dungeon, just because of your blood..."

"I can guess." She stared into the fireplace. "So many of our people vanished into those dungeons...a few survived. Some sit on the Enclave now. An entire generation broken and scarred...I know what they did to Healers especially...shattered their hands, from whence the power flowed."

It was David's turn to shut his eyes tightly against the memory: how many times had he seen Deven wake from a nightmare and then spend hours compulsively rubbing his hands together?

Lesela's voice drew him back to the present. "And then there is Deven, a creature unique to all the realms. Part Elf, part human, turned into all vampire, but still retaining the power of our kin...Nico may be the first of that kind born from full blood, but I believe Deven was the first of the Dark Elves."

"You say that like you expect there to be more."

She turned her eyes back on him, and he nearly started. There was something strange in her eyes, a light he'd never seen before...but her expression, somewhat blank yet totally laser-focused, was one he'd seen on the face of nearly every Consort he'd ever met.

"I do," she said. Her voice had taken on a faint hollowness... like something was blowing through her, like she was a musical instrument. "Only through the union of all our blood can we rise from the burning to come and create a world...both new and ancient...and Kai...Kai..."

David leaned forward, listening keenly as her voice fell to a whisper. "What about Kai?"

"This has all happened before," she said. "The Prophet has a plan...now, as he did then, so long ago..."

He tried not to make any noise and shake her out of it, but inside his heart had fallen down to the ground with a resounding thud. Of course...Morningstar had Kai. Who else could it be? The Prophet had done his experiments with Nico because Nico would survive them, but Kai couldn't regenerate like a vampire could. Whatever they'd been trying to do to Nico was just the rehearsal. Now they were ready for opening night.

All they needed was power. All of their high-caliber magic so far had needed the death of a Signet...and David hadn't heard any news of a kidnapping or murder this week. It was likely that, whatever their plans, Kai was still alive.

For the moment.

One day David hoped he'd live in a world where "still alive" didn't always end in "for the moment."

Lesela had fallen silent, but suddenly she said, "I know what you plan to do."

He raised an eyebrow. "Oh?"

"With Deven. To break the barrier."

David sat back, resting his elbows on the chair, and regarded her gravely. "And you think we'll fail?"

Her eyes burned into him for just a second as she Saw whatever it was Elves Saw when they looked at him. "I can help you succeed."

He couldn't help but laugh—not at her confidence, but at the mental image. "Can you now."

229

"Your Queen, the one with Weaving talent. She knows what to do, and you know how to anchor her. But there is something you have overlooked: Although Deven cannot feel it, his is no longer the only barrier between them. In his anger Nico has built one of his own, though he would not recognize it as such. If you only knock down one, and Nico sees what you are doing, he can put it back up again."

Dismayed, David said, "As strong as Deven's is, how are we supposed to take down two, especially against Nico's will?"

"You will need to generate a lot of power. How much confidence do you have in your...talents? Or your Queen's?"

"Absolute," he replied. "Miranda's Weaving skills might not be honed just yet, but she and I are not just some ordinary Pair. She's remade a soul bond with her bare hands. We are Thirdborn—the only two in existence."

"For now," Lesela said softly. "But as I said...not only must you take down two barriers at once, you must do it swiftly."

"I don't think this is the kind of thing you can do with a quickie."

"Then you must find a way to incapacitate Nico so you have time to complete your task. Make him sleep, somehow, and keep him that way. For that you need a Healer."

David nodded, understanding. "So once we manage to convince Deven we know what we're doing, you can put Nico under, and by the time he wakes up it will be done."

"Yes."

"Then we do have a plan."

"Do you, now?"

David froze at the voice and forced himself to look up toward the door. As he did, he caught Lesela's eye, and saw her calm determination turn to fear.

Nico leaned against the doorframe, arms crossed; Deven must have left the door open when he ran off. The Elf was watching them both with open disdain, but David could see that roiling anger in his eyes that hadn't abated since he'd murdered his way out of Morningstar's clutches. He seemed to feed on it more than blood.

She had never seen him as a vampire, let alone as one like this. As if that weren't enough, Morningstar had shorn off his hair, a symbol among Elves of age and wisdom; most never cut theirs at all, or if they had practical jobs where it would get in the way, cut it only to the waist and kept it braided back. David wasn't sure whom he'd gotten to even out the ragged remains, but while he looked absolutely gorgeous with short hair it was, to say the least, a radical change.

Slowly, her hands shaking slightly, Lesela stood and turned to face him. "Nicolanai," she said, swallowing hard. To her credit she squared her shoulders and took a careful approach: "I am glad to see you. We need your help, my friend...your brother is missing."

Nico didn't seem to hear her. "Come to see the show, have you? To carry the news back to Avilon that the Enclave was right to excommunicate me?"

David took a deep breath. It was the first time he'd heard Nico refer to that directly—David had been pretty sure he knew, even though Kai hadn't told him. How could he not know?

David, too, stood up slowly, keeping his distance. "Kai is missing, Nico. We think Morningstar has him. You can help us find him."

"I'm sure he's better off wherever he is," Nico replied dismissively. "The other options are pretty depressing, aren't they? He could be in Avilon, surrounded by sycophants and scared old men, or here, trying desperately to fix his broken brother even though we all know the truth." He pushed himself off the doorframe and took a step forward.

Lesela took a step back, instinctively edging closer to David. David very deliberately moved to put himself ever so slightly in front of her, standing between her and Nico. David drew himself up to his full height and did the same with his power-aura, subtly raising it to where the Weaver had to be able to feel it.

Just that little bit of space helped Lesela speak again. "It is not too late for you to make all of this right," she said. "Your friends love you, and you have a place among them far greater than any place you ever had in Avilon. You are well quit of that realm. Here you can truly make a difference as you always longed to. What could you have done there, and what can you do here, if only you choose to?"

Nico just looked at her, eyes going silver at the edges. David shifted again, shielding Lesela visually with his body. Even in this place of rage and blood where Nico dwelt, instinct would tell him not to try anything with David there.

Or it should have.

"What can I do here?" Nico asked her. "That's a fantastic question, Lesela. Would you like to see the answer?"

"Nico," David said in a low voice, a warning in the word. "You need to remove yourself from this room right now."

Nico laughed.

It was a cold, nasty sound that sent a chill through David.

"You," Nico said, "Are not the Prime of me."

"Am I not?" David took a step forward and completely blocked him from Lesela. "All right, then, show me I'm not. Come through me. Go ahead."

"I'm starting to think you're not taking me seriously," Nico replied. "All of you seem to think if you just say the right thing or stage the right intervention you can turn me back into the poor sad creature I was, and I'll go back to simpering after you and he both. You don't seem to get that I *like* this. It's truly liberating not to need love from someone who can't love you, or need approval from those whose standards you can never meet. I want the old me to stay dead, and I intend to make sure he does. Obviously I can't kill Deven, and you...well...I don't even really know *how* to kill you. But if you're all planning to team up and drag me back into what I was...I'm afraid I can't let you do that."

David gave him a smile as cold as his own. "You're not going to stop us," he told the Elf evenly. "I refuse to let you go on like this—and not only because I care about you. You are a danger to everyone in this Haven and every human in Austin, and that is not acceptable. As Prime of this territory I will do what I must to neutralize the threat you pose. For the moment at least that means bringing the real you back. Keep pushing it and it might mean putting your ass in a coma and keeping you there."

Very few people had ever been able to stand up to the look on David's face—nearly all of them had fallen dead to the ground for trying. Most were either insane or had nothing to lose. It was difficult to say where Nico fell along that spectrum.

Nico glanced toward the left, and David barely had time to register what he was doing before a large vase shattered and the shards flew toward Lesela's face.

He wasn't Prime for nothing, though—his reflexes kicked in and he ground the shards into powder with his mind before they could reach her. Half a breath later a table next to the chair he'd been sitting in collapsed and broken pieces of wood, ends in splinters, sailed toward him.

David held up a hand and combined a shield with telekinetic energy to block not only the broken wood but anything else Nico might throw at them. "Stay behind me," he commanded Lesela, who was all too happy to obey.

David held up the shield with part of his mind and reached toward Nico with another, trying to get hold of his neck and break it—it was the only way to put him out that would last more than a few minutes. But Nico had already observed, dissected, and learned how to do what David was doing, and shut David out.

Something bright glowed in the corner of David's eye, and he realized what it was just in time: embers from the fireplace. David shored up the shield and they bounced off, but he also had to concentrate enough to extinguish them before they burned the house down.

Nico looked annoyed. "Fine," he said. "We'll do it your way."

"What does that—"

David pulled his attention back to Nico just as a fist of energy struck him, and it felt like the room was being sucked out from under him. His vision greyed out and everything lurched forward—

He tumbled into the grass, hitting the ground rolling and coming back up to his feet with his sword already drawn...but he wasn't looking at Nico anymore, or the guest suite at all.

David spun around trying to get his bearings. Where the hell was he? Nico had apparently learned the trick of how to Mist someone else the way David and Miranda did on the New Moon. Normally he'd be impressed, but right now he had to hurry.

He recognized the trees around him—he wasn't far from the Haven. He shut his eyes and grabbed hold of the memory of the guest room, lassoing it with energy and hauling it toward himself with enough force that he was sure he'd regret it later.

Even passing through space, between worlds and beyond reality, he heard a scream.

David reappeared exactly where he'd stood, expecting to be thrown again or at least have something fly at his head.

Nico was gone.

Breathing hard, David sheathed the Oncoming Storm and looked around—where was Lesela? That must have been her screaming, so...

A soft whimper got his attention, and he found her on the other side of the bed where she had apparently run in a futile attempt to escape. The thick smell of blood hit him like an earthquake a split second before he saw it spilled all around her where she had fallen.

He knelt beside her, desperately trying to remember how Miranda had healed her cat, how Deven did it all the time—surely he could too.

One look at her and his heart sank. The tears in her throat were huge and ragged, but they weren't her only wounds; he couldn't say for sure what the weapon was but she'd been stabbed as well, right through the abdomen. There was so much damage it would take Deven to heal her, and there wasn't time.

Nonetheless, he hit his com: "Deven, get back here *now*. Lesela's down."

Suddenly a hand seized his forearm— bloody, shaking, but with an iron grip born of the desperation of her final minutes. He covered her hand with his, meeting her pain-glazed eyes.

"Help is coming," he said. "Just hold on another minute."

She gave him a soft, regretful smile. "Tell him…"

He knew what he was hearing.

Last words.

He leaned closer, still holding onto her hand, his other touching her face, trying to offer some comfort, any comfort. "Go on."

She took as much of a breath as she could and murmured something in his ear that, at first, didn't make much sense. He simply filed the words away and kept his attention on her until—

"Well now…where were we?"

David lifted his head and looked at Nico, who had returned to the doorway, covered in blood but still utterly indifferent to his own actions.

Before the Prime could say anything, though, the Elf's head snapped around to the left with a horrible crack, and he dropped to the ground, silence falling with him.

Behind him, Deven's eyes were pure silver, almost burning, and his teeth were out.

He was at Lesela's side in a heartbeat, but he had to know, as David had known, that it was too late. The light had gone out of the Elf's eyes, and her hand went limp in David's.

David checked for a pulse, though it was unnecessary. He met Deven's eyes. The elder Prime didn't seem to know what to do.

"She said something," David told him quietly. "Something I should tell you." At Deven's raised eyebrow, David repeated, "'The child of the evening still lives.' Does that mean anything to you? Was it prophecy?"

"The child of the evening..." Deven looked down, shaking his head, but not out of ignorance.

"That's what she told me."

"It's not a metaphor...it's a name. Elendala Seara."

"Is that someone you know?"

"No," Deven replied, closing his eyes. "It's my mother."

Chapter Fifteen

The door of the interrogation room slammed shut with the reverberating finality of a tomb.

"If he so much as twitches, break his neck again—don't give him a chance to regain consciousness until I permit it."

The four Elite he'd assigned to guard Nico's body bowed in assent. They all looked as bewildered as he felt, and uneasy about what they'd been ordered to do. Neck snapping was considered fairly extreme as a sedative among vampires; it worked, yes, but it was difficult to heal and could take days before the victim regained the full range of motion. Anything involving the nervous system was tricky. Doing it over and over again could cause long-term, though not permanent, damage to the body, and had been known to permanently affect the mind. David could only assume that Nico would come out of it faster than the average.

But they had few alternatives. The tranquilizer Deven had dosed him with last time only worked for half an hour at most, and a few doses in Nico had already started to develop a tolerance. There was no place here they could keep him that he couldn't escape, if he was conscious and able to move; he could Mist anywhere he liked, and even if he couldn't he could build a portal without breaking a sweat and vanish into the city to unleash his wrath upon the entire population.

David stared through the window at his lover, who had been chained down this time despite the wrongness of it. Hopefully he wouldn't wake to find himself bound; but if he did, and lashed out, the chains gave the guards a moment to get into the cell and put him out again. It was awful, sickening, and David didn't know what else to do.

A moment later Deven reappeared. He didn't look well at all - God knew what echoes he was catching from his Consort's broken mind. And while he might be pretending not to care much about Lesela, he had insisted on taking care of her body himself.

"Did you bury her?" David asked quietly.

Deven shook his head, eyes on the window. "We need to send her back to Avilon, but we don't know when or if that will be possible, so...I had her burned. There are guards keeping watch who will collect the ashes."

He looked at Deven curiously. "She's not a vampire, though - sunlight won't burn her, and doesn't it take an incredibly high temperature to reduce a non-vampire to ash?"

"I know how to burn a body, David," Deven snapped. Then, he gestured vaguely and said, "Sorry."

"Don't be. How are you holding up?"

"I'm not." Deven couldn't seem to look at him—he often had trouble with eye contact when he was in tears or otherwise overcome. "I can't take this anymore. I was barely holding it together as it was, and now..."

The emotion on Deven's face was one David had only rarely ever seen—one most people didn't think he was capable of. *Fear.*

Unable to resist the urge to do something, anything, David reached over and took his hand, squeezed it. "You're not alone."

"What else can be taken from me? Who else can I lose? Miranda? You, again? Who else do I love? And none of this would have happened if -"

"Stop right there," David told him firmly. "You're free to feel however you feel, but at least do it from the truth, not from this delusion you have that you're some kind of immortal plague rat. We are all culpable in all of this to one degree or another. And besides...not an ounce of blame is going to get us out of this." David took hold of his chin and forced their eyes to meet. "So stop being a dick to someone I love, and get your head back in the game."

Deven looked away, eyes bright. "I've got nothing," he said. "If you have some brilliant plan now would be the time to share it."

He was right. There was no more time to lose. Miranda might not have had a chance to work on her Weaving, but they had to trust that she could do it—Persephone had believed she could, and it was She who had given Miranda the ability in the first place. This was the place for a leap of faith if ever there was one.

"Come on," he told Deven, taking his hand again. "We need to talk and we can't do it here. Miranda will be home shortly."

Before Deven could reply, David hauled him along into a Mist, emerging in the Signet Suite where everything was so normal, so peaceful, it made the whole night seem even more painful.

David took off his coat and disarmed, then went to change; he returned from the closet with some of Miranda's black cotton off-duty wear and handed it to Deven.

"You're all bloody," he told Deven. "Go wash off and get comfortable. I think you need to stay here with us tonight."

Deven gave him an incredulous look. "Here? With you?"

David recognized the worry in Dev's expression and sighed, mentally tapping on his com and saying, "Star Two."

A second later Miranda replied, *"Star-Two."*

"Deven's in a fairly dreadful state and I think he should sleep in our room tonight, but I want him to hear your opinion."

"Of course he should! Dev, get in bed. As your Queen, that's an order."

A smile flickered on Deven's face. "You're not really my—"

"The hell I'm not. Now do as you're told."

Deven smiled a little more. "Yes, my Lady." He gave David a look of faint amusement.

David pointed silently at the bathroom.

Almost laughing, Deven did as the Queen had commanded.

David flopped down on the bed and took care of a few odds and ends while he waited for Miranda to get home and Deven to return; he ran a quick check on the sensor network, scanned the patrol reports for the night, checked for any urgent messages from Jacob that would indicate a Signet had gone down. The night-to-night work of running most of the country never stopped, not even for Elf emergencies.

They apparently had a moment's reprieve; nothing dramatic had occurred that night at all outside the Haven, either in his territories or overseas. He was surprised—in their lives shit-storms were almost always Category 4.

Deven emerged from the bathroom in a cloud of steam. The sleeveless shirt David had filched from Miranda gave him a magnificent look at Dev's tattoos—and biceps. David decided to pretend that wasn't why he'd picked it.

Again, the Prime looked reluctant to follow David to the bed, and said halfheartedly, "I could take the couch..."

"Don't be ridiculous." David stretched out and lifted the covers, patting the mattress. "Look, I know you don't want to cause a problem, but in case you haven't noticed, there isn't one. Not anymore. Miranda would be thrilled to have you here under any circumstances, and I'm not complaining either." More quietly, he added, "I know you're on the precipice. You can lay it all down here, for now. You need to feel safe, and we can protect you. Nothing that comes through that door will survive the walk across the room with the two of us here."

Finally, Deven acquiesced, and lay down next to him, letting David tuck him in and draw him close. David had to smile—it was the first time in a long time they'd been in bed together like this, without any shame lurking around the headboard just waiting to pounce. Things were so different now...different from a few years ago, yes, but also different from decades ago, when their relationship had been anything but safe.

"I think you're wrong," Deven told him softly, still able to pick up on his thoughts. "We damn near killed each other on a regular basis and did unspeakable things to each other's hearts, but when we were together like this, in the quiet of the morning...I knew I was safe. You were the only lover I would ever trust to protect me."

Something dark and frightened crossed his face, and he shivered and buried his head in David's shoulder, fingers digging into David's arm.

"I think he might be gone for good this time," Deven said in a harsh whisper. "Before, underneath the anger, at least there was some flicker of who he was...I can't feel that anymore. All I feel is hate...for me, for you, for everyone and everything. I think he would kill me, or himself, except he wouldn't get to enjoy watching me die. But the second we let him wake he's coming after you."

"Not if we come after him first," David replied. "We do have a plan, Dev...it was better when Lesela was here to help, but I think what's among the three of us will be enough, and the circumstances are as ideal as they're going to get. But...you're going to have to trust us, more than you ever have before."

"I trust you as much as I am capable," Deven said tiredly, closing his eyes. "I hope that's enough."

"It's a start."

Finally, he murmured, "I'm scared, David...of what else he might do, who he might hurt...scared I won't ever get him back and have a chance to make this right...and scared that even if he does come back, he'll be so broken he might as well have died. How is he supposed to live with all of this? The guilt is going to destroy him...assuming it's not too late already."

"You'll have a chance," David told him with a kiss to his forehead. "I give you my word."

A slight smile. "Well, if I have the word of David Solomon, fate had better watch its back."

"Damn right."

"Can you forgive me for how I've behaved?" Deven asked, shifting back to look in his face. "I know you were avoiding me this whole year, and I'm rather glad you did, given how I treated everyone."

David smiled. "I forgive you. I'll always forgive you. There are things that I've come to accept about us in these few years. I wasn't ready to own up to most of it until Miranda made it clear it was okay, that she wasn't going to get angry at whatever I felt."

"And...what do you feel?"

"I should think it would be perfectly obvious," David said wryly. "I love you, never stopped, can't stop, won't. That's just how it is, and I'm finally okay with that. I need you to be, too, if you can."

Pale eyes lifted up to his. "I think I can now."

"Good."

He felt Deven's body gradually go slack, and lay in the warm darkness for a while, listening to him breathe. He could feel Miranda's presence drawing closer, and once she had arrived at the Haven, it was only a matter of minutes before there was movement at the door.

The Queen swept in in full Miranda Grey the Celebrity regalia, carrying her guitar case but still armed to the teeth. She paused just inside to remove some of her gear and hang it near the door, but stopped when she saw Deven was asleep; she caught David's gaze and raised an eyebrow.

He wasn't quite sure how to convey the situation in a gesture, but luckily he didn't have to; she could see it on his face. He'd told her what happened in a quiet phone call while waiting for the guards to finish chaining up Nico. He wasn't sure how to classify her reaction to learning Morningstar had Kai, Nico had just killed Deven's grandmother, and their timetable had accelerated drastically, but she had been, and was still, calm and in command.

To think once upon a time he'd been unsure if she could handle bearing a Signet. In a lot of ways she was better at it than he'd ever been.

She nodded, then said quietly, "How are you?"

"I've been better," he replied. "Everything settled out there?"

"I think so. Having Maguire and Myers there was a good idea. I could sense a lot of hostility toward the police but I think seeing all of us up there together helped. If nothing else I made it clear that anyone harassing the detectives will answer to me."

David smiled. "That should do it, then."

She paused by the bed and looked down at its occupants, sadness edging the satisfaction from her eyes. "Are you keeping him under?"

"No. He's just that tired."

"Poor kitten," she said, very lightly touching Deven's sleeping face. "You're right...we can't wait any longer."

"Do you think you can do it?"

"I have to, don't I?" She stepped back and went to remove her boots. "If we're going to find Kai, stop Morningstar, get that ritual from the Codex done, move forward at all...we can't do it like this. We need our Weaver back, and we need everyone at full strength. No matter how you look at it the first step is to get that barrier down." She looked at him. "Did you talk it over?"

"Not yet. I thought it best if you were here."

Another nod. "I'm going to take a shower...let's let him sleep a little longer. If he's going to do his part he needs to be at least somewhat alert."

She definitely had a point. Left alone again in the comfortable quiet with someone he'd long, long missed having in his arms, David let himself drift off too, trying to pretend for a moment that nothing existed beyond the suite door.

She could feel her Prime falling asleep as she stripped off her clothes and waited for the shower spray to heat up. After the night he'd had, she was thankful he could catch even a few moments' rest...and she needed a moment as well.

She'd been holding it together pretty well, she thought, for most of the last hour. She'd felt what David would describe as a "great disturbance in the Force" but couldn't figure out exactly who or what it was about until her phone rang and he unloaded, as gently as possible, the night's events.

Kai missing, presumably in the hands of Morningstar. Deven's grandmother here, then gone, but gone forever, at Nico's hand. Nico chained in a cell with his neck broken. It was a lot to process...too much, it turned out.

Miranda sagged against the shower wall and let herself cry for a while. She could have let it out in front of the boys—they'd hardly judge her for it—but she wanted to be careful about the atmosphere in the bedroom for the next few hours. She knew Deven was dangerously close to another breakdown, and this time they probably wouldn't get him back.

And would they ever see their Nico again? And even if they did, how would he live with himself? Lesela had been his friend, once his lover. It was her prophetic gift that had sent him to the Shadow World. Not to mention she was his Prime's only living relative, the only one who could answer the questions Miranda knew Deven had about his history. Now they would never get to know each other; she would never have a chance to see beneath the angry exterior to the wonderful creature in which it turned out her family line had ended.

And Kai...Miranda wept into the shower spray as she imagined him being torn apart as Nico had been...cut open, violated in such intimate and agonizing ways...stripped of every defense, including sanity, and left with...what? What would be left of Kai? Would he end up like his brother? She pictured him that way, his confidence and that stubborn will broken into shards...Elves healed quickly, but not always completely. They could scar. Kai didn't have Nico's vampiric regenerative ability. If they did to him what the Inquisition had done to Deven all those years ago, broke his hands...he would never play again...assuming he would even want to.

She shut her eyes and leaned sideways against the tiled wall, praying silently to anyone out there that Kai wouldn't have to face what Nico had, wouldn't be tortured, and wouldn't lose his life's work because of them. It was bad enough that their war had swallowed Nico—at least he'd come here and gotten involved willingly. Kai had only left Avilon for his brother, not to join the fight against Morningstar and certainly not to become a pawn for either side.

The bathroom was dense with clouds of steam when she reached for her towel. If they failed tonight...if she failed...she shuddered at the thought and wished she could do something like crossing herself or knocking on wood that would actually help.

The Queen pulled on her bathrobe, holding her breath steady. She had to stay grounded. She closed her eyes and groped after the image of the Web she'd managed to find at her piano, just to be sure it was still there.

It took a minute, but once she relaxed her mind's eye enough there it was, hovering quietly around the edges of her awareness. She wasn't able to See very far—she could follow the threads from her own part over to David and See him pretty clearly, and she could feel the tangled knot that represented Deven, but to do anything to help she would have to get close, get her hands dirty.

"Okay," she said into the empty room, trying to inject confidence into her slightly shaky voice. "Here we go."

Both Primes were still asleep when she returned to the bedroom. She stood at the foot of the bed for a moment, one hand on the bedpost, both getting a better look at the energetic situation and admiring the scene.

They had, in the time she'd been in the shower, shifted so that both lay on their sides, David acting as the big spoon with one arm around Deven's middle, their fingers entwined. She had to smile: David's hand was so much bigger than either hers or Deven's, though they didn't seem terribly large in and of themselves.

Dev's other hand had wrapped itself around David's other wrist—David had told her about the heartbeat thing. Where did that come from, she wondered? She was glad David didn't seem to need that kind of reassurance with her; if she'd woken with his hand around her neck she probably would have broken his arm.

Such an odd pair, her boys. Standing over them she felt a surge of affection and protectiveness...and maybe just a little possessiveness, if she let herself admit it. Life had already taken enough from them both...from them all. She was going to find a way that they could all be happy, even just for a year or two, and if she had to move Heaven and Earth to do it, she would do so gladly.

The situation in the Web was pretty straightforward, though it looked like it might be even direr than they'd expected. She could see herself and her Pair bond with David, as well as Deven's connection that led off to Nico. She turned her attention very slowly toward Nico until the barrier came into view.

It was closer to Deven's end than the Elf's, and the sight of it made her stomach clench.

She couldn't See the level of detail that Stella could; Stella said she Saw the Web in full color, where what Miranda was looking at was mostly threads made of blue-white light. It made her think of the stars: what looked to ordinary eyes like white dots of light were, on closer inspection with the right equipment, a nocturnal rainbow.

She could See it well enough to be intimidated. The barrier was such a small thing, just a shadow that had wrapped itself around the bond and twisted it almost totally shut, but the imbalance building up on either side was inches from disastrous. This was going to take an enormous amount of power…power she could only hope they had. Without any real experience she couldn't say for sure if they were strong enough…they had to be. They were out of options and out of time.

She shook herself out of the vision; if she kept staring at it she was just going to second-guess herself into paralysis. She didn't have to keep the vision "up" the whole time as long as she could visualize it clearly when it was needed—she'd gotten that much from Stella, though now she wished she'd found the time to sit the Witch down and grill her about technique.

Taking a deep breath, Miranda sat down on the edge of the bed where she could reach over and run her fingers lightly through David's hair.

He stirred, eyes opening halfway, still dazed with sleep, sharpening when he saw her.

She wasn't sure how to wake Deven in a way that wouldn't get her stabbed, but David was way ahead of her; she felt him reach over and tap lightly on Deven's mind.

Dev started and woke, gaze fixing on Miranda.

Once when she was a kid Miranda had visited the Houston Zoo, and amid crying about how sad the animals must be, she had caught the eye of a wolf as he woke from a nap in the sun. In the space of about two seconds she saw the analysis: *Not a threat, not food, all is well.*

244

The exact same thing passed over Deven's face, his eyes flashing from lavender to silver to deeper violet and back to lavender. Again, it was almost instantaneous, but it was the sort of thing one predator would always notice in another.

Given the situation she decided not to overanalyze how attractive it was.

"Hey," she said softly. "You okay, more or less?"

He dropped his head back into the pillow and said, voice muffled, "Not especially." After a moment he looked back up at her. "I'm told you have a plan?"

David and Miranda exchanged a look. "Okay," she began, groping for words for a second, "Like you said before, just knocking the barrier over would overwhelm you both, and assuming it didn't kill you, that much energy isn't something we need in Nico's hands right now—which is why now is the best time to act, while he's out. In the state you're in, with you two all unbalanced and on emotional hair triggers, even if you wanted to do it by yourself, it'd be dangerous. This isn't just a shield, it's a strangled Signet bond."

"Yes, and?"

"For us to help you, we have to get in past your shields to a much deeper level than anyone's probably ever gone besides Jonathan. David thought of a way to make it easier for you to let us in, and to let us take control of your energy and hold the balance."

Miranda couldn't help but enjoy the expression on Deven's face as once again he looked from Prime to Queen, a lot of things began to come together, and, slowly, understanding dawned. "You are out of your goddamned minds."

"Are we?" Miranda asked. "Fine, then—try and open your shielding on your own right now. As scared and freaked out and grieving as you are, go ahead, let us in and we'll go from there. Go ahead. We'll wait."

She sensed Deven trying—the stubborn bastard would scarcely even admit he needed help, let alone with such basic energy work. But just as emotional burnout could cause someone's shields to fail, they could do the opposite and turn them to stone. Neither situation was easy to fix. The best and sometimes only way to deal with either was to find a skilled psychic to help the way David had once shielded Miranda. It was the same problem, just the opposite manifestation. Too much pain, too much fear, too long alone—and years of hiding and running.

Deven's hands clenched, and he bent all his considerable will toward opening his shields, but every time he got close to them he started shaking harder, until a sound very like a sob escaped him and he gave up, putting his hands over his eyes.

"I can't," he whispered helplessly. "I didn't realize it was that bad...I avoided looking so I could avoid feeling the guilt...you're right, I can't."

"It's okay," Miranda told him gently, stroking his forehead. "We can help you. Plus, let's face it...didn't you think we were going to end up here eventually anyway?"

That at least earned a weary, but genuine, chuckle. "I suppose I did."

"And, just in case it turns out seven hundred years of history outweigh a mostly untested attraction to one's best friend, we've got a ringer." She tilted her head toward David.

A hint of uncertainty—of a different sort than before—entered Deven's voice as he said, "So...how exactly is this supposed to work?"

Miranda grinned. "Do we need to draw you a picture?"

"I mean the magic."

David picked up the thread. "There's something that Nico does—Stella apparently calls it 'Elf Tantra'—a way of taking the energy generated by sex and directing it. It's almost exactly the same as what we do when we shag our prey—we use their own arousal to heighten the power in their blood so we don't need to take as much. Nico said that it wasn't unheard of for his people to actually Weave with that energy—and that the results could be nothing short of miraculous." David looked over at Miranda and added, "I have enough experience with that end of things that even without Sight I can feed Miranda whatever power we raise, and she can funnel it into the Web."

Miranda nodded. "Once I have the power, I can use it to stick me and David in between you and Nico and hold all four of us equidistant so that when you let the barrier down, the surge will hit all of us equally with each of us absorbing a quarter of the impact. The link between Nico and David will help redistribute the energy so nobody gets overwhelmed."

Deven looked at them both like they were spouting nonsense. "You *think* it will. You don't actually *know*—in fact neither of you has the slightest idea if any of this will work."

"Do you have a better idea?"

"Just about any idea," Deven retorted, but as soon as the words were out, his protest seemed to die. "But you're right...we have to do something now, before Nico regains consciousness and kills us all. We've got one chance before everything slides even further into hell. And we have to use the tools we have...just us. We each have different skills and strengths, and we haven't had a chance to learn how they fit together." He shook his head, defeated. "But you do understand that I have just about every reservation in existence, right? None of us has ever done anything like this before, and I mean that on pretty much every level."

David laughed quietly and leaned down to kiss the hollow of Deven's throat, eliciting a shiver, and not one of strain or fear. "Speak for yourself," David said. "Don't worry...I've been choreographing this very event in my imagination for years." He followed that kiss with another, then still more in a line up to Dev's ear, where David paused and nipped lightly where, in slightly different circumstances, it would have been pointed.

A gasp. David had mentioned Elves had extremely sensitive ears; apparently that bred true just like the eye color.

Miranda focused on her breathing for a moment—she'd been concentrating so intently on being outwardly relaxed so that Deven wouldn't bolt that she'd let herself knot up with tension on the inside. The whole thing had seemed like a workable, and hopefully at least enjoyable, idea, but now...*we're really going to do this. Can I do this?*

She started to untie her bathrobe, but to her consternation her hand was shaking. Frustrated, she couldn't get the knot undone.

A hand covered hers. "Stop right there," Deven said gently, sitting up and locking eyes with her. "I will have no part in this if you're not 100% sure it's what you want—to hell with anything else. If we have to find another way we will."

"There isn't one," she said. "Not powerful enough, and not that we can implement in time."

"I don't care. I'm not sacrificing you for the rest of us. Not ever."

Miranda smiled. "You're amazing."

"I'm not. But you've lost enough already. Given enough."

"I wonder," David said, not seeming worried in the slightest, "If perhaps a different approach is called for. We're being too clinical, too focused on the magic." There was a glint of mischief in his eye as he added, "Look at us. We're in bed together. With *intent*. If we let our overall purpose consume our thoughts there's no way any of us can let go enough to actually make it work. So...for starters, the two of you need to relax. Tell me, beloved...when you imagine this particular scenario, how do we proceed? Are we all three involved? Is anyone just watching? If we can't talk about it we sure as hell shouldn't do it."

Miranda bit her lip, looking away, then said, "Well...it started out vague, right around the time I turned Thirdborn...you remember that night, right?"

"Probably better than you do," Deven pointed out.

"Then picture that...the three of us warm under the blankets, everyone safe and protected. In the real world I kissed you, and even though I was basically delirious I remember you kissing back. It seemed...sincere, for lack of a better word. I don't know if anyone else caught on."

"Jonathan did, and he wasn't even there at the time." Dev's voice was wry. "He kept bringing it up the whole way home, he claimed out of curiosity, but I wonder now if he'd seen something in a vision and was trying to figure out if it was real or symbolic."

"Oh, I noticed it too," David added. "In fact I thought it was one of the hottest things I'd ever seen. Go on, Miranda...if you'd had your way, what would have happened next?"

She could feel her face growing redder. "Instead of going back to sleep, I'd keep kissing you. I had one of you on either side of me, and...I thought about how it would feel to have you both...Dev, you know how he is in bed, when things are really intense. He treats you like the most precious thing in all creation and also like he plans to eat you alive. I imagined both of you doing that...I think that's part of why I'll probably never actually sleep with anyone else...I can't imagine anyone touching me that way, like I'm a living treasure, or letting anyone that close. And I'm not willing to settle for anything less."

Now, she smiled, and took one of Deven's hands, laying it on her neck under the edge of her robe. "But you...with you I wouldn't be settling. I know that like I know my own name."

Taking her tiny bit of guidance, he untied her robe with the other hand, and then carefully, very slowly, pushed it off her shoulders, baring her skin a little at a time.

Before he could get too anxious about being presented with an unwrapped naked woman, she curled a hand around his neck and kissed him hard.

She wasn't sure who made the soft noise of surprise—it could have been David just as easily as either of them. She could feel how it affected her Prime, seeing his two greatest loves touching each other, and that only made her bolder.

Miranda shifted forward, completely out of the robe, and into Deven's lap, winding her legs around him and pressing her body against his so he could feel what he was getting into while his clothes were still on. She felt his arms move around her, hands gliding up her back; he broke the kiss long enough to bend and taste her throat, lean her back slightly to kiss his way down her sternum.

To her delight, she found it wasn't going to be as difficult as she'd feared to get his body interested in a woman's, and she rocked her hips against his just to enjoy the effect.

Grinning impishly, and earning a quiet laugh, she tugged his shirt—hers, actually—off over his head. This was the first time she'd actually seen the full extent of his tattoos, and she could easily have gotten off track trying to pick out every little detail. They were exquisitely rendered, the lines sharp and stark against pale skin, but the one that caught her eye first was the image of a Nighthound like Cora's—designed to look like it had emerged from an illuminated manuscript, it howled up at a waning Moon from the edge of a darkened forest where a serpent coiled around the branches of a tree. Hound, Moon, forest, and snake were all drawn with a loving hand stretching from his collarbone down over one pectoral muscle, balancing a similar scene on the opposite side.

"May I..." She tapped his arm with one finger.

"Do you really have to ask at this point?"

She smiled, leaned down, and touched her tongue lightly to one of the lines. It was slightly raised, just like David's raven. She followed the outline along his collarbone and up to where neck joined shoulder.

There was a tug at the back of her mind, and she glanced over at David, who was watching with the kind of intensity that always, always went straight between her thighs. He smiled slightly and she felt him urging her: *Bite him.*

She nodded and returned her mouth to Deven's throat, ghosting her teeth over his skin—her canines took that as a signal to extend, and quick as a snake, she bit down.

The sound that elicited had the same effect as David's stare—but the effect on Deven was just as immediate, and before she could even take a drop of blood, her back hit the mattress and he was biting her in return with a low, animal growl.

She clamped her lips on the puncture wounds and sucked forcefully. Her hands slid up around his waist, and she tried to pull off the rest of his clothes but found her hands had gone uncooperative—all they wanted to do was claw and clench, not coordinate.

Luckily, as she'd said, they had a ringer; laughing quietly at her sudden clumsiness, David pushed himself up and got Deven undressed with the kind of efficiency that could only come from years of practice. He took the opportunity to add his own teeth to the situation and bit Deven's neck on the opposite side. Miranda had managed to only use her front pair, but either the angle was weird or David didn't care about such niceties, as there were four holes on his side, wine-red blood glistening as it rose up and began to trickle down over Dev's skin.

Miranda and David smiled at each other and flipped things around a bit, planting Deven firmly on his back, each of them bending to lick the wounds.

They went on like that for a while, drinking each other over and over, hands moving languidly in the dark. Miranda could feel Deven's shields falling open layer by layer—it was working.

David noticed too, and began to carefully draw off tiny sips of energy and let them build within his own aura. It took concentration, but he was obviously quite happy to watch more than participate, periodically unable to resist taking her mouth, or Deven's, for a moment.

She wasn't sure what was more of a turn-on; Deven's strong, clever hands on her body, gingerly learning unfamiliar terrain, or watching the two Primes kiss, hoping that eventually—if not tonight, then eventually—she'd get to watch a lot more than that.

Deven's mouth and hands followed each other over her skin, leaving fire in their wake, and he was clearly pleased at the effect. She felt like every inch of her body was burning—there were so many sensations hitting her at once, not just him, but her Prime, whose desire for them both was a force of nature too strong to deny. He was still holding back, though, enough to pay attention to his task, and she could sense the reservoir of energy building just as they'd planned...if a little more slowly than she'd hoped. As much as she wanted this to last, the longer they took, the more dangerous the situation became.

Fortunately she knew a few ways to move things along.

She wrapped one leg around Deven and rolled them both to the side so he was beneath her, blinking in momentary surprise at the abrupt reversal. She grinned and moved back until her hips reached his.

Miranda slid one hand down between them, closing around him gently—she reminded herself next time she wanted to see Stella turn bright red to tell her she'd been absolutely right about the fury of this particular army—and glanced over at David, who took her wordless hint and reached up to pin Deven's arms up over his head. Deven's eyes were closed, his breath coming in gasps, and the golden light from the fireplace emphasized every movement of his muscles, tiny tremors and a slight straining against David's grasp.

She kept stroking with her hand for a moment before tilting her hips and guiding him into her body, one scant, teasing inch at a time. The Queen moaned softly at the slow collision; she could barely breathe, she was so focused on that single point of convergence and the almost painfully delicious feeling of rocking her hips forward and back, barely even moving at first, tightening and relaxing her muscles in time.

She caught her husband's eye. The way he was staring, lips slightly parted, pupils blown wide and shining black in the firelight, almost seeming astonished by what he was seeing, made it even better.

David lost his focus for a second and almost lost hold of the energy reservoir, but he was no amateur—he clamped down on it quickly and brought himself back to attention, returning to his work. He was careful not to take too much power at once, lest he drain the arousal right out of them, but it had already doubled in volume, growing more with every second.

She leaned forward onto her hands, then lowered herself until she was resting mostly on top of Deven, whose nails were clawing little half-moons of blood in David's forearms. He, too, rocked his hips to meet hers, the two pushing harder and harder against each other until it felt like her pelvis was going to shatter.

It was incredible.

David's free hand snaked between the two of them to stroke her with his fingertips, each touch sending waves of electricity through her. The power reservoir was practically overswelling its banks.

He leaned in close to Deven and murmured to him—she couldn't hear much of it, but she could guess the subject matter. David was, among his many skills, the Zen master of dirty talk.

David's eyes flicked to Miranda and back as he asked, softly, "How does that feel, my darling? You both look so beautiful…" His voice lowered again, but whatever he said next drew a ragged, desperate noise from Deven, muffled as David covered his mouth with the kind of kiss that could shake the foundations of the earth.

That was enough for Miranda. She barely had time to send David a warning before her entire body felt like it was exploding, the pleasure that burned everywhere they were touching her turning incandescent, into bliss.

She wasn't the only one, and though he was completely silent except for breath, she could feel it—and she could feel David catching hold and pulling an astonishing amount of energy out of them, into the pool he had built.

Miranda's muscles all went liquid, and she collapsed with a grunt.

Deven was panting. She couldn't remember ever having seen him actually sweaty. "Holy…Jesus…woman…"

She was so wildly giddy she nearly went into a giggle fit—she'd managed to switch on his accent. "Not bad, then?" she asked.

The kiss, while not terribly eloquent, was a definite affirmative.

"All right," David said quietly. He was tense; the amount of power he was controlling right then would have scared the hell out of Miranda if she'd let herself think about it. "I think it's ready…are you two, or do you need another minute?"

"I could use about five hours, a shower, and some Taco Bell," Miranda managed, "But here…hang on…" She reluctantly pushed herself off of Deven and onto her side facing the boys. His fingers wound through hers and held on for dear life.

She hadn't noticed until then how widely he'd opened himself—she could feel, when she slowed her breathing enough to separate her senses from theirs, so much more from him than she ever had. It really was beautiful, being able to connect to someone this way even for a moment. The courage it had taken to trust her so completely…

Their eyes met briefly. His were a dark violet, almost black, flecked with stars that might have been reflections from the fireplace…she decided not to think about it just then, and closed her own eyes tight.

So much love…and pain, yes, sorrow so deep she couldn't see its end…but so much love. At this exact moment, Deven felt safe, loved. She hated to destroy that, but it was unlikely that bliss bubble was going to last once they got to work.

Miranda closed her eyes and pulled up the Web. She could see the reservoir clearly, a white sun burning in her mind.

She had next to no experience with Weaving, and not much technical knowledge, but her instincts, she knew, were good; she'd known where to put her hands last time, known how the threads would behave. It was all very logical—there were ebbs and flows, balances to maintain, threads branching and supporting other threads like cables holding up a bridge. It was difficult as hell to do, but not that hard to understand. As vast and complex as the universe was it operated by fairly simple rules.

David extended his energetic "hand" toward her, and she took it; seconds later the power they had raised began to flow into her along their Signet bond.

After a minute or two the power was singing through them both, flowing in a circuit from one to the other and back. Just like they were situated in the real world, she took up position on one side of Deven with David on the other, the energy stretching between them and forming a sort of net that would catch, but not block, whatever wave crashed through the barrier. The energy would still move through them, but the net would slow it down, gentle it—as long as they held fast.

"Okay," she said. "I think that's it. I hope that a simple solution is a good one in this case. Dev, when you're ready, if you can…"

Even with the openness and calm that they'd created in the last hour, he was still nervous as he went inward to pry open the barrier. She could See him looking for the right place to hit it—somewhere that would cause a break but not topple the whole thing at once. The more they could slow the wave down, the better.

"Got it," he said softly. She could feel his fingers squeezing hers almost painfully, and squeezed back, trying to reassure him. "Brace yourselves."

Miranda and David grasped each other's "hands" as strongly as they could, taking a breath—

—Deven hit the barrier with the strength of his will, like a sledgehammer hitting a stone wall, and she could hear the stones breaking, crumbling. She watched his part of the Web with her heart pounding. A pinpoint of light appeared, spreading out radially from the point of impact, the gaps in the "stone" growing brighter and brighter—

She knew there wasn't a sound in the actual room, but something like a sound erupted through the Web, one she knew too well from the night the Haven in California had exploded. Stone cracking loose and tumbling, a rain of jagged pebbles flying outward, dust choking the air. Everything around her shook.

It was like being hit by the entire ocean, yet not like water at all; it was like being swallowed by a wall of fire, but didn't burn. She'd never seen, Seen, or felt anything like it, but there was no room for fear under its onslaught.

The wave hit the net so hard it nearly swept her away with it, but she grounded harder than she ever had, wrapping her own energy around the surrounding threads of the Web to shore up her own strength. She couldn't hear, couldn't speak—all she could do was hold on, to the Web and to David and to herself.

It was working…or it did at first. The wave acted just like she'd thought it would and got momentarily caught up in the net of energy. The flow was squeezed from a flood into a river, and she watched it move through and past them, down the Signet bond on its way to Nico's inert form.

There had been no useful way to test her plan—she had assumed that any barriers Nico had put up would be easily broken by the wave on its way into him. As strongly as Deven had blocked him out, there was barely even a trickle of energy reaching him, enough to sustain their lives but only just. How much of a wall could he create with that?

What she hadn't taken into account was the force of his rage. Whenever he had put up his shield, he'd done so with magic made of steel. She couldn't have seen it from outside; from where they stood it just looked like the same kind of construction Deven had used. But inside, it was reinforced and impenetrable.

The power hit the barrier and bounced off.

But it did more than bounce; Nico had built some kind of counterattack into it, so that whatever impacted with its surface was thrown back toward its origin with twice as much force.

"Oh God," she gasped, "Hang onto something! It's coming back!"

She felt their fear just a heartbeat before the returning wave struck.

Now, it did burn.

She could hear herself screaming. It felt like she was being torn apart, every cell in her body breaking away from the others. Her grip on the surrounding Web was ripped away, leaving her only David to cling to, and he to her; and while their bond was one of the strongest of its kind ever to exist, even it couldn't stand up to the wave.

Miranda felt Deven grab hold of them both, and they all rooted themselves in each other as deeply as they could. If they could connect all three as deeply as a Signet bond, they might have a chance, but -

As she struggled to maintain any sense of herself, even just her own heartbeat, Miranda saw something she could scarcely believe. It was as if someone had struck a match and lit their part of the Web on fire, specifically those threads that connected all three of them as part of the Circle. Miranda flung herself at the light, seizing the threads and wrapping them around each other, reaching beyond them and to the entire Circle for help.

She felt a response almost immediately, without hesitation. One by one, the other four Signets extended a hand, providing a rock solid foundation to stand on.

Miranda was trying to redirect the wave, or at least divert it somehow, but there was too much, too fast—she wasn't a Weaver, not the kind they needed.

We're all going to die. I can't hold on any longer—

Far away, so faintly she could barely feel it, something flickered. Something was struggling, fighting its way toward them, clawing through paradoxical distances and its own fear.

She had nothing left. She reached out with her heart to the others, saying she was sorry to have failed them, that she hoped they -

Hands seized the power from her. She didn't have time to ask questions or even hope for a miracle, but then, she didn't need to.

Power, absolute and unending, slammed into the center of the deluge. The wave broke around it into a dozen tributaries, its overall strength split and twisted so that it flowed back into the presence that had appeared among them. That presence drew the entire wave into itself, then with a single push, sent it into the four of them equally, as she had planned to do in the beginning. In a matter of moments, the tide ebbed, and with another push, it was sent into motion, flowing among them as if it always had.

Miranda's waning strength returned, redoubled. She felt stronger than she ever had, and she knew the others did too. She sensed the four far-flung Signets withdrawing, and soon the endless night of the Web grew quiet except for the sound of three vampires trying desperately to catch their breath.

They were all falling back out of the vision, into the real world again, but just before she let go, Miranda looked up at their savior.

Deep violet eyes full of power and pain met and held hers.

"Nico," she whispered, and woke.

Chapter Sixteen

The first thing he was aware of was being paralyzed...and trapped.

He struggled for several minutes, panic seizing him, but he could barely move; some parts of his body obeyed, but others he could not even feel. The metallic cold of chains rubbed his skin raw as he tried in vain to break free.

He heard himself cry out in fear. A moment later a door opened, and he heard boots approaching, driving that fear to a fever pitch -

"Stop!"

The footsteps halted. "Sire, you said that if -"

The voice was calmly authoritative even though it sounded like it was coming from far away. *"I'm aware that he's awake, Elite— stand down. In fact, stand back."*

"As you will it, Sire."

The room faded away, both sound and light, and he fell back into the darkness willingly.

The next thing he felt was softness. The unyielding steel and bright light had given way to a quiet, gentle dark, illuminated by a fireplace nearby. All around him were warm and comforting scents and sounds: the even breathing of slumber, the scents of laundry soap and not a small amount of sweat and sex, and the sound of rain hitting the metal shutters outside.

He tentatively tried to wiggle his fingers. It worked, with some delay between thought and action, but additional experiments made it clear that he was still at least partially paralyzed.

What happened to me? Where am I? Why can't I move?

It felt as though a huge chunk of information had been torn from his mind. When he tried to remember how he had ended up chained, he couldn't. Everything in his head was jumbled around itself and fragmented in places.

What he did know: at some point an incredible amount of power had rushed through his body. He could feel its traces even now, a faint vibration under his skin even in the parts he couldn't otherwise feel. And there was something new pulling lightly at his mind, similar to the link he'd had with...

...*had.*

Panic gripped him again.

The energetic link to David was gone. That must be why he was so weak. And without it he would weaken further still, losing his magic again, losing the Web, and eventually his will to live. Who had broken it? And why?

"Easy, *en'tela*," came a soft voice near his ear. "Look deeper. Don't be afraid."

The Elvish term of endearment was strangely calming. It meant "half of me," and had the connotation of a beloved as cherished as one's own soul. He had never been called that before, but just hearing his own language helped ease the anxiety trying to claw its way free.

He did as he was told and groped around inside his own mind to try and touch the strangeness. He might not be able to move his arms, but this he could do, and to his surprise, it was easy; from a magical standpoint he was at full strength...or more.

What in the...

When he found it, he jerked his mental hands back in shock. He'd come round to where the Signet bond joined to his being, but at first he didn't recognize it at all. He had grown used to the strangled energy that barely filtered through, that tiny trickle all he had to live on. That whole part of him had felt shriveled and grey, as much of a wraith inside as he was outside.

This...this was not that.

He had to be dreaming, or hallucinating—perhaps even dead and waiting for whatever came next. But if so, the powers that be had given him the kindness of a lie, and were showing him what could have been, if only...

Not only was the bond still where it belonged, it was no longer choking. Energy flowed in and out of the connection as naturally as breathing, steady and even, a moonlit violet shaded with silver-black. That darkness should have been frightening, but its strength was reassuring. When he touched it, it seemed to recognize him and grin puckishly, then wash over him with a light kiss as if nothing had ever been wrong.

That would have been comfort enough in his dying moments, he supposed, but they'd done him one better. If he reached out along the bond, he found that it didn't just flow in one direction, but two—clockwise and counterclockwise along a circuit that held them within it...

...all four of them.

When he realized what he was looking at he would have gasped, but he physically couldn't. Instead he just marveled at it. Such elegant, beautiful magic had been worked here—first with clumsy yet powerful hands, and then with those hands as well as a greater power's guiding them. Whoever it was had taken down the barrier and set up a flow, but that wasn't enough; the second presence had taken hold of them all and...

It wasn't possible. Theoretically it could work, but in reality the amount of power required simply did not exist. Such things simply did not happen, not without direct—and therefore nearly unheard-of—Divine intervention.

Still, this product of his dreaming mind had been crafted with a master's touch; it was a circle in perfect balance, seamless, whole. He'd never seen its equal.

If only it could be real...such a thing would be achingly beautiful.

He could hear low voices around him now.

"How is he?"

"Working things out...I think he thinks he's dreaming."

"How long until he can move, do you think?"

"A few more hours. Full recovery could take days. It's best not to rush a spinal injury—and he hurt himself worse trying to fight before you got him out of there. He definitely needs the rest."

"It doesn't feel like he remembers much."

"Not yet, thank God. Hopefully not ever." A pause. "She's still out, too."

"Yes. We all should be—lie back down and rest, Dev. He's safe now—we all are. I know you're tired."

"You do...I know you do. I..."

"Shh...don't think about it too much yet. Just rest. We'll figure all of this out tomorrow."

Good advice. He decided to follow it.

He didn't think again for quite a while.

The Queen's dreams were often made of memories not her own; it was a hazard of having a Signet bond. She dreamed scattered moments of a dour little village long since fallen into dust; she dreamed college campuses, beds, and battlefields she'd never set foot on.

All of those images and sensations had the same general feel to them, as if she was watching them all through a slightly tinted lens. Dreams that came from her own subconscious were in full color.

That morning, though, there were new memories, and they were nothing like what she had dreamed before.

She saw high stone walls; those walls were bound up in the smells of beeswax and dampness, the feel of a wet winter's chill. She heard the click-click of wooden beads. She felt her hand cramping from hours of slow, methodical writing, and her eyes ached from focusing too long in too little light. These were human aches and pains; she remembered what they felt like, but from a distance. The emotion, though, echoed throughout time no matter what kind of creature experienced it: in those long hours of writing, or praying...chanting the Divine Office... she felt happy, at peace, just for a while.

Everything had a faded, almost sepia quality to it—more than just history, ancient history, leached of most of its color after hundreds of years.

There was a boy in those walls whom she caught staring at her more than once. They both blushed and turned away with pounding hearts. Both reached for the same sheaf of papers, and both turned scarlet when their fingers brushed. Shy smiles across the chapel. Almost forgetting for a moment—almost—that if anyone saw, if anyone found out...

She knew, without having to see, that it would end in blood.

A stark contrast: trees whose tops soared so high overhead they disappeared into the fog; everything soft and blue, no sense of foreboding...but also no excitement, nothing to make her heartbeat fly into the treetops. Quiet life, same life, year in and year out.

"Are you sure?"

"Yes...I am sorry...I cannot tell you how to place it in a greater context, I can only tell you what I saw."

Even in the liquid silver syllables of the language, she could hear resignation in her own voice: *"I am going to die."*

"Yes, but...not for long."

That quiet life fell into nothing the night she stood amid the filth and decay of the human city, her attention riveted on the slender figure wandering the streets and sinking slowly to his knees in the one place he knew he could find silence, even as an apostate. She watched his hands press into the pavement, sorrow wailing up from every cell of his body, and she knew her time had come...time to step forward, to reach down, and...

"You called...I am your answer."

Miranda opened her eyes slowly, not trusting her senses to tell her where she actually was—or when. Her mind was tumbling over itself showing her too many things at once, but luckily she remembered at some point that she was dreaming, and apparently woke herself up.

She kept her eyes shut for a moment and just listened and felt. It was still raining outside, cool air from the windows meeting the warmth of the fireplace. The weight of the comforter was long familiar, though she wasn't entirely sure what had happened to the sheet. The strangest thing was the feeling of not one, or two, but four presences in the bed.

Well...no, that wasn't the strangest thing.

Not by a long shot, which was saying something.

Not only could she feel the physical solidity of two extra bodies with her, she could sense the energy and emotions of both of them. As soon as she turned her awareness to them the "noise" intensified, and she nearly panicked; she couldn't fully shield from it because it wasn't hitting her from all sides the way crowds of people did...it was hitting her from *inside*. Even the strongest barrier would give way under that much energy. There was no escaping it, nowhere to go.

Ground. Ground, Queen. You're not some newborn vampire amateur. Ground.

As soon as she got herself re-centered and firmly grounded, the noise migrated to the background, the same way her bond with David always had, ready to be drawn upon or touched any moment but not interfering in her own identity.

That was when she fully understood what Nico had done.

She remembered seeing him just before she'd lost consciousness. How had he woken, and moreover how had he woken as himself? What had changed? How could he have just stepped in and reworked the Web after everything he'd been through? Was the Web like the dreamtime, where Persephone could reach them and help?

In the end, the reasons and mechanics were secondary to the unbelievable, inescapable truth:

The Pair, so briefly a Trinity two years back, was now Four.

What did it mean for the future? Was it permanent? Why just them and not the entire Circle? How was it supposed to work now?

All the questions were dizzying. She forced herself to breathe more slowly, to stay grounded. There would be time to figure it out. She had to stay calm, for their sake if not her own.

It occurred to her to actually stop and evaluate what she was getting from everyone; she was used to David's emotions, and there were no warning bells ringing on his end. In fact, all she could sense from him right now was a quiet sort of happiness…a feeling mirrored in the first of their new bond-mates, while the second was still deeply unconscious and likely to stay that way for a while.

She heard a murmur to her right, and a quiet chuckle, and cracked open one eye…then smiled.

The Primes of the South and West—whatever the hell that even meant now—lay tangled up in each other and in the sheets, kissing slowly and sweetly, an almost lazy desire in the way they touched. She might have thought it was post-coital, but she'd have felt that, she knew, especially this close.

David lifted his head and smiled down at Deven, but neither spoke for a while.

Really, there didn't seem much to say, at least not now. Right now, nothing had to exist beyond the fortunately gigantic bed and its tumble of linens and limbs. The love in their eyes—as full of wonder as it was any other emotion—was beautiful, if only because it was free now...free to show itself without fear. None of them had to look away anymore, or struggle to be "over" each other.

"It's impolite to stare," David said with a grin, looking over at her.

She grinned back. "Don't mind me. Carry on."

Dev stretched out an arm and gestured for her hand; she gave it, and he asked, "How are you feeling, love?"

"Amazing. You?"

"Same. It's ridiculous, really—I can't seem to quit smiling."

Miranda shook her head and asked, "How did this happen? How could it?"

"There's only one person who can answer that," David replied, "and we've got at least until sunset before he's healed enough to wake again. He was with us for a few minutes earlier, but still way too confused for questions."

"Theoretically at least it makes sense we'd be okay for now," added Deven. "An even number is far more stable. It's easier to knock over a table with only three legs."

"But that wasn't the only problem last time—remember why it didn't work?"

"Because Deven was suicidal and crazy?" David frowned. "Wait, you're right...there was something else. You're not Thirdborn. Neither is Nico. The whole system should collapse...but it's not. It's as stable as any Signet bond I've ever seen."

"Maybe because there's two of us and two of you?"

Miranda caught David's eye, and he lifted an eyebrow, then nodded and gently pried Dev's mouth open with one finger. Now it was Deven's turn to give an eyebrow, but he opened his mouth wider so David could poke lightly at one of his canines.

The tooth extended as it should, along with its mate on the other side, but then -

"Whoa!" David jerked his hand back as the teeth behind the canines lengthened slightly as well. "When the fuck did *that* happen?"

Miranda's heartbeat stepped up at the sight. Deven's eyes went wide when he felt the change, and he touched his tongue to first one side then the other in disbelief.

"I have no idea," he said. Miranda noticed that even with his teeth lengthened his diction was as precise as always; she always felt like she sounded like a kid with braces when she tried to talk with her fangs out, but then she hadn't been practicing for seven hundred years. "That feels so weird."

Miranda groped sideways for her phone on the bedside table and checked the time and date before dropping it back where it had been. "I think you were asleep long enough to go through the transition," she observed. "You must not have felt a thing. It must have been an easy passage for once."

"Given what the two of you went through, I'm not exactly upset about that," Deven replied wryly, moving his mouth around as his teeth returned to normal. "It does bring up a difficult question, though." He glanced over to his right, where Nico slept on his back with his hands folded.

Miranda got what he meant and her heart sank. "How are we going to tell him?"

Dev sighed. "We'll worry about that when he's healed. Right now there's nothing we can do about it."

"Are you hungry?" David asked. "You know how the change has to be sealed."

"No, not yet. I should be, just in general...but I'm not. I think all the energy running through us is clouding anything else, which would explain why I didn't sense anything different. That's good, though; it means there's time for him to rest and finish healing...and for us as well. We've all been running at the edge of our endurance for weeks. I think the world can save itself for a couple of nights while we get some sleep."

"Sleep," Miranda said with a raised eyebrow. "That's certainly what it looked like to me."

She managed not to burst out laughing at the instantaneous worry on both of their faces, until Deven said uncertainly, "We weren't actually..."

Now she giggled. "You're not seriously going to act self-conscious *now*, are you?"

"We haven't sorted out the rules for all this," Deven pointed out, "Or even if there *is* an all this. For all I know it was a one-time thing, and waking up to find the two of us making out isn't much of a 'good morning' for you."

"Yeah, well, for all I know, this was a one-time thing, and you've had enough girl for another seven centuries."

"Except for the part where you *do* know," David retorted. "Let's settle it: would you like to keep this going after today?" He pointed at Miranda.

"Hell yes," she said.

He pointed at Deven.

"Definitely."

David nodded and said, "So would I. There. Not to mention, if any of us is unhappy, we'll all know now. You're right about the need for rules, of course—the clearer we are, the fewer problems might arise. But at this particular moment I don't think you need to worry."

"I suppose you're right." Deven looked thoughtful, and added, "Of course all of this is subject to change once Nico is awake and himself again. I can't imagine he would object to anything we decided, but still, at that point I think we need a sitting-up, clothes-on discussion."

Miranda laughed again. "I never thought I'd see the day I had the kind of relationship that required a board meeting," she said. "But I'd rather be overly cautious than risk someone getting hurt when a little honesty could have helped avoid it. Right now, though...I think we can all agree that the two of you need to kiss some more. For starters."

The boys looked at each other. "She's determined," Deven noted.

"You got your daydream," Miranda told her husband reasonably. "Shouldn't I get mine?"

The Primes' eyes met again. "What do you think?" David asked. "Any objections?"

"Only that you're not already kissing me."

David glanced over at her again. "All right, do you have any limitations, requests, things you'd rather not see...?"

She thought about it for a moment, and then smiled slowly—the kind of smile that made a faint flicker of anticipatory concern cross David's face. When she spoke it was to Deven. "I've heard so many stories about you two, it's hard to know what to ask for."

"Have you now," he said, looking up at David, who shrugged good-naturedly.

"About how you tore each other apart like animals...but not always. Sometimes, when it stormed outside and you locked the doors, and stayed in bed for days...the only words he could give me for that were 'drowning' and 'dissolution,' and I remember thinking how odd that was…I mean, I've seen him lose himself in the two of us, and I've seen intense and heard a lot of noise, but dissolution…what would that even look like? Do you remember how you managed that?"

Deven met her eyes. Oh, yes, he definitely remembered that. He had catalogued every second, just as she'd hoped. He smiled.

"Show me that," Miranda asked, touching his face. "Show me our Prime undone."

David looked the tiniest bit alarmed at both her choice of words and her facial expression, and asked, "Don't you want to help with that?"

"I might. In a bit. Right now I just want to see what you two do to each other. I want to see drowning and dissolution."

Deven bowed his head almost formally. "As you will it, my Queen."

In those hours before he regained full consciousness Nico had some very odd dreams, mostly about the others having an impressive amount of rather athletic sex that was at turns deliriously passionate and prone to fits of giggling.

It would have been extremely arousing if he hadn't been so weak and confused, but as it was, the best he could manage was to be comforted by the idea of everyone together, and happy, without him.

He had decided, in the course of half-waking and half-dreaming, that he was almost certainly dead. His memory was so blurry he couldn't explain his surety, but he felt so far away from the world, so alone…and he knew he deserved it.

Something very bad had happened. He had done something…he didn't know what…but he could feel it, a second skin of crawling guilt he had no idea how to cope with.

He'd wronged others before, carelessly, when he was young— not nearly as often as his blade-tongued brother had—but he had learned from those apologies, and it had been many years since he'd done anything unacceptable enough to feel actual guilt. The emotion had its uses; it could be a catalyst for change…but one of the first things he had understood about the human world, and its

Shadow equivalent, was that people here wrapped guilt's folds around themselves and wore it underneath nearly every outfit.

It made more sense now. In Avilon there were few things he could do that would hurt someone as much as humans hurt each other. Cruelty simply wasn't something the Elentheia were normally capable of, especially after having so much of it visited upon them by the Inquisition. Only the truly aberrant among his people would be able to willfully cause pain.

Humans didn't know how to forgive themselves. Forgiveness must be asked both through a window and before a mirror, but all the glass here was dark.

He feared he was beginning to understand that too. Whatever had happened had been *that* unforgivable.

Wrestling with these thoughts drove him toward wakefulness, and finally, he started awake in a blind panic, expecting that when he tried to move his limbs would still be chained down...

They were not. In fact, he was comfortable, and felt...

The word took a moment to arise. The room was warm, dimly lit, familiar—it was his own, he realized. He'd been living here for two years now. He had chosen the linens himself, and had been told to change whatever he liked, so he'd asked for more bookshelves, and for plants that could bear the continual shadow in the room. The twin smells of chlorophyll and vanillin from leaf and paper were like a soothing balm for his frayed nerves.

Safe. He felt safe.

Well, he could discard his theory. He was clearly alive. No one dead could ache so much. He felt like he'd been clenching every muscle in his body for days, especially in his neck and back. He could move everything now, but it hurt so badly to try.

Slowly, painfully, he sat up, rubbing his eyes to clear them though it didn't really help. His vision wasn't the problem; his mind was.

Thus he only sensed a presence a mere second before the words: "Hey sweetie."

Nico turned toward her with a half-smile. His voice was a bit croaky as he said, "Stella...you have no idea how glad I am to see you."

She hesitated for a moment, her eyes searching his, but then hugged him. Her warmth and the quick beat of her heart were another comfort. She smelled like she always did, squeezed him tightly like always.

"You've been out for days," she told him. "Do you...what's the last thing you remember?"

Nico frowned. "I..." He groped for the memories, any memories, but everything seemed to be happening at once in his mind, and he couldn't place anything recent in context or time. "I don't know...everything is...damaged."

"You don't remember anything?" She actually sounded hopeful.

Dear Theia. "Stella, what did I do?" When he didn't get an immediate response he went on, "You can barely look at me, and you apparently *want* me to have amnesia. All I know is I have this sense of terrible things that happened and I was involved, but I don't understand what or why."

Stella bit her lip. "We'll get to that...first, you might want to take a look at the Web."

He might have accused her of dissembling, but her tone was too serious, so he obeyed, bringing up the Sight effortlessly in the time it took to blink. It didn't occur to him that was odd until he had already turned the vision to where he could see himself.

Nico felt himself go pale as he stared at it, unbelieving. "What...what happened here?"

"What does it look like to you?"

"My magical strength has more than doubled—I'm easily where I was before I left Avilon...no, stronger. How can that be with the bond...strangled like...oh."

Now she cracked a smile at what was no doubt a memorably gobsmacked look on his face. "Yeah."

"But..." He could only think of one appropriate phrase. "What the fuck?"

Stella giggled in spite of herself. "To give you the short-short version, Miranda took her second stab at Weaving, to bring down the barrier between you and Deven."

"Did Deven know she was going to do that?"

"He helped, sweetie. The three of them, well, apparently they used the world's oldest magic to fuel the work. It was actually a really sound plan, except they didn't know how strong the barrier you made was."

"I made."

"Yes. In the last week things have been..." She had to stop and take a deep breath, and when she looked at him again, her eyes were bright. "Bad things happened. You kind of..."

"Went batshit crazy," came a voice.

Nico turned toward the door in surprise to see the Prime standing there, looking very different from before. Nico remembered the last time he'd seen Deven, that night David had brought him home and they'd bathed and dressed the elder Prime together. David had shaved off the facial hair, but that was it. After that, Deven had apparently taken over for himself. His hair was black again. He looked ten times healthier, and there were metal loops in his eyebrow and another in his nose. When he spoke Nico caught a flash of silver in his mouth.

"Miranda held the balance as well as she could, but it overwhelmed her. It almost killed us all, but then, you happened."

Nico stared at him. "I happened how?"

"You woke from a coma and fixed the whole thing like you were untying a shoelace. I don't know if you were working alone, or had help, but regardless, you not only restored our Signet bond, you—"

Nico drew an astonished breath when he followed the line of the bond from where it had been half-dead and starving for energy. It flowed like water from one of them to the next...and the next...and the next.

He shook his head, hard; it was too much to comprehend, too much to accept. "That's not possible. No one is that powerful. Not even me."

"Like I said," Deven replied, "I think you had Help."

Nico heard the capital H. "Oh."

"The upshot is, we're a bit of a quad now, in more ways than one."

His mind had gone from blurry and empty-feeling to far too full. He had no recollection whatsoever of doing any of that, but it *felt* like it had happened. And when he touched the lines of the Web where magic had been worked, he could feel his own energy signature, and Miranda's. He didn't sense anyone else, but there was clearly something else at work within the threads; as he'd said, no single being could work at that magnitude, that quickly, and that perfectly, and live to tell of it.

"Are the others okay?" he finally asked, blinking out of the vision.

Deven smiled. "Very."

It occurred to the Elf that the sex dreams he'd been having before he woke had probably really happened.

Nico thought back to those flashes, and felt himself blushing furiously. He'd been there, then—asleep, mostly, but there, while...

Apparently the entire world had changed profoundly in the last few days and he'd missed *all* of it.

"Stella," Deven said, "Would you mind giving us a moment alone?"

The Witch looked from one of them to the other and nodded. "Of course. I'll be in my room if you need me, Nico."

"Thank you." He caught her hand and squeezed it as she climbed off the bed and left the room, closing the door quietly behind her. She gave him a strange parting look that might have been worry, or fear, though at what, he wasn't sure.

Deven came over and sat down on the edge of the bed, regarding him in silence for a while. Nico didn't know what to do with himself under that stare. He settled for looking himself over— something seemed off about his body, but he couldn't pinpoint what it was, not even well enough to ask about it.

"Your hair," Deven told him.

Suddenly Nico understood: his head felt too light, there was no weight on his shoulders, no constant movement on his neck. For centuries he'd moved through every day unconsciously drawing it out of the way; all Elves did. Now, when he shook his head nothing moved. It wasn't falling into his face. He reached up, hands trembling, and touched what was left. It was perhaps two inches long.

"Who did this to me?" he asked.

"I evened it out. It was ragged and torn out in places." The Prime crossed his arms, seeming to weigh several unpleasant options before choosing one. "You remember nothing about the last ten days?"

"No. My memories are washed out like a drawing left in the rain. I know something terrible has happened, but that's it. The last thing I remember is..." It came to him, and relieved, he finished, "leaving the concert hall with Stella and Kai after Miranda's performance. We were to meet the others at the car, but something…yes, it was the human police; they came and snatched the Queen. What did they want?"

"To charge her with murder," Deven answered almost flippantly. "That's all dealt with now. I wish I could say you'll never get those memories back, but traumatic amnesia is a mercurial bastard. You might get flashes, whole days, impressions, all of it, or nothing at all, and it might take years or minutes. I've seen it before, and the ones who got through it with the least damage were those who already knew about the events they'd experienced and were prepared for what they might see. So I'm going to tell you, flat out, most of what happened. You don't need all of it now."

"All right," Nico said around the knot in his throat that was rapidly sinking into his stomach. "Simple is best—just give me what's important."

This was already one of the longest conversations they'd ever had, and it made Nico nervous. After a minute or so of choosing his words, Deven spoke, and every sentence made Nico's heart grow colder and colder, wanting not to believe, but unable to deny a word.

"The night of the concert Morningstar took you. They had you for a day, and in that time they tortured you so unbearably you snapped. It was some of the worst I've ever seen."

"Coming from you," Nico murmured, trailing off.

Deven nodded. "I've seen bloodier, more violent. I've seen psychological torture that didn't leave a mark. But this was beyond that—it wasn't just torture, but defilement. David says they vivisected you. They were trying to learn things about you. Pain tolerances, primarily. They cut you open and did exploratory surgery…and you were awake for all of it."

Nico felt suddenly nauseated—the memories still did not come, but he could feel their echo, and hear the echo of his own screams…for hours…cold metal, and the stench of his own blood, and that man…standing over, his giddy enjoyment obscene and humiliating.

"I feel it," he said hoarsely, putting his hands over his eyes though it did nothing to help. "Just…keep going. How did I get away?"

"Miranda and I rescued you, sort of. You had already broken out, but we had to knock you unconscious to get you home.

You…you killed the men who hurt you, except for the Prophet—he got away unscathed. By the time we reached you, you were completely out of your mind. The next few days were terrifying. You stayed, but you were a different creature entirely. Full of hate and anger you'd turn on anyone…and did."

The peculiar inflection of the last word startled Nico. He swallowed hard. "Whom did I kill, Deven?"

The Prime took a deep breath. "Lesela."

He shook his head, again denying, though the truth was raw in his mind. He remembered a familiar energy that wanted only to heal, and that compassion had enraged him so much…

"David and I fought," Nico whispered, head in his hands. "And then I killed her…I killed her…she only wanted to help me, and…no, no…no."

He heard something strange and new in Deven's voice: the need to reach out, himself, and try to heal what could not be healed. Deven had never reached for him before, never wanted to get that close.

"There's more…but only one thing you really need to know for now. It's not something you did, but you need to know."

He was shaking already, limbs drawing in, curling up on himself like a contracted muscle. Maybe that was why he'd been in pain when he woke.

Deven pushed the words out as if saying them quickly would get them into the air where they could evaporate and do no more harm…but words never went away, any more than actions did. Even those never written on paper were written in the Web to be read for all time.

"Kai sent a message to Lesela asking her for help. She expected him to follow it home, but he didn't, and she grew worried. She had the other Weavers Gate her here, thinking he had stayed to watch over you…but he wasn't here. He never made it home. We're pretty sure…we think Morningstar has him. David's theory is that what they did to you was to figure out if a regular Elf could survive whatever they have planned—they needed to practice on someone they couldn't kill. But we don't know. David's been searching the whole region for any sign of him but so far there's nothing. He's just gone."

Nico had been turned into a vampire in the most painful way imaginable. He'd been rejected by the person whose soul was joined to his. He'd spent two years drained and depressed, nearly suicidal, knowing he could never return to Avilon again.

Now this.

If he had snapped, that was why. No one thing was too great for him to bear, but all together, these months were a burden so heavy he could not stand beneath it. He was a tree whose roots had been carved away one by one until there was nothing to hold him up.

Now there was nothing left to snap. It was all broken.

He closed his eyes and lay back down, curling the rest of the way into a ball the way his body seemed to crave, folding his arms over his head, uselessly warding off blows that had already come.

There was a long moment of silence.

Then, he heard, softly, "Oh no you don't."

He felt weight shift on the bed, and a hand came to rest on the nape of his neck—bare now, exposed. Nico sensed energy shifting as well, moving in a slow and gentle wave from Prime to Consort...the way it was supposed to work...

It was *working*, he realized, feeling it in a way he hadn't when he was just looking at the Web. After all these months and so much sadness, amid all this destruction and despair, the thing he had longed for—nearly died without—had found him.

The palm of Deven's hand began to heat up. Healing power. He'd said he couldn't heal minds or hearts, though...

A chuckle. "With you it's a little different. I can't fix it, but I can give you some room to breathe."

Nico managed a nod, but his thoughts were in a whirl as the current of energy reached him, lapping silently at the boundaries of his soul, asking without words for consent. Again, he nodded. The tide came in.

It wasn't dramatic, and as Deven had said, it didn't fix anything. But that wasn't his responsibility.

"Yes it is," Deven said in a whisper touched deeply with sorrow. He lifted his hand, but didn't take it away; it lay back down on Nico's head and stroked the remains of his hair. "I did this to you, after you gave everything for me. I cannot begin to atone for the last two years, Nico. I expect nothing from you. All I ask is that you let me help when I can, now that I can. Just don't shut down. You've seen what happens then."

"I don't know if I can survive this," Nico said in a hoarse, hollow voice.

"Of course you can. I know you don't see it now…but you, my love, are stronger than I could hope to be. And you're not alone. As long as you don't shut us out, you'll have all the help you need."

My love. He called me 'my love.' He called me…

Unexpectedly—but perhaps not—tears overcame the Weaver, and then he fell into helpless sobs, face buried in the pillow while the combined misery of the last few days, even the parts he couldn't remember, flooded his heart.

And sure enough, through the storm and all around him, he felt love from all sides, holding him up, offering their strength in any way he needed it. *We are here*, it said in three voices. *We are your family…together we are Four…and we are unstoppable.*

He cried himself to sleep with Deven sitting at his side, just being there, touching him without any sort of demand; and by the time Nico slipped back into oblivion, he was almost, almost smiling.

Chapter Seventeen

"Tell me something true."

Deven looked at her over the rim of his coffee cup, pondered a moment, and said, "I used to be a backup dancer for Michael Jackson."

"What in the *what* now?" Miranda wasn't sure whether it made perfect sense or he was screwing with her, and she made sure it showed on her face.

He grinned. "No, really." He took a sip, wrinkled his nose, and dumped more sugar into the cup. "Periodically I take time off from life as an assassin and murder pimp and seek out training that I feel would add to my skill set. I've studied almost every form of martial arts on the globe, and branched out from there into other forms of movement." Another grin. "You'll love this one—the most recent was tribal fusion. Belly dance."

She laughed. "Well, that explains your abs. You realize you have to prove that with a demonstration. Stage outfit required."

Deven laughed too. "Maybe sometime. Being a vampire is a huge advantage for a dancer—so is being in a body that stopped developing at seventeen."

"Oh, I wouldn't say that. You don't move like any seventeen year old I've ever met."

"I take that as a compliment. Have you seen teenage boys lately? They're hairy dumb elephants."

Miranda giggled and took another bite of the chocolate croissant she'd ordered with her latte. It felt wrong to be having fun given what was happening at home, but David had all but thrown them out of the house so he, Nico, and Stella could work on the search for Kai without Miranda and Deven hovering around fretting.

Everyone was a bundle of raw nerves. One day had turned into two, then three, and there was no trace of Morningstar, or the Bard, whatsoever. They'd tried magic, technology, both together; they'd used the seeking spell Stella and David had bastardized to find Nico and coupled that with the twin connection between the brothers. There was no hint of Kai's presence anywhere in Austin, or Texas, at all.

It was a strange counterpoint to everything else going on. After a preliminary group discussion about their new reality, things seemed to be working remarkably well; the consensus had been to play it by ear for a bit and then have another meeting when everyone had given serious thought to their own boundaries and needs—and after they'd found Kai.

Miranda was fairly sure she wouldn't be back to the Suite tonight, though ostensibly this was just a shopping excursion. Deven's old wardrobe had been blown to shit with the Haven, and since coming to Austin he'd been dressing in Normal Guy Drag; he'd asked her to come with him to town to start rectifying that, giving them time to decompress and the others time to work.

She sincerely hoped David would be able to persuade Nico to have company for the day. She didn't want the Elf sleeping alone when so many horrible memories were so close to the surface.

"Your turn," Deven said, shaking her out of the dervish whirl of her thoughts and reminding her that they'd agreed to talk about anything but their Elf crisis. "Tell me something true."

Miranda thought about it for a minute. "I doubt I have anything as interesting as the stories you could tell."

"Not the point."

"Yeah, I know. Um...okay, I've got it. I once had sex in a Burger King bathroom."

He gave her a long blink. "Like in the song?"

"Yeah. My first ex in college was...well...basically awful in the sack. Toward the end I started suggesting weird places just to keep from falling asleep. Burger King, the roof of a parking garage, Mt. Bonnell...typical stuff."

"That bad, was he?"

She nodded, and added around a bite of croissant, "Near as I could tell he thought a clitoris was like the B-button on a video game controller and he was Super Mario in one of the swimming levels."

Miranda had the immensely gratifying experience of seeing the Prime of the Western United States inhale his coffee and then laugh himself silly. It didn't take her long to lose it too, and for a minute they relaxed and gleefully annoyed the other patrons of Slim Shaky's Espresso Bar.

"I suppose David was quite an education, then," Deven noted once they'd fallen quiet again. "Whatever his faults, our boy can shag like a champion."

"No kidding. I'm pretty sure he's got at least a Master's Degree in the subject." She frowned. "Is it weird for us to talk about this?"

"Why would it be?"

"I don't know. I guess I'm still used to 'normal' relationships, whatever those are."

Deven gave her a conspiratorial grin and indicated a nearby couple with a tilt of his head. "Look at Mr. and Mrs. White Bread over there—when they get home she's going to strap him to a bed frame in their refurbished basement, put on a vinyl cat suit, and spank him with a pancake turner until he can't sit down tomorrow. And that fellow over there, the one in the owlish glasses and the extremely sober button-down? Not only is he into gay porn, he writes it—Harry Potter fan fiction. An accountant by day, Bottom!Remus77 by night."

She lifted an eyebrow. "Are you making that up, or do you actually know?"

"Yes. The point is, even people who claim to have normal relationships have their kinks and twists. There are four of us, yes, but compared to a lot of people polyamory is weak tea."

"Are you sure you don't have any fetishes you're hiding? Getting off to chanting monk CDs, maybe?"

Another long blink. "My God...how did you know?"

At her widened eyes, he laughed again.

After a moment of companionable silence, she told him, "One more time...tell me something true."

He smiled and took her hand, eyes sparkling. "I adore you."

She knew she was practically beaming, and was about to reply when her com chimed. "Star-Two," she said.

"Sorry to cut your date short, beloved, but...I've got something."

Miranda and Deven's eyes locked. "We're on our way."

"I do not take orders from you," Nico ground out, poison in every syllable. He started to get back to his feet.

A boot came down solidly on his neck.

"Yes. You. Do."

"...didn't work, but I'm starting to think we're trying the spell too soon. We have to narrow the field—even assuming they're in Texas that's a huge area to search. It's...Nico?"

The pressure on his neck turned out to be the gentleness of a hand, not the definitive statement of a boot, and he lifted his head to see David regarding him with concern. "Are you still with me?"

He nodded, shaking the images away. "A memory...it will pass."

They both knew that was a lie. In the last few days, Nico had stayed as busy as he could, refusing to give up the search for Kai, but his motives were as selfish as they were motivated by fear for his brother. Every time he was still, in every silence, more of the recent days returned. He'd hoped they would wait until Kai was found and he could breathe again, but he was not given to good fortune these days.

At David's raised eyebrow Nico said wearily, "The gods are infinitely imaginative in their cruelty. Each time I think things cannot get any worse...somehow they do."

"Careful," David responded. "You're starting to sound like Deven."

"Perhaps his fatalism is not so extreme after all."

Nico could tell that David resisted pointing out that Deven had been much less fatalistic since they'd gotten Nico back; but Nico lowered his eyes, sighing, and went back to toying with the stone in his hand.

Apparently curious, the Prime put a hand over his and turned Nico's palm over so he could see it: a flat oval-shaped stone, transparent but for pale bands of blue, purple, and green. "Fluorite, yes?" David asked.

He nodded. "My people have been known to employ it for help in emotional healing."

"Where did you get it? Oh...I see. Deven gave it to you."

Nico smiled a little in spite of himself. "Yes. He said there is a shop in town that sells all sorts of stones with mystical properties." He had no idea if it was actually working or not, but he had to admit having it in his hands made him feel better, if only because of where it came from. "He is giving me a wide berth...but whenever I go to bed I find gifts like this in my room, everything very deliberately chosen. Distractions, I suppose, to make me smile in the midst of all of this pain."

Now David smiled. "He's courting you."

"So it would seem."

"And how do you feel about that?"

"I don't know." Nico sighed and pocketed the fluorite. "Our timing is apparently doomed no matter what. Even two weeks ago, I would have been overjoyed...now, I...I can hardly feel anything but fear for Kai. He might have been dead for days...and that might be better than the suffering they will bring him. Kai has hurt no one...he is not part of this war...he only wanted to take care of his broken brother. I cannot turn my heart anywhere right now but to finding him."

"You shouldn't blame yourself, Nico."

"Perhaps not...but I do, all the same."

The Prime pulled him close for a moment. They had something far more profound now than a magical connection—that was a capillary compared to this artery. Nico didn't want to rely on the others...he had been weak long enough. But at the moment he was flat-out exhausted from lack of sleep and too many attempts at the seeking spell; there was no way he could keep going without help.

After half a dozen tries Stella had finally run out of energy and fallen over sideways, the Prime's lightning reflexes the only thing that kept her from cracking her skull on what was no doubt a very expensive piece of computer equipment. David had ordered the Witch to bed for at least a few hours. He'd known better than to try and do the same to Nico.

"You know you can lean on us," David murmured, the low vibration of his voice soothing against Nico's ear. "We're here to take care of each other."

"You've given me so much already."

"And do you see me regretting it? Or my strength flagging? No, and you won't. We're here to care for each other—and I'm here to care for all of you. I will be the fixed point in our turning world no matter how fast it spins. Maybe you're not ready to trust Deven, and maybe you don't know Miranda well enough yet to trust her...but you can trust me."

Nico leaned back to look at him, hearing something odd in his tone, and...

"What?" David frowned...and as soon as he blinked, his eyes were blue again.

"Nothing," Nico half-whispered. "I'm just tired."

"Understatement, love. If I thought we had time I'd send you to bed like Stella."

He started to ask David why he'd stopped working, but remembered that the Prime had sent for the others and was no doubt waiting until they arrived to move forward. David was cautiously optimistic about his discoveries but needed their input to draw any conclusions.

Nico watched him return to his seat behind the big desk, heard the system beep and chirp in happy acknowledgment of his presence, and tried not to look as shaken as he felt.

"Does the name Elendala Seara mean anything to you?" David asked suddenly.

Nico started, blinked. "Elendala Seara? It's Elvish, but...I know no one by that name. Why do you ask?"

"It's Deven's mother's name. There's been...a suggestion...that she's still alive. I don't know how that would be possible—she'd be seven centuries old by now and she was only half Elf."

Nico shrugged. "Half is enough. In the human world, she would most likely age and die. If she went to live in Avilon or one of the other Sanctuaries the magic there would prevail over her human half and she would, after a while, be almost indistinguishable from the rest of us."

"What about one-quarter Elf?"

He smiled. "That, I could not say. I've never heard of it happening, but in theory at least it could if the person was strong enough."

Nico didn't ask where David had heard of Elendala; he was pretty sure he knew, and didn't want to think about it...not yet. *Keep that memory at bay a while longer...please. I cannot fall apart now.*

"Then again," Nico went on, crossing his arms over his chest against sudden cold that didn't come from outside, "if she escaped to Avilon that long ago and took a new name, I might know her and not realize it. Are you planning to look for her?"

"Not without Deven's permission. I was just curious. I suppose it would be a ridiculous coincidence for you to know her."

"Do we even have coincidences anymore?" Nico asked.

"Good point."

Before Nico could say anything else, the office door opened; Miranda and Deven had arrived, looking purposeful and grave.

Nico tried not to appear as relieved as he felt upon seeing the Prime. It was like looking back to that brief time before Nico had left California, when Deven had recovered from his breakdown and was himself for a while. Odd how black leather, metal studs, and edged weapons could be so comforting.

Deven caught his eye and offered a small smile. Nico felt himself flushing and looked down, unable to hide a smile of his own.

David cleared his throat, and when Nico looked up, he was watching the Weaver with amusement in his eyes. "I've had an insight, but I need all brains on deck."

Miranda took position next to Nico and Deven took the other chair. Nico had seen what happened when someone besides David sat down behind the desk—Stella had forgotten she wasn't logged in, and the computer system had, in David's words, freaked the fuck out.

"We've tried the spell six times, and gotten nothing," David said. "We even managed to amplify the spell throughout the sensor network—that's all over the country. But all the power in the world isn't going to help if we don't know what direction to look in. Right now we're blindfolded and swinging at a piñata the size of a honeybee."

"How do we narrow it down, then?" Miranda asked. "Is there another spell? Something in the Codex?"

Nico shook his head. "So far there is no practical magic in the Codex. We may yet find some, but there's no way to know until it's decoded."

"The answer might not be magic at all," David told them. "At least not yet. What did we do before we had Elves and Witches around?"

Deven's eyes were on the sensor map of Austin, projected up onto the wall. "Follow the money trail."

"When we destroyed Morningstar's base last year I had the Elite bag and tag every receipt and piece of paperwork they found. I had it all scanned, and the data filed away in case I ever needed it. Well, if we operate on the assumption—admittedly a problematic one—that their current operation is at least the size of the old one, we can run all of that data against businesses and utilities and look for a location that is using approximately the same amount of electricity, food, uniforms, et cetera."

Deven gave him a dubious look. "That's kind of a long shot."

"That's the only kind of shot we have at this point. That's why I called you back—I need more parameters. Something to narrow it down further. Right now there are over a hundred possible locations just statewide. There's no way we can raid them all. Give me more to go on."

"Weapons," Deven suggested immediately. "They've all got standard-issue swords; upper mid-range quality, mass-produced. Not disposable but not our caliber."

"I don't suppose you noticed—"

"Koneko, model 42."

Nico watched as the map on the wall expanded to show the entire state, with dozens of red lights representing the possible loci. After a moment over half of them vanished.

"Wait," Miranda said, "that many places ordered that exact sword?"

"No—that many places put in orders to weapons dealers in the price range of at least twenty of that sword. Getting actual shipping manifests from Koneko is going to take time. Any more suggestions?"

"Magic."

They all looked at Nico, no doubt wondering what he was on about considering they'd been using magic in the search all week.

"Your network records magical energy. It is likely, given their track record of doing blood magic to take power from Signets and brainwash their soldiers, that they intend something arcane for Kai. Looking for magic alone wouldn't necessarily help, since in any given human settlement there are spells going on every night. But we know that in addition to their base out in the middle of nowhere they also commandeer abandoned buildings—see how many of your loci are supposedly empty but still drawing electricity, and cross reference them with large spikes in magical usage in the last week."

They were all still looking at him, but now with appreciation. "Have I told you lately that you're brilliant?" David asked.

Nico smiled. "It does sometimes bear repeating."

David returned his attention to the computer, and the screen split into several windows, each with its own activity. Nico had learned a good deal about how computers worked, and David had shown him different types of technical languages, but what the Prime was doing now was a little more complicated than Nico could grasp without serious study.

"How are you feeling, Nico?"

He looked over at Deven. "I do not think that is a fair question, my Lord."

Miranda reached over and put her hand on his shoulder. "Is there anything we can do?"

Nico put his head in his hands for a moment, saying quietly, "Only one thing, and you are already doing all you can."

He heard the chair creak, and then felt hands on his, drawing them away from his face so dark violet eyes could meet lavender.

"We're going to find him," Deven said. "I give you my word."

"Clever of you not to specify 'alive,'" Nico muttered, looking away. "Or 'sane.'"

One hand took gentle hold of his chin and brought their gazes back in line. "I can't promise the latter for certain, given what we know they might do. We didn't bring you back sane, after all—but alive, I can promise." His thumb brushed lightly, so very lightly, over Nico's lower lip, and Nico couldn't help it—he shivered. "I've failed you too many times. Not this time. If I have to decapitate every last one of those bastards, I'll bring your brother home."

They stared at each other until Nico offered a slight nod, closed his eyes, and, taking a risk, leaned his head against Deven's shoulder. He heard a quickly indrawn breath and, after a few second's astonished pause, felt arms slide around him.

Miranda had been pretending not to watch them, but David had been absorbed in his work and spoke again without looking up. "All right...I've got it narrowed down to five likely locations."

Deven stepped back away from the desk to turn toward the screen again. Nico fought a surprisingly forceful urge to drag him back and then wrap himself around the Prime and not let go until the world stopped running out from under him.

David went on, highlighting the places he'd found. "One in Fort Worth, one about ten miles from McAllen, another in an abandoned warehouse in Beaumont, and two here in Austin. I've got satellite footage of the first two—one's a slaughterhouse, hence the large order of what turns out to be various sharp devices for hacking animals into chunks. The other is an old scout camp, which was apparently abandoned because of flooding, making the roads impassable for all practical purposes. Thermal shows twenty humans at the former, none at the latter."

"Who the hell is doing magic at a slaughterhouse?" Miranda asked.

"I have no idea. But that cuts the list to three. Beaumont's a good candidate—looks like it's between owners but the lights are still on. I'm sending Lieutenant Sadh and a team from the Houston garrison to check it out. I just dispatched teams to the two Austin locations as well." Seeing the alarm on Miranda's face he added, "Strictly recon. No engagement. We should know something within the hour."

Nico sat staring up at the map, listening with half attention to the others—David commanded the entire Elite to be on high alert, Miranda made sure they had a driver on standby and contacted the Hausmann to inform them there might be an emergency patient tonight.

"I can probably heal him," he heard Deven say. "But we have no idea what to expect, and I've never tried it on an Elf before. And even if I can, a night of monitoring and fluids would be helpful. The less I have to do, the better I can do it."

Nico kept his eyes on those three red dots. Kai might be in one of them. He could be there right now, suffering, wondering why Nico and the others hadn't come to save him. So alone...he must be so afraid...even with all his bravado he had no more idea how to deal with torture and terror than Nico had. He might have already lost his mind...might be dead...might wish he were dead.

All those possibilities made Nico's head swim, and he put his face in his hands again, holding back premature tears of grief. Whatever they had done to Kai, his life before this place would be over, and everything from now on would be the "after." Nico knew how it felt to have life split in two like that. He'd had it happen half a dozen times in the last two years.

"*Star-One,*" came a male voice. "*This is Lieutenant Sadh reporting.*"

David hit some sort of directive on the computer that routed the voice out where they could all hear it. "Go ahead, Lieutenant."

"*I'm afraid this location is a bust, Sire. The warehouse is populated by squatters, not soldiers—some of them managed to patch into the city electrical grid. I had my people interview some of the locals and got confirmation. Suspicious activity for the metro PD, but not for us.*"

"Well done, Lieutenant. Call back your team and return to your protocol."

"*Yes, Sire.*"

David sighed, disappointed. "I suppose it's just as well— Beaumont's hours away."

"*Star-One, this is Second Lieutenant Mendez reporting. I think we may have something.*"

They all leaned closer, though no one had any problem hearing. "Go ahead."

Mendez sounded faintly out of breath as she said, "*At first everything seemed innocuous. There's nothing in the building itself, just a big empty space. It's one of the smaller warehouses in the area, and we're in a sketchy neighborhood where people tend to look the other way. I was about to call them back when Elite 71 saw several humans clad in BDUs leaving the building.*"

"Are you sure it's not a drug cartel?" Miranda asked, leaning in farther. "The Quintana-Rios clan has been busy this year and APD busted one of their smaller operations in that neighborhood."

"*Positive, my Lady. They were wearing swords. I suspect thermal imaging will show a pretty decent-sized group underground.*"

"Stand by, Second Lieutenant." David made the map shrink to one corner of the screen and pulled up another that looked like just that individual building. "Switching to thermal scan...now."

Suddenly dozens of lights appeared inside the building, moving around what appeared to be multiple rooms.

"Two days ago the sensor network registered a significant spike in magical energy at this address." David's expression became grimly determined. "I think we have a winner."

"What do we do, then?" Miranda asked. "Attack in force? Send a stealth team?"

Deven, however, was frowning.

"What is it?" David asked.

"This isn't right."

"How so?"

Deven shook his head. "We already broke into an underground base of theirs once. Doesn't it seem convenient that they'd do exactly the same thing again? If Kai is important to them, and they know we've found them once, wouldn't they have taken him out of the city, or even out of Texas? These are people who've managed to take down half a dozen Signets—*Signets*. They're clearly not stupid."

"So you think it's a trap," Miranda concluded, deflated. "You don't think they have Kai there at all."

"Actually I think they do. I think they've had him there the whole time—and they want us to know."

"Bait?" David asked.

"Maybe. Or maybe it's a show of strength—I didn't want to suggest this before, but...it's possible they did to Kai what they've done to the other Signets and stole his power to do something massive. Or..." Deven looked over at Nico, took a breath, and went on, "or they're still doing it. They might be using him as a battery for something, which is why they'd want to know what he could tolerate, so they'd know how much and how long to drain him before he gives out."

"God," David muttered. "What do you suggest, then?"

Nico almost missed the shift in Deven's expression; it was there and smoothed over so quickly and with such iron control. But for just a second, his eyes went silver, his hand tightened around Ghostlight's hilt, and something predatory and fierce came over his face.

Hatred. Long-seething, scarlet hatred twisted around rage.

He'd never doubted Deven's power or authority, and he'd seen him angry and half-mad from grief, but this was the first time he'd ever found the Prime *terrifying*...and all the more terrifying because it was so alluring.

It was then that, after days of thinking only of Kai's fate, Nico remembered he wasn't the only one who had lost someone to Morningstar.

By the time Deven turned to face the others, he was as calm and collected as always, though there was something ever so slightly feral in the way he said, "I have an idea."

The endless rain had finally cleared over Austin, leaving bitter cold beneath crystalline stars. Even with the chill the sudden lack of deluge had drawn the city's denizens outside, wide-eyed and bleary like they'd woken from hibernation.

The drastic increase in activity was worrisome to the Queen, who waited by the car while the others got out, leaning sideways so she could see down the street where the warehouse stood, the very picture of dereliction. She certainly wouldn't have picked it out of a lineup if she had to guess which building on the block was the headquarters of a small army.

She knew that the Elite were busy cordoning off the block—not with pylons, but with their own presence. In this neighborhood human traffic was pretty low at night, due in part to the cartel she'd mentioned before. Even if the whole thing went profoundly south on them, civilian casualties were unlikely.

She still didn't like it. It was reckless. Deven was out for blood, and though that feeling of secondhand anger drifting through her was gratifying, it didn't leave her clear-headed, which meant it probably didn't Deven either.

"He knows what he's doing," David said, coming to stand beside her. "Even without any of our inherited power he could take them all in his sleep."

She looked over at her other two bondmates, who were wearing remarkably similar expressions at the moment. She'd never thought of Nico as looking particularly dangerous, but in a long coat with his hair short showing off both his ears and the tattoo on his face, he cut an impressive, and vampiric, figure.

She imagined him armed. *Damn.*

She glanced at David. He was biting his lip against a grin. "Stop reading my mind," she said.

"Oh, I didn't need to. I know that look."

"You act like you haven't already planted a flag in that particular mountain," she replied, eliciting a snort from her Prime.

"I highly recommend the climb," he said with a smile.

She started to make a sardonic comment, but the momentary respite was broken. "Let's go," Deven said. "David, you have the toy surprises?"

David held up a silver briefcase. Unfortunately for Miranda's sense of the stereotypical he didn't have it handcuffed to his wrist. "Ready."

"Remember, stay back unless I call. The fewer targets we give them the better."

Much as she preferred a straightforward battle, Miranda had to concede the point he'd made on the way here: if Morningstar killed one of them they weren't just fracturing the Circle anymore, but killing all four of them in one shot, leaving what was left of the Circle crippled and without its leader. Miranda and David were immune to heart-shots with wood, but they had no idea if that extended to the other Pair, and there really wasn't a good way to find out.

The plan was simple enough: draw as many of Morningstar's soldiers to the front of the building as possible while two teams of Elite went in the back way from different directions, doubling the chance that one of them would find Kai. They were to vacate the premises the second the order came, even if they hadn't found him. They weren't planning on a big battle, but that didn't mean they wouldn't get one.

Miranda wasn't sure what Deven intended to do in order to catch their attention, but she had a feeling it would be theatrical.

There was an empty storefront across the street from the warehouse. Its front window was boarded up, but had gaps aplenty they could watch through, and the half-rotted plywood and 2x4s would be easy work if they needed to break cover.

It was pretty disgusting on the inside, having served at some point as a drug den and, possibly at the same time, a toilet.

"What is it with bad guys and warehouses?" Miranda muttered, taking up position at one of the gaps. "Can't someone who wants to kill us operate out of a nice bungalow or something?"

David echoed her motion, except that he took hold of the bottom half of one of the boards and snapped it off, making the gap wide enough to get his arm through, and wide enough that they could all see out of it. Nico stood just behind him, arms crossed, anxiety written both in his face and posture.

"Here we go," David said. "Both of you—strengthen your shields."

Miranda would have asked why, but they all fell silent watching the solitary figure stride purposefully into the middle of the street.

Deven stopped right in front of the warehouse, in the glow of the streetlights, cold and impassive with his Signet out where its own light was visible. He turned his back to their hiding place and faced the warehouse.

Miranda remembered, just in time, to do as David had said, and thank goodness she did.

A voice thundered through her head, loud enough to rattle her bones—but completely silent. She could feel it seizing every mind it could latch onto in the building.

COME OUT AND FACE ME.

She knew the words would easily reach underground. If she hadn't been solidly shielded it would have been incredibly painful—she would have expected it to knock everyone unconscious except it was expertly modulated, exactly loud enough that it couldn't be ignored.

Out on the street, Deven pulled back the side of his coat and drew Ghostlight before speaking again.

NOW.

Miranda stared, amazed, at its source. "Did we know he could do that?" she asked.

"Telepathic projection," David said. "Any telepath can do it, but it takes power to get it that loud."

Nico leaned in closer. "Is being frightening something all Primes strive for, or is that just the two of you?"

David smiled without looking away from the window. "Where do you think I learned it from?"

The moment stretched out long enough that Miranda started to think they had been wrong about the warehouse, and—

Movement.

She saw shadows detach from the building...dozens of them. Then she heard the telltale creak of crossbows being raised.

"Go ahead," Deven said. "Get it out of your systems."

Clicks bit into the air like hailstones hitting pavement. She watched at least thirty arrows fly out from the warehouse, sailing toward the oh-so-easy target—all in black, in the middle of the street, they barely had to aim to hit him.

Miranda felt a pull at her mind, and she, David, and Nico all opened themselves up. Energy flowed out of her, and she grinned, watching Deven push the energy out around him in a circle as if he did such things everyday.

Every last arrow hit the barrier and snapped in half, clattering to the ground harmlessly.

"Send out the Prophet," Deven ordered. "And bring me the Elf."

"I'm afraid I can't do that," came a voice.

A man in cleric's clothing stepped out into view.

He didn't seem at all concerned with the situation; his demeanor was actually affable, like he and Deven were old drinking buddies.

"I know you," Deven said. "You're the Shepherd I met in California."

"I am indeed," was the reply. "I'm touched you remember me."

"Where is the Elf?"

The Shepherd stuck his hands in his pockets a little too casually, but it didn't look like there was anything in them. "Don't worry—he's perfectly safe with us. I think you'll be pleased with how well he's been treated."

"The only thing you can do to please me, besides die in a pool of your own blood, is bring him to me."

"What will you do if I refuse?"

Deven said, "Do you really need to ask that?"

"I suppose not. Well, it turns out you're in luck—the Prophet wants to meet you."

"That's not what I asked for."

"I'm afraid it isn't my call. I'm only a soldier of God like anyone here; a leader of men, perhaps, but still a servant. I'm happy to, say, order explosives set at a Haven, and make the call to arm them, but ultimately the Word comes from the Prophet, and I work his will, as he delivers it from the Highest."

Deven laughed quietly. "Are you suicidal, or is your Prophet trying to get rid of you? Because either way..."

A whistle, and the Shepherd flew backwards, knocked off his feet by the dagger protruding from his chest. Miranda stifled a gasp with her hand over her mouth—she hadn't even seen Deven move. She ought to be used to that kind of thing by now—she'd done it herself more than once—but it still blew her away.

"Now," he said, more loudly, "If the Prophet wants to speak to me, let him come forth. I'm running out of patience, and since I don't have enough knives for all of you, your ends will be far messier."

There was a slow clap from the warehouse's open door.

"Excellent," someone said. "Truly, very impressive."

Miranda froze.

She knew that voice.

Next to her, both Nico and David had gone very still as well. She saw Nico grab David's arm in a death-grip.

No...no, no, no.

David said softly into his com, "Elite teams fall back—you have two minutes."

"As you will it, Sire."

Miranda barely heard them. All she could do was stare.

The Prophet walked out into the light, smiling as if this was all a play written solely for his amusement. He wore all black, like the Shepherd, but instead of a clerical collar, there was an amulet hanging from his throat, glowing a strange, sickly blue.

A Signet.

That wasn't all he'd stolen.

He walked around Deven in a slow circle before coming to stand about ten feet in front of him—an easy striking distance...but the Prophet knew there was no way in hell Deven would attack him.

His dark violet eyes fixed on the Prime's. "Please, do go on," he said. "I love a good threat display, especially when it's empty."

Deven's reaction to the man standing in front of him was shocking, but echoed exactly what they were all feeling.

He dropped his sword.

"What...the hell...is this?" he demanded softly, hissing the words and taking a step back.

The Prophet smiled again. Miranda felt nausea washing over her. How many times had she seen that smile—only nothing like this, not nasty and cruel, not enjoying someone else's pain.

"It is remarkable," he said, holding out his arms, looking at his hands with what looked like genuine pleasure. "I've worn many bodies in the last two thousand years, but they were all human. Humans are so fragile, and so disposable—you have no idea how many I burned through in the last year alone. Then I had a delightful idea: Use another breed. Obviously I couldn't take one of yours. Your flesh is beneath me. But the Elentheia...once I discovered they still exist, I knew I had to at least give it a try. The Sanctuaries were still inaccessible, so I had to work with what I could get. I knew they were strong, but I couldn't be sure they would be able to contain me any more than a human."

"Who are you?"

"Oh, come now. Don't you have a guess? You're nearly half as old as I am...or, perhaps older, in a way, given how little of that time I was awake. We've been asleep for a very, very long time, thanks to your merry little band's first incarnation."

Deven shook his head. "You're insane. That's just a myth—"

"So is Persephone, so are Elves, so are vampires. You'll have to do better than that, boy. I know you're used to being the apex predator around here, but..."

Before Miranda could register the motion, the Prophet had crossed the space and wrapped his hand around Deven's throat, hauling him up off the ground. He shook his hand hard like he was shaking a rag doll, and Miranda heard a dull crack.

Deven went limp.

"It would be very easy for me to kill you right now," the Prophet said. "But I have much more entertaining plans for all of you. Before I'm done, you will all kneel to me."

He dropped the Prime on the ground—Deven was still conscious, but Miranda knew his spine was broken. The Prophet stood over him, and moved as if to step on his neck.

She didn't have a chance to react. She heard the storefront's door slam, and next thing she knew, the Prophet was thrown aside, where he hit the ground rolling and was back on his feet in seconds.

"Aha!" he said, pleased. "I was wondering if you'd survived."

"Keep your hands off of him," Nico snarled, standing between him and Deven. "And *get the hell out of my brother!*"

"Fascinating," said the Prophet in Kai's stolen, melodic voice. "You're actually willing to hurt your twin's body to save your Prime's. I suppose it's to be expected—mere self-preservation would drive you to protect that pathetic little creature you're anchored to."

"Give him back, you bastard."

He went on as if Nico hadn't spoken. "But I know that if you think there's even the slightest chance he's still in here, you won't lay a hand on this body. Is he? Or did I annihilate his soul to make room for my own? How could you ever possibly know?"

Miranda, breathing hard, looked at David. "We have to do something."

But he was way ahead of her; he'd snapped the briefcase open, exposing three spherical devices in a nest of foam. He hit a switch at the top of each, and she felt him tap firmly on the back of Nico's mind. *Ready.*

"You'll be happy to know that thanks to your contribution, your dear brother didn't have to suffer nearly as much as you did in the process of emptying out his body. Well, not physically anyway. Having all the power sucked out of you is pretty hideous, or at least it sounded like it was."

"You know," Nico said, regaining his calm in spite of the Prophet's baiting, "I've learned a lot about good and evil since I came here. I learned that the first, and most obvious, flaw of evil is something none of you can seem to help."

"And what's that?"

Nico smiled. "Monologuing."

Nico threw himself backward, turning so he landed covering Deven, and across the street, David took the three spherical devices from the briefcase and, drawing on both Nico and Miranda, threw them, hard, with his mind.

The second the devices hit the building, they exploded.

The force of the blast shattered the remaining glass in the storefront window. Miranda dropped to her knees, covering her face with her arms, and felt glass shards hitting the sleeve of her coat. The air was thick with smoke and dust, and distantly she heard screaming.

She knew at least a few of the soldiers had survived, but if she had her way right now they would *all* be burning.

There was a grunt from both impact and pain. Nico and Deven lay on the floor where the Elf had transported them, the Elf still shielding the Prime.

"What did he do?" David demanded. "Can he Mist?"

"I think so," Nico ground out hoarsely, rolling sideways. He was sooty and bruised, his coat badly singed. "I know he lived. Stolen or not, I would have felt it if he died that close to me."

"Let's get out of here," Miranda said. "The police and AFD will be here any minute. Harlan will be at the rendezvous point—we'll have to carry Dev."

"No," David said. "I've got it."

He didn't finish the sentence. Miranda felt a sickening lurch, and next thing she knew, she was tumbling to the ground next to the Escalade.

Groaning, she turned a gaze of astonishment on her husband. "Did you just Mist four people at once?"

David had sagged back against the vehicle, looking faintly ill, but he nodded. "It was faster."

Miranda shook her head. "I don't even know how to react to that."

From the look of it, neither did he.

Nico, too, was leaning on the car, ghostly white, breathing hard—from exertion or shock, or both, she wasn't sure. She pushed herself to her feet, went over, and hugged him hard.

"We'll get him back," she said. "We'll find a way."

"What was he talking about?" Nico asked. "I don't understand—how can he be two thousand years old?"

"It's all connected," David said, passing his hands over his face. He picked Deven, who was unconscious now, up off the ground and with Harlan's help got him in the car. "The original Circle—they defeated Morningstar, but not until Morningstar buried Persephone...the way She had once buried them."

"Oh my God," Miranda didn't want to believe it; it was too big, too strange. But if she put together everything she'd heard about vampire history, it made sense.

They had all assumed that the origin myth of vampire kind and the story of the first Circle were two separate things...but they weren't.

She, David, Deven, and Nico were Thirdborn. The iteration of vampires that had given rise to the Signets were Secondborn.

And according to myth, hidden deep in the earth by the Goddess Herself, were the Firstborn.

Chapter Eighteen

Over the next few days Nico fought his way out of nightmares over and over. Someone else spoke to him with Kai's voice. Lesela fell to the ground with her hands at her throat, whispering, *"Why?"*

In the dreams he killed them both with the same blade; he'd murdered Lesela and left her dying alone, so far from home and family and anything beautiful, merely as bait for the others. He could remember the hot splash of her blood, the intoxicating power of it. He never wanted to feel that again...but he knew he would.

He would, but now he would have to finish it...he would have to kill, every month, forever. The need was building in him even now—more slowly than they'd expected, but building all the same.

Lying in bed shaking violently and feebly fighting off soul-choking despair, he had to force that reality away from his mind. If he let himself think about now it he would lose his sanity, and there would be no coming back. His heart had taken too many blows in too little time.

David came to see him and give him updates: Only about a dozen bodies had been pulled from the warehouse's wreckage. David had chosen his explosives very deliberately to cause the hottest fire possible and destroy as much evidence as they could. He had pored over a schematic of the building to find the precise spots to hit so the whole front would come down. The back of the building faced a row of stores that might yet have had humans in them; as far as they knew there had been no casualties among the innocent.

There was no sign of the Prophet—not that they'd expected

295

any. David had contacted practically every vampire he knew of great age or wisdom, trying to find more than myth and legend about the Firstborn, but it would take time and persistence. It was likely their best hope was the Codex, and their second best the Order of Elysium, if he could convince them to talk. Since Deven had massacred the Cloister and Eladra, they wanted nothing to do with the Signets, but they might not have much choice if they wanted vampire kind to survive.

Not to mention that while they might hate Deven, there was no way they could deny David for long. He would get the truth from them in whatever way he had to. Nico prayed his reputation was widespread enough that they would understand exactly what that meant and offer up whatever they knew before Deven became the least of their enemies. Deven would probably never raise a blade to the Order again no matter how dire the circumstances. David had no such reluctance.

David lay down with him for a while, offering his endless reservoir of strength as he had so many times before. Nico clung to him, but though it was comforting, he couldn't let his grief show for fear of drowning in it. He knew that David wanted to stay, mostly to keep an eye on him; everyone was treating him like he was made of spun glass and might break into splinters at any second.

He just might. He was not the strong person he had been when he set foot in California. Oh, magically he was more powerful than he had ever been—the other Weavers, always envious of his abilities, would be genuinely frightened of him now. But emotionally he was pathetically weak. There was only one place he might find solace...in the Signet bond...but he was afraid if he let them close, they would see what a failure they had in their midst...how could anyone want him now?

Everything was broken. What fate had not destroyed he had killed on his own. He had failed at everything he'd turned his hand to.

He told David he wanted some time alone. The Prime frowned, not agreeing in the slightest, but didn't gainsay his wishes. "Call me the minute you change your mind," he said lovingly, kissing Nico's forehead. "At your word, I'll be with you in a heartbeat or less."

It was quite remarkable how the Prime could be such a gentle, kind lover and still be a just but terrifying monarch. He brought many of the same skills to both.

A strange thing, being loved so much. Nico didn't deserve it, but nothing as silly as shattered self-esteem would hold the Prime back from one he loved. Nico envied him his confidence...always had. David was a force of nature matched only by his Queen, and they were the hands of the Goddess, and in many ways Her very being here on Earth.

The third night, Nico stood in the hallway staring at a door for the fourth time in the last few days. He wanted to knock...he wanted to flee. The first two days he could make the excuse that it was too soon. Not so tonight.

It took all the will he could summon, but he rapped lightly on the door, heart in his throat. At first he didn't think there would be an answer.

He was only too ready to retreat, but the door swung silently inward a few inches, an invitation without words.

As he stepped into the room, lit only by fire, he heard music.

Nico expected to see someone in the bed, but there were only rumpled sheets; his eyes fell on the armchair, where a slender figure sat cross-legged, eyes closed, a faint look of concentration on his face. The music was coming from a phone plugged into a set of speakers.

The Prime looked both angelic and saturnine; he was all in black, the sort of casual wear that the others favored, though with a t-shirt bearing the worn, faded logo of something called Beatles. The stone of his Signet shone soft green against the dark fabric. One bare foot was visible, and something about that made Nico feel a little too warm for the room.

"I can come back later," Nico said lamely.

Pale eyes opened and met his. "It's all right," Deven said. "Come in, sit."

He did, suddenly unsure what to do with his hands. "Should you be up?" he asked. "It's only been three days."

Deven had been essentially comatose, placed carefully in bed where he could recover without moving. They'd done the same thing to Nico, before...but Nico had woken in chains. He'd been so scared, and in pain, with no memory of what was happening or why.

Had Kai been scared and in pain when the Prophet overtook his body? Had he known what was happening, felt himself dying? Had it felt like drowning, suffocating, or had he just lost consciousness? Was he still in there fighting desperately to exist?

Deven smiled, bringing Nico back to the room. "Well, I won't be in fighting form for another few days, but I'm mobile, just stiff."

He watched Nico for a while before asking, "I don't remember what happened...after he broke my neck. How did I get away?"

Nico, a little sheepish because he knew what the reaction would be, answered, "I sort of...attacked him."

"You did *what?*"

"I broke cover and threw him—with my mind, I mean—then kept him talking long enough for David to arm the explosives, grabbed you, and Misted out."

"You could have been killed!"

"Yes, well, whatever he had planned for you wouldn't have been pleasant for me either."

"Still...you shouldn't have done that, Nico."

"I didn't stop to weigh pros and cons," Nico retorted. "You were lying there on the ground, helpless. That was all I could see."

He expected more admonishment, but Deven stared at him for a second and then relented, shaking his head. "You are a wonder," he said with undisguised affection. Nico felt his ears turning red, but couldn't think of a reply.

"Thank you for having the presence of mind to retrieve Ghostlight," the Prime added. "I don't think I've ever dropped her like that before."

"I don't blame you. We are all still reeling."

"I'm going to keep my promise. One way or another. I meant it."

Nico just nodded. He couldn't say that he had lost all hope for a happy outcome for his brother or anyone. That he wanted to have faith in Deven, but even that was beyond his strength now. That when everything that had mattered to him for five centuries had been stripped away, and everything that had brought him here had fallen apart, what was left to believe in?

"Stop," Deven said quietly.

"Stop what?"

"Stop thinking you're weak and a failure and whatever other poisonous nonsense is going through your head. I can feel it, you know. Nico…" He sat forward, wincing slightly but moving without any hesitation. "I know you've had your heart broken a thousand times since you came here. I know I did much of the breaking. But you can't give up. We need you here, now. I need you."

They were silent for a while, and the music changed tracks. "I recognize this," Nico said, looking away from the intent gaze fixed upon him. "I think the Queen performed it onstage the night…that night."

A smile. "She gave me this playlist—songs by other artists that she's covered onstage."

Nico nodded mutely. He didn't really know what to say or do now, how to act, even how to feel. Perhaps it had been a mistake to come here so soon; perhaps he wasn't ready to say what he needed to say, or hear what he needed to hear. Perhaps it was too late for either to make any difference.

Another pause. Then Deven asked, "Do your people dance, Nico?"

A bit taken aback, Nico looked at him again. "Yes, of course…though probably not the way people do here."

"There are a lot of variations…but slow songs like this are pretty easy." He stood.

"In silent screams, in wildest dreams
I never dreamed of this…"

Nico started to protest that he shouldn't be active yet, but it didn't look like Deven had any trouble, and the thought of saying anything about it died on his lips when the Prime held out a hand.

Caught off guard, Nico took it. Deven pulled him up out of the chair, and once he was standing, moved closer and placed his hands on Nico's, lifting them to his waist. Nico was too overwhelmed by the unexpected physical proximity to disobey, and Deven rested his hands on Nico's shoulders with a slight, amused smile at Nico's stunned expression.

"Basically at this point you just sway," the Prime said, drawing him into the beat of the song. "See? Easy."

"Lantern burning, flickered in my mind for only you
But you're still gone, gone, gone…"

If the point had been to distract him, Nico had to admit it was a brilliant idea: it was impossible to think about anything, in that moment, but the pressure of hands on his shoulders slowly winding around the back of his neck, and the warmth under his own palms.

Deven looked up into his eyes, and what Nico saw there was almost miraculous. The broken creature who had endured a perpetual funeral in his heart for the last two years had become something else, and not the person Nico had met, the one slowly disintegrating under the weight of his own immortality; this was something new, something that contained those other Devens but was stronger than any before. There was a gentleness in his eyes just now that Nico suspected few others would be privileged to see, but with it came a new, quiet self-assurance.

Somehow in the midst of everything that was wrong, something had gone very, very right. And perhaps…just maybe…if Deven could find himself again in the midst of all this pain, Nico could too. It was an outlandish thought given the circles his mind had been trapped in for days…but there it was, a sliver of possibility.

"Thank you for saving me…again," Deven said softly.

Nico smiled. "You are welcome, my Lord."

"Your kiss, my cheek, I watched you leave
Your smile, my ghost, I fell to my knees…"

He nearly stopped breathing when Deven leaned against him, head on his shoulder, both still swaying, holding onto each other. Everywhere they were touching felt like it was on fire, frozen, and electrified all at once. Nico was shaking, and worse yet flushed with embarrassment for it, but gradually he felt a light wave of energy washing through him, calming the tremors, soothing his fear.

Deven leaned back to meet his eyes again. "It's all right," he whispered. "It's all right, *en'tela*…I've got you."

Nico nodded, not trusting himself to speak, but then, he didn't really need to. He just held on.

Still, words had their place. Deven touched his face, his expression somewhere between bemused and reverent, and said, "I love you, Nico."

The world halted on its axis. "You…you do?"

"From the moment you took my hand and lifted me up out of the dark…and every second since. I just wish it hadn't taken me so long to understand."

"Well," Nico said wryly in spite of everything, "You can be kind of an idiot."

His heart did a wild somersault off a cliff as Deven gave him the most beautiful smile he'd ever seen, and then covered Nico's mouth with his own.

They had only ever kissed once, that night on the terrace in California, a moment of desperate desire that had ended in heartache that never truly eased...until now.

Months and months of sadness seemed to fade into nothing. Nico found himself near tears again, but this time for a very different reason, something he hadn't felt in so long he'd forgotten what it was like: *Joy.*

After a moment Deven drew back just enough to speak in his ear, and asked, "Will you stay with me tonight?"

Swallowing hard, Nico said, "I will."

Deven smiled and stepped back, drawing him along by both hands until they were right by the bed; then he hauled Nico down for another kiss, this one dizzyingly deep and born of a need that had existed among their kind since the first Prime reached out to his Queen—the need to fit one's soul to another's, to fill the lonely, empty places that mortals only knew in pale imitation...an emptiness that could go on for millennia...unless the Signet spoke for someone, and suddenly forever was not long enough.

"I don't think I ever realized how tall you are," Deven noted as his fingers found their way to the buttons of Nico's shirt and started undoing them.

Nico laughed. "I can get you a box to stand on if you like."

"I have a better idea—" Deven gave him a hard shove, and somehow got one foot behind Nico's, tripping him backwards onto the bed. Nico landed on his back with a grunt that turned into another laugh.

He intended to make a sardonic comment, but quite suddenly found himself unable to speak, as lips took his again, and the heat and weight of a body stretched with almost serpentine grace along his.

Deven finished unbuttoning and drew back the dark linen, exposing Nico's Signet. He stared at it for a moment, then leaned down and lightly kissed the stone before turning his attention to Nico's throat.

Nico worked his hands up underneath Deven's shirt, reveling in the phenomenal strength in his back and shoulders. Barely two minutes of touching and he felt drunk; what kind of bliss bubble, to use Stella's phrase, was he in for after an hour? Or a whole night?

Fortunately there was only one way to find out.

Grinning, Deven pulled the shirt off and tossed it aside. Nico took the opportunity to pull him close and roll sideways, reversing their positions, affording him a much better angle from which to run his hands slowly over Deven's skin, and follow his hands with his mouth, learning the landscape without any hurry. Meanwhile Deven got him shirtless as well with his usual ruthless efficiency.

He could feel the Prime's heartbeat—it was racing as fast as his own, though whether out of nerves or arousal, he couldn't say.

Oh, wait...he *could* say. All he had to do was open himself. He'd been trying not to intrude, holding back; every time he came close to accepting the bond's full power he stepped away, still afraid. He'd connected to it energetically, but emotionally...

"Now who's the idiot?" Deven took hold of his chin, as he had before, and met his gaze almost sternly. "That's what it's for, Nico. Let it in...let *me* in. I can't promise I'll never hurt you again...you know what a disaster I am. But I can promise never to abandon you again, and I will do everything in my power to keep you safe, by my side, where you belong. Just try to trust me, if you can."

"This love left a permanent mark
This love is glowing in the dark
These hands had to let it go free
And this love came back to me..."

Nico rested his forehead against Deven's for a moment, relaxing his hold over his emotions, truly letting the connection between them speak. He'd felt things from it since it had been unblocked, but he'd done so with as much distance as possible. Deven was right...he hadn't trusted it. He didn't know if he could yet. But he knew without doubt that it was worth climbing over his fear...worth working for...worth living for.

When he let go and opened himself to it, there was only one thing reverberating through it that mattered. There was so much love between them, even after so much sorrow, and its light was enough to banish even the darkest of those days. He breathed it in like the first gasp of oxygen after near-drowning. Indeed it felt like breaking through the surface of dark water, finally feeling the free air again.

"I love you," Nico said softly.

A smile, touched with the kind of happiness they'd both denied themselves but could have found, all this time, in each other. "Good," he replied. "Because I'm afraid you're stuck with me."

"And you with me," Nico pointed out, kissing him again before adding, "You're never driving me away again."

Deven's eyes were sparkling as he slid his hands down Nico's back. "I should hope not," he said, lifting up to speak in his ear as if the words were both a secret and a promise. "You are my Consort, after all."

Miranda opened her eyes with a contended sigh. Waking up sore and lazy with her limbs all-akimbo seemed to have become a habit...a very satisfying habit.

She shifted slightly backwards to remind herself how she'd fallen asleep. There was no mistaking David half-draped over her; he didn't snore, but his breathing pattern was one she knew as well as her own, as was the scent of his skin and the familiar weight of his arm around her.

Meanwhile in front of her, Deven mirrored her position, Nico curled up against his back asleep with a tiny smile on his face. She'd so rarely seen the Elf smile, and she'd been afraid after finding out Kai's fate he would completely break down, but she had underestimated the overwhelming, all-consuming rush of falling completely and incandescently in love.

The Pair hadn't even come out of Deven's bedroom for two days. Miranda had practically squealed like a schoolgirl when she realized what was happening on their side of the bond, and she and David had high-fived.

And that was before she'd had a chance to watch the way they touched each other. Merely thinking about the afternoon they'd all just spent together sent delighted shivers through her.

Her eyes burned watching them sleep. They were so happy. All of them were, just for a minute. The outside world would intrude again so soon, and the world would go back to tearing itself apart, but for a few precious days they'd been able to let go of the sorrow and anger and responsibility and just...be.

After a minute she became aware of the sound of purring, and looked around for Jean Grey, who sounded like she was up on the bed, and probably behind her; she very slowly moved her head to look back over her shoulder. She had to stifle a giggle: the cat was actually resting on David's hip, eyes closed, kneading the comforter that was thankfully thick enough that he didn't feel her claws.

Miranda turned back over. She had to wonder what the cat thought about the additional people periodically spending the day in what the cat no doubt considered *her* bed. Did it annoy her, or did she just relish the extra hands available to pet her?

The Queen herself would definitely agree with the latter.

She saw Deven's eyelashes flutter, and he opened them slowly. There was nothing predatory in his eyes this time—just sleepy, even peaceful. He smiled and slid one hand over to touch her face.

As he slipped back into slumber she took his hand and held it to her chest. It twisted in her grasp until the palm was flat to her skin—feeling her heartbeat, she realized. Curious, Miranda reached down with her other hand to take hold of David's arm and pressed her fingers against his wrist until she could feel the pulse beneath. It was strangely reassuring, all the more because, if she listened, she could hear all four of their hearts in the darkness...all steady and strong. Being able to hold onto it made her feel safe, and the hands gently touching her for the same reason made her feel not strangled...but cherished.

"Go back to sleep, my Queen," she heard David murmur into her hair. "All is well for now."

Miranda smiled, closing her eyes. Yes. Yes, it was.

Epilogue

Back again.

The portal opened and closed without any fanfare. There was no one on the empty, wind-swept cliff to notice.

Miranda remembered the sound of the wind among the redwoods, the trees whispering and laughing to each other down below her line of sight. It hadn't been long since she had stood here, but that visit had been for her own grief—this was more important.

She stood still, watching, taking David's hand. He looked stricken as he stared at the bare ruin of a place he'd once called home. The last time he'd been here was two years ago, when the central building was in ruins but some of the surrounding structures still stood. It was one thing to know the whole property had been razed, another to see it like this, just an empty parcel of land overlooking the forest.

As soon as they landed, Deven walked off into the misty, cold night—he knew exactly where he was going. Nico hesitated a moment, not wanting to intrude, but finally he looked over at Miranda, who gave him a slight nod.

Steeling himself, Nico followed his Prime.

She and David exchanged a look and then followed him.

Miranda also knew where they were going, and sure enough soon she saw the memorial, exactly as she'd seen it last time.

She grabbed Nico's arm with one hand and David's with the other, willing them both to hang back for a moment. They understood and waited.

She wished she could see Dev's expression, standing there, looking at all the tokens and letters that had been left, not just for the murdered Elite and servants, but for Jonathan, and for him. He could have pretended that his entire life here was just a waking dream, since he hadn't seen what was left of it until now. Now...now it was real, and it was forever.

All she could see was a silhouette whose head was bowed. They were all practically holding their breath, afraid to break the silence.

After a long moment, Deven lowered himself to his knees in front of the memorial. David's hand tightened in hers—he was waiting, she realized, for her to give the okay to approach. She had to smile at that.

She tugged sideways and, little by little, they moved off to the right to see better without interrupting. Nico drew his hand back from hers—if anyone should go first, he should, but he stayed where he was a minute longer.

From the side she could see that Deven's eyes were dry, but his face bore sorrow and longing deep enough to break her heart. He reached out a hand and carefully plucked a sprig of evergreen needles, brown and sodden, from the bottle of whiskey that had been left for Jonathan. Then, he took something out of his coat pocket and pressed it down into the dirt; it was too small to see what it was.

She heard him speak very softly even through the wind.

"...yours. I'm keeping your name, just so you know. I couldn't ask for a better part of you to carry with me. It's the most important thing you ever gave me...yourself."

Now, she saw tears, but he ignored them for the time being and went on in a slightly shaky voice. "But this life, the one we built together...there's nothing left of it, and almost nothing left of who I was. What there is...that's the part of me you loved best. So I'm keeping that too." He wiped his eyes with a sleeve. "I don't know what's going to happen to this place. It won't stay bare forever. I'll make sure you have a spot no matter what I do with it. But...I have to go now, my love. You're gone...so this isn't my home anymore."

Then Deven rose, took a step back. A shiver ran through him; he turned partway, looking for the others anxiously, and saw Nico, who had moved closer until he was only a few feet back.

Seeing the look on the Prime's face Nico went to him, and

Deven buried his face in the Elf's chest, curling his hands into the lapels of Nico's coat.

David squeezed her hand again, and gave her a look that clearly said, "Now?"

She nodded.

They joined the Pair before the memorial. Miranda wrapped her arms around Deven from the back, and David did so where he could hold on to both him and Nico with one hand extended to take Miranda's.

They stood that way for a long time. She and David fed energy into Nico, who gave it to Deven—they could do it directly along their four-way bond, but so far the best approach they'd found was to consider themselves two Pairs who were joined together, not four individual people. They could share in whatever direction they liked but it seemed to work most efficiently from that perspective, taking advantage of the kind of energy work Pairs knew by instinct.

Finally, she felt Deven shift, and stepped back. David did the same. Nico gently wiped Dev's eyes with the end of his scarf, earning a sweet smile and a kissed hand. Finally, Deven turned to face all of them, calm and centered.

"Thank you," he said. He cast a glance at the cliff and let out a breath. "I think we can go now."

That answered the question, then. They'd all been wondering what would happen to this property; would Deven want to rebuild the Haven and return to his territory? Would he want to move it elsewhere? Or would he want to leave it all behind?

She was relieved that it seemed he'd chosen the third. She wanted them near her. And while Nico had said he could make them all Gatestones that would travel to and from California in minutes, with everything that could happen, it still felt right for the whole Tetrad to stay close to one another.

Miranda started to say as much, but Nico frowned and stepped back away from them, looking alarmed. He reached into his coat pocket.

"What is it?" Deven asked. Something about Nico's face had made his hand fly to Ghostlight's hilt, and that worried Miranda enough to do the same with Shadowflame.

Nico pulled something out of his pocket—a stone. It was just starting to glow faintly red in the night.

"Is that the Gatestone you made for Kai?" David asked.

The Elf shook his head. "No, this is the Speaking Stone—the one that summoned me here to Earth. I think someone might be..." He held it out on his palm, where it glowed brighter and brighter, pulsating, as well as vibrating in his hand, practically dancing.

Instantly Miranda felt intense dread clawing through her. She wanted to tell Nico to throw the stone over the cliff and then transport them all home, and not to hear its message under any circumstances, but she couldn't get the words out.

Then a voice erupted from the stone, ragged and weak, like its owner had been badly hurt and was barely hanging on. Miranda didn't recognize it...and she didn't recognize the words it spoke either. She hadn't had time to learn much Elvish except for the absolute basics and the sort of things they said during sex.

Whatever it said, Nico dropped the rock like it had scorched his hand. He had gone ghostly white, hand over his mouth in shock. He started to tilt sideways and probably would have passed out if Deven hadn't immediately pulled him close and offered something strong to lean on.

"What is it, Nico? Whose voice was that?"

Nico looked at her, eyes near-panicked. "It was my mother," he said.

"What did she say?"

He gripped Deven's arm so hard she was sure it would be bruised. Deven had apparently understood, as had David, and both were as pale and stunned as Nico. After a few deep breaths, Nico steeled himself, and repeated what his mother had said:

"Avilon is burning."

Made in the USA
San Bernardino, CA
03 April 2016